"What will you be doing while I sleep?"

"Watching you."

"Are you serious?" Do you really think I want you watching me when I'm probably drooling or some other unattractive thing?

"I like looking at you. I like looking at your bed-mussed head, knowing that it was created by your thrashing in the heat of lovemaking. With me. I like seeing you snore softly through lips that are swollen from my kisses. I like the sex flush that still colors your face and neck."

With each reason he gave for watching her, Miranda's jaw dropped lower and lower. But what she said was "I do not snore."

He grinned. "Whatever you say, dearling."

"Said like a man who wants more sex."

He shrugged. "I do."

SANDRA HILL

KISS OF WRATH

A DEADLY ANGELS BOOK

AVON

An Imprint of HarperCollinsPublishers

AVON BOOKS
An Imprint of HarperCollins*Publishers*
195 Broadway
New York, New York 10007

Copyright © 2014 by Sandra Hill
Excerpt from *Vampire in Paradise* copyright © 2014 by Sandra Hill
ISBN 978-0-06-221046-3
www.avonromance.com

First Avon Books mass market printing: June 2014

Avon Trademark Reg. U.S. Pat. Off. and in Other Countries, Marca Registrada, Hecho en U.S.A.
HarperCollins® is a registered trademark of HarperCollins Publishers.

Printed in the U.S.A.

10 9 8 7 6 5 4 3 2 1

This book is dedicated to all those single parents who march on each day with the grueling task of raising children on their own. They understand best the struggle, and joy, ahead for my heroine who becomes an instant mother to not one, or two, but five children.

And this book is dedicated as well to those parents who have ever lost a child. They understand best how my hero's grief can go on forever.

And to those who enjoy a good love story sprinkled with both smiles and tears. The best kind of all!

There is joy in the heavens over one sinner that repents.
LUKE: 15:10

Now war rose in heaven, Michael and his angels fighting against the dragon. And the dragon and his angels fought back.
REVELATIONS 22:7

Prologue

The Norselands, A.D. 845
When men turn beastly . . .

Mordr Sigurdsson, best known as Mordr the Brave, led his battle-weary men up the steep incline from the fjord to Stonegarth. His wooden castle and the surrounding village sat atop a high motte, a massive, flat-topped earthworks mound in the Frankish style, rising high above the surrounding area.

He'd already anchored his longships. Later, but not too much later, the ten vessels would be brought ashore to winter. Already, ice crusted the edges of the narrow waterway leading to his aptly named grim estate in the far north where naught grew except boulders and hardy evergreens, which was fine with him. He obtained all he needed to subsist and prosper by trading, serving in the army of one grab-land king or another, or going a-Viking. A good life!

He and his men had been gone nigh on a year now, longer than he usually spent away from his homeland. In truth, they'd waited too long in trying to outrun winter for their return voyage, having to crack thickening ice ahead of them in many places, but that one last monastery to plunder had been too tempting. As a result, they were not only exhausted but cold to the bone, with frost painting their fur cloaks and hats, not to mention beards and mustaches. Like Norse ice gods, they were. Their breaths froze into snowflakes on leaving their mouths, and below their noses snot formed icicles into miniature tusks.

They were home now, though, and he for one intended to dig in for a long stay.

As if sensing Mordr's thoughts, his *hersir*, Geirfinn the Fearless, said on a frosty breath, "My Aud best have the fire stoked for my arrival because I intend to burrow in 'til the spring thaw."

Atzer Horse Teeth, one of Mordr's hirdsmen serving under Geirfinn, guffawed from his other side. "Which fire would that be? The cook fire, or the fire betwixt your wife's thighs?"

Mordr and other hirdsmen close by laughed, causing more frosty cloud-breaths.

"Did I not mention burrowing?" Geirfinn replied with a grin, hardly visible through his huge, walruslike, ice-crusted mustache. "I do my best work beneath the bed furs . . . burrowing."

More companionable laughter. Ah, it was good to be home.

"First off, I want a horn of ale, or five," Mordr declared, joining in the levity. "A warm bath to wash away the battle filth."

"And lice," someone called out behind him.

Lice were ever a problem for fighting men ofttimes forced to bed down in unclean places and unable to take their customary baths. Norsemen did tend to bathe more than other men. 'Twas one reason women of all lands welcomed them to their beds. That, and other reasons, Mordr thought with silent humor at his own jest.

"Then I want a hearty meal in my great hall," Mordr went on to encourage his men onward. Many of them wore heavy hauberks of chain mail. Plus swords and battle-axes and shields added to the weight on the climb upward. "Yea, you are all invited to my welcome feast . . . after your burrowing." He smiled before continuing, "Then a long night betwixt the thighs of my favorite concubine, Dyna."

"Dyna of the big bosoms?" Atzer teased.

"Precisely," Mordr said. "Forget a long night. Mayhap I will need a night and a day afore I am sated. I might even favor my wife, Gulli, with my attentions if she is not in her usual nagsome mood."

There was much nodding. They all understood the pain of a shrewish wife.

But, nay, Mordr realized belatedly, there was something more important than all those appetites. Most of all, he yearned to see his children, Kata and Jomar. Though only one year apart, being six and five, respectively, his little mites were naught alike in appearance or personality. Kata had pale blond hair that would no doubt darken over time into dark blond or light brown like his own. She was a saucy wenchling with an impish grin, always up for some mischief or other. Jomar, black-haired like his mother, Gulli, was more serious but always willing to participate in Kata's childish adventures.

Yea, that is what he had missed most about Stonegarth. His children. He pictured himself, first thing, tossing Kata and Jomar into the air, giving them huge bear hugs and playful tickles. Was there aught more glorious to a man than the giggle of a child, especially when the boyling or girling was fruit of his loins?

He'd brought Kata dozens of ribands, all the colors of the rainbow, and for Jomar, there was a miniature sword crafted of hard wood with its own belted scabbard, so small it would fit around a man's thigh. Mordr couldn't wait to see their joyful appreciation. Also, both of them would delight in an intricately carved board game of *hnefatafl* with silly game pieces . . . giants, and trolls, and such rather than the usual king, his defending soldiers, and the opposing foemen.

His first clue that something was amiss came with the realization that none of his housecarls, or even any villagers, rushed to greet them. The second clue, which had his comrades-in-arms unsheathing their weapons, was no smoke rising from the roofs of his keep or any of the longhouses and outbuildings that comprised Stonegarth on the flat-topped mountain. Always there should be hearth smoke, even in the summer months, from cook fires, if not for heat. The ominous silence had them all on alert.

And then they came upon the first of the macabre scenes. In the outer courtyard lay the dead bodies of his guardsmen, frozen into stiff, grotesque postures, eyes open, mouths agape in horror. The cold even preserved the blood of their wounds in splotchy patterns. Which gave Mordr evidence that the attackers must have come just afore the more recent freeze. No more than three sennights ago.

"Was it Saxons?" someone asked.

"Those cowards would not travel this deep into our territory," another soldier replied. "Mayhap Huns."

"Nay! 'Twas Norsemen. Look at this sword. Pattern-welded in the Viking style," Atzer pointed out.

"Hordssons!" several men concluded as one.

"Those slimy outlaws do not merit the name Viking. They have lurked about for years, waiting for a chance to attack," Geirfinn said. "Damn them all to the fires of Muspell."

Mordr heard these remarks through the roar that was growing in his ears. "Kata? Jomar?" he cried out even as he began to sprint toward the keep. The other men began rushing in all directions, swords aready, though, from the state of the frozen corpses, it appeared the invaders were gone, for days, if not weeks.

Despite his heavy armor, Mordr ran like the wind across the courtyard, up the steps, and through the open double doors leading to his great hall, where the three hearth fires were cold, the logs long burned out. Tapestries had been ripped from the walls, benches and trestle tables wantonly hacked into kindling. Along the way, he jumped over the corpses of his housecarls and servants, male and female both. In the corridor betwixt the solar and the scullery, he found Dyna's body, her gunna torn from neck to hem, her breasts bearing dark bruise marks, as did her widespread thighs. Mordr would warrant that many men had participated in the rape, if the bloodstains on her thighs were any indication.

His wife's body bore similar signs of mistreatment when he found it in a storage room where she must have hidden, or tried to hide.

And no sign of his precious children.

With foreboding, Mordr vaulted up the steep stairs to the upper level of his wooden keep where there were three sleeping chambers. In the first one, he found Jomar, who must have been hiding, facedown, under the bed when he'd been found by the invaders. He'd been dragged out by the feet, and his skull cleaved almost clear through from the back by a broadsword. Mordr prayed gods that it had been a quick death.

He dropped to his knees and gathered his little

boyling up into his arms, keening with grief. His heart felt shattered like glass, sharp slivers cutting into his soul. But he could not fall apart yet. First, he must find Kata. Laying Jomar carefully onto the bed, he spread his own fur cloak over the body, as if to warm him in death.

Kata's nude, frozen corpse lay in the next chamber. No sword blow to her perfect body. Instead, from the quantity of blood pooled betwixt her thighs, he concluded with horror that she must have bled to death from her girl parts. From numerous swivings by beastly Hordsson males.

What kind of men killed women and children? What kind of men found pleasure in raping little girls? Why had they not taken women and children, or healthy males, as valuable slaves, a practice employed by even the most vile villains? The slave marts in Hedeby, and Birka, and Kaupang would have welcomed them in a trice. Had that been the case, Mordr would have had a chance of recovering his children, by ransom or sword.

This was an act of violence, of evil, pure and simple. Aimed at him. Monetary gain had not been the goal, leastways not totally.

Mordr stood, arms raised to tear at his own hair. The roar of outrage, "NOOOOOOOOOOOOO!" that came from him could be heard even outside the keep and beyond, into the village. Some say that was the day that Mordr the Brave became Mordr the Berserker.

One

Hell hath no fury like a Viking wronged . . .

After being restrained by his men—it took Geir-finn, Atzer, and three other burly fellows to hold him down—and after being forced to drink horn after horn of *uisge beatha*, that potent, prized Scottish brew, Mordr fell into a deep, alehead sleep. When he awakened, the rage was still in him, but he restrained it inside himself in silent, cold fury toward the Hordssons. He began to plan.

No matter what he did—walk down the incline to check on the landed longships, eat a hunk of cold boar shank, bathe his filthy body, feel the warmth of the hearth fire—images of Jomar and Kata were ever with him. And those images were not of the laughing, happy children he had left behind at Stonegarth a year ago. Nay, all he could see was their bloody, defiled bodies and sad, frozen, tormented faces.

Their deaths, all the deaths at Stonegarth, must be avenged. Thus it was that, two days later, in his great hall, which had been cleared somewhat of the destruction, Mordr raised a hand high in the air and declared,

"War on the Hordssons! To the death of every misbe-gotten cur bearing that name!"

A loud cheer went up from the men. There were no women or children present, of course.

Within a sennight, Mordr and his reluctant followers—reluctant only because winter was not the best time for warfare and his hirdsmen would have preferred a springtime march to battle—had razed the sorry keep and village of the Hordsson clan. Not a single Hordsson male over the age of ten survived the surprise assault. Some women, too. Mordr, even in the berserk madness that overtook him when fighting started, had no taste for killing females, but if they got in his way, they were fair targets, to his rattled mind. Never young children, though. Never!

For a year and more, he sought out Hordsson kin in other parts of the Norselands—Hordaland, Jutland, Vestfold, Halogaland. It did not matter if they had par-ticipated in the raid on Stonegarth; if they had Hords-son blood, Mordr decreed they must die. Then there was word of some Hordssons in the Irish lands; he traveled there and wreaked his still raging vengeance. Still others lived and died at Mordr's hands in Nor-thumbria where a Viking king ruled that portion of Britain. After that, he moved onto the Orkney Isles.

Hundreds of dead Hordssons lay in his wake of terror. Others shook in fright and changed their names to escape Mordr's path of retaliation.

Though it had not been his aim, Mordr gained far fame for his berserk skill with a sword named Ven-geance and a battle-axe named Fury. Every man with a speck of sense, even those not named Hordsson, avoided his path for fear of doing or saying something to set him off. 'Twas a well-known fact among fighting men that you never engaged a warrior, whether he was a berserker or not, who had no care whether he lived or died.

In truth, Mordr welcomed the road to Valhalla. Or did the Christians have the right of it? Followers of the One-God believed there was an afterlife where good deeds whilst living gained an entry into heaven. According to their Holy Book, after death a man could meet up with those who'd gone before him. If that was the case, Mordr was lost. He'd never been baptized, and too many misdeeds would bar him from the heavenly gates. Alas, he would never see Jomar and Kata again.

By then, many of his men wearied of the vendetta and went back to Stonegarth, with Mordr's permission, led by Atzer. Mordr never returned to his home, though he had heard years later that the estate prospered as the men under Atzer took wives, had children, and drew villagers and cotters to newly built longhouses. Even his six brothers, who joined him at first from their estates scattered across the Norselands, gave up after a while. It was not their fight.

"Mayhap you need to swive a lusty maid, or ten, to calm your mind," his brother Ivak suggested before departing.

"Ivak, you think every problem in the world can be solved with your cock."

"Can it not?" his halfbrained brother asked, and he was serious.

Vikar, the oldest of the Sigurdsson brood, gave his usual sage advice, sage in his own not-so-humble opinion. "Your pride has been assuaged. Accept the wergild offered by King Haakon to halt your vendetta, and use it to start over again."

"Dost think this is about pride? Dost think I care for bribe coins? Dost think I could truly start over?" Mordr stormed. "I can never replace my two children."

That shut up Vikar . . . for a while.

His brother Cnut mentioned the widow whose prosperous lands adjoined his in Vestfold.

"Would that by chance be Inga No Teeth?" Mordr asked with growing impatience.

"Well . . ." Cnut stammered, then said defensively, "You know what they say about all cats being the same in the dark."

"Whoever said that did not know cats, or women," Ivak interjected.

They all turned to stare at Ivak.

"I am just saying," Ivak defended himself. "Besides, there are advantages to a toothless woman in the bed arts."

They all gaped at Ivak with incredulity.

"I am just saying," Ivak repeated, this time with a grin.

"I do not need another wife," Mordr said with growing impatience.

"You could go exploring with those Vikings who seek new countries to settle beyond Iceland," said Trond.

Mordr arched a brow at Trond, who was the laziest Norseman ever born. Trond would never go exploring himself because it would require too much energy. "The only way I am going to Iceland is if there is a Hordsson sitting on an iceberg thereabouts," Mordr declared.

Sigurd the Healer made one of the most outrageous suggestions. "Methinks you should let me drill a hole in your head. Trepanning, it is called. Mayhap all your body's bad humors would be released, and you would lose this madness."

His other brothers were as stunned as Mordr.

"I like my madness, thank you very much. You come within an arm's length of me with a drill, and you will find that instrument lodged in one of your body parts, the one where the sun does not shine, lest it come up from a privy hole."

Harek, the most intelligent and most wealthy of all his brothers—he was a moneylender and tax collector—said, "If you're going to continue on this path of self-destruction, can I have Stonegarth?"

Mordr could not be angry with his brother. Harek was what he was, a greedy Viking bent on amassing enough treasure to establish his own kingdom.

"I've already given it to Atzer," Mordr told him.

His brothers left him eventually, as did many more of his followers. In the end, Geirfinn was the only one of his original *hersir*s to stay. When Mordr could find no more Hordssons to kill, Mordr, Geirfinn, and a handful of loyal comrades-in-arms hired themselves out as mercenaries to kings and chieftains of many lands. For a while, they even became Jomsvikings, but Mordr chafed under the rigid rules of that monastic-like living.

Thus it was that five years after the invasion of Stonegarth and the death of his children, Mordr found himself in a battle against a band of Saxon villains. There were only twelve men with Mordr now, but thirteen powerful Norse warriors could handle twice, mayhap thrice, that many foemen. But not today. They were outnumbered five to one, and the gods were against them, pelting rain down on them in cold misery. If that were not bad enough, Thor raised his mighty hammer Mjollnir, causing lightning to flash, as if foretelling doom. Already vultures—ravens of death—circled overhead, just waiting to pounce on the human carrion.

The field became slippery with sword dew, as well as mud. The air rang with the clang of metal weapon against metal weapon, the death screams of the fallen, the grunts of soldiers brandishing heavy broadswords, and his own roars of berserkness.

Mordr cleared a path through the fray in front of him, trying to get to Geirfinn, who was being attacked from both sides. When he was almost there, he saw his good friend go down from a lance thrown from behind by yet another Saxon villain. A death blow, it had to be.

With a bellow of outrage, Mordr tossed his shield and leather helmet to the ground. Storming forward, he wielded his heavy broadsword in his right hand and his battle-axe in his left. One foeman got his head lopped off. Another Mordr speared through the heart with the sharp butt end of his battle-axe. Still another would ne'er swive any maids in the future, for Mordr firmly planted his sword Vengeance in the soldier's groin.

As he was pulling his sword back out of the groaning man's body, Mordr made a huge mistake. Ne'er turn your back on the battlefield. Someone had come up behind him, quickly reaching around and garroting him from shoulder to shoulder. Blood gushed forth, and he felt a flush of heat race across the skin of his entire body, as if he had been scalded. His arms went numb, and his legs gave out, causing him to fall forward. Soon, the sounds of battle faded as he felt his blood soaking the ground beneath him. Someone rolled him over with a booted foot and laughed. "King Edmund will give me a great boon for having felled this vicious Viking."

But then Mordr heard nothing as he sank into a dark slumber, and it was not a peaceful sleep as he'd expected death would be. It sounded like beasts gnashing their teeth all around him, just waiting for the cue to devour his flesh and bones. *Is this death then? Why am I not on the road to Asgard? Where are my Valkyries?*

Why am I not being welcomed into Odin's great hall in Valhalla?

"Because thou art not in Valhalla, Viking," a voice boomed above him.

Mordr hadn't realized he'd spoken aloud. In truth, how could he speak with his neck nigh split through to his nape? He blinked his eyes open. He was still in the middle of the battlefield. Fighting was going on around him. Rain still came down in stinging sheets. Except for the circle surrounding him where a tall man stood over him. Instead of wearing a battle helmet and *brynja* of chain mesh, this lackwit wore a white robe, similar to those worn by men in eastern lands. It was tied at the waist with a golden rope, and his dark hair hung loose to his shoulder. Most amazing of all, a light emanated from the man, like a full-body halo. Mordr knew about halos, having once seen a Byzantine church mural depicting a saint, but that fellow's halo had been surrounding his head only. This must be an important saint.

"Are you a saint?" Mordr asked, oddly unsurprised that he could speak.

"You could say that," the man said, and from his back suddenly unfurled a massive set of pure white wings.

"Bloody hell! An angel?"

The man—rather, the angel—nodded. "I am St. Michael the Archangel, and you, Viking, are in big trouble."

Mordr noticed that the angel did not say "Viking" in a complimentary way. "What do you have against Vikings?"

"You are a sorry lot of men. Vain. Prideful. Greedy. Vicious. Fornicators."

"We are also brave in battle. Good providers for our families. Yea, I know what you are going to say. We provide by plundering, but that is not so bad when you consider we are doing a good deed by relieving your churchmen of the overabundance of wealth they garner for themselves. As for vanity, some could say that your God made Norsemen beautiful; therefore, 'tis not our fault that we are proud of ourselves."

Michael's eyes went wide before he shook his head as if Mordr were a hopeless idiot.

In fact, Michael said, "Idiot! Thou art in the greatest trouble of your life, and you dare to make excuses."

"What would you have me do? In truth, I am not sorry to have my life end."

Michael's face softened for a moment. "Your children are safe and in a happy place."

For the first time since he'd come across the ravaged bodies of Jomar and Kata, tears filled Mordr's eyes and streamed down his face, mixing with the blood on his neck. A small sob slipped from his slit threat.

"Weep not for your children, but for yourself. You are a grave sinner, Mordr, as are your six brothers."

Mordr stiffened, as much as a dead body could. "Are my brothers dead, too?"

"If they are not dead, they soon will be."

"Why?" Mordr asked.

"You know why, sinner."

Mordr did not need to think before nodding. "My berserkness. The killing. It started with the assault on Stonegarth, with the murder of my children. I had good cause to—"

"Foolish Viking! Vengeance is the Lord's, not man's," the angel said in a steely voice. Then, "Do not try to excuse your actions. Even if you could be forgiven for killing those who killed your children, and I am not sure it ever could be, there have been so many other lives you've taken. Many of them innocent of any crime."

"I understand why I must be punished, but you mentioned my brothers, as well. Why must you take all of us at one time?"

"Because you are grave sinners, each guilty in a most heinous way of the Seven Deadly Sins," Michael explained with growing impatience, "as are many of your Norse race. God in His anger has decided to use you seven as examples, and—"

"Lucky us!" Mordr muttered.

Michael cast a black look his way for the interruption.

No sense of humor.

Michael continued, "In truth, there will come a time in the future when the Viking race will no longer be. That is the will of the Lord."

Mordr's numb brain tried to comprehend what the angel told him. "How exactly are you—or rather, your God—going to use me and my brothers?"

"Ah. I thought you would never ask." Michael smiled, and it was not a nice smile. "God has commissioned me to establish a legion of vangels to fight Satan's Lucipires, demon vampires. And, at the same time, to save those humans fanged by the Lucipires with a sin taint afore they commit some grievous act, a grave sin." Michael motioned with his head to a sight directly behind the circle of light that surrounded him.

Mordr recalled, when he'd first emerged from his death sleep, the sound of gnashing teeth, like leashed beasts. He saw now what had caused that noise. A band of grotesque beasts were trying—unsuccessfully, so far—to break into the halo barrier. They were huge, animal-like humans, tall as upright black bears, with scaly skin oozing slime. Their eyes were red, and their open mouths showed elongated incisors, like wolves, but longer and sharper.

"Lucipires?" Mordr asked.

"Precisely. You do not want to be in their clutches, believe you me."

Mordr believed. With typical Viking self-confidence, Mordr knew he could fight off three or four foemen, but these were not men, exactly, and they numbered in the dozens. He thought for a moment, then burst out with a chortle of laughter, which only caused more blood to spurt from his mouth. "You said you would turn me and my brothers into angels. Now there is a task! Turning Vikings into angels."

"Tsk, tsk. You do not listen carefully. I did not say angels. I said *vangels*."

"And they are?"

"Viking vampire angels."

"Huh?"

"For hundreds and hundreds and hundreds of years, seven hundred years to begin with, you would serve the Lord as a vangel."

"Seven hundred years?" Mordr exclaimed. "You mean, I would live for centuries."

Michael nodded. "Mayhap even thousands."

"Do I have a choice?"

"Of course. You can choose to be a vangel, or join the other side."

"The other side? Oh. Oh no!" Mordr realized that Michael meant he would be taken by those beasts, slobber dripping from their fangs, their eyes glowing like torchlights as they tried to break the barrier to get at him. "I choose vangels. Definitely."

"So be it!" Michael said, and extended a hand over Mordr, causing him to be lifted to his feet.

Mordr put a hand to his neck and felt the skin intact. "Thank you."

"Do not thank me yet, Viking."

Mordr blinked several times. The golden halo was gone, as were the horrid beasts. In fact, the battlefield was now a clear field. No fighting soldiers. No dead bodies. There were so many questions riddling his mind, but he asked the most inane one. "Will I have wings, like yours?"

Michael hooted a short laugh. "Not yet. Maybe later. Probably never."

That was clear as mud. "By the by, what is a vampire?"

Michael graced him with another of those smiles, which were not really smiles.

Immediately, Mordr felt a fierce pain in his mouth, as if his jaw were being broken and pierced with fiery tongs. When the pain went away, as suddenly as it had hit him, Mordr felt around his mouth with his tongue and realized that he now had a long—really long—tooth on either side of his front teeth on top. With horror, he said, "You made me into a wolf? I hate wolves. They are the most devious creatures, and they smell bad."

Michael shook his head. "Not a wolf. A vampire."

Then more pain hit him. On his shoulder blades. He reached behind him, over his shoulders, and discovered two bumps there. He arched his brows at Michael. "Please do not tell me that you put teeth in my back."

"Thickheaded dolts, that is what these Vikings are," Michael muttered. Then, he told Mordr, "Do not be ridiculous. They are bumps. Where your wings *might* emerge someday."

"There is hope for me then?"

"Viking, Viking, Viking! Didst not know, there is always hope? Are you ready to begin your penance?"

Penance? Ah. He means punishment. Still, Mordr nodded, hesitantly. What choice did he have, really?

The angel took him by the hand, and Mordr found himself rising above the ground, higher and higher, spinning, through the clouds, across the skies, over countries. Where he would land, Mordr had no idea.

One thought emerged through his battered brain. *I have been given a second chance. Praise the gods! Nay, that is incorrect. Praise God!*

Michael smiled, and this time it was a good smile.

Some inheritances are better than others . . .

Dr. Miranda Hart, psychologist, prided herself on always maintaining a dignified calm. She did a half hour of yoga every morning, after all, and she gave lectures on stress management. Even so, she stared with stunned horror at the lawyer in front of her and practically screamed, "Noooooo!"

"I'm sorry, Ms. Hart." Bradley Allison, elderly Cincinnati lawyer and longtime family retainer, clearly was not sorry. In fact, he recoiled, obviously disgusted with her reaction. "I thought you'd be pleased at this 'bequest.' The highest compliment!"

"Are you crazy?" Miranda asked, immediately realizing that she was the one who sounded crazy. And *crazy* was not a word that a mental health professional should be using. She inhaled and exhaled several times, finding her center. "You have to understand, Mr. Allison. I'm thirty-four years old. I've never been married, by choice. It's taken me eight years to pay off my college loans and establish a successful practice in Las Vegas. Not Cincinnati, by the way. I live in a luxury high-rise apartment with two bedrooms, one of which has been converted into an office. I have no desire for children . . . or a dog." She shivered with distaste.

"It was your cousin Cassandra's wish that you adopt her five children. If you decline, there's no option but to put them in foster care. Cassandra's neighbor is unable to care for them for much longer. She has a big family of her own. I must warn you, if the Jessup children are adopted, I'm sure they will be separated."

The oldest of Cassie's children was eight-year-old Margaret, or Maggie. One set of twins was six-year-old Benjamin and Samuel, Ben and Sam. The other twins were three-year-old Linda and Larry. Mr. Allison was right. Miranda would bet her hard-earned degree that there would be two separate adoptions for the twins, and Maggie might not be adopted at all because of her age.

Miranda steeled herself not to care. "What about Roger's family?" Roger Jessup, Cassie's no-good husband, was in prison for assault and battery, and not for the first time, which had been news to Miranda when she'd arrived for Cassie's funeral three days ago.

"No family," Mr. Allison informed her. "Just you." By his seventy-five-year-old nose raised northward, she could tell what he thought of her. She knew for sure when he added, "Perhaps they would be better off in foster care, after all."

Miranda didn't have a maternal bone in her body, but she didn't like some old codger pointing out her flaws. Besides, she didn't consider a lack of desire for procreation a flaw.

Despite his obvious misgivings, the lawyer tried a different tack. "If money is the issue, the family home could be sold."

She waved that remark aside. "I own half the house, our grandparents' to begin with, and Cassie and I both signed contracts years ago that, if one of us died first, the home belonged to the remaining cousin. Even if her husband were around, Roger has no claim on the house."

"He might try," Mr. Allison told her.

"Let him." After what she'd recently learned about

Roger, she would welcome the fight. "Cassie made a good living as a nurse, but, as you mentioned earlier, there's only a few thousand in her bank account. Roger is welcome to that. Let's hope that satisfies him."

Mr. Allison nodded. "You do not need to tell me what can or cannot be done with the family home. I am very aware of the circumstances surrounding the house, young lady. Your grandfather was a good friend of mine. I drew up that contract."

Boy! Talk about pole-up-the-ass irritable! They have a syndrome name for it, in fact. Irritable bowel syndrome. *Oh God! I can't believe I am making psychiatry jokes with myself. Must be the thought of sudden motherhood. To FIVE children! I need a Valium, or a fast train out of town.*

"Will you or will you not be taking responsibility for the children, Ms. Hart? It's Friday afternoon. If you're going to reject your cousin's wishes, I need to contact social services." Bradley pursed his lips and twitched his nose as if there was a foul odor in the room.

Miranda wasn't ready to make that decision, and the old fart's pressuring her didn't help at all. "Argh! What woman chooses to have five children today, anyhow?" Miranda wondered aloud, not really directing her thoughts at anyone, least of all the judgmental lawyer. "My cousin Cassie always was a ditz. Any stray animal—dog, cat, bird, rabbit—found its way into her house. She and her family lived down the street from me in Cincinnati, and their home was like a zoo. Cassie's mother, Aunt Mary, was just the same. Apparently, Cassie extended her bleeding heart to popping out children."

Mr. Allison looked at her as if she were a species of smelly bug. "Be that as it may—"

"Who says 'Be that as it may'?" she inquired meanly.

"*Be that as it may*, your cousin died. Her husband

is in prison, and even if he weren't, Cassandra did not want them to be in his custody. You might want to read this letter that Cassandra left for you before making a final decision."

"Why didn't you tell me there was a letter?" she asked coldly.

The lawyer shrugged. "I mistakenly thought you would do the right thing before reading the letter."

She took the sealed envelope from him. "Do you know what's in the letter?"

"I can guess."

Oooh, she was developing a real dislike for the man. Turning away from the lawyer, she opened the envelope and unfolded the letter, which was dated a year ago.

Hey Mir:

If you're reading this, I'm no longer around. Sorry we didn't keep in touch more after college, but I always felt close to you when we did talk. I love you like a sister. Remember that time we did the blood oath thing up in Willy Markle's tree house? "Sisters to the End!"

Well, cousin, I need your help now. I have cancer. Looks like I won't make it past another year. I know, I know, I should have talked to you about this. But it's hard to admit that your life has been a huge mistake. Except for the kids, of course.

Suffice it to say, my asshole husband Roger is an abuser. The beatings started after Maggie was born. The usual pattern, violence followed by profound apologies and promises to never do it again. As a nurse, I should have known better.

Miranda stopped reading and turned to the lawyer, who was watching her from behind his antique lawyer's desk, with his bony hands tented in front of his mouth. "The assault and battery that landed Roger in jail this last time—was it for beating Cassie?"

He nodded. "Broke an arm, cracked several ribs, and knocked out a tooth. He also hit Maggie so hard with a belt that it broke the skin on her back." Mr. Allison glared at her, as if Miranda should have done something to stop the abuse. "Thankfully, we have a judge here in Ohio who has a low tolerance for wife abusers, and even less for men who hit children. He gave Roger Jessup the maximum of five years. With good behavior, Roger might be out in two or so years. You can see why the issue of the children needs to be settled before that."

"No one ever told me," she said defensively. "Cassie could have come to me at any time, and I would have helped."

Mr. Allison arched his unruly white brows at her in silent recrimination. *Like now?* he seemed to be saying.

Miranda returned to the letter.

Even knowing that I have cancer, Roger's rages haven't let up. In fact, they seem to be getting worse. For the first time, last month, I called the police and had him put in jail. Aside from hitting me, he also lashed out at Maggie when she tried to intervene. He beat her with a belt. Can you imagine? The poor girl has scars. And he locked the twins—all four of them—in a closet. I fear the direction his rages might take in my absence if he did this when I was around. That is a travesty I will never allow. I should have stopped this horrible pattern long ago, for my children's sake, if not my own.

The cancer will probably get me before Roger is released from prison. And so, dear cousin, I am asking you to please, please take care of my precious children. I know what a huge favor I am asking of you. An im-

position of the highest order to your single lifestyle! Do it for love of me, please.

Your cousin,
Cassandra Hart Jessup

Single lifestyle? Did Cassie even remotely think I was so selfish as to choose my "single lifestyle," whatever that is, over helping her? Miranda had tears in her eyes when she turned back to the lawyer. "Where do I sign?" she asked.

For the first time, the lawyer smiled at her. "You'll never regret this decision, my dear."

Miranda wasn't so sure about that.

Two

In the year of Our Lord, two
thousand and fourteen . . .
From cruiseship to casino, a vangel's
work was never done . . .

Mordr arrived at the castle shortly after dawn, in
the year 2014, one thousand, one hundred, and sixty-
four years since he had "died." No one was up and
about yet. Which was remarkable considering there
were roughly seventy-five vangels in residence at any
one time, and probably twice that number today with
Mike flying in for a meeting, and, yes, Mordr meant
that literally. Mike was the irreverent name the vangels gave to St. Michael the Archangel, their heavenly
mentor.

There must have been hot times at the old castle
last night if so many of the occupants were sleeping
it off. Or the vangels might have been busy fighting
Lucipires somewhere. Lucipires were Satan's very own
demon vampires, the reason for vangels' existence
here on earth. Wipe the Lucies out, and vangels could

go off to their heavenly rewards. Presumably. One never knew what Mike would dream up next.

Guards patrolled the hundred acres surrounding the castle, of course. To keep out any Lucies that might stumble onto the so-far secret estate and any of the wacky townsfolk who were always sneaking around trying to take pictures of the "vampires" up on the hill. You'd think the photographers would be satisfied harassing the Amish in the area, who also abhorred picture taking.

Mordr was amazed at just how wacky the townsfolk were, but then what could you expect with a town named Transylvania? No, not Transylvania, Romania. This was Transylvania-frickin'-Pennsylvania, an economically depressed town that turned itself around five years or so ago by changing its name and jumping onto the vampire craze sweeping the country. A tourist trap of the vampire persuasion. Hah! Mordr would like to see some of these idiots have real fangs for a day. Then they'd know just how uncomfortable and unattractive they really were.

He parked his Hummer in the underground parking garage in the back, which had been his brother Vikar's latest project here at the run-down castle he and his minions had been renovating the past few years. It was a never-ending job, which Vikar hated, which was probably Mike's intent in assigning him here. Mike was all about pushing them beyond their comfort zones in the name of personal growth, or so he said, endlessly. Their brother Ivak was supposed to be renovating an equally run-down plantation house in Louisiana to be their southern headquarters, but apparently a snake problem was slowing him down. A *big* snake problem.

Mordr, ever vigilant to his surroundings, noted twenty-nine other vehicles parked in the underground garage. Vangels could teletransport, but they usually saved that for emergencies, like when rushing to aid a fellow vangel surrounded by a herd of Lucipires. It was important that vangels not call attention to their extraordinary skills, whenever possible.

Tapping in the codes on the security box, Mordr entered a steel-encased corridor. He walked quietly past closed doors that were once dungeons and wine cellars but were now padded-wall training rooms. There were also sleeping quarters, including large barracks-style ones for the younger vangels, those only a few hundred years old, unlike Mordr and his brothers, roughly twelve hundred years old, give or take.

When he entered the kitchen, he could smell coffee, even though no one was about. Lizzie, the cook, should be up soon. That was Lizzie Borden, the axe murderer. Now reformed, she wielded a sharp blade in a new fashion, cleaving meat and such. When she'd first arrived, one vangel had made the mistake of teasing her about her axe background; that vangel now had one less finger.

He went over to the massive coffeemaker, which had been set on an automatic timer, and poured a cup of the bitter brew. Sitting on one of many stools lined up before the pristine island that ran the length of the kitchen, he sipped at his coffee, just to occupy his time until everyone awakened.

Aside from the coffee, the smell of fresh fruit permeated the air, coming from the bowl of oranges, and apples, and bananas, and clusters of green and purple grapes in front of him. He plucked off one of the fat purple ones and popped it into his mouth, making a small sound of surprised pleasure at the succulent sweetness.

Ticking away the seconds was a new wall clock with a yellow smiley face in its center. Someone had a warped sense of humor around here. Surely not Lizzie, who wouldn't know a smile if it hit her in the face. Not that Mordr was inclined to humor himself, but he didn't surround himself with silly smiley faces, either. He could see how the ticking of the clock would be rather soothing, or irritating, depending on one's mood.

The sun was just beginning to come up, peeping through the large windows, which looked out over a wide lawn leading to a gazebo. Someone had been doing some landscaping. Probably Vikar's human wife, Alex. What Viking would ever waste space on such a frivolous structure, lest it was to store firewood for the cold winters in the Norselands?

He had hoped this peaceful atmosphere would calm his always fuming rage. Even after all these years, his berserkness lurked just below the surface, waiting for the least trigger to set him off. Modern people referred it as carrying a chip on one's shoulder. In Mordr's case, it was more like a boulder. It was a curse, really.

Vikar strolled in then, announcing his presence with a wide-mouthed, jaw-cracking yawn. "Hey, brother! You're early."

Mordr shrugged. "The sooner I got off that friggin' boat, the better."

"Tsk, tsk, tsk!" Vikar clucked. "We are Vikings, Mordr. We grew up loving water and our longships. You have a dream job."

"Pfff! Not my dream!"

"Remember the time you were assigned to those Quakers in Philadelphia. You in the midst of pacifists? Now, that was a flinch-worthy job for a berserker!"

Michael liked nothing better than putting the vangels in positions the opposite of the sins they had committed.

"Yea, I remember well. But you have suffered just

as much. Like the time Mike forced you to prowl the poor streets of Britain as a leper. You wore ragged, stinksome garments, and even got lice. Folks made a wide path to get around you. Or when he made you a humble priest in a Russian monastery." Vikar's sin had been pride. Immense pride.

Vikar shrugged. "I still say a ship should be a welcome change for you. How would you like to be landlocked like I am here in the middle of nowhere, my arse tied to this moldering castle?" Vikar poured himself a coffee and scratched his belly as he leaned against the wall, watching him. Vikar was barefooted, wearing only a pair of sleep pants. Gone were the days when men were men and could walk about naked if they so chose in their mostly male keeps. Not that they subjected females, other than wives and concubines, to their nudity back then, either, unless they were *drukkinn*.

"First of all, I'm on a cruise ship, not a longship. Dodging every other minute the dozens of husband-hunting females."

"You never fail to amaze me, Mordr. A Viking who dislikes women!"

"I did not say that I dislike women in general, but these are desperate females. A man likes to do the hunting, not be the hunted."

"I do not know about that. In the old days, mayhap. Now, a little role reversal is not unwelcome, if you ask me."

Mordr laughed. "Role reversal? You are becoming too modern by half." Actually, Mordr was trying to steer the conversation in another direction. Unlike most Vikings—bloody hell, unlike most men in general—Mordr did not like to discuss sex. Too close to a reality he avoided thinking about. Truth to tell, while his brothers and many of the vangels found their forced celibacy to be a hardship, Mordr did not have all that much interest in mating these days. That particular urge was overshadowed by the always simmering rage inside him. He feared he would hurt any woman he took to his bed. But if his brothers got even a hint of his "problem," there would be jokes aplenty about his lance having lost its steel, or his candle having no wick. Which would probably cause him to go berserk and hurt one of them for the jest.

"By the by, where is your entourage of vangels?"

"Someone needed to stay behind to maintain my undercover security force there, and Mike didn't precisely request their presence here. Only that of the VIK." The VIK was an acronym for the seven Sigurdsson brothers, leaders of all the vangels. "Besides, they, unlike me, enjoy cruise ships."

Vikar arched his brows.

"Efrim has developed a taste for bikini-clad women. Gissur is in the ship's kitchen making caviar tarts fit for a king. Halveig sings like an angel as part of the shipboard entertainment. Teit has been showing off his talent on a high board, diving through a ring of fire. Haki is teaching a class on swordplay."

"Sounds like they fit right in."

"Like lackwit pegs."

"Dammit, Mordr! I just noticed your paleness. Are there no sinners on those cruise ships?"

"Plenty," he said, "but the hot Caribbean sun counteracts all the repentants I am fanging."

A vangel's skin changed from pale, even translucent, to a healthy tan after they saved human sinners, partaking a small amount of their blood, or when they destroyed (not merely killed) Lucipires.

Vikar opened the commercial-size refrigerator, taking out two cartons of Fake-O, the synthetic blood invented about fifty years ago by their physician brother, Sigurd, to supplement the needs of vangels. Mordr quaffed them down quickly, followed by several swallows of the hot coffee to kill the putrid taste. It was questionable which tasted worse. "Son of a troll! Could Sig not add some flavoring to this scum? Tastes like curdled piss!"

"Actually, some of the younger vangels have requested strawberry or chocolate Fake-O. Armod wants carbonation added, like Pepsi."

Mordr gaped at Vikar to see if he was serious. He was.

"Can you imagine thickened, bubbling, slimy, Pepsi-flavored Fake-O?"

He and Vikar both shivered with disgust.

Speaking of the devil—uh, angel—Armod, a young Icelandic Viking with slicked-back, black hair, walked into the kitchen. Rather, he moonwalked into the kitchen.

Mordr was the one gaping now.

Vikar laughed as Armod gave them both a wave, mid-moonwalk, and went over to a cabinet where he pulled down a box of Froot Loops. He poured the sweet cereal into a bowl and covered it with milk. "Armod fancies himself Michael Jackson reincarnated. He moonwalks everywhere he goes about the castle, plays that 'Thriller' music ad nauseam, and wears his braies so short his white hose is exposed."

"I've met Armod many times before," Mordr reminded Vikar, "but I thought he would have outgrown this foolishness by now."

"Hardly. In fact, he is gaining a following."

Mordr shook his head at the image. "Really, Vikings moonwalking? Or rather angels moonwalking?"

"Don't forget vampires."

"You complain about your arse being tied to this moldering castle," Mordr said, "but I would wager my best sword that your arse enjoys being tied to your wife's bed, moldering castle or not."

"There is that." Vikar grinned.

"Can you imagine how much worse it would be if we were in the real Transylvania?"

Vikar made an exaggerated grimace. "I met Count Dracula one time when we vangels were still time traveling. He was one scary dude, and you know we Vikings are rarely scared."

Dude? Vikar really is becoming too modern. "Speaking of scary, I heard a rumor that Mike is thinking about turning Ivan the Terrible into a vangel," Mordr said, popping a few more grapes into his mouth and crunching loudly.

Just then, Lizzie came ambling into the kitchen. She wore the same Victorian gown she'd worn in Victorian times and carried a cleaver. For chopping meat, Mordr hoped. A half dozen kitchen ceorls followed after her.

Lizzie must have heard the tail end of their conversation because she muttered, "He better not send Ivan here. I have enough to do cooking for Vikings. I draw the line at learning Russian cooking."

Vikar just smiled. "It's just a rumor, Lizzie."

"Besides, Ivan was no Viking," Mordr pointed out, "and vangels thus far have been only *Viking* vampire angels."

"Thus far." Vikar homed in on just those words of Mordr's. "Remember, Mike insinuated to Zeb last time he was here that, if he fulfilled his duties for another fifty years, he might make him a vangel. And Zeb is a Hebrew, a far cry from a Norseman."

Zebulan was a Lucipire who acted as a double agent, so to speak, for Michael. Zeb had done some favors for Mordr's brothers Trond and Ivak in recent years, which had apparently impressed Mike, not an easy thing to do.

Mordr and Vikar watched with fascination as Lizzie ordered her kitchen staff about with an authority that would do a Viking chieftain proud. "Alov, get four dozen eggs. Hove, five slabs of bacon and five pounds of sausage and no dawdling. Freya, start toasting and buttering bread. Torgny, whip up some of those biscuits you do so well. We'll need ten quarts of orange juice. Someone start the juicer. Hurry, hurry, we don't want to be eating when Michael gets here." Soon, Lizzie was using her cleaver on the cutting board to expertly make thick, uniform slices of bacon, and the kitchen was being filled with delicious smells of cooking. "I forgot. Armod, go get that scrapple you and Mistress Alex bought at the Amish market. It would go good with syrup. You did buy a gallon of that good maple syrup, too, I hope." Armod nodded, his mouth full of that sickeningly sweet cereal, and moonwalked off to do as he was ordered. They all did, except for the moonwalking, despite where they fell in the social strata of the castle. The lowest of them all, thralls, who were actually mere servants (slaves per se not being permitted in modern times) were rushing about setting placemats, dishes, and cutlery along both sides of the fifteen-foot island, working around Mordr and Vikar, and in the dining room. The vangels would eat in shifts, or fill their plates and go into other rooms, or outside.

Mordr's brother Ivak, a minister of sorts in a Louisiana prison, strolled in, wearing rubber thong sandals, shorts, and a sleeveless muscle shirt over a clerical collar, which he best remove before Mike arrived. The archangel would not see the humor in the attire. Ivak saluted Vikar with his middle finger.

"I assigned him and his wife to different bedchambers last night," Vikar explained with a grin. Another warped attempt at humor. Really, vangels had too much time on their hands.

To Mordr, Ivak said, "Welcome, Brother Grim. I have missed your merry countenance."

Mordr started to rise to go after the fool, but Vikar held him back. "Temper, temper," Vikar warned.

Laughing, Ivak went over to the stove, where he kissed Lizzie on the cheek. *Eeew!* Then, the fool snuck a piece of crisp bacon and popped it into his fool mouth.

Lizzie smiled.

"Did you see that?" Mordr asked Vikar. "In all these years, I have never seen Lizzie smile. I did not even know she had teeth. Well, except for fangs."

Vikar shrugged. "Ivak always had a way with women."

And a lot of good it did him, too. Ivak was guilty of the sin of lust. Not that he would be having lustsome thoughts about the old woman. Or would he? "Anyone else sneaking a bit of food risks her axe— rather cleaver—hitting a body part," Mordr grumbled.

Just then, the sound of giggling could be heard coming from down the hall, soon followed by two little mitelings, Vikar and Alex's "adopted" children Gunnar and Gunnora, who skipped into the kitchen. "Unca Mord!" the twins squealed as one.

What was it about children and dogs, that they always sought attention from people who favored them least, or were skittish around them? *That is me. Skittish. Damn, damn, damn!*

"Gun. Nora," Mordr greeted them. Then, feeling trapped, he stood abruptly, knocking over his stool. His ears rang, and he felt light-headed as the little ones ran toward him, arms outstretched as they anticipated being swung high in the air, as all their uncles were wont to do. Except Mordr.

He swiveled on his boots and began to take long strides toward the back doorway.

"Why doesn't Unca Mord like us?" he heard Gun ask his father in his little boyling voice.

Mordr's heart, what was left of it, nigh broke, but he did not stop.

"Maybe he found out that you pick your nose," Nora replied.

"Or that you cry like a baby when you fall," Gun countered.

"Mordr!" Vikar called out with concern as he leaned down and took one child in each arm, lifting them up to his bare chest.

"Daddy, why don't you have boobies, like Mommy?"

"Ask your mother," Vikar advised with age-old male wisdom.

Mordr waved to Vikar over his shoulder, indicating he was all right. "I just want to check out the gazebo."

Lackwit, lackwit, lackwit, Mordr berated himself as he walked around a huge hole in the backyard—*another renovation project?*—and sat on a gazebo bench, rubbing his face with both hands. *When will I be able to bear being around children again? When will I stop seeing Kata and Jomar's faces in every little person I come across? When will the pain of their loss end?*

Vikar left him alone, thank God! And Mordr watched silently as more and more vangels awakened and went about their work, awaiting Michael's arrival. He could hear Lizzie's voice raised stridently as she continued to prepare breakfast for the horde. Laughter abounded as vangels who hadn't seen each other in a long time got reacquainted.

What is wrong with me that I cannot be like all others?

Why am I always so grim? Why am I without humor? Why, why, why?

Michael finally arrived. Mordr knew that because he could hear the sound of many wings. Apparently, the archangel had brought a legion with him this time. They better not be expecting breakfast. By the sounds of the morning activities, Lizzie would have breakfast over by now and the kitchen cleaned up. He would like to be there if Mike asked her to prepare an impromptu angelic feast. Mordr almost smiled at that image. Almost.

Soon after, Vikar came to get Mordr.

"I did not mean to upset the children," Mordr said right off.

"It is all right. The little ones recover fast."

"I brought them some gifts from the ship store. A kaleidoscope and a microscope."

"They will be pleased."

The two brothers sat side by side in silence for a moment.

"What's with the big hole?" Mordr asked.

"Swimming pool. First, it was going to be a small above-ground pool for the children, but somehow it's turned into an big-ass, Olympic-size pool for everyone. As if I don't have enough to do with these castle renovations. Last month, the plumbing backed up and we had to dig up the back courtyard. That's when Alex got the pool idea."

Mordr turned to look at Vikar. "Do you do everything she wants?"

"Just about," Vikar agreed happily. "Oh, by the way, Mike wants to see you in an hour."

"Me?" Mordr exclaimed. "Me, in particular?" No vangel wanted to be singled out by their heavenly pain-in-the-arse.

"You, in particular." Vikar arched his brows with amusement. Easy for him to be amused when he was not the one in the archangel's crosshairs.

Mordr stood wearily.

"You lucky devil, Mordr! I mean, you lucky vangel! Guess where Mike is sending you next?" Vikar asked with barely controlled laughter.

Uh-oh! Mordr did not like the expression on Vikar's face.

"Well?"

"Sin City."

"Oh shit! He's sending me to Hell. What have I done lately to merit such a punishment?"

"Not Hell, you halfbrain." Vikar was laughing out loud now. "You are going to Las Vegas."

Where's Mary Poppins when you need her? . . .

Dr. Miranda Hart was late. Again.

"George?" she said into the speaker on her cell phone that sat on the hall table as she wobbled on one foot, then the other, stepping into a pair of high-heeled pumps. "Can you take my nine a.m. appointment with P. Jack Sloane? I'm running a little late."

"Again?" She heard George—Dr. George Jensen, her boss at Nevada Psychiatric Services—sigh deeply. "You used to be the first one in the office."

"Well, I'm cashing in on those credits now." She glanced into the mirror over the table and cringed. Her curly red hair, a gift from some long-ago Irish ancestor and the bane of her onetime orderly life, was already coming loose from the French knot she'd pinned it into a mere half hour ago.

"Miranda," George said on a long sigh.

Miranda knew as well as George that canceling appointments with depressed/exuberant/obsessive-compulsive/bipolar emotional wrecks could cause huge crises. It was a professional no-no. In P. Jack's case, she was not worried, though, and George wouldn't be, either. P. Jack, a high-stakes baccarat dealer at a Las Vegas casino, had been married and divorced thirteen times, and he was trying to understand through therapy what his core problem was. He had, of course, proposed to her several times.

"I already have another appointment scheduled for that time, Miranda. We'll have to cancel Mr. Sloane and reschedule for later today. Unless you have other pressing plans, like a peewee badminton game."

Miranda groaned. It was not like George to be sarcastic. She suspected he was reaching the end of his rope with her. Now was not the time to correct him, and say it was peewee baseball, not badminton. Even as she repinned the loose strands of hair back into place, she argued her case, "Listen, I'll stay late today. Tell P. Jack I can see him at five, if he's available."

George agreed, then added ominously, "Please tell me you completed the monthly records that were supposed to be filed two days ago."

Miranda glanced over at her briefcase near the front door where she'd dropped it when she came in yesterday. "Of course," she lied.

No sooner had she ended her call with George than her phone rang again. She would have ignored it and let her answering machine kick in, except that the caller ID said "Bradley Allison, Esq." with a Cincinnati number. Reluctantly, she answered, "Hello."

"Miranda? How are you doing?"

"Fine." *Surviving.*

"And the children?"

"Flourishing." *Driving me up the wall.*

"Did you get the parole hearing notice?"

"Uh." Quickly, she shuffled through the pile of un-opened mail on the hall table, and there it was. An official-looking envelope with the return address of Ohio State Penitentiary, Youngstown, Ohio. Ripping it open, she read the short notice: "Inmate Roger Jessup is being recommended for parole. As an interested party, if you have any objections, you are welcome to attend the hearing on June 22. Please notify our office by June 15 if you plan to attend." It was signed by the assistant warden. "Yes, I got the letter, but I can't possibly go on Monday. Can you go in my place?"

"I could, but, really, I don't think it would do any good. It was important that you go last year. His first year of incarceration was riddled with bad behavior. Uncontrollable rages. It wasn't surprising his petition was denied."

Miranda knew only too well about Roger's rages. He'd called her unlisted number (how he'd gotten the number, she had no idea) whenever he had access to a prison phone (way too often) and yelled at her about all she had done to him. (Taken his children. Stolen his house. Turned his kids against him. Lied about his abuse. Yada, yada. In his deranged mind, Miranda was responsible for every bad thing in his life, including Cassie's death.) So it had been imperative that she attend that first parole hearing. The look he'd given her that day had been scary, even with him in cuffs.

"So, what's different this year?"

"He's become a model prisoner. Not one single in-fraction. No rages. No fighting. In fact, he volunteers in the prison ministry. He's been born again."

Miranda scoffed at that last. She knew all about prison religion.

"Bottom line, he's going to be paroled this time

whether you protest or not. I suspect he'll be in a halfway house as early as next week. On probation, of course."

With a sigh, Miranda said, "I know he's unhappy about my adopting his children—"

"—and selling the house, although you had every right to do so."

"And my objecting to his parole last year and my unwillingness to let him speak to his children. Actually, it was the kids that didn't want to talk to him, but he didn't believe that."

"I wouldn't be surprised to find him petitioning the courts for restoration of parental rights, or at the least visitation."

"We've talked about that before, and I took your advice about hiring Gloria Alvarado, that L.A. lawyer who wrote the book, literally, on fighting tough cases in family court. She's a shark. She believes that the most Roger could ever get is supervised visitation and that the children can't be forced to comply if it traumatizes them."

"I hope she's right, Miranda," Bradley said skeptically. "In any case, you know very well, as a psychologist, that men with rage issues can hide their violent tendencies very well until something triggers an explosion. The courts are full of cases where seemingly peace-loving men, and women, go berserk."

"Are you trying to frighten me?"

"Just be prepared. Hope that he's changed and is willing to let you raise his children, but take every precaution to make yourselves secure."

"I put in a high-tech security system around my house. I block any unknown phone numbers. I screen the mail." Although she hadn't done a good job with the mail lately, as evidenced by her missing the prison letter. "The only thing I'm missing is a bodyguard."

"I hope it never comes to that."

"Well, if it does, maybe I could get a Kevin Costner look-alike," she joked, referring to the *Bodyguard* movie.

"Who?"

"Never mind."

After clicking off, she braced herself and headed for the kitchen, where she could hear the sound of chaos. Unfortunately, the norm since Guadalupe, her Spanish homemaker/babysitter/housekeeper, quit a month ago, presumably to go to graduate school in Mexico City, but Miranda suspected she had gone no farther than two blocks away, getting away from the Hart-Jessup household being her only goal.

Miranda opened the kitchen door and stood, unnoticed at first, as her five nieces and nephews trashed the wonderful stainless-steel kitchen that had been a huge attraction for the house she'd bought two years ago, after selling both her apartment and the house in Cincinnati. The kitchen had been spotless when Miranda had gone to bed late last night. In some delusional lifetime, when Miranda had bought the house, she'd imagined herself having peaceful family meals with the children around that big table. She hadn't realized what a mess children could make, unintentionally, just by pouring cereal into a bowl or buttering a piece of toast.

With Bradley Allison's phone call looming in her mind, she stared at the five children. Despite all the problems they caused, and there were plenty, and despite the lack of order they created just by breathing, she loved them unconditionally, something she'd never expected when she'd taken on responsibility for their care two years ago. Her heart constricted at the thought of ever losing them. No way in the world was Roger

Jessup going to get his hands on these children again, she vowed.

Maggie, her oldest niece—which was how she thought of the children, although technically they were second cousins—pushed her glasses up on her nose as she slathered peanut butter and jelly on five sandwiches and put them in baggies. She also kept swiping at the hair that kept falling onto her face. Maggie shared Miranda's unfortunate red hair, and hers was even curlier. Like Annie with her finger in a light socket. Totally unmanageable. One of these days, when Miranda had a free moment, she was going to take the little girl to a hair salon where they would try to find a style that worked for her. At ten years old, Maggie was like a little mother to her younger siblings and had been for several years, helping her own mother, Miranda's cousin Cassie, while she suffered the end stages of cancer. As indicated by her making sandwiches for them all.

It would be better if the kids just bought their lunches at school, but with the government's new emphasis on nutrition, they'd all turned up their noses. As the youngest, Linda, had explained, "They want us to eat green flowery things."

Miranda assumed she meant broccoli.

Sam, instead of getting ready for school, was demonstrating his new talent, flapping his bent elbows at his side like a chicken, making obscene noises. To an eight-year-old boy, Miranda had come to learn, anything resembling a fart, a belch, or flying snot from a sneeze was considered cool.

His twin, Ben, was on the floor wrestling with his younger brother, Larry. "You killed my tree frog," Ben accused.

What tree frog? Did we have a frog in this house? Eew!

"It was an accident," Larry said, squirming out from under Ben and putting a chair between them.

"Why did you put those two crickets in the aquarium?" Ben narrowed his eyes and chased Larry around the table.

Ah, so that's what the fight is about.

"'Cause Johnny Severino tol' me that frogs eat crickets."

"Johnny Severino is a retard."

Oooh! That is not a word we use in this house.

"Is not!"

"Is so! He picks his nose and eats the boogers."

Eeew!

"So what?" Larry put both hands on his little hips, very brave now that he noticed Miranda had arrived.

"Those big-ass crickets ate my frog."

Did I just hear an eight-year-old say "big-ass"?

"Frogs are s'posed to eat crickets," Larry argued. "I looked it up on the Internet."

"Not crickets big as tree frogs."

Sam, now over his burst of frog grief, pulled a waffle from the toaster, then put some squirt butter all over the top and on a good portion of the counter as well, with enough syrup to give a small country a sugar rush.

Larry's twin, Linda, unfazed by the activity around her, slurped up huge spoonfuls of Froot Loops. So much for the organic steel-cut oatmeal Miranda had made early this morning before going upstairs to shower. It was still warming on the stove, probably congealed into concrete.

The dog Ruff, a mostly white mutt the size of a small bear, lay splatted out under the table, also unfazed by the chaos around him. He was waiting for food scraps to drop from the table. There were plenty.

But then Linda glanced up and saw Miranda. "Aunt

Mir, Larry got skid marks on his undies again. He hid them in the back of the bathroom closet."

Larry gasped and cast an icy glare at his twin, then turned to Miranda. "Linda flunked her spelling test."

Linda was the one looking betrayed now. "I am never, ever speaking to you again."

Enough was enough! Miranda clapped her hands. "Hey, guys, the bus will be here in ten minutes. Time to get this show on the road." Usually, Miranda had the gang dressed, backpacked, lunches in order, and out the door waiting on the corner for the bus. Although she employed a house cleaning service, everything else, like meals, had been out of whack since Lupe had gone.

Just then, she noticed that Maggie was weeping silently as she bagged the various sandwiches.

"Honey," Miranda said, going over and putting an arm around Maggie's thin shoulders. "What's the matter?"

"Saturday's my birthday," she said on a sob.

"I know that." Miranda pointed to the calendar on the fridge with a big red heart circling Saturday's date. "Remember, I asked you if you wanted to have a birthday party, and you said you only wanted family."

Maggie nodded. She was morbidly shy and had few friends. Another problem Miranda needed to address as soon as she had time to breathe.

"So, what's the problem, sweetie?"

"Kids who have their birthdays on the weekend get to bring birthday cupcakes in during one of the school days."

"And your day is today?" Miranda guessed.

Maggie nodded again.

"Did you tell me about this before?" Miranda knew the answer before Maggie could nod yet again. *I am such a failure as a mother.* "Okay, here's what we're gonna do.

You go to school, and I'll go down to Shakey's Bakery and get some super-scrumptious cupcakes and drop them off before I go to work." *And be even later.*

"But everyone will know they're not homemade."

Good Lord. Shakey's cupcakes probably cost three dollars each. Two dozen, about seventy-two dollars. Whereas it would cost only a few dollars to make the whole batch at home. Plus, hers would probably taste like crap. She thought for a moment. "I'll put them in a Tupperware container."

Maggie smiled hesitantly. "That would work."

"Aunt Mir, I can't find my retainer," Ben said.

"In the downstairs bathroom on the sink."

"Aunt Mir, can I have five dollars to sign up for hockey?" Sam asked.

"In the cookie jar."

"Did you wash my soccer shirt?" Larry was adjusting his massive backpack onto his shoulders.

"In the laundry basket."

"Can I go to Sally's house after school?" Linda asked.

"As long as Sally's mother is there, and you do your homework when you get home."

Soon an almost miraculous silence came over the house as the kids rushed out. Miranda sank down into a chair and put her face on the table. Something sticky hit her forehead. Probably syrup. Under the table, Ruff let out a loud burp.

Miranda would have cried if she had the energy. Something needed to be done. What she needed was a household manager. A babysitter, but much more than that. Someone who could organize her home, do the grocery shopping and cooking, supervise the children, chauffeur the kids to all their various activities, and generally take some of the weight off her shoulders. *A wife. I need a wife. No, no, no, that is so sexist. I'm a psychologist, I should know better. What I need is a Mary Poppins, do-everything kind of home helper.*

She recalled Bradley Allison's phone call then with the threat of Roger looming on the horizon, and amended her wish list. *What I need is a Mary Poppins, do-everything kind of home helper who is, oh, let's say, an ex-Marine the size of a bulldozer with special forces fighting skills.*

But where could she find such a person?

Three

Mission Impossible it might very well be . . .

Michael the Archangel sat in a wingback chair in the first and biggest of three parlors in the castle, looking around at what he had come to regard as his children. The seven Sigurdsson brothers, who comprised the VIK, the high council of all the vangels, sat in a half circle of chairs, facing him.

Vikings! Was there ever a more boisterous, wild, sin-prone race of men to walk the earth? Who would have predicted that a heavenly being, such as himself, would grow fond of such creatures?

Not that he would ever admit to softening his sentiments toward the miscreants. Devious opportunists that the Vikings were, they would use it against him.

He hoped his fellow archangels never found out. A saint bonding with Vikings? It was embarrassing, really.

The seven brothers were still atoning for their original mortal sins, but being Vikings, they could not help themselves from erring more, which accounted for more and more years being added onto their initial seven-hundred-year penances. In fact, their nervousness now as they waited for him to speak was telling. Not knowing the purpose of this meeting, each was worried, having committed some wrong or other. He would bet his wings that they would be vangels until the end of time.

Raising his hands high, he prayed, "Lord, bless this gathering and give these men wisdom, courage, and determination to carry out your will in their missions." *And give me the wisdom, courage, and determination to deal with these idiots.* "For they are stubborn as mules, prideful as peacocks, wanton as rabbits, greedy as hogs, dumb as dinosaurs, and irritable as bears with wind in the bowels. Amen."

The seven brothers—grown men of great height and, by the grace of God, handsome appearance—raised their eyes and waited in nervous silence for the axe they expected to fall on one, or all, of their fool heads. Except for Mordr, that was, who muttered something about lackwit animal metaphors. He would get to Mordr soon enough. The dour Viking would have reason to mutter then.

"Vikar," Michael said, calling first on the eldest.

Vikar flinched.

He does not hesitate to war with fiercesome demon vampires and yet he cringes at my singling him out. Holy heavens! You'd think I was going to wield a whip or rain down locusts. "Pray tell, what is that vast hole in your back bailey, Vikar? Art thou digging a tunnel to Hell? Is that how you plan to fight Satan's Lucipires now?"

Vikar's face, a healthy golden tone today due to some recent vangelizing, flushed with heat. "Of course not. It is to be a swimming pool," Vikar explained in a low voice, scarcely a murmur, as if embarrassed. As well, he should be!

Michael arched his brows. "You were ordered to

renovate this castle into a suitable accommodation for vangels. Not a luxurious spa."

"Hardly luxurious!" Vikar protested. "Alex . . . I mean, *I* . . . wanted a pool for the children to swim in."

Michael laughed. "Please! Those little ones are not yet three feet tall, and by my estimate, your pool will be at least thirty cubits. Pfff! Next, there will be a hot tub."

By the increasing color on Vikar's face, Michael assumed the pool would be even larger and that, indeed, a hot tub was in the plans. In truth, Michael did not mind a swimming pool, or even a hot tub, if it kept the Vikings out of trouble. Still, he cautioned, "Pride, Vikar. Remember, pride is e'er your downfall."

Vikar nodded. "All right. I'll skip the wet bar and fake palm trees." He immediately realized his mistake when he noticed his brothers snickering at him.

"Cnut," Michael said then.

Cnut's head shot up, and Vikar breathed a sigh of relief.

"What is the latest tally on vangels-in-training?"

Cnut, too, looked noticeably relieved since it was not one of his sins that was being exposed. Yet.

Cnut was in charge of military training—in particular, training to fight Lucipires, which was all together different from regular military skills. The only way to destroy one of Satan's demon vampires—destroy, not just kill, which did not prevent their return at a later date—was to pierce them with swords or bullets treated with the symbolic blood of Christ or the symbolic splinters of the True Cross. Holy water was a deterrent, but it only burned the skin off the vile creatures, and regular weapons merely killed them, allowing them to be resurrected over and over as demon vampires.

"We now have five hundred and seventy full-fledged

vangels, and twenty vangel trainees about to graduate into the ranks. Another fifteen of the newly turned need additional training. At least a month more."

Michael nodded. "I will be sending a hundred more shortly."

Seven jaws dropped at that news.

"And, no, Ivan the Terrible will not be one of them." Vikings were great ones for rumormongering. Like old women they were betimes. They had yet to learn that he heard everything.

"Is it necessary to expand our ranks?" asked Vikar. "I mean, we annihilated a large number of Lucies on that Southern mission at Angola Prison a few months back."

"They're like roaches," Sigurd, the physician, explained, to no one in particular. "Kill a roach in one spot, and five others spring up in another."

Michael nodded. "With Satan's help, in the Lucipires' case. Word coming up to the heavens is that Lucifer has given Jasper another thousand of his demons." Lucifer had been Satan's name when he'd been an archangel. Jasper, Lucifer's cohort in heavenly crimes, was also a fallen angel, once a friend of Michael's, now king of the demon vampires.

"I do not have room for another hundred vangels here," Vikar griped.

"Ivak, have you not made ready the Southern headquarters for the vangels?"

"I'm trying," Ivak contended. "Workers keep quitting on me because of the snake problem. The repulsive reptiles seem to multiply by the day. Like Lucies."

"Has it never occurred to you that they might be just that?" Michael asked.

"Huh?" Ivak said.

"Asp, Garden of Eden, original sin. Ring any bells, Viking?" Verily, Vikings could be so thickheaded.

When Ivak still stared at him with lack of understanding, Michael continued, "Have the plantation renovated enough to house fifty new vangels within six weeks."

"That is imposs—" Ivak started to say, then quickly amended, "As you wish." And bowed his head with seeming meekness, which was fooling no one. Vikings did not do meek well.

"By the by, how is the baby coming?" Michael asked. To Michael's consternation and total surprise, Ivak was soon to be the father of a human baby. Vangels were not supposed to be capable of begetting children.

"Not soon enough. Gabrielle looks like she swallowed a wild boar, whole."

"Mayhap it will be twins. Or triplets," Michael offered.

"Whaaaat?" Ivak looked as if he was the one who swallowed something . . . something unpalatable.

Actually, Michael knew that it would be only one child. A boy. In fact, he had informed Ivak of that fact sometime ago. Ivak must have forgotten.

Michael left Ivak squirming in his seat as he moved on to another of the Vikings. "Cnut, you will help Vikar train the other fifty into vangels here in this very castle. Later, we will have to consider establishing another principality on the other side of the world. Possibly Italy, near the Vatican. Or the Holy Land. The Lord does have a fondness for Jerusalem."

They all cringed, wondering if they would be the one landed with that task. There would be incredible pressure to succeed in that favored country of the Lord's.

"Now, the reason for our meeting today." Michael speared the grim-faced Viking at the far end of the semicircle. "Mordr."

Mordr lifted his head, unafraid like some of the

others of whatever task Michael would assign him. He should be afraid. The Lord liked his archangels to test humans and vangels . . . especially Viking vangels . . . with tasks they hated.

"Thou will go to Las Vegas where there is a family in need of protection."

"Las Vegas!" Harek interjected. "Let me go. Las Vegas is my kind of place. Why can't I go on this mission?"

"Because you would enjoy it too much," Michael told the too smart, too greedy Viking who was teaching him to use a computer. "Besides, you have yet to put up a website for me."

"I could do that and take care of whatever task is required in Las Vegas," Harek persisted.

"Harek, Harek, Harek, have you been gambling again?"

Harek pretended to be affronted at the question. But then admitted, "Only with the stock market."

"Remember, Viking, thy sin is greed."

"Any profits I make go back into the vangel treasury," Harek contended.

He was fooling no one, least of all Michael. Yea, he contributed greatly to the VIK coffers, but he also amassed a vast fortune for himself. For what purpose, Michael had yet to discover. Harek's time would come. Later. Still, Michael could not help but prod Harek a bit more. "Now that I am learning computers, I noticed something odd on the Internet. 'Twould appear that someone is selling angel wing feathers as holy relics. I cannot imagine who would do such a sacrilegious thing, can you, Harek?"

"Um," Harek said.

"Since ten thousand seem to have been sold thus far, methinks they must be fake angel feathers. Mayhap goose feathers. What do you think, Harek?"

Harek knew enough to shut his mouth. No more pleas for a Las Vegas posting.

"Harek!" Trond exclaimed with mock horror. "I am shocked."

"And how goes your Navy SEAL training, Trond?" Michael asked.

Trond immediately realized his mistake in calling attention to himself. "All right," he answered, "but I have never worked so hard in all my life . . . or death. My aches have aches."

"Good," Michael said. The slothful, lazy Viking needed to ache, and where better to do that than in a society of fighting men who ran five miles in heavy boots afore breakfast?

Turning back to Mordr, who still maintained his grim-faced demeanor, Michael said, "There is a situation in Las Vegas. Some people are about to be threatened by an evil person. You are to protect them." Michael passed a piece of paper, which was handed down the line until it reached Mordr.

"One-eleven Crescent Street. That is all?" Mordr asked. "What kind of protection? What kind of evil? Is it Lucipires?"

"Possibly. You will have to ascertain the facts."

"That is all? Just go to this address and protect whoever, or whatever, is there?" Mordr inquired with a surly attitude that Michael did not appreciate. Not one bit. "Does it not make more sense to concentrate our efforts where there might be a large number of Lucies . . . like we did on that Sin Cruise, or at the SEAL base in Coronado, or at Angola Prison. I mean, one household? Really?"

"Really," Michael replied.

"Am I to offer protection only, or should I attempt to save the attacker threatening their safety as well?" Sometimes Lucies fanged and drained a human who was already evil, a quick and easy conversion to Lucie Hell. Other times, a human might have committed some bad act or was contemplating some heinous act; a fanging by a Lucie then gave them a sin taint, thus pushing them over their tipping points to mortal sin. It was the latter that vangels were sometimes able to help, if they could redeem them before crossing that final line. "Is this villain redeemable?"

Michael shrugged.

"Aaarrgh!" Mordr growled.

"I heard that."

Mordr frowned with frustration. "Can you not give me any more details?"

"Thou wilt know when thou wilt know."

Mordr muttered a foul word under his breath. Just so long as he did not take the Lord's name in vain, Michael could ignore the rudeness. For now.

Michael stared down the resistant man.

"As you wish," Mordr finally agreed.

"Now," Michael said. "Which one of you is guilty of the sin of lust?"

Six faces turned blood red.

All except Mordr, who had problems in that regard that would soon be tested. Mightily.

Some bribes are sweeter than others . . .

"**D**arla?" Miranda said into her cell phone as she barreled down the Strip in her green minivan toward Caesar's Palace, where P. Jack was apparently having a meltdown.

"Uh-oh!" Darla, her best friend since she'd moved to Las Vegas, said at the other end of the phone line. "Two-thirty in the afternoon? Can mean only one thing. An emergency with the rug rats."

Miranda couldn't be offended. At one time, she would have referred to kids in general as rug rats. She still did, at times. "P. Jack is having a crisis," Miranda said. "He's about to marry wife number fourteen, a stripper he met last night who is his soul mate for life. I'm on my way for an intervention."

"Good luck!" Darla laughed. Miranda had been telling her P. Jack stories from back when they'd been roommates in a one-room apartment five years ago on moving to the gambling mecca. A petite five foot two, compared to Miranda's five foot ten, Darla, a former karate instructor, was a bouncer, of all things, at one of the smaller casinos, Lucky Lou's. She knew P. Jack, too; in many ways Las Vegas was a small community, where the residents and employees all knew one another. In fact, Darla was the one who had referred P. Jack to Miranda's clinic. Darla had, of course, also been the recipient of one of his marriage proposals . . . between wives eight and nine, as Miranda recalled.

"What's up?" Darla asked.

"The agency is sending over the answer to my prayers this afternoon," Miranda continued. "A world-class household manager, please God. She does everything from child care to laundry to carpooling to homework supervision. Even cooking."

"Sounds like a wife to me."

"Exactly. And for what she charges, there may very well be a division of assets. Just kidding. But, really, I'm willing to pay for the right person." She paused. "This person has another unique qualification that I'm in need of. Ex-military."

Miranda's words were met with silence. Then a worried "Roger's out?"

"No, but he soon will be. Good behavior and all that. A halfway house at first."

"Maybe he's reformed. Maybe he's sorry for what

he's done and will leave his kids alone. Maybe he'll wait for the kids to grow up and contact him, if they ever want to."

"Do you think so?" Miranda asked hopefully.

"No."

They both laughed, halfheartedly.

"Anyhow, the job applicant will be there at four."

"So you need me there, not so much for the kids, as to arm wrestle this Mrs. Doubtfire to the floor so she won't escape 'til you get home."

"Yes. And to make sure the kids behave."

"The first I can handle. Not so sure about the latter."

"Oh, Darla, you know how much the little gremlins love you."

"Don't try to butter me up."

"Seriously, hon, can you cover for me? I shouldn't be much later than four-thirty." As an incentive, she added, "I'll bring Chinese for dinner. And Shakey's sticky buns for dessert."

"Consider me buttered."

Whatever happens in Vegas better stay in Vegas . . .

Once again, excitement reigned in Horror, the icy palace headquarters of the Lucipires in the far Arctic regions of the world. The prospect of a new mission to bring vast numbers of evil humans into their ranks had them salivating with anticipation. Literally.

Not a pretty sight, thought Jasper, shivering with distaste. Now king of the demon vampires, Jasper had once been a beauteous archangel, one of God's favored ones, afore being expelled from Heaven along with Lucifer and his other rebel followers. The one delegated to expel them had been St. Michael the Archangel, Jasper's most-hated enemy.

And it wasn't just the drooling that repulsed him. When they were in their demonoid forms, whether they be high haakai, mungs, imps, or hordlings, their skin was scaly, their eyes bloodred, their hands and feet claw-like, with slime oozing from every pore, and then there were the fangs. Of course, they could morph into the most attractive human forms, when needed.

Jasper walked purposefully down the Corridor of Change, where he usually slowed down to enjoy his unique collection, but not today. Too much on his mind.

Both sides of the hallway were lined with giant butterfly jars in which "dead" humans were pinned through the heart like, well, butterflies. They hung inside, flailing their limbs, screaming their no-longer-beating hearts out. Eventually, they would reach a state of stasis, at which point they either willingly became Lucipires or entered the torture dungeons where a little, or a lot, of painful persuasion usually brought them around to Jasper's way of thinking.

"Shall I take that one out for you to play with?" asked Beltane, his French hordling assistant. He pointed a clawed hand toward the right where a new human had just been placed the night before. A blond woman who had been active in a worldwide sex slave trade specializing in young girls and boys. *Very* young.

"Later," Jasper snapped, then softened his tone, realizing that the young Creole—young, as in only one hundred and fifty years old, compared to Jasper's ancient age—had only been trying to please him. "Mayhap you and I can both play with her later."

Beltane gazed at Jasper with the adoration that was his due, but in the young hordling's case, the affection appeared to be genuine. Jasper's cold heart warmed a bit at the prospect. This must be the paternal feeling humans talked about regarding fathers and sons.

If only all his minions regarded Jasper with the same high regard, if not at least deference. He was thinking, of course, of Heinrich Mann, who stood in the open doorway of the conference room up ahead, waiting for him. Heinrich, whom Jasper not-so-affectionately referred to as Heiney, was a former Nazi general, who had somehow gained the confidence of Satan, and become a personal thorn in Jasper's backside.

If he gives me one of those Hitler salutes, I swear I am going to puke.

"'Master," Heinrich said, bowing low. "It is good to see you again."

Liar, liar, your swastika's on fire.

"Welcome, Heinrich," Jasper said in a tone that told the German weasel just how unwelcome he was. "Please come inside and be seated."

The open doorway was still blocked by the German, who was only seventy years old, having died when in his thirties, serving as a Nazi officer during World War II. Unlike Jasper, who was almost two thousand years old. A prime candidate to become a Lucipire, Heinrich had been, but the biggest pain in Jasper's hairy behind he'd been ever since then.

"The other members of the council are already inside," Heinrich informed him, as if Jasper were not already aware of that fact. And since when had Heinrich become a council member? As far as Jasper knew, and he knew everything about Lucipires and their commanding council, Heinrich was a mere liaison with Satan. Well, not exactly "mere," but not a council member, either. "I wanted to have a word with you in private."

Uh-oh!

"Satan is displeased by the discord between us."

"Us?"

"You and I." Heinrich's scaly face flushed with color.

Jasper hadn't known that Lucipires could blush. Amazing. And alarming when you considered why Heinrich would be blushing. It did not bode well for Jasper, he would bet his best thumbscrew.

Jasper arched an overly thick brow at Heinrich.

Heinrich shifted uneasily from foot to foot.

Uh-oh! Jasper thought again.

"The solution might be for me to stay here."

"Here?"

"At Horror."

Jasper was horrified. "Why?"

"Well, I was thinking that since we lost one of the command council members last year that . . . well, uh, maybe I could familiarize myself with all the duties of a high haakai by studying under you here at Horror and, uh, eventually be appointed to fill that spot."

Heinrich wanted to replace Dominique Fontaine? Holy Lucifer! She had been one of his seven high commanders until her permanent annihilation last year by the vangels led by those seven loathsome Sigurdsson brothers who comprised the VIK leadership. She'd operated out of a New Orleans mansion named Anguish that housed a five-star restaurant on the first floor and torture chambers that would impress the Marquis de Sade on the upper floors. Creole by birth, she'd been six feet tall with café-au-lait skin. Gorgeous when in human form. Evil to her rotted bones. Not that evil was a bad thing. Heinrich was evil, too, of course. They all were, but the German couldn't begin to fill her seat.

"So, you think to nominate yourself for council membership?" Jasper asked.

Heinrich nodded enthusiastically. The dumb asswipe!

Over my dead body! "Heinrich, you're a mung. Council members are commanders of high haakai standing."

In the Lucipire society, there were a few Seraphim

Lucipires, like Jasper, who had been archangels at one time and expelled from Heaven. Next came the high haakai, haakai, mungs, then the imps and hordlings, which were like foot soldiers to the demon vampires. Mungs were usually of large size, as much as eight feet tall, their scales oozing a poisonous mung, and dragging a tail. Well, all the Lucipires had tails, to Jasper's discomfort. Try sitting on a toilet, for example.

"Couldn't I be the first mung to serve on the council? After all, I have the ear of Satan. That should be an asset."

"Did Satan come up with this idea?"

"No, but he might be convinced to favor my appointment if you back me."

Was Heinrich delusional? Did he not know how much Jasper despised him? His ambition, his ladder climbing, his ass kissing . . . well, tail kissing. With more patience than the lackwit Lucipire deserved, Jasper said, "This is not a discussion for today. Let us revisit the question sometime in the future." *Like the far, far future. Can anyone say eternity?* "The most important thing today is the proposal for our new mission."

"That is another thing," Heinrich said.

Jasper rolled his eyes. If Heiney did not soon move from the middle of the doorway, Jasper was going to make him a foot taller by putting him on his favorite rack.

Quickly, Heinrich explained, sensing Jasper's growing impatience. "I do not think targeting casinos is the best thing to do. Not with all the heightened security related to terrorism."

Ah, now Jasper understood why Heinrich was really here. The proposal up for discussion at this special meeting of the council had been generated by one of his favorite Lucipires, the Hebrew Zebulan. Since Zeb was a Jew, Heinrich, a Nazi, hated him with a passion. Perhaps that was why Jasper liked Zeb so much. Because Heinrich didn't. How perverse was that? Or maybe it was just a case of: The enemy of my enemy is my friend.

"Enough! Move aside, Heinrich, and take thyself back to Hell. I have no need of you at the moment. Tell Satan I will report to him directly after this meeting."

Heinrich was about to protest, but Jasper rose to his full seven-foot-two height, his fangs elongated, and raised a clawed hand. With a mighty swipe, he cast the Nazi aside. Not that he had anything against Nazis, mind. Their particular kind of evil had been like chicken soup to a devilish soul.

Before the idiot could respond, Jasper entered the council room where Beltane was holding his chair out for him. Jasper slammed the door behind him, and locked it with a mind transmittal, which came in handy when dealing with bothersome gnats like Heinrich. Jasper could hear his frustrated scream through the thick wood, and smiled.

"Good day, gentlemen," he greeted the council members warmly, looking around the U-shaped table at the four high haakais waiting for him. Each, garbed in magnificent capes over their demonoid forms, rose and bowed to him. There was enough slime in this room, oozing from porous scales, to lubricate a locomotive. The smell of sulfur, the bane of Lucipires, was rank in their midst. Jasper had grown accustomed to it. In fact, on certain occasions when he coupled with a female Lucipire, it rather turned him on. "Master," the council members said as one.

Hector, the former Roman soldier, lived in the hidden catacombs beneath the Vatican; his headquarters were called Terror. The Arab Haroun al Rashid, had been a Silk Road merchant who specialized in slave trading; his luxurious tent city in the desert was called Torment. Yakov the Russian lived in Siberia in a dwelling he called Desolation. And Zebulan the Hebrew, his favorite, dwelled in volcanic ruins in Greece that he deemed Gloom. Jasper's own palace was alternately referred to as Despair or Horror. Same thing.

"Sit, sit," he said to his comrades. "We have much to accomplish today. But first, have you all been offered a beverage?"

Nubile naked humans, both male and female, who would eventually become Lucipires, stood ready with trays of pure virgin blood in crystal goblets. His council members declined his offer, pointing to drinks already placed in front of each of them. He waved for a young girl to bring one for him and for Beltane, who sat to his right, but back farther from the table. The girl's nipples were pierced with rings from which hung small silver beaded weights. Through her waxed genitalia, he could see that her labia had also been pierced, the folds stretched apart with a slim bar, the clitoris prominent and always exposed. He'd personally participated in the torture of this woman and patted her rump appreciatively for the pleasure it had given him. She flinched slightly and he licked his lips with anticipation. He looked forward to her further punishment. Although she'd reached the stage of stasis, she'd not yet accepted her fate. She would. Before nightfall.

The other naked humans had vibrating phalluses protruding from their vaginas and anuses that could be turned on or off by remotes sitting in front of his council members. To entertain council members until his arrival and later, if they were so inclined. By the expression on some of the humans, he could tell they'd been well titillated so far. Some still were.

"Shall we have reports first?" Jasper suggested.

One by one, they told of the "kills" in their areas.

"Kills" were not really kills in the usual sense whereby a soul went to Heaven or Hell or Purgatory based on their life deeds. No, this was something entirely different. Long, long ago. Satan had put together bands of demon vampires to harvest human souls before their time, before they had a chance to repent.

Lucipires generally only attacked those who had already committed some grave sin or were contemplating such. Everything from bad to truly evil; the Lucipires weren't particular. They just helped the victims along the path to Lucipiredom by fanging them with a sin taint. If the humans were already advanced on the road to Hell, that's all it would take to kill them, making their bodies disappear and be transported to whichever headquarters was to handle the torture and change to Lucipires. Many of these victims were referred to as missing persons in the human society. Few humans accepted their new lives as Lucipires, not right off. They needed convincing.

Haroun reported prosperous harvests in his part of the world. Not surprising with the wars that still raged in the Middle East.

Hector was concentrating on sinners who journeyed to Rome hoping to have all their bad deeds absolved. Not if Hector and his Lucipires could fang them first.

Yakov said his job was somewhat easy because the Russians loved their vodka, and everyone knew that liquor was the gatekeeper to Hell. They should call vodka Satan's Handmaid.

Zeb stood then, and Jasper preened. He didn't know why he was so fond of the Jew. It wasn't as if he had more kills than any of the other haakai. In fact, his present assignment to the Naval Air Base in Coronado, California, had been decidedly unsuccessful.

"Have you managed to turn any of the Navy SEALs yet?"

Zeb shook his head. "No, but I'm working on two of them who are wavering on the side of extreme sin. But there are more than ten thousand men and women at the Naval Amphibious Base there who are away from home and thus easily tempted."

Hector was looking at a paper in front of him. "Your numbers are not that great there, Zeb. Do you consider that site a lost cause?"

"Absolutely not. Yes, it is taking me a while to turn a SEAL, but we never thought it would be easy. Loyalty, faithfulness, dedication, and all that crap. Damnation, but how do I fang men or women who run five miles, twice a day?"

"Run after them," Yakov suggested, and they all laughed. Hard to picture Lucipires jogging with their tails dragging. Of course, Zeb would be in humanoid form there.

"In my defense," Zeb continued, "remember our discussion before I relocated to Coronado? One SEAL kill would equal a hundred others. Maybe several hundred. A real coup!"

"You're right, Zeb. Continue your work there," Jasper said.

"But what is this proposal you are making here today?" Haroun wanted to know. Even as he spoke, he was fussing with a remote and watching a red-haired Irish girl on the other side of the room as she began to squirm. A buzzing sound resonated in the momentarily silent room.

"I followed some military men for a weekend trip to Las Vegas recently, and it occurred to me that casino cities like Las Vegas or Atlantic City or Reno or Monaco or Macau would be prime hunting grounds for sinners."

Everyone sat straighter with interest.

"You could be right, Zeb," Jasper said. "They don't call Las Vegas Sin City for nothing."

The others nodded.

"And Macau in China is being touted as the new Las Vegas," Hector added.

"We must proceed cautiously this time," Jasper said, not wanting to bring up the last three failed missions. A Sin Cruise, the SEALs, and then Angola Prison. "Planning will be everything. What do you have in mind, Zeb?"

"Well, let us try to hit several of the casino cities at once. That way, the vangels will have to divide their ranks to fight us, assuming they learn of our plans."

"There are four of you here," Jasper pointed out. "Each of you can handle operations in Las Vegas, Reno, Monaco, and Macau. I will oversee operations. We can leave Atlantic City for some other time."

They all had suggestions for how to proceed, and Jasper loved how they worked together. Not like it had been when Dominique was around, always creating discord.

"We will immediately infiltrate the casinos with some of our Lucipires," Zeb said, apparently having put some thought into this already. "They can work in many capacities. Everything from maintenance to roulette dealers to showgirls to—"

"Well, if you're going to have some of our female Lucipires be showgirls, you might as well let some of them be hookers. Is that not what they call paid harlots in this time?" Haroun grinned, which was not a pretty thing on a demon vampire. The fangs and long tongues got in the way.

"They would like that," Yakov agreed. "In fact, some of the men could hook, too."

When the council finished making initial plans and agreed to meet again in one week, Zeb asked Jasper for a private moment.

"Would you agree to my taking a few days off?"

"At the beginning of a mission?"

Zeb shrugged. "I feel a bit burned out."

Odd statement for a demon! "Where would you go?"

Zeb shrugged again. "Somewhere warm, I think."

Jasper had heard rumors that Zeb had a secret hideaway which he escaped to on occasion. Thus far, Jasper hadn't felt a need to investigate further. "I could go with you," he surprised himself by saying.

Zeb was shocked, but he immediately regained his calm. "I do not think that would be a good idea. Not this time." He waggled his big eyebrows at him. Even as a demon vampire, Zeb was rather handsome.

So, a woman was involved. "Anyone I know?"

Zeb shook his head.

"A Lucipire?"

"Not yet," Zeb said, and that sealed the deal for Jasper.

"Have a good time, then work hard to make this new operation successful," Jasper said, patting Zeb on the shoulder.

Once his council members had departed, Jasper sighed with satisfaction, thinking, *Betimes it is good to be me.* Then he turned to Beltane and said, "Care for a game of eyeball Ping-Pong?"

Four

Even Vikings get lost sometimes . . .

Mordr was in a foul mood.

He had walked from one end of the famous Las Vegas Strip to the other. All he had was a blister on his heel and a stupid address. At first he had cruised the gambling mecca in the cool air conditioning of the Lexus SUV with blacked-out windows that Trond had lent him, but the GPS was malfunctioning. So, he had reverted to the age-old method of transport. Walking. Even a street policeman he had approached had no idea where Crescent Street was. Must be a new development, the cop had said.

"Develop what?" he'd asked.

"Move it, buster." The cop must have thought he was jesting. Like Mordr ever jested!

At an all-you-can-eat buffet palace (though there was naught about it that resembled a palace), he'd eaten so much that the manager gave him dirty looks. He'd dirty-looked the lackwit right back, then flashed his fangs, something that was not only immature but forbidden to vangels in less-than-dangerous situations. He was inordinately pleased to see the miscreant scurry away in fright.

He'd been propositioned three times back on the street. One time the offer had involved some explicit sexual activity that defied imagination. He was not interested, though he was curious. He would have to ask Ivak later. Ivak fashioned himself the expert on all things of a sexual nature.

In a casino, bored to the bone, he put a dollar in a Wheel of Fortune machine and, to his embarrassment, heard bells and whistles go off all around him. Folks turned to stare at him. Apparently, he'd won some kind of jackpot. Five thousand dollars. Michael would have his skin if he knew he'd been gambling.

He'd stopped two young men from picking the pocket of an elderly woman in denim braies, high-heeled boots, and a cowboy hat. The woman, who was eighty if she was a day, also tried to proposition him, as a reward. Not if his eventual wings depended on it!

One hotel pretended to be a Roman palace (Las Vegas had a thing about palaces—Caesar's Palace, the Palace Café, the Palace Wedding Chapel, Palace Deli, Palace Pedicures). Another hotel claimed to be a riverboat. In the middle of the desert! Yet others were an American frontier town, a circus, a Greek spa, even a Viking world, complete with a longship in the lobby in a miniature pool that churned out waves, like an ocean. That particular hotel was called—what else!— Valhalla. The waitresses were dressed up as some halfbrain's idea of what a Valkyrie would wear. As if Odin would allow his females to half expose breasts pushed up nigh to their chins by some artificial means or other. They wobbled about in heels so high their buttocks arched out. He supposed some men might consider them a lustsome sight. Mordr did not!

The last straw for him was when a half dozen Elvis

clones riding bicycles almost ran him over and didn't even stop to see if he was all right. Disgusted, he went into a little tavern where he ordered a cold beer. He was sitting there when an exceedingly tall woman came in and sat on a bar stool beside him. She was what was known here as a showgirl . . . or a prostitute. It was hard to tell the difference in this town. With feathers in her big blond hair, thick makeup including red pouty lips and eyelashes so long and curly they had to be fake, and a skimpy outfit that was three sizes too small, she let out a long sigh. Without her placing an order, the bartender, who obviously knew her well, passed over a tall glass of iced water.

"How're tricks, Trixie?" the bartender quipped.

"Tricky." The woman shrugged and used a napkin to pat the perspiration from her forehead. "Only a dozen people in the audience today. If we don't get more business, the show will close down."

"The economy," the bartender concluded.

"Tell me about it."

As she sipped at her drink, being careful not to smear her lipstick, the woman turned to him and said, "Where you from, pal?"

You do not want to know. Just then, Mordr noticed something. Under the thick layer of paint on the woman's face was a faint hint of . . . whiskers? He arched a brow.

"Yep," the woman—uh, man—replied with a grin.

Mordr burst out with a short laugh—at himself for being so easily duped.

"Jack Trixson," the man-woman said, stretching out a hand in greeting.

A nice Viking name, Mordr decided, and shook the man's hand. "Mordr Sigurdsson."

"Great hair, Mordr!" Jack remarked.

Mordr did not think much about his appearance.

His hair was long in the Norse style with war braids framing each side of his face, but to him the color seemed a dull blondish brown and unremarkable. Normally, he would have scoffed or done violence at such a compliment, especially from a man, but he needed to tread carefully in this strange city. "Thank you. Yours is quite . . . um, impressive, too." Impressive it was, indeed. Big and blond, reaching down to his wide shoulders.

"A wig," Jack informed him with a grin. "Looks real, doesn't it? Pantene conditioner. You oughta try it. It'll give your hair more body and luster and take care of those split ends."

Split ends? I have split ends? What are split ends? This was the strangest conversation Mordr had ever had with a man . . . or woman. He could not contain his curiosity then. "Are you a man who likes women? A man who likes men? A man who likes both? Or . . ." He tossed his hands in the air. "I mean no offense. Truly."

"No offense taken. The first of those, actually. This is just a job. I have a wife and two kids to support, and my acting career was going nowhere. So, we left Hollywood and came here. Until the economy hit the toilet, I was doing well as a female impersonator."

They talked for some time until Jack had to return for the second show of the day. Mordr declined his invitation to attend. In the end, it was Jack who gave him directions to Crescent Street. Turns out it was right around the corner from Jack's own home in a new development, which was why Mordr had been having trouble finding it on the GPS, as the policeman had suggested earlier.

By mid-afternoon, Mordr got to Crescent Street. He was surprised to find a residential neighborhood, and 111 Crescent Street, the address Michael had given him, was a two-story home of impressive proportions with a wide lawn being currently pampered by a sprinkler system, which was unusual in the afternoon. Most of these contraptions operated only at night. And wasn't that another strange thing about modern times? Wasting water to grow weeds, which was what grass was, really. He could just imagine King Olaf telling one of his servants, "Go water the weeds in the courtyard so the horses won't bruise their hooves on the hard-packed dirt when they come back from battle."

Not sure what to expect when he came here today, Mordr was armed with a back holster pressed against his white T-shirt, under an unbuttoned black shirt worn over cargo pants with all the appropriate pockets for knives and other specially treated weapons. Normally, he would have worn a cape to hide his armaments, but that would be too obvious in this desert heat.

He walked up the sidewalk to the front door, unsure whether to first circle and study the property to assess any potential danger. There were Bulldog Security notices in various windows, tiny cameras placed in strategic locations, what was probably a motion detector that was operational at nighttime, a numbered panel next to the door frame to bar entry by strangers. Definitely a place in need of protection, for one reason or another. He sniffed the air for the sulfurous scent of Lucies. Nothing. No scent of lemons, either, which would indicate a person hell-bent on . . . well, going to Hell, who might already have been fanged with a Lucie sin taint but not yet crossed over to the dark side. In other words, a human he might be able to save.

While he was pondering his choices, the door flew open and a young girl of no more than ten years took him by the arm and, with surprising strength, yanked him inside. He had only a brief moment to notice her bright red curls and blinking, owlish eyes behind wire-rimmed glasses. She had water spots on her red blouse, as if she'd just run in from a rain shower. "You're late," she accused. "That's no way to get a job. I may be a kid, but even I know that tardiness is a no-no in job hunting."

"Late for what?"

The little girl rolled her eyes, as if he were a dunderhead. Which he felt like at the moment. "Oh well. Thank God, you're here. Finally."

"No. Thank Michael."

"Is he the head of the agency?"

"You could say that." God's special agent.

"You better come with me. Ben and Sam are about to do something really dumb."

"Who are Ben and Sam?" Mordr knew of no Ben or Sam.

"My brothers," she said with decided disgust. "They're eight-year-old twins who are always in trouble. Idiots! Ben thinks he's Evel Knievel. One time he tried to roller-skate off the garage roof onto a mattress and almost cracked his fool head open. Sam thinks he's a born gambler. He'll probably try to con you into a game of blackjack. Don't play with him. He cheats."

All Mordr could think to say was "Huh?"

"This could be dangerous. C'mon. You need to stop them." She tugged on his arm, trying to move him down the hallway toward what sounded like a party or something in the distance. A crash, like a trash can falling over. Loud voices, like a television set, with screams and shrieks and laughter. Farther away, young voices, human, mixed with screams and shrieks and laughter.

"Laughter? That does not sound like any kind of danger requiring my help." He was about to warn her that it was dangerous for a young maid to invite a grown man, a stranger, into her house.

Before he could speak, she tapped a foot with impatience. "Ben can't start the barbecue and he's looking for gasoline to help him. I hid the can under the patio umbrella in the shed, but he could find it any minute now. Ben thinks that, just because Sam is running the hose, it will put out any explosion. Did I mention that they're idiots?"

Ah, the water spots. He gave a brief nod of understanding, though he didn't understand much.

"I told them that they would be in big trouble. I told them gasoline wasn't the same as lighter fluid, which is also dangerous, but they wouldn't listen to me. Said they were hungry for hamburgers from the grill and that they knew what they were doing. Boys!" She shook her head as if the entire male race of the younger set were hopeless. Him, too.

Despite himself, he was starting to admire the warrior lass. She had ballocks, trying to rule her brothers.

But wait. Did she say gasoline? The house could be afire soon. "Where's your mother?" he demanded, quickly scanning the hallway and the living room and dining room off to either side, both of which were empty. He would have something to say to a woman who would neglect her children so.

"Dead."

Oh! "Your father?"

"In prison."

That is not good. "Well, who in bloody hell is caring for you?"

"I'm pretty sure 'bloody hell' is cursing. You're going to have to put a quarter in the swear jar."

"Aaarrgh! Who in bloody hell is caring for you?" he repeated.

"Tsk, tsk, tsk!" she had the nerve to chastise him before explaining, "Aunt Mir cares for us, ever since Mom died, but she got delayed at the casino—"

A casino! A sin palace, for a certainty. Not that I have any room to judge. But what kind of mother, even a foster mother, gambles, leaving her children to fend for themselves? She will probably arrive home drukkinn.

"—and her friend Darla came to watch us 'til she gets home." The girling was midway down the corridor, continuing to talk as she waited for him to rush to her assistance, while he stood in place by the front door. Shoving her glasses up higher on her little nose, she blinked. "Or 'til you got here."

"Me?"

"Yep. Our new nanny."

"A nanny? Are you calling me a goat?"

She closed her eyes and appeared to be counting. When she was seemingly in control of her temper, she explained very slowly, "Well, household manager then. That's the title the agency gave Aunt Mir. Darla is supposed to keep you company until Aunt Mir can interview you. Aunt Mir said you're the answer to all our prayers and Darla was to sit on you if you tried to escape, but I think she was kidding. Don't you?"

"Don't I what?" *Did she really say I am the answer to someone's prayer? Hardly! More like the opposite. And anyone trying to sit on me is going to have trouble getting me to the floor first.*

"Are you a Viking? You look just like those men on that series we watched on the History Channel."

"Yes, I am a Viking, but I am not a house person, like you mentioned. Nor am I the answer to some fool prayer. You have me mixed up with—" *Oh no! Mike, you didn't!*

"Whatever." The girl, who probably thought he was arguing about the title, not the job itself, was jumping up and down with agitation. "You need to help us. Now! Hurry, hurry, hurry."

He reached up to pull at his long hair in frustration, but restrained himself. Instead, he fisted his hands at his sides and counted to ten, in Old Norse. "Where is this Darla person?"

From upstairs, he heard a pounding, like someone knocking on wood. And muffled curses.

The girl's face got red as she looked everywhere except upward.

"What's that noise?" he asked, narrowing his eyes suspiciously.

"It might be Darla," she said, looking everywhere but up at him.

"Why is she yelling?"

"She might be locked in the bathroom." Still not making eye contact with him.

"Why?"

"Don't worry about that now. We have to stop Ben and Sam first."

With a snort of disgust, he followed the girl through the kitchen, which looked as if a horde of Huns had swept through. There was food and books and a spilled pitcher of some red drink . . . not blood, he was certain. Well, fairly certain. The source of the television sounds came from a small set on the counter showing a lack-wit sponge that talked. He'd seen his brother Vikar's children watching the same show on numerous occasions. And people thought Vikings had been strange for believing in gods and trolls and dragons and such.

Outside, a big white dog, which resembled a polar bear, was barking as it galloped in circles around the backyard, over and over and over. It was being chased by a boy, about eight years old, in a red St. Joseph's Academy T-shirt who had a running hose in his little hands. Another boy in a blue St. Joseph's Academy T-shirt, the twin of the hose wielder, was standing over a cold barbecue, striking match after match, trying to set the grill afire. The matches must have been wet because not one of them ignited. Thank God! The two boys were as soaked as the dog. An even smaller boy, about five years old, with blond spiky hair and a freckled face, was bemoaning the fact that he'd been unable to find the gasoline can, so far. And suddenly latched on to Mordr's thigh was a little girl, about the same size and similar appearance to freckled boy number three. Not identical but possibly another pair of twins. Her hair was long and blond and held off her face with butterfly clips, and she was missing two front teeth. He glanced down and saw her soulful greenish-gray eyes gazing up at him as if he were some hero come to save their personal planet.

"Are you my daddy?" the little one asked.

"Don't mind Linda. She asks every man that," Owl Girl informed him.

In that instant, he realized that for the first time in a thousand and more years he was face to face with not only a little girl, roughly the same age as Kata had been, looking for a lost father, but also a boyling, or several boylings, much the same size as Jomar had been. *Before their deaths.* Blood drained from his head, his legs turned to butter, and he reached out for the door frame to brace himself. "I . . . have . . . to . . . go," he gritted out.

"You can't go," Owl Girl howled. "You're a Viking. Practically a superhero. You have to help us."

"He's a Viking?" all three boys said as one. "Wow!"

The still-running hose was turning the sparsely grassed plot of the backyard into a pool of mud, but none of them seemed to notice, even though they were barefooted.

"We're getting a Viking for a babysitter!" Red Shirt remarked with obvious pleasure. "Cool, dude!"

"Do you have a sword?" Blue Shirt wanted to know.

"I can't wait to tell Johnny Severino. This beats his pet snake any day," said the smallest boy.

"I have to pee," the gremlin attached to his leg whined.

"You guys are in *big* trouble!" Owl Girl yelled.

The three boys made a rude gesture at her that involved sticking out their tongues and blowing.

"Aaarrgh!" she screamed with frustration, then put her hands on her narrow hips and tapped a foot impatiently, like she was some mini-adult, or something. "Are you going to help us or not?"

"Let the Darla person help you."

"I told you. Darla is locked in the bathroom," she replied, as if he were too thickheaded to understand simple English.

"Unlock her then."

"We can't," the boy in the blue T-shirt said. "The dog ate the key."

They all turned to look at said dog, a huge mongrel of an animal, who was presently sitting with a big doggie grin on its face.

"Enough! Who is responsible for this . . . this disaster?" he hollered, stepping out onto the stone-flagged patio.

All five children jumped at the volume of his voice.

"Ben did it." The boy in the blue shirt pointed to his twin in the red shirt.

Red Shirt stuck out his tongue at Blue Shirt.

"Can you jump rope?" the one with a death grip on his thigh asked. Apparently, peeing was no longer of imminent importance. *I am a Viking. I cannot believe I am saying—thinking—the word* pee. *Is this to be my punishment then? No doubt this is Michael's brand of humor. Warped.*

"Don't be silly. Vikings do not jump rope."

"Betcha they can."

"They're too fat."

What? Mordr sucked in his flat belly.

"They're not fat. They're just big," Owl Girl said in his defense.

Just then, he felt a wetness on his feet. Damn! Did the little one piss on his shoes? Glancing down, he stepped aside, realizing with relief that it was just a small puddle from the increasing pool in the yard.

"I'm gonna ask Santa for a sword next Christmas."

"It won't fit in your stocking, dumbbell."

"It will fit under the tree, dumbbell."

"Can you braid my hair like yours?"

Just then, one of the older twins got a bright idea. Dropping the still running hose to the ground, he shouted with glee, "Slip and slide!"

The other boys cheered.

Soon they were covered, head to toe, with mud as they ran fast, then slid face first across the mud. Mordr noted that the pool of slimy mud was getting deeper. Even the dog, chasing the children, did a slide. On its rump. The little girl clinging to him giggled. Only Owl Girl disapproved as she murmured, "Aunt Mir is going to have a fit."

Enough was enough! The little trolls weren't his responsibility, but someone had to take control. He walked over to the faucet and shut off the hose. Then he bellowed, "Get out of that damn mud, and come here. At once!"

Five heads shot up, and Owl Girl muttered, "Finally!"

The three boys, dripping mud, came to stand before him.

Using his most menacing voice, he demanded, "Who is responsible for this mess?"

They all spoke at once.

"Sam started the barbecue."

"Linda said she wanted a hot dog."

"Larry let the dog loose."

"Ben hooked up the hose."

"Maggie dropped the key that Ruff ate."

Owl Girl, whose name was apparently Maggie, hissed with outrage, "It was an accident. I was trying to help Darla."

"Well, you're all going to clean it up," he declared, "starting with that kitchen."

There was some muttering, and Maggie said at his side, "That's not fair. I didn't—"

He glared at her. First, she wanted his help. Then, she wanted to tell him how to help.

She pressed her lips together, but she was not happy. She probably regretted having let him in the door.

As if he cared!

"Before you do anything, though, you need to get hosed off."

The three boys smiled.

"And I am going to do the hosing."

The smiling boys no longer smiled.

But just then, the boy in the red shirt said, "Holy shit! Look at Ruff. I ain't never seen a dog do such a big dump before."

"Swear jar, swear jar," Blue Shirt hooted.

The huge dog was, indeed, squatting near the bushes at the side of the yard, doing his business. And it *was* an impressive dump.

"Someone better check his poop for the key," Red Shirt pronounced, and five sets of eyes turned to him.

Fortunately, or not so fortunately, a female voice spoke sharply behind him. "What the hell is going on here? And who the hell are you?"

He turned as best he could with the girl still clinging to his thigh and almost staggered backward at what he saw. A woman with flaming red hair stood in the kitchen doorway holding a broom aloft, as a weapon, he supposed. She was glaring at him through icy green eyes, like a mother bear whose cubs were threatened. A red belt cinched in the narrow waist of a black linen dress on her tall, shapely figure. The dress came down to her knees, which were bare and led to smooth and softly curved calves, then shiny black high-heeled shoes.

He'd seen more beautiful women before. More voluptuous ones, too. But there was something different about this one, something he couldn't quite define. Except that he knew one thing. Blood rushed from his wildly pumping heart to all his extremities, including the one that had been slumbering since oh, let's say, the Dark Ages. For the first time in what seemed like forever, lust passed over him in waves so powerful he could scarce contain the urge to toss the wench over his shoulder and carry her to the nearest bed furs. The worm betwixt his legs became a snake, hard and huge and throbbing. He had to have this woman. He had to!

"You heard me, buster. Who the hell are you?" she demanded. "And where's Darla?"

He was called back to his surroundings then, aware of the children watching his every move. Now was not the time for lustsome actions, or even lustsome thoughts. Later, he promised himself. For now, he knew that he had to choose his words carefully in responding to her question. But then, he recalled what Owl Girl had said to him on first opening the front door.

"I believe—" he started to say, then had to clear his husky throat. "I believe I am the answer to your prayers."

Five

The answer to prayers comes in many
forms, some bigger than others . . .

𝕬 short time ago, Miranda had walked into the
kitchen, which appeared to have imploded onto itself,
and turned off Nickelodeon's annoying SpongeBob
on the blaring television. No one had been around to
notice.

Stepping up to the sink, she'd looked through the
window to the backyard and had done a double take.
She couldn't believe what she'd been seeing.

To the right, an open barbecue, where the children
had been expressly forbidden to touch the outside grill.

To the far center, Ruff had been raising his tail high,
depositing a large pile of matter right next to a rose-
bush. She sure hoped doo-doo was a good fertilizer,
or another bush in this once nicely landscaped setting
would bite the dust. And it was not easy growing anything in this desert climate.

Front and center, a running hose had lain at the
edge of a huge mud pool that had previously been her
grassy backyard. Okay, somewhat grassy backyard,

considering the pounding it got from three rough-housing boys. The kids had been begging for a pool for some time. Looked like they'd taken matters into their own hands. Ben and Sam and Larry were covered with the brown goop from head to bare toes. It was going to take hours to shower off the mud that no doubt filled every bodily crevice. The stains would never come out of their clothes. And God only knew if Miranda would be able to repair the damage to the grass. She might be forced to install a pool, after all.

To the left, Maggie had been coming from the garden shed. She'd been mud-free but had a clothespin on her nose and the pooper scooper in her hand heading toward Ruff's latest "gift." The children took turns every week with this distasteful task.

In the middle of all this, Linda, also mud-free, had been and still was clinging like Saran Wrap to the monstrously big thigh of a monstrously big man. Long, brownish-blond hair with crystals or gems of some kind intertwined in the two thin braids that framed a face with sharply sculpted Nordic features. About six foot four. Muscles apparent everywhere, even under cargo pants and an unbuttoned black shirt over a pure white T-shirt. A modern-day Viking, by the looks of him. Hey, she and the kids had watched the Viking series on the History Channel like millions of people. An educational as well as entertaining experience. Did he work for Valhalla, that new casino? If so, what was he doing here?

Amazing the things a woman noticed in the flash of a moment. But then, this kind of guy probably got lots of notice from women. Not that she was looking at him in that way. Much.

With delayed realization, like dominoes falling in her brain, several facts became apparent. There was a man here. A stranger! On her property! With her children!

Oh my God!

Was he a threat?

Of course he is. Look at the boys lined up like little soldiers staring up at him with fright. The man had a hand on one hip and was wagging a forefinger of the other hand at the boys, giving them some kind of lecture.

Where was Darla?

Oh my God!

Was Darla tied up in some closet? Or dead? Or lying upstairs on one of the beds, sated and boneless after hours of hot sex with a Viking? No, Darla wouldn't be that irresponsible with kids in the house. Well, not usually.

The boys were the first to notice her as she stepped through the open sliding glass doors. Instead of looking relieved that she'd come to their rescue, they looked even more frightened. And guilty. Oooh, she knew that look well. What had they done now? Aside from turning the yard into a mud-wrestling arena? Could they have played some trick on this man as he walked innocently through the neighborhood and then he'd tracked them down here and now he had some sort of retribution in mind.

Over my dead body! She narrowed her eyes with menace and picked up the closest weapon. A broom.

"What the hell is going on here? And who the hell are you?" she demanded.

Normally, the kids would have been yelling, "Swear jar" at her for that slip of the tongue, but not now. Another clue that they were scared of this stranger. Or of her.

The man turned and froze. With a mixture of shock and wonder, he gazed at her through oddly sad, crystal blue eyes as if she were some heavenly apparition that had landed here, just for him. A gift from the gods. Not the usual reaction she got from men these days. Not when she often forgot to comb her hair or didn't have time to apply makeup. The expression on his face soon turned to one of dismay, though. Was it her "weapon" or her scowl that brought about the transformation? Or had he got a better look and come to his senses? It didn't matter.

"You heard me, buster. Who the hell are you?" she demanded. "And where's Darla?"

"I believe . . . I believe I am the answer to your prayers," he replied hesitantly and not at all happy about his assertion.

"Oh Lord! That tired old line!"

Before she could say more, the children all began to speak, at once.

"He's the new nanny," said Maggie, who had taken care of her doggie chore and had come up to stand beside her.

The man scowled at Maggie.

"Household manager," she corrected. "Jeesh! I'm tryin' to help you here. You could at least smile."

"He's a Viking, and he's gonna show me his sword," Larry declared.

The man scowled at Larry.

Larry ducked his head, then raised his chin defiantly. "Well, he *is* a Viking. He said so."

"Don't hurt him," Linda said, peeking around the man's leg. Poor Linda had been less than three years old when her father had been sent to prison, and she had no real recollection of him. She'd probably wiped out any bad memories as a defense mechanism as many children in abusive households did. As a result, she looked for a father figure everywhere. She'd no doubt asked this strange man if he was her daddy. In fact, Miranda glanced at Maggie and she nodded, as if understanding her aunt's unspoken question.

"She couldn't hurt me, little one," the man said in a

deep, rumbly voice, lifting Linda into his arms, gently, then setting her down on the patio chair.

"Is that so?" Miranda said, adjusting the broom better so the wooden handle was aimed roughly in the region of his flat belly.

"Are you planning to sweep up the mud with that broom, or attempt to spear me, or are you a witch about to mount your broom and ride away? What about these *neglected* children?" he asked without giving her a chance to answer.

"We're not neglected," Ben tried to say.

"Neg-neglected?" she sputtered out. How dare he make such an accusation? She launched herself at him, broom first.

He stepped aside at the last moment. As she slid forward on the mud, dropping the broom, and almost landing face first in the mess, he caught her with an arm around her waist. Then, holding her up by both forearms, her feet dangling off the ground, he glared at her and said, "These children are a menace, and you are the biggest menace of all. For shame! Off gambling and drinking and whoring whilst your children nigh kill themselves?"

"Whass a har?" Linda wanted to know.

"Whass a man-ass?" Larry asked with a grin. "Hey, us guys are man-asses," he told his brothers. Now they were all grinning. Their fears seeming to have disappeared.

She brought her attention back to the Viking man. "Are you crazy?" she spat out. Not a word her profession approved of ordinarily, but this was a situation that called for the out-of-ordinary. "I'm a psychologist in a town with more gambling addicts than blades of grass. The last thing I would do is gamble myself. As for drinking, my beverage of choice is diet soda. And I won't even dignify that remark about whoring."

Despite her indignation and anger, Miranda noticed the most compelling scent coming from this man. A mixture of sandalwood and limes and fresh air.

Huh?

"Are you aware that these children were about to start a cook fire using gasoline?" he asked her.

"What?" Alarmed, she turned to the boys, who all hung their heads with guilt.

"I hid the gasoline," Maggie told her, "but I asked this nice man to help me just in case they found the can."

"Are you serious?" Even dangling from this stranger's arms, she managed to narrow her eyes at the boys. "Now you have gone too far. I swear, you will be grounded for life."

"Grounding? Is that a new kind of punishment? I think a swift whack on a bare arse would suffice," the Viking commented.

"I do not believe in physical violence," she replied.

"Pfff! Mayhap that's why this nation is so soft."

This was an absolutely ridiculous conversation. "Put me down. At once. I swear I am going to sue your pants off for trespassing and . . . and . . . scaring little children."

"We're not scared," Sam interjected.

"What's a har?" Linda repeated.

The man ignored the children and spoke directly to her. "Foolish woman! You are in no position to make threats. Mayhap you should just ground me, whatever that is."

Instead of putting her down, he raised her even higher, as if to emphasize how high off the ground she was. How tall was this guy anyhow? And strong? He could probably bench press a bus with all those muscles.

"Besides, those bratlings scare me. Not the other

way around. Place a battle-axe in those boys' hands and they'd make good Huns."

"Hunz? What's a Hunz? Oh, you mean Huns. Never mind," she said as she recalled the Viking series once again.

"You have a battle-axe, too?" one of the boys asked, hopefully. *Boys!*

"Are you trying to say my boys are bad?" It was one thing for her to call them bad boys, which they were not, at heart, just mischievous, but it was quite another for a stranger to malign them.

"Nay, they are boys being boys, but, you, m'lady, have much to answer for." His unusual blue, sad eyes iced over with condemnation of her.

She gritted out, "And assault. I'm going to have you arrested for assault. How dare you glower at me like that?"

He cocked his head to the side. "Assault by glowering?"

"And abuse . . . I'm going to have you arrested for child abuse, too. What did you do to make them listen to you? They never stand still like that. If you hit them, I am going to personally strangle you with those pretty braids of yours, then stuff them down your throat."

He didn't stop glowering, but his lips did twitch at her words. "You think I am pretty?"

"Not you. Your hair."

More lip twitching. "Even with split ends?"

"Huh?"

"You are going to be very busy with all this 'arresting' and strangling. Meanwhile, neglecting your children. Again."

"Aaarrgh!" She tried to squirm out of his hold, to no avail. Even when she kicked him, her pointy high-heeled Jimmy Choos hitting him mid-calf, he didn't even flinch.

Just then, there was the sound of breaking glass

up above somewhere. It was the bathroom window being broken from inside. The handle of a toilet brush emerged, pushing out the remaining shards. Then Darla stuck her head out and shouted, "Hey! You! Put my friend down. I have a gun and I know how to use it. I can shoot your ass off."

Viking man glanced up and arched an eyebrow at the toilet brush Darla was waving in the air. "Nice gun," he remarked, but he did lower Miranda to the ground, though he kept a pincer grasp on one forearm to prevent her from running or doing him bodily harm, she supposed. If she could! But the broom was now out of reach.

"Darla, I presume," he said to Miranda.

"Yeah, and she really does know how to use a weapon. She's in security."

"Really? So am I."

"Huh? You are?" She waved a hand dismissively then, as if it didn't matter. Craning her neck upward, she asked, "Darla, honey, why did you knock out the window?"

"Because I'm locked in the damn bathroom."

She lowered her gaze to Viking man.

"Don't look at me," he said, raising both hands in the air. "This is the first I've seen the woman."

Her gaze moved to the children then, especially the three mud pies still standing at attention at the end of the already drying mud patch.

"It was an accident," Sam said.

"Hah! Likely story!" she remarked.

"The bathroom door always sticks," Ben added.

"That's why the key is always in the door," she said, as if they didn't all know that.

"Ruff ate the key," Viking Man said.

"What? You were here? You look like you could knock a door off its hinges with a fingertip."

"Sarcasm ill-becomes you, wench."

"Wench? What century are you living in?"

"I don't know. Sometimes it's hard to remember."

"Huh?" She was saying that an awful lot today, she noticed with what was probably hysterical irrelevance.

"We're waiting for Ruff to poop out the key," Larry interrupted.

All the children looked to Maggie, who'd just finished the latest pooper scooper job. She shrugged. "Nothing yet."

"I'm hungry. Can we have hot dogs and mac and cheese?" Larry asked, rubbing his little tummy, in the midst of all this chaos.

"I could barbecue hamburgers," Sam had the nerve to offer. Then he ducked his head sheepishly. "If someone could start the grill for me."

"If you go near a fire today, I will personally paddle your arse," Viking man said.

She did not advocate physical punishment, but when she noticed all three boys straighten to attention, she curbed the admonition that was on the tip of her tongue. For now, anyway.

"Hey, folks! Remember me. Lady locked in bathroom," Darla yelled down to them, still waving the toilet brush.

"There's another key in the top drawer of my desk. Go get it, Mags." Turning to the boys, she said, "Don't any of you dare go near the house until I'm done hosing you off. And, no, you are not hosing each other off. You'll have the house turned into a houseboat before you're done."

Turning, she addressed the stranger then. "Who are you?"

"Mordr Sigurdsson. And you?"

"Miranda Hart." She folded her arms over her chest, then wished she hadn't when those incredibly blue, sad eyes latched on her, there. Ignoring his intense scrutiny, she tilted her chin so she could address him directly. "What are you doing here?"

"I was sent."

"By the employment agency?" she asked incredulously, trying in vain to recall if she'd ever told them she only wanted females.

"No. A different . . . agency."

Just then, a feminine voice called out, "Yoo-hoo!" from the side yard where a gate was being opened, immediately followed by the ringing of an alarm bell. It was part of the security system that Miranda had paid tons of money to install and which apparently hadn't stopped a person from opening the gate, only breaking the eardrum of everyone within a half mile. Quickly, Miranda went over to the box on the wall near the patio door and punched in several numbers. Immediately, the ringing stopped.

Still standing there, inside the gate, stunned, was a big Amazon of a middle-aged woman with graying hair and a supermarket carry bag. Despite her big shoulders and military bearing, she looked like what a nanny was supposed to look like in a perfect world. Clearly the candidate Blue Star Employment Agency had sent for the job. Not a piercing or tattoo in sight. (Miranda had seen more than a few of those on the candidates she'd interviewed so far.) She probably had an apron in her bag for making marvelous home-cooked meals and from-scratch apple pies. (One of the candidates had looked as if she did double duty nights wearing an apron and nothing else. Still another had mentioned her specialty being brownies with a special ingredient. Wink, wink.). This woman had a good-size lap and an ample bosom, perfect for cuddling a crying youngster. (One of the women Miranda had interviewed had big breasts, all right. The kind that cost about ten thou each and were mostly for show, which she'd done a lot of in a braless tank top. Ben and Sam's eyes had about popped out.) Most of all, she looked as if she could handle a bunch of unruly kids.

"Sorry I'm late, but there was a pile-up on the Interstate that had traffic backed up for . . ." The perfect nanny's words trailed off as her jaw dropped, taking in the scene before her. The homemade swimming pool. The mud-covered boys. A giant of a glowering man and a cowering girl once more attached to his thigh. Not to mention a screaming female above wielding a toilet brush. Ruff, who had just noticed the newcomer (some watchdog he was!), began to gallop toward her, barking wildly, tongue lolling, drool flying, about to plant a big wet one on her.

But the woman turned on her heels, letting the gate slam after her, and began to fast-walk, calling over her shoulder with the lame excuse, "Sorry, but I don't do dogs."

The man looked at Miranda. She looked at him. Miranda burst out laughing, and the man pressed his lips together to avoid smiling. For some reason, probably the hopeless despair in his pale blue eyes, she knew . . . she just knew . . . that this was a man who rarely laughed, and she felt an inordinate pleasure in having a small part in lightening his spirits, even if only momentarily.

Suddenly he turned somber again. "Go inside with the girls. Rescue your friend and clean up that mess in the kitchen. I will hose off these bratlings. And then we will talk."

"We can hose ourselves off," Ben said with consternation, his eight-year-old pride wounded.

"Yeah," Larry said, already contemplating more slipping and sliding, Miranda could tell.

"Betcha a dollar we could hang the hose from Ruff's

collar an' we could chase after him to get clean." This bright idea from Sam, the gambler.

"Here's an idea," the Viking said. "You three stand still as statues and I hose the skin off you. This is a man's job." Then he had the nerve to turn to her. "Go. There is much woman's work to do inside."

"Woman's work?" she sputtered. Who did this bozo think he was? Giving her orders? Delegating her to woman's work? "What century are you living in?"

"You asked me that afore. Repetition is a sign of dotage. Mayhap you are older than you look."

"I beg your bleeping pardon! And what's with the mayhap?"

"Maybe, mayhap, same thing."

"Can I stay with you?" Linda asked the man, whom she was clinging to once again.

"No, little one, you must go with the ladies," he said.

"But, Daddy . . ." Linda whined.

Okay, this had gone far enough. "Linda, this is not your father. You have to stop—"

"Yes, he is," Linda insisted, holding even tighter onto the man's thigh. "He called today and said he is coming pretty soon, and then he came, and . . ." Linda began to sob.

Red flags unfurled in Miranda's brain. "Linda, honey, did you pick up the telephone today? You know that we have a rule about answering the land phone when it rings. That's why we have a cell phone."

Linda stopped crying and said, "Oops!" But then she raised her little chin. "But it was Daddy! It was!"

"It's okay, sweetie," Miranda soothed Linda. She would have a talk with her and all the other children later about the dangers they faced, being careful not to paint Roger as too much of a villain. He was still their father, after all.

Still, the fact that Roger had discovered her new, private number was chilling. He might have pretended that he was calling to talk to one of his kids, but he was making a point loud and clear. To Miranda. He was out there and coming.

So, it is starting already, Miranda thought as a shiver of dread swept over her. She raised her eyes and noticed the big man staring at her with questions in his startling blue eyes. He knew, or at least sensed, that there was some danger. Then, with a strangeness that was remarkable in this day of strangeness, he nodded to himself and said, "Ahhh, that is why I have been sent here. Some danger is threatening you, is it not?"

She nodded, hesitantly.

"You need not fear, m'lady. I am here to protect you."

Six

Take this job and love it! . . .

Mordr stood in the backyard on a patch where there was still dry grass, not mud and muck. With a hand on one hip and hose in the other, he was watering down the mudlings, the whole time lecturing them sternly. In the old days, he would have just tossed the errant youthlings in the fjord until they learned their lessons or were clean, or both. Today, this misguided society would deem that child abuse.

At first, the boys had protested and tried to run from him, but once he'd convinced them that he meant business by picking them up by the scruffs of their filthy necks, they stood still and let him hose off the layers of mud that had already started to cake in the hot sun. Even the dog sat at attention, tongue lolling, while Mordr sprayed his fur.

"What are your names?" Mordr growled out. *I am going to have a thing or ten to say to Mike next time I see him. Putting me, who has avoided children for centuries, in the midst of not one or two but five of the little ones . . . it is barbaric, that is what it is.*

Mordr could swear he heard a voice in his head say, *Get over yourself!*

"My name is Ben," said Blue Shirt. "I'm eight, and I'm the oldest boy."

"Sam," said Red Shirt. He was identical in appearance to Ben except for a small mole beside his left eye, Mordr made note for future reference. "And don't pay any attention to Ben. He's only five minutes older than me." He elbowed his brother, and his brother elbowed him back.

Mordr narrowed his eyes at the two of them, hosed both their fool heads, and told them, "Behave yourselves lest you raise my ire. I have not been around children for a good while and I am not in the mood for misbehavior." The two boys, water streaming down their faces from their plastered hair, went back to standing erect, elbows to themselves, for the moment.

Last came the little one . . . the one who resembled his beloved Jomar. Except for the freckles. Jomar hadn't had freckles, as far as Mordr could recall, although Mordr had rarely been home in the summertime. Too busy a-Viking. So, the sun spots might have popped out then and faded by winter. Even so, the little boyling was very like Jomar in age and height, except for the blond hair. Jomar's had been black. . . . *Oh, please God, let there not be dimples when he smiles so innocently at me.*

The little boy hitched up his wet shorts, which hung precariously on his tiny hips, and smiled up at him. Yes, to Mordr's dismay, there were dimples, but only on one side. One saving grace, at least. "I'm Larry. But you can call me Lar." He sounded out the nickname to sound like *lair*, as in bear's lair.

The dog barked then, and Larry patted its wet fur, which smelled rank. "This is Ruff," Larry said.

Mordr arched a brow. "Rough? Because he is rough with you children?" Mordr had witnessed on more than one occasion the bodily damage a vicious dog could do, especially to small persons.

They all laughed.

Mordr frowned, seeing no humor in his question.

"Not that kind of rough," Ben explained. "More like ruff, ruff!"

Ruff flashed Mordr a doggie grin and barked, "Ruff, ruff!"

The boys chimed in and they produced a chorus of "ruffs."

They are too frivolous, by half. I will go mad if I have to stay here for long.

He turned off the hose and told the children, "We are going to clean up this yard. Sam, roll up the hose. And do not turn the water on again, if you value your life. Larry, pick up all the shoes and socks lying about and put them on a pile by the door. Ben, come with me to see what damage was done by that grill." He paused, then gave each of them a dark look, "If one of you dares step in that mud again, you will find yourselves hanging from a tree, bare naked, with red bottoms."

Jaws dropped on three little faces at that picture.

"We don't have a big enough tree," Sam pointed out.

"That is irrelevant," Mordr said.

"Red bottoms? You mean, like Rudolph the Reindeer has a red nose, we'll have red asses," Ben had the nerve to say. It was clear to Mordr that this boy was the *hersir* of this small *hird*. A ringleader. What he did or said, the others followed. *Much like my Kata.*

Mordr sighed. No, he could not think of that now. No, no, no!

"Swear jar, swear jar," his laughing brothers hooted at Ben.

He picked Ben up by the waist and tossed him over his shoulder, swatting him once on his rump. Over his other shoulder, he ordered the others, "Get to work. Now!"

Ben's slim body, which weighed no more than a small sack of meal, was quivering. With fright, or laughter, Mordr wasn't sure. Putting him on his feet near the grill, Mordr hunched down so that they were eye to eye.

The boy wasn't afraid of him, not one bit, which was rather alarming to Mordr. First of all, a Viking man did not want to lose his ability to frighten his enemies. Not that these little ones were his enemies, but they *were* combatants whom he had to conquer, in one sense. Secondly, a good soldier, and a good child, must have fear of some things, lest they mistakenly fall into danger. Fear was a man's friend, truly.

"Listen and listen good, bratling. If you ever defy me again, you will get more than a soft pat against your buttocks. I do have a sword, and I know how to use it."

Well, that was not a nice thing to say to a child.

Ben nodded his head, no longer grinning.

I guess "not so nice" is needed in some cases.

"Now, tell me, what the he— what in heaven's name were you going to do with the grill?" Mordr asked, straightening to stare at the open grill, burnt matches, and charred newspaper.

"We . . . I . . . wanted to surprise Aunt Miranda by cooking dinner. I watched her barbecue hamburgers lots of time. But I couldn't get the grill to start."

It was a gas grill, which should have started with a mere click of a button. Mordr leaned down and examined the propane tank underneath. "Did it occur to your dimwitted brain that it might be out of gas?"

Apparently it hadn't because Ben's face reddened and he said, "Oh. So I guess it wouldn't have started even if I poured gasoline on it? A little bit of gasoline," he quickly added on seeing Mordr's horrified expression.

"Do you realize the damage you could have caused? Not just to yourself and the other children, but to the house itself. The siding could have caught afire like tinder, and a mere hose might not have been able to put it out."

"I'm sorry! I only wanted to do somethin' good for Aunt Mir. She works real hard for us, and she's not even our mother." Ben's eyes filled with tears.

That was all Mordr needed. Making a child cry. Quickly he patted the boy's shoulder and said, "We learn from our mistakes. Do not ever do that again."

"I won't," Ben said, swiping at the snot dripping from his nose with a forearm. "Do you really have a sword?"

"Yes, child, I do."

"Will you teach me how to sword fight?"

A sudden image came to Mordr of the wooden sword he had brought home for Jomar, a gift he never got to see. But this boy wouldn't know that. "I will make you a wooden sword to practice swordplay, not sword fighting, *if* you behave yourself."

"Yay!" Ben said and turned to no doubt lord it over his brothers that he'd gotten something that they hadn't.

"I will do the same for your brothers, if they agree to the same terms."

Ben's shoulders deflated for a moment, but he quickly got over his disappointment and gave his consent, "Okay." In the way of children everywhere, his brain skittered to another subject. "I wish my hair was long so I could have braids like yours on each side of my face."

"War braids."

"Huh?"

"They are called war braids."

"Cool!"

"One more thing. Can you tell me why your mother—I mean, your aunt—looked so fearful when Linda mentioned a phone call from your father?"

Ben's face reddened, again, not with embarrassment as it turned out, but anger. "Because my dad's an asshole."

Mordr just caught himself from saying, "Swear jar."

"That is not a nice thing to say about one's sire . . . father."

"My father isn't a *nice* man. He beat my mom, before she died. A lot. And he locked me and Sam and Larry and Linda in the closet one time when we tried to help, and then he forgot to let us out, and it got dark, and we were . . . afra— mad. He even beat Maggie's back with a belt when Mom wasn't home."

Owl Girl was beaten with a belt?

A rage rose in Mordr and he could practically feel the steam coming out of his ears, but he caught himself just in time before going berserk. When he was calm again, he remarked, "But your father is in prison, is he not? That is what your sister told me."

Ben nodded. "Yeah, but he's gettin' out soon. That's why I need to learn how to use a sword. Or a gun."

Oh, hell in a basket! I hope there are no guns about. Forget about the danger of a barbecue fire, this child is going to shoot his eyes out, or someone else's.

At Mordr's order, Ben went over to sit with his brothers. They looked like little angels . . . sodden, dirty angels with cowlicks and freckles and enough energy to launch a longship. Just to punctuate that thought, one of them let out a loud fart.

Mordr was shaking his head at the daunting task of trying to turn those mischievous boys into well-behaved young men. It would be like trying to harness a whale and riding the seas on its back.

He was putting the cover over the barbecue grill when Miranda came out. She had changed to black denim braies . . . *tight* black denim braies with a sleeveless red shirt. Her wild red hair was piled atop her head with a claw-like thing. She was barefooted, and he noticed that her toenails had been painted a pale peach color, like little shells.

The woman was not young—at least in her thirties, probably older than his thirty-one human years. She was slim, and he preferred a little meat on the bones of his women . . . well, back when he had women. She had small breasts while big ones were more desirable, in his opinion, leastways ones that filled a man's hand. And of course there was that red hair. Still, once again, Mordr felt a punch to the stomach, and lower, just gazing at her. What did it mean? Well, he knew what it meant, but why now? Why her?

She took one look at the boys sitting elbow to elbow, behaving, and demanded of him, "What did you do to them?"

"Disciplined them. As should you, if you were not gallivanting off to casinos." *Gallivanting* was a perfect word he'd picked up from some old lady in Louisiana when visiting Ivak last year. Tante Lulu was her name.

"Discipline?" She bristled. "Did he lay a hand on any of you?" she asked the boys.

Mordr saw Ben consider telling her about the slap to his buttocks, but reconsidered. The three boys said, "No."

"He's jus' gonna hang us from a tree," Larry offered.

"Whaaat?" She turned to Mordr.

"It was a jest." He favored Larry with a dirty look, and the boy just grinned at him.

By the runes! I am losing my fearsome demeanor.

"He is going to give us each a sword, though," Ben chirped in, "if we behave."

She gave Mordr a look that would have intimidated a lesser man, but not him. He just flashed the same look back at her. "You will not give these boys weapons of any kind," she said evenly. "Not a sword, not a gun, not a knife, not brass knuckles, not anything that could kill or maim. Do you hear me?"

"They heard you in California."

The boys were protesting loudly. "Please, Aunt Mir. Please, please, please."

"We're gonna be real good. I'll even change my underwear every day."

"I'll do my homework, even when I don't wanna."

"He's a Viking. He kin show us how to use a sword without cuttin' off a finger or nothin'."

"Absolutely not!" she said vehemently.

"Don't you think you are overreacting?" Mordr asked. "Even little ones need to learn how to protect themselves."

His mention of protection seemed to give her pause. But then she reaffirmed her opposition, "Not with a deadly weapon."

"Son of a Saxon bitch!" he exclaimed. "Since when is a wooden short sword a deadly weapon?"

"Wooden?"

"Did I not mention that they would be wood?"

"Uh, no! I think I would remember that. But I don't care if they're made of bubble gum. No swords, big boy."

Big boy? Does she mean me? "Sarcasm is not an admirable quality in a woman," he pointed out.

She breathed deeply, in and out, as if he were trying her patience.

Which caused her small breasts to press against the tightness of her shirt. He noticed that the nipples were prominent under the stretchy material, which compensated for her flat chest, he supposed, though it would take a lot to compensate for that red hair. He would wager his best sword that she was red down below, too.

A shot of lust hit him again, like a sharpshooter's bullet to his groin. Erotic tingles radiated out from his ballocks to all his extremities.

This had to stop. He shook his head like yon wet, shaggy dog to clear his brain and other body parts.

While his mind had been wandering to places it hadn't been in centuries, she had been reprimanding the boys, ending with "I want you boys to go in the house and take a shower," then quickly added, "one at a time. Then, you will go to your bedrooms and do your homework. After dinner, we will decide what to do about your behavior today."

Once the children were gone, Miranda turned on him. "Darla and I have some questions for you." Hands on hips, she tapped a foot impatiently, just as Owl Girl—Maggie—had done earlier.

"Darla of the broken window and long-handled brush weapon?"

"Darla of the pistol that she is even now filling with bullets, one of which has your name on it, if we find out you're a crony of Roger's. I made her stay inside to wait for us because the mood she's in, she might just shoot off those fool braids of yours."

"I thought you liked my braids."

"Don't try to distract me."

"Who is Roger?"

She darted a quick glance at him to see if he was being honest. "The children's father."

"I thought he was in prison."

"You know an awful lot about us. How did you know Roger was in prison?"

"Child chatter."

"Did they also mention that he is out or about to be released?"

"Yes. Do you know when?"

"No, I'm not sure."

Another woman, Darla, he presumed from the pistol dangling from one hand, stuck her head out the kitchen door and yelled, "Either you come in here, or I'm coming out there."

He agreed and followed Miranda into the house, not because he was afraid of the short woman with a ferocious frown, waving a gun, but because it was past time he found out exactly why Mike had sent him here. He observed, with typical male irrelevance, that Darla was shorter, plumper, bigger-breasted, rounder-rumped, with black, not red hair. For his sins, Mordr did not feel one tiny bit of lust.

Suddenly, he noticed a most pleasing fragrance wafting back at him from Miranda. Faintly floral. Familiar. Ah, he recalled now the scent of the flowers Alex had shown him in her garden last summer. As if he cared a whit about flowers! Lilies, they were called. It must be her perfume, he decided.

As they walked through the kitchen, he saw Maggie washing dishes in the sink. She pushed her glasses up her little nose when she saw him. He winked at her, a sign of assurance. Why he did that, he had no idea. She just blinked in acknowledgment, then smiled. And it was a wondrous smile that transformed her plain face.

The little one, Linda, was wiping the now clear table with a wet sponge. She gave him a toothless smile. All he could do in return was nod his head, his heart was racing so fast.

As a result of his distraction, he almost ran into Miranda's back as she slowed and entered the door of a room off the corridor. Not the formal parlor he'd seen on first entering the house, nor the dining room, which had been converted to a family room with low sofas and a flat-screen TV. He knew all about flat-screen TVs. They had what Vikar called "the biggest, badass, flat-screen TV in the universe" back at the castle in Pennsylvania. This one of course measured about a tenth that one's size. No, this was a home office, complete with desk, floor-to-ceiling shelves lined with books, a Persian rug, and two armed chairs.

Miranda sat behind the desk, while he and Darla sat in the opposing chairs in front of the desk. He stretched out his long legs and crossed them at the ankles.

Darla, who still had the pistol in hand, barked out, "Are you carrying, buddy?"

He looked pointedly at his open hands.

"You know what I mean," Darla insisted.

Actually he did. "Yes, I am carrying."

"You got a license to carry?" This Darla person was like a bulldog tugging at a rope, never letting up.

At first he was going to tell her it was none of her business, but then he recalled some document Mike had given him a long time ago . . . well, long by human standards. Three years ago. Taking a wallet out of his back pocket, being careful not to open his shirt too wide and expose his weapons, he took out a folded piece of paper and handed it to her.

Meanwhile, Miranda just glared at him, arms folded across her chest. Did she think she could cower

him with a dark look? He was the master of dark looks.
"Wait. Let me see that," Miranda said, reaching across
the desk for his wallet.

At first, he was going to resist, but then recalled he
had nothing incriminating on him. Except for a folding sword, two knives, including a K-Bar used by the
SEALs, and a Sig Sauer, all of which had been specially
treated to kill Lucies, as well as evil humans when the
need arose.

"Mordr Sigurdsson, 777 Colyer Lane, Transylvania,
Pennsylvania," Miranda read aloud from his driver's
license. "Are you joking? Transylvania?'"

He shrugged. He got that reaction all the time.

"I thought Transylvania was in Romania," Miranda
remarked.

"This is a different Transylvania." Totally, incredibly different in a most ridiculous way, truth to tell.

"Mordr," Darla said, leaning over to scan the license
in Miranda's hand. "What nationality is that?"

What did a twelve-hundred-year-old angel vampire
answer to that? "I am Norse by birth."

"A Viking? Like the kids said?" Miranda laughed.

He saw nothing funny about being a Viking and so
he replied with ice in his voice, "Precisely."

Darla pulled the laptop computer on the desk so
that it was turned in front of her and poised her fingers
over the keyboard. "You should know, I'm the director
of security for a small casino off the Strip. I have access
to all kinds of information."

Was that supposed to intimidate him? "I am in security, too."

"Really?" both women said.

He nodded hesitantly, already regretting having
brought up that sore subject.

He was right to be hesitant because the next question from Miranda was, "Where did you work security most recently?"

He felt his face heat as he revealed, "Director of security for a cruise ship."

The jaws of both women dropped.

But Darla narrowed her eyes at him. "What's your social?"

"Social? Even though I worked a cruise ship, I am not a very social person." More like anti-social, according to his brothers.

"You know very well what I mean. Your social security number," Darla snarled. "Never mind." She took a small card from his wallet and began typing on the keys of the laptop.

While she was doing whatever she was doing with the laptop—Mordr didn't understand the things himself, though his brother Harek was an expert in that field—he gave his attention to Miranda. "What is this danger you are facing here?"

She appeared startled by his question. "How do you know there is danger?"

"I would not have been sent here to protect you if there were no danger."

She tilted her head to the side, causing some curls to escape from the red pile atop her head. He had to admit it wasn't a bad shade of red, not that orange-ish red that he hated. Still, it was red. "*Who* sent you?"

How did he answer that question? Not Michael the Archangel, for a certainty. She was not ready to hear about angels and vampires, or demons, for that matter. "A friend."

"Of yours?"

Hardly. "Yours."

"Who?" she demanded, her face heating with color. Just then, Darla exclaimed, "Oh my God!" as she stared at the laptop screen, which he could not see from his position.

He was about to tell her that it was unwise to take the Lord's name in vain, but, before he could speak, she turned to Miranda and said, "He's former CIA and a decorated special forces hero with two tours in Afghanistan."

"I am?" he said, then quickly amended to "I am." He was always surprised to learn how Michael changed the vangels' credentials with all his special connections.

"And you're here to protect me . . . and the children?"

"Did I not say so afore?"

She bared her teeth at him, before curbing her temper.

"Did my lawyer send you? Bradley Allison? That's it, isn't it? Oh, the dear man!"

Mordr said nothing. Let her think her lawyer sent him. Better that than for him to mention St. Michael the Archangel.

He noticed that Darla had set aside the pistol, no longer considering him a threat. Foolish woman. He could be a villain pretending to be someone else.

Well, he *was* pretending to be someone else, but that was different.

"Do you have a résumé?"

"A what?"

"A résumé. You know, a summary of all your education—."

"I never had any education. Leastways not formal schooling."

"Your skills?"

"I can fight like a mad grizzly with his foot in a steel trap. There isn't a weapon I can't use and do it well.

When I say I will protect someone, I will do just that. I never fail." *Except for the one time when it mattered most.*

"Whoa! Someone has a high opinion of himself," Darla commented, but she was eyeing him like a hungry bitch for the new dog in the neighborhood.

He was not interested. Not one bit. "Before this goes any further, exactly what or who would I be protecting you from? The children's father?"

The two women nodded.

"He's been released or about to be released," Miranda explained.

"Has he threatened you?"

"Not lately," Miranda admitted, "but the first year he was in jail he sent me numerous threatening letters. He blames me for keeping him in prison. For adopting his children. For not letting the children visit him while incarcerated; that was their decision, by the way. For stealing his house."

"And you think he will come here?"

"Absolutely," Miranda and Darla said as one.

"I'm a psychologist . . ." Miranda started to say.

Oh, wonderful! A mind doctor. Another person to pick at his brain, digging for hidden emotion.

". . . but you don't have to be a professional to conclude that Roger has serious emotional problems. At the least, rage issues and the need for anger management. At the worst, he's psychotic and unable to control his impulses."

Mordr wondered what she would think of *his* "rage issues." That's all he would need, a psychologist probing his mind, trying to discern the cause of his "problem." Asking questions, like "Did you suck your thumb as a child?" He knew this because he watched Dr. Phil on the television when he was bored between missions. It was either that, or watch Armod's endless

Michael Jackson videos until he wanted to hurl the contents of his stomach. Even so, he saw an amusing picture in his head of Armod teaching three little trolls and two girlings how to moonwalk. If he were not so somber, he would smile at the image.

Mordr called his attention back to the present. He had to stop these mind wanderings.

"The thing I fear most is that he will harm the children," Miranda said with a wobbly voice.

That raised the hackles on him like nothing else could. "Why would he harm his own children?"

"Some men do," Darla pointed out. "You read about them in the news all the time."

And it revolted Mordr every time he heard about it.

"Roger was a wife beater and he wasn't a model father, even before he went to prison." Miranda grimaced with revulsion. "Verbal abuse of the kids, certainly. And occasional physical abuse, like the beating he gave Maggie. His rages were escalating, and I think Cassie, my cousin and the kids' mother, realized that. Cassie didn't have to be a psychologist to know that Roger would be physically abusing all of them in time. That's why Cassie turned him in."

"A nithing," Mordr said.

"A what?" Darla asked.

"A man who is less than nothing, below contempt."

"That's for sure," Darla concurred.

"I've done research on his personality type, and I believe he will overreact when faced with rejection from the children," Miranda expounded. "Assuming the courts even allowed him visitation, the first time one of them whined about not wanting to go with him, or wet the bed, or failed to do something he ordered quick enough, it would likely trigger one of his rages."

Mordr had his own triggers, but she didn't need to

know that, and his certainly didn't involve children.
"I understand. You are wise to be concerned," Mordr
said.

Miranda nodded, then got down to business. "If I
hire you, it has to be as my home manager. If you're
here as a guard, it would alert Roger. Like waving a
red flag in front of a bull."

"You mean nanny. Speak plainly, wench."

Miranda would clearly relish knocking him aside
the head with a hard object, but she was probably desperate for his help, or becoming so. Thus she held her
sharp tongue. "Well, they're the same thing, except a
home manager does more than care for the children.
There wouldn't be many cleaning chores, though, because I have a housekeeper come in for two hours five
days a week."

*That is good because I would not have a clue how to run
a vacuum, and I don't want to learn.*

"There are two more weeks of school and they get
the bus in front of the house."

"How safe are they at school?"

"I've given orders to the administration and teachers that they are not to release the children, under any
circumstances, to anyone but me or Darla, and definitely not to Roger. I've filled them in on the safety
concerns."

He nodded, but was unsure if that was enough.

"They need supervision while at home, and they're
all involved in after-school activities for which they
will need to be transported. Karate, soccer, swim team,
ballet, chorus."

Modern parents spoiled their children overmuch, in
his opinion. Why did they need all these extra activities? What was wrong with mere play? But he would
not speak of that, for now.

"You would have to prepare some meals. Plus, the kids like to take bag lunches to school."

His eyes widened with surprise. "You want me to cook?"

"Yes. Can you cook?"

Not even a boar's leg over an open fire. "Of course."

"They don't need anything fancy."

Good. I will have to call Alex and get some tips, or Lizzie Borden. No, Alex would be best. Lizzie never did like me much, always holding on to that cleaver when I am about. Says I eat too much. I am a big man. What does she expect? And what is a bag lunch, anyhow?

"Listen, you two iron out all those details," Darla said. "I have to be off to work." She stood and gave him what she must consider a menacing look, "If you do anything to hurt Mir and the kids, I'll be after you like your worst enemy."

Lady, I know more than you could ever guess about enemies. He quelled his irritation and assured her, "They will be safe with me."

With that, Darla departed, and he was left alone with Miranda.

"You will have to live in, of course," she said, twisting her hands in her lap.

"Of course."

He could tell she was nervous being alone with him. Truth to tell, he was a mite nervous himself, and nervousness was a new experience for him.

"We can discuss all your specific duties later. Don't you want to know what your salary will be?"

"Not particularly."

She smiled. "Bradley's influence again, I suppose."

He shrugged and leaned back in his chair, linking his hands behind his nape, just looking at her. He liked looking at her.

She stared at him, too. Rather dazed, he thought. But then she shook her head, as if confused. "Let me show you to your room. It's off the kitchen, not very big. Nothing fancy."

"I do not need big or fancy." Many, many times over the centuries, he'd slept on the hard ground or in hovels. He'd also slept in palaces and luxurious hotel suites. None of that mattered to him.

They both stood, and Mordr was staggered by the smell of lilies and cloves as she walked around the desk toward him. It seemed to enter his nostrils and sweep through his body, causing his blood to heat and the fine hairs to stand out on the back of his neck. Without thinking, he said, "Your scent enthralls me."

At the same time, she said, "You smell delicious. Like sandalwood and lime. Is it cologne?"

Mordr had never used cologne. Never ever. The most scent he'd ever put on his body would have been in his soap, and he did not recall the scent of sandalwood, or fruit, for that matter. *Delicious? Me?*

Just then, Mordr realized what it was, and he almost reeled with disbelief. His brothers Vikar and Trond and Ivak, all of whom were married to life mates, claimed that at one point before the mating, a special scent emanated from couples. A sure sign of soul mates.

No, no, no! This cannot . . . will not . . . happen to me.

"Stop looking at me like that," she said, no longer dazed. "Let's make one thing clear. There will no sex involved in your duties. I am not interested."

"As if you were asked!" he scoffed. "For your information, I have been celibate for a long, long time." *Damn, damn, damn, when did I develop a loose tongue?*

"How long?"

"Longer than you can imagine, and then more than that." Think two hundred and fifty years, give or take.

Her face softened. "I deal with problems like this all the time. Are you able to masturbate to orgasm?"

Surely, *surely*, she did not say what he thought she did.

He must have looked confused because she started to say, "Masturbation is the practice of—"

"I know what masturbation is. Are you demented? Asking a man such a question!"

"There are remedies for impotency today. I'm a professional. Like a medical doctor. Everything you tell me is confidential. No need to be embarrassed."

Mordr went rigid with consternation. "I am *not* impotent." Leastways, he did not think he was. "It is a choice."

"Oh," she said, though she clearly did not understand.

"How would you feel if I asked you whether you pleasure yourself to a climax?"

"I would answer yes." She put her hand on the doorknob and motioned for him to follow.

At first, he was too stunned to move. *She masturbates? Why am I surprised? After seeing what is on modern television, Sodom and Gomorrah look like Mayberry.* And, yes, he was familiar with that old television show. In fact, that Barney Fife character reminded him of a Viking he once knew, Lars Lackwit.

She opened the door, and he followed, entertaining the most delicious mind fantasies.

Five little bodies almost fell back on their little rumps. Apparently, they had been pressed against the door, eavesdropping. He hoped they hadn't heard *everything*. At least they were clean, having taken showers as ordered, he assumed. Except for Ruff, who was still dirty as his fur dried in matted clumps.

"Yay, we have a Viking nanny!"

"When do I get my sword?"

"I like peanut butter and jelly on my sandwiches, but only strawberry jelly. And no crusts."

"Can you tell bedtime stories?"

"What's for dinner?"

"I need help with my multiplication tables."

"It's my turn to bring cupcakes for snack time."

"We're out of milk."

"The downstairs toilet is plugged up. I think someone used too much paper."

Miranda looked at him. "Welcome to my world."

Seven

**Talk about the BFF (best friend
forever) from Hell!...**

Roger Jessup sat fuming in front of an ancient computer sitting on a battered desk in a shared living room of a shabby duplex in Akron, Ohio. It was Heaven's Gate, the bullshit name for the halfway house he was "sentenced" to. "Hell's Armpit" would be more appropriate.

During the day, he was employed for minimum wage as a maintenance worker for the city, despite his having been a licensed electrician until a few years ago. Apparently, no one wanted to hire a convicted felon to wire their houses. It wasn't like he was an axe murderer or anything, but that didn't seem to matter.

Once a week he had to sit in a class of misfits listening to some jackass teach him anger management. Hah! He had learned a thing or two about anger and how to manage to survive after serving two years in prison. Now, *there* were some psychos who needed anger management!

No, none of those things were what had Roger's jock strap in a twist at the moment. It was what he was reading on the computer screen. "Son of a fucking bitch!" he snarled.

"Whassup, Jessup?" Without looking his way, Clarence Farrell chuckled from the recliner where he was watching another of the endless reality TV shows he was addicted to. This one was *Amish Strippers*. Before that, it was *Gay Soldiers*. Some days, Roger wished the cable box would explode and stay off, giving those voices in Roger's head some blessed silence, a chance to think.

"Nothing special," Roger grumbled.

A person didn't want to get on Clarence's bad side. He was a mean-ass repeat offender who'd just served ten years in Ohio Pen for assault with a deadly weapon, rape, kidnapping, robbery, and a long laundry list of other crimes committed against an ex-girlfriend. Caused the woman to lose an eye and sliced one ear half off. Eew! And it wasn't his first offense. Clarence had been in the halfway house for a year now and would be released about the same time as Roger.

"Whoa! Wouldja look at that? I like it when they bend over like that. Don't you?" Clarence was licking his big lips.

Roger glanced at the TV set. "I grew up in Ohio Amish country, and I ain't never seen an Amish woman with tits like that," he commented, just to be amiable. Or to avoid Clarence's fist, which often shot out at random for the least offense.

Roger went back to scowling at the computer in front of him, and he might have made a growling noise.

"So, what poker you got up your ass this time, man?" Clarence asked in his usual insulting manner.

Roger gritted his teeth at Clarence's tone and would have liked to tell him, *Bite me!* But Clarence might do that, literally. Instead, Roger told him, "My wife's cousin sold my home while I was in prison, and I just found out from the real estate transfers online that the bitch pocketed a cool two hundred and fifty thou."

"Whoa! And they call us robbers!" Clarence had the irritating habit of chewing on the ice in his glass after drinking his soda, which he was doing now.

Crunch, crunch, crunch!

Roger felt like clubbing him over the head with the remote Clarence held on to like it was his personal possession. Just because he was bigger than the rest of them, and mean as a junkyard dog, and sported two gold incisors that he claimed to have yanked out of the mouth of a bookie who tried to steal from him, didn't mean he had the right to hog the TV. And make them all watch these crackpot reality TV shows.

Crunch, crunch, crunch!

Holy hell! I feel like he's scratching my eyeballs with sandpaper.

Besides that, Clarence had a nerve putting Roger in the same class as Clarence and robbers. Roger had never robbed anyone. All he'd done was smack his wife around a little when she got out of hand. And his kids . . . well, kids needed a good smack once in a while to grow up right.

"I sunk a lot of money into that house, even if it was in my wife's name. Rewired the whole two stories. Installed a patio, stone by fucking stone. Painted till I 'bout died from the fumes. Put in a second bathroom. That house wasn't worth shit when we moved in, and now Miranda Fucking Hart gets to reap the benefits."

"You oughta try to get some of that cash back. It ain't right."

Crunch, crunch, crunch!

How much damn ice can one glass hold? Roger flexed the tension out of his fingers, barely restraining himself from putting his fingers around Clarence's neck, and squeezing, squeezing, squeezing. "The courts are on her side. She's a psychiatrist or psychologist or something. Has lawyers in her pocket. Probably in her panties, too."

"I didn't mean to get your money back through the courts, dude."

Crunch, crunch, crunch.

I'm going to tear that ice maker out of the fridge first chance I get. "Oh. I intend to. Believe you me. She'll pay. And not just for stealing the house. She took my kids, too. Moved them to Vegas."

"Whaaat? Are you shittin' me, man? Your kids? I didn't know you had kids." Roger had Clarence's full attention now.

"Yep. Five of them. Three boys and two girls," Roger said with pride. He felt kind of manly when he talked about having five kids, like his swimmers were especially potent.

"Well, that settles it. You and me gotta go to Vegas. We'll show that ballbuster what's what."

"Uh," Roger said dumbly. Yeah, he planned to go to Vegas. And he planned to get his kids back, along with the money for his house. Plus, Miranda was gonna pay big-time for what she'd done to him, including her testimony at his parole hearing last year, claiming he was a psycho with rage issues. He was going to kill her, but he was going to be careful how he went about it so he didn't get blamed. What he didn't need was a six foot two, two-hundred-and-fifty-pound black guy with an attitude along for the ride.

But Clarence was already on a roll. "In fact, I got a buddy who lives on the Strip. In an apartment over a pizza shop. We can stay with him while we case the situation."

Oh hell! How am I going to tell Clarence I want to go

on my own? "Listen, I appreciate the offer, but I really think that—"

Clarence waved a hand airily, "You don't hafta thank me, Rog." Roger hated when people called him Rog. "What are best friends for, huh?"

This was the first Roger had heard that they were best friends.

Roger stood, bracing himself to tell Clarence that he didn't need his help, but Clarence was already on his cell phone, telling, not asking, the dumb schmuck in Sin City that he would be there soon with his good buddy, meaning Roger, and to make sure he stocked up on beer and a hooker or two.

Then he turned to Roger and flashed a gold-toothed smile. "Vegas, here we come!"

Crunch, crunch, crunch.

You gotta love a resourceful man . . .

Miranda awakened from a deep sleep when her alarm went off at six a.m. She sat up and stretched, totally refreshed. For the first time in ages, she'd slept for a full eight hours.

All thanks to her personal Viking. He'd told the kids at nine o'clock that it was time to go upstairs. By ten, they were all in their respective beds. And they didn't even protest, as they usually did. Well, they did start to complain, but he gave them such a quelling scowl that they immediately obeyed. It must be some kind of Norse magic.

Miranda concluded that the children reacted differently to Mordr because he was a man, an authority figure to them, while she was just softhearted Aunt Mir. She had to admit that one reason she'd slept so well was the presence of Mordr in the house and the protection he offered. She felt safe.

The sun was creeping up over the horizon while she took a quick shower and brushed her teeth. Coffee, that's what she needed now. She put on underwear and grabbed a robe, tiptoeing silently out of her room, not wanting to awaken the children so early.

She couldn't resist, though. Peeking into each bedroom, she looked lovingly at the children, who were innocent angels when asleep. Maggie and Linda in the pink bedroom. Ben and Sam in bunk beds and Larry in a single bed in the largest bedroom of the house, which was decorated in blue and white stripes, a compromise to all their differing tastes.

The girls' room was somewhat tidy, unlike the boys' room, which looked as if a cyclone had blown through. Clothes on the floor. A half-eaten apple on a windowsill. Homework scattered about the three desks. Closet door open. A Thomas the Tank Engine track at the foot of Larry's bed, some of the engines under the bed. An opened can of fish food for the ten-gallon aquarium that cast the only light in the still dim room. Even the goldfish appeared to be asleep, hiding behind a conch shell.

Miranda's heart tightened with the love she felt for these five little people, each so different and yet linked with a bond of family. How could she ever have considered walking away from them when Bradley Allison told her of Cassie's "bequest" two years ago?

She closed the door quietly, letting them sleep until their alarms went off at seven. The school bus didn't arrive until eight. Much as she'd come to love the gremlins, she cherished this short, silent respite from the chaos to come.

The coffeepot was perking, and five paper bags were lined up on the counter.

What?

She peeked in one bag. Peanut butter and strawberry jelly sandwich, a squeeze yogurt, an apple, and a Capri Sun. Others differed with bologna and mustard, ham and cheese, boxed raisins, a banana, Cutie oranges. Twinkies.

Mordr must have done this.

But how did he know of the kids' differing tastes?

She glanced out the window and saw that the muddy patch had dried nicely. The damage might be minimal. No need to call a landscaper to reseed the backyard.

Then she did a double take as Mordr walked into view, coming from the side of the house. He was out there in his bare feet, wearing nothing but low-riding, slim pants. Taking pictures of her house with a cell phone camera. All the suspicions she'd had about him initially, then put aside, came rushing back.

Walking outside, she confronted him. "What are you doing?"

"Taking pictures of your house," he said calmly, ignoring or not registering the coldness of her question. He continued clicking away, big as you please, and he was plenty big, walking about the house, taking more pictures of the building and the yards, back, sides, and front. Once she could have sworn he took a picture of her.

She followed after him, trying not to notice the breadth of his shoulders, the narrowness of his waist and hips, the tight butt, and long, long legs. And the scars! Oh my God! His body was covered with long-healed scars. How did he get so many wounds? She decided to save that question for later. Instead, she asked, "Why are you taking pictures of my house?"

He stopped walking and addressed her directly, "My brother Cnut is a security expert. The best! Homes, business, governments, everything. I would have him come here to assess your circumstances, but he's in Russia at the moment. Next best thing is that I describe the situation and send him pictures."

"Oh," she said. "Is he your only brother?" Like that was important!

"Pfff! I have six brothers."

"And sisters?"

He shook his head. "Six brothers are enough, believe you me."

"I'm an only child," she said, surprised that she'd revealed something about herself without being asked. Quickly, she backtracked, "I'm always fascinated by the dynamics of a big family."

"I do not know this dynamics, but you certainly have your own big family now."

"That I do." They were headed toward the kitchen door.

"Don't you think it's inappropriate to walk about half naked?"

His eyes widened with surprise. "Half naked? I would have you know that I donned braies this morning in order to be 'appropriate.'"

Did that mean that he slept naked? Of course it did. Yikes! "You have to be careful not to be naked around the children."

He gave her a look of consternation, as if he would ever do such a thing. Then, "Is it acceptable to be naked around you?"

"Of course not." *Is he serious, or teasing me? His expression reveals nothing.*

They were back in the kitchen, where he picked up a short-sleeved black shirt hanging on the back of a chair. Putting it on, he left it unbuttoned, leaving exposed a path of light brown hair on his chest that led down in a V toward, well, just downward. Happy trail, for sure. How could a man this virile be celibate?

Stop it, Miranda. No more ogling! No more speculation on his sex life. "What are brays anyhow?"

"Braies are breeches or long pants."

She nodded. "I'm confused by your language," she said. "One time you speak modern language, and the next you throw out ancient words, like braies."

He shrugged. "At heart I am Viking, and Old Norse words seep into my speech, though I know better when I have a chance to think on it."

That made as much sense as, well, a Viking in Las Vegas. "Thank you for making the children's lunches. I haven't been that efficient for a long time."

He leaned back against the counter and arched a brow in question.

"Lack of efficiency is a natural result of being overworked, overstressed, trying to do too much, having no help for the past few weeks," she said defensively. "I would be the first to say that I'm spread too thin."

"That problem should be solved now that I am here."

She hoped so.

"Why do you work so much?"

Silly question! "I have to support my large family."

"Have you never wed?"

She shook her head.

"That is odd."

"Why?"

"Most women your age have been wed for many years with five or more children of their own by now. 'Tis the husband's job to support his family."

"What century are you living in?"

"Let me say that a different way then. Why is a woman of your beauty not married?"

"Please! I know I'm not beautiful." She tried to remember if she'd combed her hair yet.

"Well, not beautiful, but comely in a certain way."

She laughed. "That is the lamest compliment I have ever heard."

"I did not mean it as a compliment. Merely an observation."

She rolled her eyes.

Though he didn't smile, there was a certain dancing light in his blue eyes. Was he teasing her? Hard to tell with his somber demeanor, she thought once again.

"How did you know what to make for the kids' lunches?"

"Hah! First, I had to call my sister-by-marriage Alex, and ask her what a bag lunch was."

Apparently he wasn't as well-qualified for the job as he might have led them to believe. That didn't bother her too much. Not yet.

"Then I asked the children their preferences. While I conceded to their wishes on the bag lunches, I told them there would be only one item on the menu for breakfast. Cereal and milk. They all wanted different things, ranging from bacon and eggs to fruity charms, which I only learned later was cold cereal, and a dozen things in between. Imagine the little bratlings thinking some idiot would cater to all their individual tastes!"

Yeah, imagine that! "Thanks for starting the coffee. Do you want a cup?"

He shook his head. "I drink it on occasion, but I never developed a taste for the bitter brew."

Once again she was struck by the inconsistency of his speech. *Bratling. Bitter brew.* While at the same time using words like *conceded.* "Is English a second language for you?"

"Hmpfh! More like eighth. I've always understood Saxon English. They are very similar, you know, but modern English is fairly new to me."

"You speak eight languages?" Why that shocked her, she wasn't sure. Was she guilty of racial bias? As in big Viking equates with dumb?

He counted on the fingers of both hands. "Actually, ten languages if you count Latin, which is a dead language. Even the priests no longer use it in their Masses."

Miranda toasted and buttered an English muffin for herself to have with her coffee. Then, without asking, she toasted and buttered another one, placing it on the table, along with a glass of milk and a glass of orange juice, in front of him. Before she had the chance to set some jam on the table, he'd scarfed down both his and her muffins and all the milk. She made two more muffins and sat down with her coffee, spreading some of the strawberry jam on her muffins. He watched what she was doing, then did the same with his own. He nodded his satisfaction.

"Don't you ever smile?"

"Rarely."

"Why? Forget I asked that. It's none of my business. What were you writing?" She pointed to the yellow legal pad with bold male writing on it. She had a pile of the pads in her office and that was one of her favorite gel pens he'd been using.

"Ideas for how to better secure your home and to protect you and the children when away from home."

She waved a hand for him to explain while she chewed on her muffin, licking some jelly off the corners of her mouth.

He just stared at her mouth, and then he licked his own lips.

Holy cow! She felt that little gesture mirrored on her own lips, and whoo-boy, it felt good. "Uh, for example?" *Focus, Miranda, focus. On the subject at hand, not the luscious male before you.*

He seemed to make a concerted effort to concentrate, too. "It would be better if you had a real guard dog, one that would warn you of any stranger on the property."

She shook her head. "There's no way I could get rid of Ruff. The children would never forgive me. And there's no way I could handle two dogs."

He conceded that point with a nod. "Cnut will assess your home security and come up with some recommendations. In the meantime, my biggest concern is the school situation. Two separate schools. Minimal security. There are only a few weeks until the end of the school year. Why not school them at home with a tutor?"

She shook her head again. "I have to maintain the appearance of normality in the kids' lives. They lost their mother two years ago. Their father is absent, in prison. I moved them from their old neighborhood in Cincinnati to this new development in Las Vegas. So many changes!"

"Well, then, I will have to assign men to watch over them when they are in school."

"You have men? How many? Surely, you don't expect them to live here."

He gave her a look that pretty much said, *What do you think?* Then he said, "The number does not matter. And they will make their own sleeping arrangements."

"I don't like the idea of the kids having guards outside the school."

"The children will never know they are there."

She tapped her fingertips on the table, considering. "All right," she agreed.

"I also don't like the idea of the children riding on the bus. A bus could be waylaid on the way from here to there, or the reverse. I will drive them to school and pick them up."

She was about to protest, but nodded again. Small, but important, concessions.

"By the time you return from your work today, I will have a more detailed plan for you. We have not even talked of your own safety, but never fear, I will manage it all." Did he really waggle his eyebrows at her before saying, "After all, I am your house manager."

"Thank you," she replied with a wobbly voice. The last time anyone offered to lift the load from her shoulders was . . . she didn't remember when. Oh, Darla helped. And her coworkers. But still, the responsibility for the children's welfare and safety was hers alone. Until now.

His concern touched her deeply. She sensed that he cared, that he would do this, even if he weren't paid. It made him look even more attractive to her. His long hair was pulled back off his face and tied with a rubber band low on his nape, calling attention to his sharp cheekbones and other Nordic features. A dark blond shade of morning whiskers dusted his chin. And of course all those muscles.

He cleared his throat.

Embarrassed to be caught ogling him, she stood. "I need to get dressed for work before waking the kids."

His attentive eyes surveyed her boldly, taking in her tall body from bed-head hair to slippered feet. She felt as if he could see through her thick terry-cloth robe, under which she wore only skimpy underwear.

"What will you be doing today?" he asked.

"For one thing, I have to testify in court on behalf of an elderly man whose children are trying to have him declared incompetent so that they can sell his house."

"Greed," he concluded.

"Definitely."

"That is my brother Harek's big sin," he mentioned.

"What is?" Somehow, she'd lost the thread of this conversation.

"Greed," he said.

"And what is your big sin?" she asked, not really expecting him to answer.

But he did. "Anger."

For a moment, she didn't know what to say, but then she told him, "We offer wonderful anger management classes at our clinic."

He snorted his opinion of that suggestion. Then, he made a shooing motion with his hand. "Go! Before I check to see what you are hiding under that ugly robe."

She smiled inwardly as she saw him begin to clear the table and rinse her mug and his glass in the sink. Her very own house husband, sort of. Wait 'til she told the women at work what she had waiting for her at home. A Viking nanny. Or a Viking house manager. Whatever. He was damn hot and in her kitchen.

Something occurred to her then. "Are you married?"

He glanced back, realizing she hadn't left yet. "No."

"Ever married?"

He hesitated before nodding. "She died long ago."

She was about to apologize for being so intrusive, but had to ask one more question. "Do you have children?"

The sudden bleakness in his eyes was shocking. His lips thinned, in anger or pain, she wasn't sure. He tossed the dish towel on the counter and sliced her with a cutting glance. "I do not ever discuss my children. Never!"

"I'm sorry."

He ignored her apology and walked stoically out of the kitchen and into the backyard. Through the window, she could see him staring off into space, his back to her. Even from here, she could see that his hands were fisted.

Who is this man I've brought into my house?

Why am I so touched by the pain he has clearly suffered?

Is this going to be the biggest mistake of my life?

Eight

(Viking) honey, I'm ho-o-o-ome . . .

Miranda checked with Mordr several times during the day to make sure everything was going all right.

At nine a.m., on her grilling him, he said, "The children are settled in their schools under the watchful eye of my men. Naught will happen to them there."

"Already your men are there?"

"Already."

"Did they get to school on time?"

"Of course."

"Larry always forgets—"

"Larry had his backpack on."

"I meant to mention the broken bathroom window."

"The glass man is coming this afternoon."

"What about—"

"Miranda."

"What?"

"Go to work."

At ten a.m., she asked what he was doing.

"I am putting motion detectors on your roof."

"Please God, don't tell me you are up on the roof."

"This is not a good time for me to talk. Oops!"

"Mordr! Mordr!" she yelled into her cell phone.

Finally, he spoke again, "I slipped, but all is well."

"Get off the damn roof!"

He hung up on her.

Oh my God! Did he fall off the roof? I hope my home-owners' policy covers this liability. I can hear my insurance agent now. "And what was a Viking nanny doing on your roof?" Heart racing, she called right back.

He sighed into the phone. "Miranda, you must stop calling me, lest I get no work done."

"Are you on the roof again?"

Instead of answering her question, he said, "Did you know your neighbor cleans her house in the nude?"

"What neighbor?"

"The pink house, across the street and over one."

He *was* on the roof! "Mrs. Edmonds? She's sixty if she is a day."

"Hmm. She is well-preserved for an elder. You should see her bend over to vacuum under the sofa."

"You're going to be arrested for being a Peeping Tom."

"I do not know this peeping person, but if anyone is arrested it will be Mrs. Edmonds for . . . oh." He released a snort of disbelief, like suppressed laughter.

"What? What now?"

"She has a tattoo of two kissing pigs on her belly, low down."

"How can you tell what the tattoo is from that distance? Are you using binoculars?"

"No. I have exceptional vision." On those words, he hung up on her. Again.

Miranda finished the paperwork in her office, put all the necessary files in her briefcase, and headed toward her van for the short drive to the courthouse. Two hours later, after testifying on behalf of Edgar Harris, her client, hopefully helping him to thumb his nose at his ungrateful children, she talked in the hall to the opposing psychologist on the case, Jerome "Call Me Jerry" Daltry. A real slimeball, who made his living as an "expert" witness in court proceedings around the country. She told him exactly what she thought of him, and he had the nerve to ask if she was free for dinner that night. "Not even if I were starving to death!" she replied.

But Jerry's mention of food reminded her that it had been five hours since her short breakfast with Mordr that morning, so she hit the drive-through at Wendy's where she got a salad and diet soda to eat back in the office, where she had client appointments lined up all afternoon. Okay, she also ordered a cheeseburger and small fries. *So kill me!*

She resisted calling home until one-thirty, post yummy lunch. "How are things going, Mordr?"

"Fine. Your cleaning person is helping me decide what to make for dinner."

"Mrs. Delgado?" The usually stoic Mrs. Delgado rarely spoke to Miranda unless asked a direct question. She wouldn't help Miranda choose dish detergent if asked, let alone plan a dinner. In fact, she'd informed Miranda on being hired that she didn't do windows, babysitting, or dinners.

"Do you have more than one cleaning person?"

"No. Are you being sarcastic?"

Another sigh. "Why are you calling, Miranda?"

She was the one who sighed now. "So, what did you and Mrs. Delgado decide on?"

"Roast pot."

Oh good Lord! Is that why Mrs. Delgado is always so dazed-looking? High on drugs? "Don't you dare bring pot into my house! That's it. You're fired."

There was murmur of conversation. Then he corrected himself, "Pot roast. Listen, wench, you need to wipe your suspicious mind lest I decide to quit this job, which is not at all to my liking anyway. What?" He was speaking to Mrs. Delgado again. "Do we have a crock?"

Huh? "Why do you need a crock?" And what's with the *we*?

"A Crock-Pot," she heard Mrs. Delgado say in the background, followed by a giggle.

Mrs. Delgado giggling? Would wonders never cease?

"The Crock-Pot is in the cabinet above the refrigerator. But you don't have to make dinner. I can stop for something on the way home."

"Did I not tell you to stop worrying, that you are under my shield now."

"What shield?"

He made a tsking sound of impatience and ignored her question. Instead, he told her, "I am making a list for Mrs. Delgado to go grocery shopping. Is there anything you need? Your larder is depleted of many things. By the by, do you mind if I drink the occasional beer?"

"Uh, no." *Mrs. Delgado is grocery shopping for us? Is this the same person who said she didn't do errands when I asked her one time to stop for milk on the way to my house?*

"Good." On that terse response, he hung up on her, yet again. Did the man not know how to say good-bye? Come to think on it, he didn't say hello, either.

Miranda found herself able to accomplish more work in the next three hours than she had in the past three days. Maybe she would even be able to attend that two-day conference in L.A. next month. No, that was too much to hope for. Still, she felt as if a great weight had been lifted off her shoulders, and at least for the time being she wasn't worried about Roger or the children's welfare. She only hoped that she wasn't deluding herself about how much Mordr could help her.

It was five p.m. by the time Miranda arrived home. Using the remote, she opened the garage doors and parked her vehicle next to Mordr's. He'd told her this morning that it was advisable not to leave their vehicles outdoors where they could be compromised in some way. She hadn't asked exactly what he meant by *compromised*, assuming he meant explosives or sabotaging the engine or simple vandalism.

She entered the house from the garage directly into the kitchen, which was neat as a pin, and empty. Usually, the kids were here making a mess of after-school snacks. At the thought of food, she noticed the delicious smell of pot roast. Lifting the lid, she saw not only a large, succulent beef chuck roast but little potatoes and carrots as well. Not just that, but she could smell bread baking in the oven.

So, where was the Viking wonder?

Scent of a woman . . .

Mordr wondered if he would be sane once this mission was completed.

Right now, the children were sitting about the floor in the family room doing their schoolwork with the television turned off, all on his orders. If they remained silent and completed their assignments, he'd promised to tell them about the first time he went a-Viking as an overconfident eleven-year-old and almost wet his braies when a shark head-butted his longship. With slitted eyes and arms folded over his chest, he dared them to speak before their half hour was over, whilst he sat in an incredibly comfortable leather chair called a La-Z-Boy. It reclined, it vibrated, it molded its cushions to his backside, and he was harboring sinful ideas about what could be done on such a piece of furniture. And, yes, a red-haired vixen starred in that mind game.

But he could fantasize for only so long. Always, his thoughts came back to the little ones he had been sent to protect. Truly, being around children was tearing at his soul, causing him to go nigh faint on one occasion, and at other times, wanting to howl to the high heavens with his pain. Several times he'd escaped their presence for a few moments just so he could breathe without gasping. Tears even welled in his eyes when they got too close. A Viking warrior weeping? It was unacceptable.

He didn't need to pray to Michael to relieve him of this particular assignment. Michael knew! And, not surprisingly, the irksome saint remained absent and silent.

Mordr was fine—well, not fine, but not screaming silently—when he was busy with specific tasks, like driving the five chatterlings to and from school. The only time they were not talking, or laughing, or giggling, or shouting, or shrieking was when they were asleep. Worst of all was the little girl, Linda, who insisted on giving him kisses. Kisses! Once last night before going to bed, and once before leaving his car and going into her school.

Another thing was their smell. Oh, not the scent of the dirt and other unmentionable things they attracted like moving magnets, but their skin when clean, especially after bathing, had a distinct child scent that was all too familiar to him, even after all these centuries.

When he'd arrived at their schools this afternoon to bring them home, they entered the car like a herd of Huns let loose from some dungeon.

"My peanut butter and jelly sandwich got smushed."

"You're s'posed to put it on top of your backpack, not under the books."

"I traded a Twinkie with Johnny Severino for a night crawler."

"Eew! Where is it? Where is it?"

"I put it on Jane Hardy's shoulder an' she screamed an' I had to do quiet time in the corner for a whole hour. During recess!"

"Farty Hardy! Farty Hardy!"

"Wish I could miss math class."

"I got ninety-eight on my spelling test. I missed *jogging*. Didja know there's two Gs in *jogging*?"

"Stop touching me."

"You touched me first."

"Ow!"

"Miss Washburn says I need to have my eyeglasses adjusted so they stop slipping."

"I'm hungry."

"I have to pee."

"I have to poop."

"Hurry, Mordr, hurry!"

"Can you build us a longship, Mordr?"

"Where would you sail it, dickhead?"

"Swear jar, swear jar!"

"We could tow it to the lake, like Mr. Bates does with his pontoon."

"I would make a good pirate. Arg!"

"Dork!"

Once inside the house, before they had a chance to throw their belongings hither and yon, all bodily functions seemingly forgotten, he ordered them to take their school backpacks to their bedchambers. What were modern people thinking? Making little ones lug around those heavy canvas bags on their backs. They would be hunchbacks before they ever reached adulthood.

After they'd washed their hands, and taken care of bladder and bowel functions, he gave them milk and an unusual sweet called cookies, or Oreos, which they broke apart and licked before dunking in milk. Mordr was going to try some later. The Oreos were one of many wonderful suggestions from Mrs. Delgado, who'd spent every bit of the two hundred dollars he'd handed her for grocery shopping. Money well spent, if these Oreos were any indication. Then on to the family room, where they were now, finishing up their school-work.

"I'm done," Maggie exclaimed, shutting her note-book. She came over and sat on the floor next to his chair, wanting a front-row seat for his story to come. Linda was already on the floor at his other side, read-ing a book about Hansel and Gretel and a witch, which seemed all together too frightening for a child her age, in Mordr's opinion. In any case, Linda claimed she did not have any homework, though Larry was work-ing out numbers on a lined paper, occasionally glanc-ing up at him with questions like, "What's two plus three?"

Mordr had to discreetly count on his fingers to give the answer.

Ben and Sam looked at Maggie with disgust as they continued to labor over their own work, a history lesson about a war between Britain and America. Those bloody Saxons continued to be war-like throughout the years, apparently, Mordr mused, whilst Vikings, who had clearly been the better fighting men, had died out as a separate race. Try to find the logic in that!

Finally, they were all done, or so they said, and he moved his chair into an upright position as they gath-ered about him.

"In Viking times, children did not remain children for long. By the time a boy was eleven or twelve, he was ready to go a-Viking with his father and brothers, and girls learned how to run a household."

"What about school?" Sam wanted to know.

"No school. We had priest tutors for a few years, but that was all."

"Wish I lived then," Ben said, making a swishing motion with his hand like he was sword fighting. "I would make a great Viking."

Mordr almost smiled. The little bratling probably would.

"How come girls didn't go a-Viking?" Maggie pushed her glasses up her little nose and scowled at him.

"Times were different then."

"Doesn't seem fair to me." Maggie continued to scowl at him as if he were personally responsible for the inequality of the sexes back then.

"How come you talk like you lived back then?" Larry asked.

Good question! "It is just a way of telling a story about our history," Mordr fabricated.

"Go on," Linda encouraged as she pressed her blond head against his knee. Although he wore blue denim braies today, he could feel the fine hairs on his legs stand on end at the sweetness of the gesture.

"So, it was time for me to go on my first adventure. I had been training with the older men, of course, since—"

"With swords?" Ben asked with awe.

Mordr nodded.

"Real swords, not wooden ones?" Sam specified.

Mordr nodded again. "We practiced with wooden swords as youthlings, my brothers and I, then moved on to short swords, then later broadswords."

"How many brothers do you have?" Larry was picking his nose and examining his find as he asked the question.

"Six."

"And sisters?" This from Maggie, of course, who was still disgruntled over girls being barred from manly ventures.

"No sisters." Then, as a concession to Maggie, he added, "I did not mean to imply that women always stayed at home. There were always exceptions. Like Boudicca, the Celtic warrior queen. And female pirates. And, on the rare occasion, a Viking woman on a longship adventure." *But only when their lackwit fathers or husbands permitted such foolishness.*

"Whoa! Pirates?" Ben exclaimed with a wishful gleam in his eyes.

"I want a real sword," Sam declared. "If Viking boys got real swords, why can't I have one?"

"Can I have a kitten?" Linda asked with absolutely no relevance.

Larry continued to search for booty in his nose and wipe his fingers on his pants. Which reminded Mordr that he should make him wash his hands afore dinner.

Maggie had her little arms folded over her little chest, still upset over the female situation in Viking times. "If I lived then, I would organize all the women to demand our rights."

And end up locked in some tower or minus a tongue. "Good for you!"

Just then, all the children spoke together, each with different opinions, each with different questions. Ben tackled Sam 'til he was face first on the floor and sat on him because Sam called Ben a wuss. And Maggie shoved Larry for making a rude remark about girls doing girl things. And Linda was singing some song for him that she had learned in school that day, something about the wheels going around. So much for his story!

Mordr put his face in his hands as chaos reigned

around him. Maybe he should suggest more Oreos. Just then, he smelled something floral. Light. Not over-powering. But compelling. Oh no! Lilies. He raised his head and saw Miranda standing in the open doorway. He hadn't even realized that she had come home.

The children's backs were to her; so, for the moment, they were unaware of her presence. Which gave Mordr a chance to study her. She wore a seemingly modest dress today. Green silk, ending at the knees. But it seemed to wrap around, one side, then the other, with a bow tied on the left at her small waist. He wondered idly—or not so idly—if that bow was the only thing holding the garment together. What would happen if he walked over and leaned down to her neck to see if the floral scent was truly her skin's natural odor or some artificial perfume and at the same time, slipped the knot on the bow, then stepped back to see what treasures lay hidden under—

"Aunt Mir!"

"You're home!"

The children jumped up and ran to Miranda, giving her a group hug, even the older boys. She smiled down at them, kissing the tops of their unruly heads. She couldn't appear more maternal if she was their real mother.

They were all talking at once then, telling her about their day. The night crawler incident was noticeably absent. She listened intently to each of them, then ruf-fled the hair on Ben and Sam and told them all, "Take your school things up to your rooms and you can play out back until dinner. Maybe you could set up that new croquet set and . . ."

Her words trailed off as the kids grabbed their books and notebooks and rushed for the stairs.

"I call dibs on the red ball."

"I get yellow."

"You always get yellow."

"Stop shoving."

"Bite me!"

Larry was scratching his butt, which prompted Ben to walk over and give him a wedgie, which caused Larry to head-butt Ben in the stomach, knocking him to the ground.

Leaning against the door frame, she shrugged with seeming apology for the children's behavior, as if she were personally responsible, then smiled at him.

Oh no! No smiles. Please, God, no smiles. Her smiles make me feel like . . . they make me feel!

"You did great today," she said. "The house looks clean. The dinner smells delicious. And the children are somewhat behaving themselves. Thank you."

"Mrs. Delgado helped."

"That's another thing. Mrs. Delgado refuses to do any more than basic cleaning for me. I noticed folded clothes in the laundry, and you mentioned grocery shopping. A miracle!"

"She is a lonely woman since her son died in the war. And bitter, truth to tell. His ex-wife doesn't let her see her granddaughter very often. That is why she is so quiet and irksome, I suspect."

"I knew Mrs. Delgado had a son who'd died in Afghanistan. A Marine. But that's all she'd ever disclosed to me. How did you get her to talk to you?"

Mordr rose from the chair and walked toward her. "Me? I did nothing to encourage talking. I do not talk much myself. Mayhap she recognized a kindred spirit. A shared pain."

He could tell she wanted to ask more—and since when did he mention his painful past, even in such a general way?—but he was close to her now, and his proximity made her nervous. And, yes, he leaned down to smell her scent. He closed his eyes and inhaled deeply. Like an aphrodisiac, it was, entering his nostrils, streaming through his bloodstream, turning him warm and—

"Are you smelling me?" she accused, although he noticed that she was sniffing, too. She'd mentioned yesterday that he had a particular scent.

He stepped back, reluctantly, and nodded. "I was wondering . . ."

"Wondering what?" she prodded when he didn't finish his thought.

I was wondering what would happen if I untied that bow and looked at your body. "I was wondering if men stop and gape when you walk down the street."

"Why would they do that?"

Would your skin be creamy soft with delicious curves? Would your breasts be small with oversensitive nipples, as I suspect? Would your nether hair glimmer in the sunlight like reddish gold fleece? "Because of your scant attire. I know it is not considered scandalous today, but where I come from, women do not expose their legs or arms."

"*What?*" She flinched. "Are you a Muslim? That sounds a lot like purdah to me."

"Have I not said it enough? I am a Viking."

"Religious fanatic, then?"

"This compelling attraction I have for you has naught to do with religion, believe you me. Unless lust is no longer one of the Seven Deadly Sins."

"I don't understand. You condemn me for my attire, then claim you are attracted to me."

"Of course I am attracted to you. Is that not what I have said?"

"Actually, no."

"Then, let me say it plain. I like your attire and how you look in it. Too much! I just wonder if I will be able to resist your temptation?"

"This is the craziest conversation I've ever had.

Temptation? I don't dress to tempt anyone. Good Lord!"

He thought about warning her not to swear, but decided to save that admonition for later. "Do not be alarmed."

"Alarmed? You practically accuse me of dressing provocatively to turn men on."

"Not men. Me. I mean, I am not saying you deliberately entice. Just that I am."

She crossed her eyes with frustration. "Am what?"

"Tempted."

"You are crossing a line with these inappropriate words."

"I don't see why my remarks would be deemed inappropriate. I am just stating a fact. 'Tis amazing, but it is what it is. I am attracted to you."

"That is the most lame compliment I have ever heard."

"I have not felt such instant . . . uh, attraction in such a long time that I am amazed. I am not saying this right."

She tilted her head to the side. "I should be alarmed by that statement, but, as a psychologist, I know that it is mere testosterone speaking. A natural attraction based on scientific principles of . . . what? Why are you shaking your head?"

"Because it is more than that. By the by, if it is mere science, are you feeling the same . . . arousal?"

"I am not!" she said, but her denial was belied by a blush that covered her face and crept down her neck to parts unknown but tempting as water to a thirsty man.

Her hair was upswept, exposing small shell ears pierced with dangling jade earrings and also highlighting the graceful line of her neck. He ran a forefinger along her jaw from ear to ear.

"Amazing!" he repeated in a sex-husky voice.

"You keep saying that. Why is it so amazing?"

"Because I have not had such thoughts in three hundred years."

"Oddly, it seems like three hundred years for me, too," she confessed.

And then he kissed her.

Nine

Trouble comes in big packages . . .

$\mathcal{M}$ordr kissed her.

Three hundred years since he last had a woman? Hah! Talk about exaggeration! If it truly had been a long time (she suspected something more like three days) since he'd last had a woman, he hadn't forgotten a thing. Kind of like riding a bicycle, except better. Way better!

Maybe it was a Viking thing. A mere kiss from him was about a seventeen on the Richter scale. The man had hidden skills. He certainly made her quake in certain places.

He was a big man. Tall, hard-muscled shoulders and chest with big workman's hands and long, tree-trunk legs, evident in a blue Minnesota Vikings T-shirt that matched his pale blue eyes, tucked into well-worn denim jeans and sockless athletic shoes. He had to bend his knees slightly to put himself on eye level with her, rather lip level. With ease he extended both arms and braced his hands on the upper curves of the archway leading from the family room to the hallway. His lips pressed to hers were soft and entreating.

She sensed that he was giving her the opportunity to resist, to shove him away and tell him he was being a jerk. That his behavior could be interpreted as sexual harassment on the job site. Instead, contrary to her usual cautious personality, she raised her hands to his shoulders and moaned.

That moan represented assent to him, she could tell.

Before she realized what he was about, he yanked her into the room and pressed her up against the side wall, raising her so that only the tips of her high heels touched the floor, the whole time devouring her with a deep kiss that went on forever. He moved his head from side to side 'til he got the perfect fit. Then he nipped at her lower lip and plunged his tongue into her open mouth. His mouth moved on hers, a constant demand that she respond. And she did.

The low growl of appreciation in his throat triggered arousal deep in her body. His hands were everywhere, making wide swaths of her back, caressing her buttocks, cupping her breasts, and strumming the nipples with his calloused thumbs.

"Oh Lord! I forgot."

"Forgot what?" She tilted her head to the side, giving him better access to that sensuous spot at the curve of her neck.

"How good it feels to hold a woman," he husked out, nibbling at her skin. "I am in so much trouble. So." Nibble. "Much." Nibble. "Trouble." He ended his nibbles with a quick bite.

Places long neglected in Miranda came alive. This was insanity, allowing a near stranger such intimate access to her body. And it was not enough. Not nearly enough.

Thus, she didn't protest when he released the bow at her side and separated her dress. In a sex-thickened voice, he murmured, "You should be careful where you wear a dress like this."

"Why?"

"It gives a man sinful thoughts."

"Are you having sinful thoughts?"

"You have no idea." His blue eyes turned silvery and his lips parted, staring down at her in nothing but a nude-colored lace bra and bikini panties. She didn't have a great body. Too slim. Breasts too small. But that didn't seem to matter to him.

"Do you know how good you look to me?"

Maybe her body wasn't so bad, after all. "You're not too shabby yourself."

He angled his head and settled his mouth on hers again. Long, lazy, but nonetheless hungry kisses ensued. She'd never been kissed so thoroughly or with such finesse. His taste was headier than champagne on an empty stomach.

Raising his head, but at the same time still holding her, he said, "For my sins, you are forbidden to me."

"Forbidden fruit?" she teased.

"Of the worst kind. Or best kind. And I am a hungry man." He looked so miserable when he spoke those words.

She raised a hand to his nape and pulled him down for a soft kiss to his lips, which were parted and moist.

"I want you," he said in a voice raw with emotion.

"No kidding!" A hardened part of his body was pressing against her belly, giving proof to his statement that he wasn't impotent. Not by a Vegas long shot.

He pinched her butt in reprimand.

She pinched his back.

He almost smiled.

"When was the last time you smiled?"

"I cannot recall."

"Really?" She cocked her head to the side. "Why? A sense of humor makes the world go round."

"Pfff! Not my world."

"You are a puzzle to me. There has to be some reason that you are always so grim. Nothing is so bad it can't be overcome."

It was as if a shadow passed over Mordr's face. He went suddenly rigid, then stepped back from her. "This was not a good idea. Sorry I am if I offended you."

"Huh? What just happened? What did I do?"

A loud ringing jarred them both, and precluded his answering her questions. The doorbell.

"Are you expecting someone?" he asked.

She shook her head.

He helped adjust her dress and pointed toward the back of the house with a silent order that she check on the children. She quickly ran to the kitchen and looked out the window. The kids were safe. For once, they had listened and were in the process of setting up the croquet course, with Maggie giving her sage advice on how it should be done, the boys arguing, and Linda just holding on to the yellow ball tightly.

She rushed back to find Mordr looking through the peephole, then undoing the various locks on the doors and clicking in the security code. "Dumb lackwits!" he muttered.

Hmm. That didn't sound dangerous.

Mordr tried to block the open doorway, but she scooted under his arm and was dumbfounded at what stood on her doorstep. Two big men wearing long cloaks with angel wing epaulets on the shoulders, over black jeans and T-shirts. Motorcycle-style boots completed the picture. One wore his long black hair with thin braids on either side of his very handsome face, similar to Mordr. The other's hair was short brown in designer disarray. Different from Mordr, but still there was a resemblance. More Vikings?

Seeing her ducking around to stand beside Mordr,

they smiled. And exposed long incisors on either side of their mouths. Like wolves or vampires.

She gasped.

"Watch yourselves," Mordr hissed.

Miranda shook her head to clear it, and when she looked again, their teeth were perfectly straight, except for slightly longer incisors. She must be in a hormone-induced haze.

"Miranda, these are my lackwit brothers, Cnut and Harek. Lackwit brothers, this is Miranda Hart . . . my, uh, client."

Client? Me? She nodded at them, acknowledging the introduction, such as it was. She was still stunned by their appearance. "Cloaks? Really? In Vegas heat?" she whispered to Mordr.

"What is wrong with cloaks?" Mordr asked her, not in a whisper. "I wear an identical one betimes. 'Tis a trait of our family."

"Cloaks have many inside pockets for carrying . . . um, certain things," the one named Harek explained.

She could only imagine.

"What are you doing here?' Mordr demanded of both brothers.

Now that was just rude.

"What are *you* doing here is the better question," Harek said. "By the looks of your lips and that bite mark on your neck, I'd say something fun."

Oh my God! What do I look like? She put a hand to her hair and groaned. It had come loose from its clip atop her head and was hanging in ridiculous curls down to her shoulders. She didn't need to wonder if she had whisker burns on her cheeks and neck, or kiss-swollen lips, like Mordr's. She probably looked like a slut.

Mordr bared his teeth at Harek, and Miranda noticed that he had slightly longer incisors, too. Since he never smiled, she hadn't been aware of that fact. She looked again. Yep, definitely a little longer than the rest of his teeth. Cute. She almost laughed when she imagined his reaction if she called him cute.

"I repeat," Mordr said icily to his brothers. "Why are you here?"

"There is trouble," Cnut told him. "Big trouble."

Guess who's coming, uh, came, to dinner . . .

"**C**an we come in?" Harek asked with a crooked grin at Miranda that some women might find attractive, but Mordr considered halfbrained. And Harek was the one who was supposed to have the biggest, sharpest brain of them all.

Cnut winked at her—*probably to annoy me*—and said in a raspy voice, the result of being nigh garroted by a slimy Saxon one time, "Pleased am I to meet you, Lady Miranda." His gravelly voice appealed to some women, or so Cnut always bragged.

"She's no lady," Mordr said.

Mordr hadn't meant that as an insult, but she chose to take it that way as evidenced by her hip bumping his side. He was momentarily shocked by her action, which bespoke familiarity, and was definitely un-lady-like. Trying for a bit of damage control, he added, "I meant, they do not use titles of nobility in this time . . . uh, country."

"Is that an apology?" she asked.

"No. Why should I apologize?"

"Still the same suave oaf," Harek remarked. "Mr. No-Personality!"

"Remember the time he asked Queen Edwina if she ever considered slicing off that mole on her nose?" Cnut said to Harek with a grin.

"Would you two Viking pain-in-the-arses care to

step into the yard with me?" Mordr gritted out, and he didn't intend to show them the sprinkler-fed grass, which was lush here in the front where the children didn't trample. In fact, he warned them, "Spew out more of those jests at my expense, and we shall see how many eyes I can blacken in two minutes."

"Aren't you worried that I might bloody those kiss-swollen lips of yours, brother?" Cnut asked with more grinning.

"Time for an intervention," Miranda declared with a scowl at him, even though he wasn't the one who started the sniping. To his brothers, she said, "You can call me Miranda. Please, come in." She stepped back to motion them in. To him, in an undertone, she whispered, "Stop behaving like a child. You're worse than Ben and Sam."

"I resent that." *By the runes, her lips look kiss-some.*

"Big deal!"

"Do not try my temper, or you may taste the flavor of my wrath." *Is there anything more sex-worthy than a woman with spirit?*

"Get over yourself!"

I would like to get over something, or on, or in. Whoo! I hope my fangs aren't showing, or another body part. All I have to do is look at her and my arousal goes up a notch or twenty.

Meanwhile, the two idiots strolled in, and, yes, it was idiotic to wear a cape in ninety-degree temperature, even though he understood why; the capes hid large amounts of weaponry. Just then, he detected a slight sulfur scent on Harek and a lemon scent on Cnut. They'd been killing Lucies and saving sinners, that would be Mordr's conclusion. And it wasn't just the odor that clung to their garments, their skin tones were healthy and tanned-looking, not the usual paleness when they'd been away too long from feeding.

And Miranda noticed, too, he could tell. When Harek passed by into the house, her nose wrinkled reflexively, as if he might have a bad case of wind in the bowels. She probably thought Cnut had been sucking on lemons, or sucking up vast amounts of lemonade.

"Miranda, why don't you go check on the children whilst I talk with my brothers?" *Is that her nipples showing as tiny, twin peaks on the bodice of her dress? Mayhap it is just a wrinkle in her undergarment. But her nipples are big, like ripe currants, or cherry pits, or . . . For the love of dirt! I cannot be thinking about nipples or that scandalous lace concoction that covers them.*

"I already checked on the children."

"Do it again."

At first, she balked and addressed Cnut, "You mentioned trouble. Is it Roger?"

"Who?" Cnut asked. "Is Roger a Lucie?"

"No, or leastways we do not know yet," Mordr answered for her.

"Lucy who?" Miranda was confused, with good reason. "Roger's last name is Jessup."

"I'll explain later," Mordr said to his brothers.

"Oh my gosh! I thought I was mistaken before, but . . ." Her words trailed off as she gaped at his brothers, whose vampire teeth were exposed again, no doubt due to reflexive lust in the proximity of a desirable woman, meaning Miranda, who was herself in an aroused state due to his stirring the embers of her desire. Idiots! His brothers were idiots, and he was the biggest idiot of them all, succumbing to temptation after centuries of self-imposed celibacy. He indicated by tapping his mouth twice what the situation was. Their fangs immediately retracted. Now, they just displayed slightly longer incisors. Naught could be done about the lust that still simmered beneath the surface of *his* skin.

Miranda blinked at his brothers. "Sorry. For a moment there, I thought I saw . . . never mind. Um, I'll just go and check on the children. Mordr, why don't you take your brothers into the den."

After she hurried off and his brothers were seated on the sofa, Mordr on the recliner, they wasted no time.

"Children, Mordr? You, around children?" Worry resonated in Harek's voice.

"Five of them," Mordr said with disgust.

"That is cruel, even for Mike," Cnut remarked.

"Tell me about it. Half the time I feel as if I am going to heave the contents of my stomach, and the other half I nigh faint."

"You have never fainted a day in your life," Harek declared, "not even that time a black bear twice your size trapped you in a cave with its cubs."

That was a memory Mordr would not soon forget, even though it happened a hundred years ago.

"And a woman, Mordr?" Harek gazed at him with incredulity. "I thought you gave up women centuries ago."

"I did not give them up precisely. I just lost interest." *By the runes! Since when do I reveal such intimate things about myself?*

"Same thing!" Harek asserted. "And equally hard to believe."

Mordr had no intention of discussing anything further with his brothers about his lack of lust. *A lack until now, God help me.* "So, what is the trouble?" he asked.

"Lucies. In Vegas," Cnut said.

"Lots of them," Harek added.

Mordr let the footrest of the recliner drop, and he sat up straight. "How can that be? I would have noticed."

"They are in the city itself, in and around the casinos," Cnut explained.

"But I was there when I first arrived a few days ago."

Harek shrugged. "They must have just come on the scene."

A sudden suspicion hit Mordr. "What are you two doing in Vegas? Checking up on me?"

"Now, why would we do that?" Harek asked. "Tsk, tsk! It's not as if you are going to commit any big sins, or anything. Right?"

Cnut pretended to be counting off on his fingers the Seven Deadly Sins. "Greed? Pride? Sloth? Envy? Wrath? Gluttony? Ah, could it be Fornication?"

"I have not fornicated," Mordr said.

"Really? The megawatt sexual current betwixt you and Miranda could heat a Siberian village. And that is saying a lot. Last time I checked on the Internet, the temperature there was twenty below zero." Harek, who was guilty of the sin of greed, was not the usual Viking. Not because other Vikings were not greedy, but because he knew stuff like computers and megawatts.

Harek was a perfect example of the contradictions he and the other vangels dealt with all the time. Ancient Norse words mixed with modern terms and knowledge.

"Back to why you are in Vegas to begin with," Mordr reminded them.

"Zeb contacted Trond and told him that Jasper has another bright idea," Cnut explained.

Zeb was a demon vampire who was trying to join the other team, meaning vangels. It had never happened in the history of the world. Once in Hell, always in Hell. But, for some reason, Michael had given Zeb fifty years to prove himself as a double agent. Then he might reconsider his devil status. Who wouldn't jump at that chance of a do-over?

"The Lucies are going to infiltrate the casinos and brothels of Las Vegas and three other cities around the world, Reno, Monaco, and Macau in China," Cnut elaborated. "Vikar is holding down the fort back at the castle, while Ivak is in Reno, Trond in Monaco, and Sigurd in Macau. We're here to help you in Vegas where, according to Zeb, Jasper's biggest contingent will be operating."

"Holy shit!" Mordr sighed. "Jasper does come up with some grandiose plans. The Sin Cruise. Navy SEALs. Prisons. You have to give him credit for finding places where sin flourishes."

His brothers nodded.

"I take it by your skin coloring and scents that you've already killed a few Lucies and saved a few sinners."

"A few," they both said.

"Where are all your vangels?" Mordr asked.

"Getting jobs throughout the city to infiltrate the ranks of Lucies," Cnut answered. "Doormen. Bouncers in nightclubs and houses of ill-repute. Dealers at roulette and poker tables. Restaurant cooks and waiters."

"Are you ready for this?" Harek grinned. "Regina is a showgirl at one of the big casinos. Wearing an almost-nothing costume with pointy high heels and a three-foot headdress. Cnut made the mistake of saying she looked hot, and she threatened to place a curse on his cock that would cause it to be tied into a knot."

Regina had been a Norse witch back in the 1200s. And not a good witch, either. She was the cauldron-boiling, black cat, broom-riding kind who could cast spells that would make the strongest men cringe. Truth to tell, she was scarier than vampires any day.

"And that's not all," Harek said with a laugh. "Armod is in rock 'n' roll heaven singing and dancing in a Michael Jackson revue at Caesar's, and Lizzie is the cook at Cougar Ranch."

"Lizzie? She almost never goes out on missions. Did she bring her axe . . . um, cleaver?"

"For a certainty!" Harek laughed. "And she's madder than a boar with a bug up its arse. Those harlots best not get in her way. She's already warned Vikar and Alex. If they dirty her kitchen back at the castle, she will be serving them gammelost with every meal." Gammelost was the stinky cheese often served to Viking warriors when out on a mission. Some said it was so putrid it turned men berserk.

Mordr almost smiled. What a weird, demented family he had, and, yes, all of them, not just the brothers, were a family. You couldn't spend all these years together and not feel a bond of sorts. Even Mordr, who disdained any kind of emotional attachment. "I assume that Michael knew all this when he sent me here."

"Definitely," his brothers said.

"I wonder, though, what the Lucies have to do with Roger. He is the father of the five children Miranda adopted." He explained the threat Roger posed to Miranda, as well as the children.

"Could Roger be a Lucie?" Harek mused.

"I do not know. Yet. I sent one of my vangels to Ohio to check him out in person."

"Ohio is a long way from Nevada, in human terms," commented Harek, as if Mordr was not aware of that fact.

"Not far enough. The man is about to be released from some halfway house, which is like a bridge betwixt prison and freedom."

"Too bad we vangels cannot just kill bad people." This from Cnut. "Instead, we must at least attempt to save them from their own evil inclinations."

Just then, there was a light knock on the door.

They all stood.

It was Maggie, who glanced up, up, up at them, and blinked behind her little glasses. Not a bit of fear, despite their much larger size. She carried a tray with three bottles of beer and a small bowl of hard pretzels. "Aunt Mir said you might like some refreshment before dinner. We're eating in a half hour. And she said to ask if your brothers will be staying for dinner."

"No," Mordr said, taking the tray from her and setting it on a low table.

"Yes," Harek and Cnut said at the same time.

"Good. We're having pot roast and homemade bread and apple pie for dessert. Mordr made it." Maggie beamed at Mordr, as if he should be thankful that she had bragged on him.

Two sets of Viking eyes went wide and turned with surprise to Mordr.

He felt like a total halfbrain. Viking warriors did not cook.

"Introduce us, Mordr," Harek encouraged.

"I forgot that you are not acquainted with Maggie, or the other children."

"Yes, we would like to meet all the children. Five, did you say?" Cnut was grinning like a *drukkinn* boar.

"These are my brothers Cnut and Harek," he told Maggie. To Harek and Cnut, he said, "And this is Margaret, or Maggie, Jessup, the oldest of the children."

Maggie pushed her glasses up higher on her nose, then walked over big as you please and shook the hands of Cnut and then Harek, both of whom were clearly amused. "Pleased to meet you," she said to each of them.

Mordr felt a swell of misplaced pride at her bravery and good manners, immediately followed by a rush of blood to his head, causing him to feel faint. He held on to the back of a chair to steady himself. All because of the quickly shuttered question in his mind of whether his Kata would be like this had she lived to ten years and more.

Cnut and Harek gazed at him with concern.

And Maggie, to his shock, told them, "It's all right. He gets like this once in a while when he's around us kids. It passes."

"Like gas?" Cnut murmured under his breath.

Mordr shot him a glance of warning.

Maggie shifted from foot to foot, and Mordr asked her, "Was there something else?"

"We were wondering if you all would like to play croquet with us . . . until dinner." Maggie's little face reddened, a perfect match to her hair, which curled wildly down to her shoulders, a trait she shared with her aunt.

"We'll be out in a few minutes, sweetling," he said, walking over to pat her on the shoulder and open the door for her, a clear hint that they wanted privacy.

Instead of being insulted, Maggie's green eyes filled with tears and she said in a hushed whisper, "You called me sweetling."

"I did?" Mordr was surprised at himself.

"I like it." Embarrassed, she scurried away.

When he turned back to his brothers, they were both grinning, *again*. And he knew why. "It was a slip of the tongue."

They all sat back down, sipping at their cold beers and crunching on the rock-hard pretzels. A person could break a tooth . . . uh, fang.

"I assume you want me to look over the house and property to check for any weakness in security," Cnut said.

He'd already sent Cnut pictures and details, but an on-site inspection would be even better. "Yes. That is why you are staying for dinner, is it not?"

"Hell, no!" Cnut said. "I would not miss a meal cooked by a Viking berserker."

"You could not get us out of here with a war horse and a battering ram. Not until we see you interacting with your five children and your life mate. A redhead! You never used to like red-haired wenches." On hearing Mordr's growl of displeasure, Harek added, "*Potential* life mate."

Mordr stiffened and gritted his teeth, barely controlling the urge to put a fist in both of their smirking faces. "They are not my children, and Miranda is not my life mate."

"Uh-huh," the two lackwits agreed, clearly not agreeing at all.

"You know what Mike said after Ivak wed Gabrielle. No more human emotional attachments for us vangels," Mordr said.

"I think what Mike said was, no more sex with humans," Cnut corrected.

"No, you are both wrong," Harek contended. "No more life mates for vangels."

"Same thing," Cnut grumbled.

Mordr felt like pulling his hair out, one strand at a time.

After drinking their beers and catching up on vangel news, Mordr led the two of them down the hall and into the kitchen, where Miranda was bent over, taking two loaves of bread out of the oven. The pies were already cooling on wire racks.

"Something smells yummy," Cnut said.

"Something looks yummy," Harek said.

Mordr's jaw dropped. Yummy? Since when did Vikings use such ridiculous words?

In an undertone to Mordr, Harek added, "Great rump!" And he wasn't talking about the meat.

Miranda had changed from her dress to a pair of

short braies that reached mid-thigh and a sleeveless blouse. Just as well. He did not want his brothers speculating about that bow on her dress. As he had, for his sins! He also didn't want them surveying her body in the skimpy attire with lustsome intentions.

He gave both of his brothers warning looks, but all he said aloud was, "Is there anything more ludicrous than a hulksome Viking male using the word *yummy*?"

"Did you just call your brothers hunks?" Miranda asked.

"No! I called them hulks. You know, big, clumsy oafs."

"Like you?" Harek asked with mock innocence.

"Precisely."

"Uh-oh! I see a problem already," Cnut said, peering out the window.

"What? What have those kids done now?" Miranda was tugging off a pair of oven mitts, about to storm out the door.

"Not the children," Cnut said quickly. "The backyard. It is a security risk."

"Still?" Mordr asked. "I thought wiring up the fence to the home alarm system and motion detectors would be enough."

Miranda had one hand over her chest and a hand braced on the table, as if she was having trouble breathing. Harek was sitting at the table, tapping away at a small electronic device he must have pulled from an inside pocket of his cloak.

"You are not to fear," Mordr assured Miranda. "Cnut is an expert in security. If there is a problem, he can fix it."

"Thanks for the vote of confidence, brother, but I'm not so sure that moving to another, more secure location wouldn't be easier and safer, at least temporarily."

"Out of the question!" Miranda exclaimed. "These

children have been moved around too much already. They need stability."

"She doesn't like to disrupt the children's lives," Mordr explained, which caused Harek to glance up from his work and Cnut to raise his eyebrows. Belatedly, he realized that he sounded like he knew Miranda really well when, in fact, he had been here for only a little over one day. Putting that aside, he went over to the window and stood gazing outward with Cnut. "What is the problem?"

"The fence would suffice for keeping out intruders, but those houses in the neighborhood are too close." Cnut pointed to a three-story dwelling that was located across the backyard and over several houses, facing another street. "A villain could stand on that roof with a high-powered weapon and do great bodily harm. At the least, using a cheap pair of binoculars, he could watch all the movements around your house."

"How would Roger get up on the Sullivans' roof?" Miranda scoffed, although she had to be thinking about Mordr being up on her roof earlier today, facing in another direction.

"It wouldn't have to be the roof. It could be through one of the upper windows," Cnut contended. "And it could be any being with evil intent, not just Roger." Cnut gave Mordr a meaningful glance. He meant Lucies.

"Mordr, do you really think Roger is that much of a threat? I mean, I know he's angry, and I know he's been physically violent in the past, and I know he blames me for the loss of his children, but you're talking about guns and shooting."

"Must be, or I would not have been sent to protect you," Mordr replied.

"So what do we do about it?"

Cnut piped in, "As I mentioned, you could stay in a more secure location until it is safe to return home."

"Like where? A hotel? Some safe house?"

"The castle," Mordr suggested.

"What castle?" she asked.

"The castle in Transylvania. I already told you about that," he said, getting increasingly impatient with all her questions.

She exhaled with exasperation. Apparently she was getting impatient, too. "You mentioned some crazy place named Transylvania, but you never mentioned a castle. I would remember that," she accused Mordr. Then, "You own a castle?"

"I do not own the castle. It is the headquarters for"—he caught himself just in time—"my family."

"Well, you could say it is Vikar's castle since he lives there more than any of us." Cnut was enjoying this whole conversation, while Mordr felt as if he were walking on eggs.

There was no way the castle would work, anyhow. Five energetic children running around in the midst of fifty or so vangels, some of whom were young, a hundred years or so, and unable yet to control their fangs. "It would be impossible."

"I know," Cnut said, more serious now. "How about Ivak's plantation in Louisiana?"

"He's barely begun to rebuild that old dump . . . uh, estate," Harek noted. "There is a huge snake problem that must be handled before the actual restoration."

"Well, then, you will have to assign some of your men to strategic spots around the neighborhood," Cnut told Mordr.

"He already has men guarding the children's schools. I can't afford that much security." Miranda looked as if she was going to faint.

"Sit," Mordr ordered. When she did and pressed both hands up to her face, Mordr added, "You can't afford not to take every precaution. Besides, it will cost you nothing."

"What?" Her head shot up.

Uh-oh! He was raising too many suspicions.

"Miranda, go outside and check on the children. We will be out soon, and all will be well, that I assure you," he said.

She stood and he noticed how kiss-swollen her lips still looked. Her nipples, even covered by an undergarment and the blouse, were evident to him, but maybe he was just remembering what he had actually seen when he had uncovered her body a short time ago.

No, no, no! He could not be distracted like this.

He would think later about what had happened betwixt them. And he might even feel guilty for his lustsome actions. Or mayhap not.

Miranda went through the sliding glass doors, and he heard the children cheering her arrival.

"You're on my team. You're on my team!" Larry yelled.

"I lost my ball," Linda cried.

"Sam is cheating already," Maggie said.

"Is Mordr coming out to play?" Ben wanted to know.

"Yeah, where's Mordr?" Sam inquired of Maggie.

"Mordr, Mordr, Mordr," all the children chanted before Miranda shushed them. The door slid shut, cutting off their words, but allowing them to still hear the sounds of shouting and laughter.

"Play? You?" Harek looked at him as if he had grown two heads.

"They want me to play croquet with them."

"Crochet? Mordr! First, cooking. Now, knitting." Cnut was genuinely concerned.

"What next? Will you be asking us if your butt is

too big?" Harek, who should know better, was also concerned.

"Idiots! I said croquet, pronounced *crow-kay*, not crochet, as in *crow-shay*. Croquet is a game that involves hitting balls with mallets through wire hoops in the ground," Mordr told them with disgust. Did they really think he was turning womanish? He should clobber the two of them to show how manly he still was.

Instead of just accepting what he had said, Cnut blathered on in another direction. "You didn't play, even when you were a boyling. You were always so serious. Until you had your own . . ." Cnut's words trailed off, but Mordr knew what he had been going to say. Until he had his own children. That was when he changed.

Mordr felt the blood rush to his head and his hands ball into fists. He wanted to hit something, hard. Only with the strongest willpower was Mordr able to control the urge to kill or do bodily harm. Just because his brother mentioned his children. Sadly, Mordr shook his head. He had thought he was past this rage.

Taking the opposite seat at the table from Harek, he asked, "What have you found out?"

Cnut was still standing by the counter, sniffing the fragrant loaves of bread and a dish of butter beside them. He reached for a knife, about to cut himself a slice.

"No!" Mordr said.

"Why not?" Cnut said.

"You'll spoil your appetite."

"You, making a jest?" Cnut put a hand over his heart, as if in shock. "Will wonders never cease?"

"Shut up, lackwit!" Mordr could tell Cnut felt bad for mentioning his children and was trying to distract him with this silliness. Mordr was getting an ache in his head from dealing with his brothers, or maybe it was from dealing with children.

"Did you really make that bread yourself?" Cnut was opening the refrigerator doors, taking out three more bottles of beer.

"For the love of an iceberg! You make a fuss over the littlest things. It was frozen dough. All I had to do was put it in the oven."

"Really?" This from Harek, who was still tapping away at his little computer or iPad, or whatever the hell you called it.

"Well, I had to grease the pans and brush some melted butter on the top of the loaves to turn the crusts golden brown. Miranda's servant told me how."

"Servant? We no longer live in the Dark Ages," Cnut chided Mordr.

"Her cleaning person," Mordr amended. "As if it matters one whit who told me how!"

"Mordr, you are turning into a regular Mordr La-gasse," Harek observed. "Remember when we were satisfied with unleavened manchet bread. Tasteless, it was, like modern pita bread."

"Or pizza dough without the toppings," Cnut added.

"By all the saints! Why are you two harping away about food? What have you found out, Harek?"

Harek took a long draw on his beer, then said, "Roger Jessup. Forty-two. Born in Cincinnati, Ohio, in 1972. Married Cassandra Hart in 2004. Five children: Margaret. Benjamin and Samuel, twins. Larry and Linda, twins. Convicted in 2011 of assault and battery, spousal rape, battery of a child, etc. Released from Ohio State Penitentiary on May 11. Currently resides at Heaven's Gate Halfway House in Akron, Ohio, about to be released, one-year probation beginning on— Holy shit!" Harek looked up at him and Cnut before announcing, "Today."

Mordr nodded. "Miranda was expecting this. Not the exact date, but her lawyer warned her that Roger would be released soon and to take precautions."

"Which is why you were sent here," Cnut guessed.

There was a light tapping on the sliding glass door, and the three of them glanced over to see a little girling with her nose pressed against the glass, watching. Linda. She gave Mordr a little wave.

Mordr sighed and took a long drink of the cold brew. "Let us go outside and face the horde."

"Do you really think you should refer to children in that manner?" Harek asked.

"I will remind you of that question in an hour," Mordr said.

The instant he opened the door, all eyes turned to them.

"Whoa! Who are they?" Sam said, pointing at Mordr's brothers, who followed behind him.

Ruff's head shot up and he galloped toward them. Mordr stepped aside and Ruff hit Harek full-on, almost knocking him to the ground. Standing on its hind legs, the dog proceeded to lick Harek's lips.

"Yuck!" Harek said. "The beast must like the taste of beer."

"Or else he just thinks you are a female dog," Mordr commented.

"He better not hump my leg." Harek laughed, trying to turn his face away from the slobbering tongue.

Ruff paused, as if considering Harek's words.

"I hope this is not your guard dog," Cnut remarked to an amused Miranda, who was sitting in a lounging chair where she had been trying to read a book.

Cnut's voice drew Ruff's attention. Giving up on Harek, he jumped on Cnut, and backed him up against the house where he began to give his mouth equal attention, accompanied by loud ruff-ruffs between licks.

"Do not dare laugh," Cnut warned Mordr.

"Daddy never laughs," Linda said, latching on to Mordr's thigh with her usual pose of adoration.

"She thinks every man she meets is her father," Mordr tried to explain to his disbelieving brothers.

"Yippee! Wait 'til I tell Johnny Severino we have three Viking nannies, not just one," Larry chirped in and did a little dance that involved thrusting hips and pumping arms. He and Armod would get along well, sharing dance moves.

"I am not a nanny," Mordr declared.

"House manager," Maggie corrected with a rolling of her eyes at her brothers, implying that it didn't make any difference but to appease Mordr's feelings.

"You are not telling Johnny or anyone else about the doings in our house," Miranda said, coming up to stand beside Mordr and his brothers.

Immediately, he was enveloped by the scent of lilies and cloves. He glanced at his brothers, but they didn't seem to notice anything. At first.

But then Harek asked, "What?"

"Why do you look as if you swallowed a sour apple?" Cnut added Mordr.

"He always looks like he swallowed a sour apple," Miranda contributed.

"Not always," Mordr told her, thus getting in the last word.

Or so he thought.

"Would you like me to get an ice pack for your mouth, Mordr?" she asked sweetly. "Your lips are all swollen and bruised."

Ben hitched up his short braies, which were hanging so low his arse crack was exposed. Undaunted, he sauntered toward them and asked Mordr's brothers, "Are you going to help us dig a swimming pool?"

"Uh," Cnut and Harek said.

"We are not digging our own swimming pool," Miranda inserted quickly.

"A longboat then. They can help us build a longboat," Sam suggested. "Mordr said he would."

"I did not!" Mordr asserted.

"You didn't say that you wouldn't," Sam asserted right back.

What kind of child logic was that?

"Tell us another story," Linda urged, rubbing her cheek against Mordr's thigh.

Ruff studied Linda's action and came up on Mordr's other side, using Mordr's other thigh as a rubbing post, causing white fur to fly about.

"I'm hungry," Larry said.

"Me too. Me too," the other children chimed in.

"Pick me up." Linda opened her arms and reached upward.

Mordr stared down at her, bleakly. He could not. He just could not. Wasn't it enough that he was here, was surrounded by all these children? Did he have to bear their touch as well?

Sensing his discomfort, Cnut picked up Linda and swung her high in the air, causing her to giggle, and Mordr escaped into the house. He wasn't hiding, exactly, but he needed some space to breathe.

From behind the closed door of the office, he heard everyone enter the kitchen. The sound of chairs scraping the floor. Water running. Child chatter. Cnut offering to slice the bread. Arguments over who sat where. Laughter.

Once Mordr was calmer, he was about to leave the office. He was embarrassed. Weak, he was, to let such little things affect him so much.

Just then, through the open doorway, he heard the phone sitting on Miranda's desk ring. One, two, three times before the answering machine kicked on. A computer voice asking the caller to leave a short message with a name and number.

First, there was heavy breathing. Then, a male crooned, "Dad-dy's coming!"

Even through the phone lines, over the miles, Mordr recognized the voice of evil and felt the berserkness he had tempered for so long begin to bubble to the surface. Like a volcano.

Would he be able to control it this time?

Ten

They could be Mickey Mantlessons . . .

𝕬 clearly distraught Mordr went into the house on hearing Linda once again call him Daddy, and his two brothers with deliberate care laid their cloaks carefully on a picnic table and moved nimbly about the yard in jeans and T-shirts, challenging the kids to a game of "killer croquet." Considering their size, they were quick on their feet, dodging this way and that, jumping over hoops, bending to get just the right shot, making their own rules.

Miranda had started to go in after Mordr, but his brothers had held her back, telling her that Mordr just needed a little time to calm down. This was nothing unusual. He would be all right shortly.

So, Miranda watched with appreciation as the two men entertained the laughing children, taking their minds off concern for Mordr. There weren't many men who came into her children's lives, and she could see how much they were enjoying the male influence.

Cnut and Harek and Mordr were similar in appearance in terms of height and blue eyes, but had varying shades of hair and body types. Mordr was more bulked up than Cnut or Harek, although they all had muscles aplenty. Cnut's hair was long and black, while Harek's was more modern, the brown strands spiked into deliberate disarray. And, of course, all three had those slightly elongated incisors, more evident on these two brothers since they smiled so often, unlike the grim Mordr.

After Harek had taken his turn, Miranda asked him, "Do all seven of you brothers resemble each other?"

Harek shrugged. "Somewhat, I suppose, though we are half brothers." At her arched brows, he explained. "Same father, different mothers."

"Seven different mothers? Was your father married to all of them? I don't mean all at once, of course."

"You have no idea." Harek laughed. "My father was a virile man, and, no, he did not wed all our mothers. He usually had two or more mistresses, in addition to his wife."

Miranda was shocked, rather outraged, and did not try to hide her reaction.

"I know, I know, you want to say that my father was not so much virile as a horndog," Harek observed.

Miranda didn't even try to disagree. "And you don't condemn your father for such actions?"

Harek shrugged. "My father is long dead. 'Twas a different time and culture."

Miranda wanted to ask more questions, but just then Cnut hit the ball with his mallet so hard that it sailed over the back fence and into a neighbor's yard. It just missed a picture window.

"Holy shit!" Ben exclaimed.

"Swear jar, swear jar!" the other children hooted.

"This is croquet, not baseball," Harek scolded Cnut.

" 'Tis boring the regular way," Cnut contended. "Betimes a man must exercise his muscles." He waggled his eyebrows at Miranda, who was scowling with dis-approval.

Harek gave his ball a good whack, too, and it rico-cheted off the top of the metal fence, almost hitting Ruff, who thought it was part of the game. The dog chased after the ball, picked it up in his big mouth, and refused to give it back.

"You're right," Harek said. "It *is* more fun this way." He and Cnut fist-bumped each other.

They were like big children. "Not if you have to re-place all the windows in the neighborhood," Miranda pointed out.

"Wanna make a bet?" Sam, ever the gambler, asked then. "First person to knock out a window. I bet fifty cents on Nut."

"Cnut," Cnut corrected.

"Rhymes with toot," Ben interjected.

"Or boot," Sam suggested.

"Or Gut, like that guy at the Amish market says, 'Gut Morning.'" Larry beamed at his own choice of rhyming word.

"Coot," Linda suggested, jumping up and down with glee over her word.

"Coot is not a word," Larry said, and stuck his tongue out at his twin.

"Is so! Is so!" Linda asserted. "Like cooties."

"Jeesh! Don't you guys know anything?" Maggie intervened. "Cnut is pronounced like the newt, an animal."

"You were named for a salamander?" Ben asked with incredulity. "Cool!"

Cnut crossed his eyes, which looked funny on such a big man.

"I still call dibs on the bet that Cnut is first to knock out a window," Sam said.

"There's going to be no betting, Sam." Miranda gave the boy a meaningful scowl. "You've been warned about that before."

"Crap! It's not like I'm takin' anyone's lunch money," Sam complained.

"Swear jar, swear jar!" the other children jeered.

The kids thought baseball croquet was hilarious, and Miranda called a halt to the games before they all tried to whack their balls up into the air and not along the ground as they were supposed to do. Someone was going to get hurt, or there would be property damage, or both.

They helped Cnut and Harek put the game pieces back in the box. No one wanted to handle the one covered with Ruff's slobber, but finally Cnut rubbed it on Ruff's fur and added it to the others. He told the children, "A real soldier must not be squeamish about body fluids, like blood or spit. One time I had to clean the vomit off Harek when he hurled the contents of his stomach on seeing a huge Saxon *hird* rushing toward us."

Five small jaws dropped. Not that they understood exactly what Cnut was telling them, but the mention of soldiers and blood was enough to impress them. Even Maggie.

Harek flashed Cnut a glance of disgust. "Believe that and I have a longship to sell you in the desert."

The kids went into the kitchen to wash their hands in the sink, an enterprise that would result in more water on the floor and counters than on their hands and a dozen soiled paper towels. While she had a chance to speak in private, Miranda asked Mordr's brothers why he reacted so strongly around the children.

"Mordr had children of his own at one time. Precious to him, Jomar and Kata were. The two little ones were killed in a most heinous manner," Harek explained.

"Oh my God! Was it recently?"

" 'Twas a long, long time ago, but the memory lives with Mordr as if it were yesterday," Harek said.

"Closure, that's what Mordr needs." Miranda was already thinking about the grief counseling group she led once a month. "How did they die?"

Cnut gave Harek a warning look.

Harek apparently agreed with Cnut's warning. "I have said more than I should have. Anything else on the subject will have to come from Mordr."

"Be forewarned, however, Mordr does not talk about his children," Cnut told her. "He can go into a rage at mere mention of the tragedy that befell his family."

"Just one more question." Miranda couldn't believe it hadn't occurred to her before. "You mentioned children. How about their mother? Is Mordr married?"

"Not anymore. His wife was killed, too." In an obvious attempt to change the subject, Harek asked Miranda, "Is there any more beer left in your refrigerator?"

"Sure. Stay here and relax until dinner." She pointed to the patio chairs. "I'll bring the beers out to you. First, I need to see how much damage my gremlins have done inside. Leave them alone for five minutes, and you never know what you'll find." Sure enough, there was water and dirt splattered everywhere, and their attempts to clean it up were making it worse. First things first. She took two beers out of the fridge.

Mordr walked in just then, emerging from the small guest bedroom she'd assigned him yesterday. He wore the same light blue Minnesota Vikings T-shirt as before, but he'd changed into a pair of navy-blue cargo shorts and leather flip-flops.

His eyes widened at the mess in the kitchen after he, or Mrs. Delgado, had gone to so much trouble to clean it so well earlier. Immediately, he took charge. "Miranda, take those beers outside to my brothers." Through the sliding doors, they could be seen talking. Harek stretched out on the chaise lounge and Cnut at the patio table. "The children and I will get dinner ready." Turning away, as if he expected her to obey his commands in her house, Mordr began ordering the children to various tasks.

"Sam, get the table extension from the hall closet."

Sam objected, "It's too heavy."

"Oh really? Mayhap Linda can do it."

Insulted, Sam stomped off. "I'll do it. Dammit!"

"Swear jar, swear jar," the other children hooted.

Muttering under his breath, Sam dug into the pocket of his shorts and pulled out a quarter, dropping it with a clink into the five-gallon amber jar sitting on the floor by the fridge. Before he did that, though, Sam shook his wet hands in Ben's face.

Ben was about to chase after Sam with a glass of water until he saw Mordr's scowl. "Toss that water anywhere but the sink and you are going to find yourself doing five laps around the house before dinner."

Ben paused, contemplating whether doing laps would be fun or not, but then he emptied the glass into the sink.

"Now, wipe off this table and the countertops and that puddle on the floor. How could you bratlings splatter water from the sink all the way over there?"

"Is bratling a bad word?" Linda wanted to know from her position under the table where she was sitting with Ruff. The dog was there, tongue lolling, waiting in his usual spot for dinner and any food that dropped his way. Linda had presumably wanted to escape the water battles.

Ben protested, "How come I have to do so much, and all Sam—"

"Now!"

Sam shot out of the kitchen, and Ben began vigorously wiping the floor. With a dish towel!

"Larry, set out nine placemats with nine dinner plates. Linda, put cutlery next to each plate. Maggie, will you help me slice the bread and set out the food?" He suddenly noticed that Miranda still stood there, a long-neck bottle in each hand. "Well? What is the problem? Are you waiting for the beer to warm up?"

"Uh."

"Back in my time . . . uh, country, we had naught but warm beer, except in the wintertime, but now . . ." He made a shivering motion. "We find it too flat and unpalatable. I know what you are thinking. Spoiled, we Vikings are becoming."

He had no idea what she was thinking. It had nothing to do with beer, but more with how attractive he looked to her. Or that he smelled good, too. That delicious limey sandalwood scent that tempted her to walk over and lean in to lick his neck. And she didn't even like limes. Or at least she hadn't in the past.

He was a tall, gorgeous package to begin with. All muscles and sinews and sharp Nordic features, with beautiful eyes and hair nicer than hers, darn it, but now that she knew a little about his past, that he'd lost two of his children, he was even more attractive to her. And that was dangerous territory for a woman who had way too much responsibility at the moment and no time for an affair.

Affair? Where did that idea come from? Mordr hadn't offered her anything like that. Just a kiss.

Hah! There was no way that was just a kiss. More like a lesson in eroticism.

If he could affect her so with a kiss, what would happen if—

"Miranda! Are we playing statues now?" Mordr said in a tone that was as close to teasing as he was capable of. "If so, dinner will be cold afore we are done."

She came abruptly out of her carnal reverie and turned on her heels, going outside. Just as she was handing the bottles to Cnut and Harek, the cell phone rang in her pocket. She pulled it out and checked the caller ID. "Do you mind if I take this?" she asked the two men.

They shook their heads and she walked across the backyard toward the fence that divided her property from a neighbor's.

"Darla?"

"Hey, sweetie, how's it going?"

"You wouldn't believe!"

"Uh-oh! Did Mordr prove to be inept or dangerous or something?"

"Nope. He's perfect. The kids actually listen to him and might even learn how to behave."

"And the problem is . . . ?"

"Well, not a problem, really. Darla, I have not one, but three Viking hunks here at the moment. Mordr's two brothers. Oh my God! You've got to come over and see this."

"Oh, damn! I'm working. This is my dinner break. Can you maybe hold them hostage or something until I can get there tomorrow?"

"Sorry. They're leaving after dinner."

"Dinner? What did you pick up?"

"Nothing. Mordr prepared the whole thing, with a little, or a lot, of help from Mrs. Delgado."

"You mean, Mrs. I-Don't-Do-Nothing-Except-Clean?"

"The same."

"A man who looks like Mordr and cooks, too. You must be in heaven. But tell me about the brothers."

Miranda surprised herself by giving a vivid description. She hadn't realized that she noticed so many details, including the slightly longer vampire-type incisors. "And they all claim to be Vikings. I mean, really, Viking vampires in Vegas."

"Oh, oh, oh! I bet I know where they've come from. There's a new revue at the Golden Nugget this month. They're called the Draculdales. A play on the Chippendales, or that Thunder From Down Under that was so popular. There's creepy music and coffins and lightning flashing before the vampiredales pop out in cloaks and fangs and then strip-dance down to just about nothing."

"Strippers?" Miranda tried to picture Mordr dancing naked. She just couldn't see it.

Darla said that she had to get back to work, promising to call the next day. Miranda went back indoors where everywhere was seated at the kitchen table, waiting for her. Mordr sat at one end of the table, and she at the other, the two brothers and five kids on either side.

To her surprise, the three men bowed their heads before eating, and supposedly said silent prayers. Then, they all dug in, enjoying the fabulous home-cooked meal, the first this house had seen in a long time. Not that Miranda couldn't cook. She was just too tired after work most days. By the time they got to the dessert, apple pie with ice cream, Mordr was about fed up with his brothers' teasing about his cooking skills. "It's just a friggin' frozen pie."

"Swear jar, swear jar," the children chanted.

Mordr stopped eating and glanced around with surprise. "*Friggin'* is not a swearword."

"It isn't?" Ben and Sam exclaimed as one, then turned to her for an opinion.

"*Friggin'* is definitely a swearword in this house."

To her surprise, Mordr got up and went over to drop a quarter in the jar, which was only several feet away from her. He winked at her before returning to the table.

A wink? From Mordr, who was always so morbidly serious?

She felt that wink like a caress along every inch of exposed skin on her body, which he seemed to be admiring. That was the only excuse she could come up with—momentary madness—for what she blurted out then.

"Are you guys strippers?"

Her question came in an instant of silence in the midst of all the talking and eating so that eight sets of eyes stared at her as if she'd lost her mind, even though Larry and Linda probably didn't know what a stripper was.

"I can barely walk with grace, let alone dance," Cnut gasped out between chuckles.

"Except for the Michael dance," Harek added, also chuckling.

"What's the Michael dance? Is it like Gangnam?" Sam wanted to know.

No one answered, especially not Mordr, who was the only one not amused by her asking if they were strippers. He stood and crooked a finger at her. "Come with me. We need to talk."

"About strippers?" she asked as she followed him from the kitchen down the hallway to her office. "It was just a joke, you know. Ha, ha, ha."

"We are not strippers," Mordr said as she followed him down the hallway to her office. "But, for your own safety, I need to tell you who we really are."

"Should I be frightened?" Miranda asked once the office door closed behind them.

"Very frightened," he replied, and he was serious.

She should have remembered. The man was always serious.

But wait a minute. Miranda was starting to get alarmed. Mordr was going to tell her who he *really* was? Had he been lying to her all along? Oh my God! In her attempt to avoid danger, had she brought even more danger into her home? "What's going on, Mordr?"

He pointed to the blinking red light on her answering machine indicating she had one message. Her eyes connected with Mordr's. "Is it . . . ?"

He nodded and pressed the button for her.

At first, all she heard was heavy breathing. But then, a cruelly taunting voice said, "Dad-dy's coming!" It was Roger.

What was Roger thinking, putting a voice message on her machine? She could go to the police and he'd be back in prison lickety-split. But then, he hadn't said anything threatening, even though she knew without a doubt that it was meant to be a threat.

She'd been expecting this, of course, or something like it. Still, she felt as if she'd been sucker punched. She had trouble breathing.

"Sit," Mordr said, and shoved her gently into one of the chairs in front of the desk. He sat down in the other.

"You're right. I am frightened," she said, once she had calmed down. "But what has Roger's call to do with who you really are? Unless . . . unless, please don't tell me you have some connection with Roger."

He shook his head. "If only it were that simple! There is no easy way to say this, Miranda. But I am a vampire angel sent to protect you."

This was the last thing she'd expected to hear from

him, and she burst out laughing. "Oh, really? Sent by whom? Don't tell me. My attorney, Bradley Allison, hired a vampire?"

"A vampire angel," he corrected. "To be more precise, a Viking vampire angel. And no, it wasn't your lawyer who sent me. It was Mike . . . um, Michael the Archangel."

She arched her eyebrows at him. "Give me a break."

"I wish I could. Personally, I need a break, too," he said. Then, "You need proof?'

"Oh yeah!"

He made a hissing sound and flashed a pair of vampire fangs at her.

She did the only thing a lady could do in the circumstance. She screamed.

Angel flying too close to the ground . . .

Mordr nigh jumped out of his skin at the shrill, loud—*very loud*—unexpected scream that Miranda let loose on seeing his fangs.

Almost immediately, he could hear the kids outside the door asking if she was all right.

Fortunately, Mordr had locked the door after them. "Everything is fine," he called out. "Go back to the kitchen."

Not that the children obeyed him. He could hear heavy breathing and muttered conversation on the other side of the door as they attempted to eavesdrop.

"Shh! Be quiet, woman! You'll scare the children. All I did was show you a little teeth." He retracted the fangs and bared his teeth at her. "See. My teeth are normal now."

"Normal? You have fangs. Well, you had fangs, I know you did. And your brothers did earlier today, too. That is not normal!" She backed away when he tried to reach for her. "Who are you people? *Are* you people?"

What could he say to that? "Yes and no."

"Aaarrgh! Get away from me. Don't you dare touch me. You . . . you . . . vampire."

"Angel."

"What?"

"Vampire angel. I prefer to think of myself as an angel, rather than a vampire."

Her jaw dropped. "Are you going to flash a set of wings at me, like you did with the fangs?"

"I would if I could, but I do not have my wings yet. Truth to tell, I might not ever have them. Vikar is the only one of us brothers who has received his, and even he cannot produce them at will. And a lot of trouble they are, too, according to Vikar. Try lugging about two twenty-five-pound weights on each shoulder and fly at the same time! Almost topped off two trees and a telephone wire the first time he attempted the feat. I could show you my shoulder bumps, though. The place where wings will eventually emerge. I hope." He paused and saw the look of confusion on her face. "I am blathering. You are turning me into a blathering lackwit."

"Me? You dare to blame me?"

"You asked for proof, and I gave you proof. I hardly think I am to blame for turning you into a chatterling." At the look of consternation on her face, he went on, "'Tis no wonder I am acting the flapping tongue. You torture me by placing me in proximity to children, which I have avoided for ages."

"I never asked you to come here."

"Someone did!" He favored her with one of his best scowls.

She just raised her chin haughtily.

And looked damn attractive when she did. "Furthermore, you torture me with seduction, even though I have been immune to bodily pleasures . . . for ages."

"Me? Seduce you? You're the one who walks around half naked, flaunting your muscles and bare feet and sexy lips . . ." She stopped talking as she realized how much she revealed and pressed her lips together tightly. That gesture, too, was damn attractive.

She thinks my lips are sexy? And my feet draw her attention? Oh, help. Help, help, help! I am sinking faster than an overladen longship on the high seas. He shook his head in an attempt to clear it of her allure. "And now you torture me with attacks on my normalcy. Dost think I want to have fangs? Dost think it was a choice of mine? I am a Viking. We Norsemen are known for our vanity."

"Vanity, thy name is Viking?" she scoffed.

"Do you dare mock me, wench?"

"It's either that, or whack you over the head with my paperweight. And I will if you call me *wench* again." She glanced pointedly at the five-sided stone object on the desk with framed pictures of the children on each side. "And I'm a pacifist, for heaven's sake. I don't believe in violence."

"Hah! That is what women always say afore they reduce a man to a gibbering idiot."

"Huh? How did we go from fangs to pacifism?"

Just then the door flew open—someone must have found a key—and five warriors-in-waiting came to the defense of their lady.

"Why did you scream, Aunt Mir?" Maggie asked, coming up close to examine Miranda to see if she'd suffered some bodily harm.

"Did you see a mouse?" Linda wanted to know, bending over to peek under the desk. "We can set a mouse trap again."

"What did you do to Aunt Mir?" Ben demanded of Mordr and punched him in the stomach, then began to rub his knuckles with the fingers of his other hand. "Ow, ow, ow!"

"Are you hurt?" Sam asked his aunt, giving her a head-to-toe survey and finding no apparent bruise marks or open wounds.

"Betcha he called her a bad name. Girls cry when boys call them bad names." This wisdom came from Larry, who was adjusting his little cock under his short pants as he talked. Someone needed to buy the boy bigger undergarments.

"What bad names?" Maggie wanted to know.

"Prissy pants! Big butt! Owl face!"

Maggie inhaled sharply with consternation at that last name and smacked Larry on the arm.

He smacked her back and soon four of the children were rolling on the floor wrestling with each other, except for Linda, who had attached herself to Mordr's thigh once again.

Mordr looked over to his two brothers for help. They stood leaning against the open door jambs, arms crossed over their chests, grins on their fool faces. At first, they just shook their heads at his apparent clumsiness in explaining the situation to Miranda.

"Come, children," Harek said finally. "You can see that your aunt is safe."

"Let us go have more ice cream," Cnut suggested.

Five heads rose with interest, then turned to their aunt for approval. She nodded, reluctantly. "Go ahead. I'll be out shortly."

No longer frightened, although she had every reason to be, Miranda turned on Mordr once the door was shut. Putting a hand on each hip, she glared up at him. "Who *are* you?" she asked, not for the first time.

He sighed. "I am a vangel, a Viking vampire angel.

St. Michael the Archangel, whom we sometimes refer to with irreverence as Mike, sent me here to protect you."

"A vampire angel! I didn't believe it before, and I don't believe it now. But just for the sake of discussion, why do you feel the need to reveal this big secret now? If I told anyone what you've said, they'd be carting you off to the funny farm."

He frowned with confusion. "Why would I go to a farm? I am a warrior, not a farmer."

"It was just a manner of speech. It means a place they take crazy people. And see what you are doing to me? I'm a psychologist. I should not be using words like *funny farm* or *crazy*."

"Nor should I call you wench," he conceded.

They nodded at each other to acknowledge the compromise.

"There would be no advantage to your telling anyone about us vangels, Miranda. First of all, no one would believe you. Second, if you shine the light of publicity on us, I would be hampered in my efforts to protect you."

"I still don't understand any of this."

"As I said before, I was sent here to protect you and your children. Leastways, I thought that was my mission. But then, Harek and Cnut arrived, telling me of the presence of Lucies in Las Vegas. Top that off with the call from Roger. Too many dangers are converging here at once. Yes, yes, I know. You don't know what Lucies are. Lucipires are demon vampires. Evil, frightening creatures that roam the earth seeking lost souls or those humans on the verge of some great sin. They were created by Satan long before the beginning of Christianity. We vangels came much later, about eight hundred years after the death of Christ. Our specific purpose is to defeat Lucipires and save those sinners or potential sinners before it is too late."

"First, vampire angels. Now, demon vampires. What next? Zombies who fly?"

"You may jest all you want, but I am telling you the truth."

"What? That we have a True Blood society here in Las Vegas, just like in Charlaine Harris's books about Louisiana? That I'm going to be the next Sookie Stackhouse?"

"Do you deliberately missay me?" Mordr was familiar with the *True Blood* series that was shown on cable television. He and his brothers had watched the program with amusement, though it was not the usual fare for vangels, being R-rated and heavy on graphic sex. In his opinion, Miranda was far more attractive than that dimwitted Sookie Stackhouse character. But suddenly one line from the opening music of the show hummed in his brain. A husky, male voice crooning, "I want to do bad things to you." An instant erection hit Mordr right where he was humming the most, and he glanced over with alarm to see if Miranda noticed.

She had not, thank the saints! She was off on her own line of thinking.

"Mordr," she said with excessive sympathy. "In my profession, I deal with delusions all the time. One of my patients is convinced he's an alien sent to this planet to impregnate as many human women as possible to create mutant ETs. Another client believes carbonated soft drinks are beverages the government invented to subdue all people into a stupor of compliance. Actually, the delusion of some fictional threat, like demons, is very common and can be cured, or controlled, with medication."

At first, he just gaped at her. Then he made a tsking

sound. "This is no delusion. Believe you me, I could not make up the specter of evil that Lucipires represent. Medication will not change anything."

She went on, as if he hadn't even spoken. "In fact, and I know your brothers said I shouldn't mention this to you, but . . ." She paused.

He stiffened, bracing himself for whatever his brothers had warned her about.

". . . grief can play games with a person's mind." She reached over and took one of his hands in both of hers. A gesture of sympathy!

He gazed at her hands on his for a long moment, savoring the sweet emotion that flooded him at the mere touch of her skin on his, postponing the knowledge of the subject she dared to broach with him. Finally, he yanked his hand away and stood. "I do not discuss my . . . grief. Not with anyone. And it has naught to do with the danger that looms around this city at the moment. You and your children need to be far away from here. Until the evil presences is gone."

She rolled her eyes. "Why should my family leave and not all the other people who live and work here? Is there something about us that calls to these . . . creatures?"

"No. Under normal circumstances, innocents have no appeal for Lucipires. They seek out those who are already evil, having committed grave sins, turning them before their normal time, giving them no chance for repentance before death. But if anyone gets in their way, whether it be you or your children, they would mow you down and take you to a world far worse than the Hell painted in Christian lore."

"There you have it then. We stay out of their way."

"That is precisely what I have been suggesting. Get out of their way. Far out of their way. Like to our castle in Transylvania or mayhap my brother Ivak's plantation in Louisiana, though neither would be ideal because young vangels cannot control their fangs and we cannot risk your children being exposed to such beings and not speaking of it when they return to their everyday lives."

"Now you are the one who is—what did you call it?—missaying me. I never suggested that we leave Nevada. I was merely thinking that the children could be confined to the house, once school is out soon for the summer, under your very fine protection."

He was the one rolling his eyes now. "Do not think to divert me with false words of praise."

She shook her head. "Not false. I do believe that you would protect the children with your own life."

"I have no life, Miranda," he said, "but of course I would protect them, and I could protect them here in a confined space. That is not the issue. What about you?"

"Me?" She tilted her head in question.

"Do you intend to stay here in this confined space until the end of the threat?"

"Of course not. I have to go to work."

He tossed his hands up in the air. "See. That is exactly my point."

"You lost me somewhere."

"You work in the city, right in the midst of the demon vampire activity. Some of your clients are probably Lucie targets. Do you work with any people who have done bad, almost irredeemable things?"

Her flushed face gave him her answer.

"Right in the middle of the fray, you would be. I cannot allow that to happen."

"Let's get one thing clear, Mordr. You have no right to allow or disallow me to do anything. I hired you. I can fire you."

He shook his head at her denseness. "You did not hire me, and you cannot fire me. Only a higher power can do that, and he is mysteriously absent these days."

"I can't believe I'm asking this, but he who? God?"

"No. Mike."

"Michael the Archangel? You're being absolutely ridiculous." She stood. "Well, thanks for explaining all this to me, Mordr, but we're going to have to agree to disagree."

"Agree to disagree? More female illogic! Go, put on clothing appropriate for the casino scene. I will take you out for the evening whilst my brothers watch over the children. I will prove to you how ridiculous I am *not* being."

She paused, before nodding her agreement. Then she surveyed his body covered only with a shirt and shorts. "Is that what you consider evening attire?"

"No," he said. "I will be wearing my cloak."

Eleven

Viva Las Vegas, demon vampire style . . .

Jasper love, love, loved Las Vegas.

There was just so much sin here. Like a chocoholic swimming in a pool of melted Hershey's Kisses, the king of all demon vampires felt himself getting not a sugar high, but a sin high.

"Kudos to the person who invented the catchphrase, 'Whatever happens in Vegas stays in Vegas.' If there is anything that encourages a man, or woman, to err off the straight and narrow, it is that," Jasper mused aloud as he strolled through one of the glitzy casinos on the Strip, ever alert to evil scents that pervaded the atmosphere. Potential victims, soon-to-be-Lucipires-in-training. It was like the proverbial shooting fish in a barrel.

Beltane, who walked beside him, gawking here and there at all the sights—gorgeous women in scanty attire, high-stakes gamblers, slot machines *ka-ching*, *ka-ching*, *ka-ching*ing, shouts of elation over big wins at the craps table, and groans of dismay by losers, blinking neon lights everywhere, and pounding music through the sound system—nodded his agreement. "A permission slip to sin, that slogan is."

"Well said!" he told his young hordling assistant, who had been taken from New Orleans in the 1700s. "By the by, you are looking very handsome today."

He and Beltane, as well as all the other Lucipires whom Jasper could see acting in various capacities as they infiltrated the casino—waiters and waitresses, dealers, players, valets, maintenance workers, showgirls, high-class prostitutes, both male and female, etc.—were in humanoid form, of course, when out in public. Beltane was wearing a gray Hugo Boss tailored suit with a crisp white shirt and red tie. A five-carat diamond acted as a tie tack. Beltane's black hair was short and styled, thanks to about a gallon of goop—half of which was splattered about the marble sink of the luxurious penthouse suite they shared—into the latest style of deliberate disarray.

"Not nearly as good as you, master," Beltane said with genuine adoration. You had to love a demon who showed such affection.

Jasper smiled and patted the boy, who was much like a son to him, on the shoulder, being careful not to touch the goop. In fact, Jasper was dressed in similar fashion to Beltane, also in Hugo Boss, but his suit was black with a black silk shirt and black tie, and a rare Asian pearl tie tack. All that blackness—hell and damnation, but he did favor the color black—provided a sharp contrast to his long, platinum-blond hair, which was pulled back off his face and tied into a queue on his neck with a diamond-studded black ribbon.

The good thing about being a Lucipire—well, one of the good things—was that when they took humanoid form, they could look like their old selves, or better, or even completely different. Jasper had once turned humanoid in the outward appearance of George Clooney. Whoo-boy, did he attract women that night! And added at least five new baby Lucipires to his killing jars, where he cured his victims until they reached stasis and agreed to become one of his legions.

They turned into the entrance of a sushi restaurant where Zeb was waiting for them at a discreet rear table. He was eating raw fish of some sort. Eeew! Jasper loved caviar, but sushi held no appeal. Beltane, who ordered some kind of eel or octopus concoction, was not so discriminating, or maybe he *was* discriminating and Jasper was the one out of sync, he conceded magnanimously, in his own not-so-humble opinion. Still, he was planning to have a nice, very rare, juicy steak later this evening, perhaps shared with that new Lucipire haakai, Delilah. No, not the biblical Delilah, but equally tantalizing with puffy red lips that could . . . well, suffice it to say, she liked to eat, too.

He noticed then how understated Zeb was in a plain black T-shirt tucked into slim denim jeans and scruffy boots, and wondered if he might be overdressed. But then he shrugged. *Anything goes in Las Vegas*, he quipped to himself.

"What's the latest report?" he asked Zeb right off once the waiter left them.

Zeb, who was heading the entire casino operation, wiped his mouth with a linen napkin and set it aside. Despite his slightly hooked nose, Zeb was a handsome man.

"Spectacular," Zeb replied. "And this after only two days in operation. Roughly three hundred kills total between Vegas, Reno, Macau, and Monaco. Hector, Haroun, and Yakov are as pleased with the results as I am. I know, that number could be a lot higher, but we are proceeding with caution this time. Kill slowly and not all in one place. No need to alert human authorities of so many missing persons on any one day, or to alert the vangels of our presence in the gambling centers."

Jasper nodded his approval. Haste had been their downfall in the past.

"Another thing. Let us set a time limit on this venture. Perhaps two weeks. Leave on a high note. Then we can return to this venue—casinos—sometime in the future."

"Excellent idea!" Jasper was becoming increasingly pleased with his choice of Zeb in this leadership role.

After Zeb left to check on his minions in Reno, a casino city less than five hundred miles northwest of Las Vegas, Jasper looked at Beltane and said, "I'm in the mood for a little blood. How about you? Or are you too full from all that raw crap?"

"I am never too full for more blood." Beltane's fangs were already starting to emerge. With a giggle, he put a hand over his mouth to hide his arousal.

"I know just the drug dealer and brothel madam who will suit our purposes."

They both transported out of the casino, leaving the slight scent of sulfur behind them.

Date with a vampire . . . uh, angel . . . uh, Viking . . . whatever, he was hot! . . .

Miranda couldn't stop looking at Mordr. She was in the passenger seat of the Lexus SUV he was driving as they approached the city. With her directions, he followed the route she took every day to work, presumably to show her the strange creatures—demon vampires, for heaven's sake—that were infiltrating the city, so that she would take his advice and stay away from town for the time being.

She had news for him. Las Vegas attracted strange people like locusts. You were just as likely to run into

"Jesus" on a street pulpit as mermaids swimming beneath the waves of an indoor ocean. Here was a further news flash: Mordr was rather strange himself.

In only a half hour, the amount of time he'd allotted for them to get ready, he'd managed to shower and shave, don a designer white T-shirt tucked into belted, navy-blue pleated slacks, and slip bare feet into loafers. He'd combed his hair back into a ponytail low on his neck, and, yes, he wore a long, black cloak similar to the ones his brothers wore. She now knew the voluminous garment hid an arsenal of scary weapons. Frightening to contemplate, but reassuring in her dire situation.

Stealing a quick, slanted glance his way, just short of an ogle, Miranda noted that Mordr looked like a Viking, of course, with his height and chiseled Nordic features, but he also looked a bit dangerous in a vampire kind of way with that cloak and his brooding demeanor. Who was she kidding? Scary or not, the man was gorgeous.

Miranda had showered, too, and quickly shimmied into a short-sleeved, scoop-necked dress of teal-blue silk that ended just above her knees. Its black belt matched her black high-heeled sandals. To save time in blow drying she'd skinned her wet hair back off her face into a figure eight chignon. From her ears dangled long aquamarine chandelier earrings that caught the light. She'd even applied makeup. Foundation, mascara, rose-colored lipstick, and just a hint of smoky eye shadow.

Coming downstairs, she'd found Mordr standing by the door, waiting impatiently for her. All he'd said was, "You did not wear the bow dress."

"Hah! That dress is retired for the duration."

"The duration of what?"

"The duration of your stay."

"Probably for the best."

For some contrary reason, she wished she'd chosen to wear the darn wraparound dress, which would forever evoke erotic memories for her.

The children had gawked at her with wide eyes. You'd think she never dressed up for an activity that didn't include them.

"Wow!" Maggie had said.

"I will second that," Harek had said.

"And I third it," Cnut had said.

Mordr had said nothing. The jerk!

"You know, sometimes you take the Brother Grim persona a little too far," she'd remarked.

"Needs must," he'd replied enigmatically.

Now it was only eight-thirty, dusk outside, but she was cocooned with him in the dim interior of his SUV, thanks to the tinted windows. Into the silence, she remarked, "A Lexus SUV, huh? Your line of work must pay well."

They could have taken her car, but Mordr had taken one look at it and said, "No, thank you." She didn't blame him. She drove a dinged-up Excursion van, a big monster of a car, necessary for carting about five little unruly passengers, two of whom had still been in booster seats when she'd first adopted them. Those booster seats were now replaced with sports equipment and other paraphernalia that children had to cart around.

"This vehicle belongs to my brother Trond. I did not want to drive my own vehicle cross-country."

"And your vehicle would be?"

"A Hummer."

She laughed. "That figures."

He arched a brow at her but reverted back to his usual infuriating silence. Even on a date of sorts, he didn't exert himself to talk unless absolutely necessary. Had he never heard of polite conversation? Okay, it wasn't a date, but still . . .

Finally, she asked, "Do you really think you can convince me that there are demon creatures skulking about town?"

"I know I can."

"Tell me again how this all came about," she said.

He darted a quick look her way as if to see if she really wanted to know or was only making conversation. It was a mixture of both.

"Many centuries ago, Lucifer created demon vampires called Lucipires under the direction of his comrade Jasper. Not being satisfied with bad folks going to Hell the usual way, after human death, he decided to speed up the process. Why not grab sinful humans, those really, really bad ones, early on, before they have a chance to repent?"

She sighed with the impossibility of accepting such a claim. Still she asked, "How do they do that?"

"The Lucies fang sinners, putting them into a condition of stasis. Then the demon vampires suck the blood out of their bodies. Once depleted, the bodies disappear. Many of the missing people reported throughout the world are actually victims now living in Horror, or one of the other Lucie haunts."

"Horror, like the horror of spending eternity in the fires of Hell?"

He shook his head. "No. Horror is the *name* of the main Lucie headquarters, currently located somewhere in the far North near the Arctic regions, which is definitely not hot. There are other Lucie command centers around the world with such names as Anguish, Terror, Torment, and Desolation."

"Creative names, anyway," she joked.

He didn't smile. Surprise, surprise.

"Sometimes, the Lucipires fang an evil human

being but are unable to complete the process, whether through the humans fighting them off, interruption, or some unexpected happening. Then, the fanged human carries a lemony scent, which is a tempting lure to any Lucie within a mile. That human can still be redeemed, and it is the job of vangels to reach them first and try to reverse the process. Usually, it is too late, but not always."

"You said the victims disappear after this fanging and draining business. Where do they go then?"

"Usually to one of the Lucipire haunts, like I said, where they are turned into demon vampires after an intense, excruciating torture training."

Good Lord! The man does tell a good story. Maybe he's a writer of fantasy novels. Stephen King in a cloak. "So, there is an afterlife?"

"Yes."

"But not just Heaven and Hell?"

"Correct."

Definitely fantasy material. "You realize this is an impossible story to believe."

He shrugged.

"You do realize that you sound like a whack job. Instead of making me understand, you're just scaring the daylights out of me."

"You should be scared," he said, not for the first time.

"Of you?"

"Me, and all others I've described for you."

She thought about his words for a moment. If everything Mordr said was true, she was afraid. But not of him. For some odd reason, she felt safe with him. "I'm not afraid of you," she told him.

He rolled his eyes. "Do I turn here?"

"Yes. See the 'Welcome to Fabulous Las Vegas' sign

right ahead. It marks the southern tip of the Strip, which runs for more than four miles. My office is one block off Las Vegas Boulevard, at the other end."

"And this is the route you take to work every day?"

"Mostly. If there's heavy traffic, I take the longer but less time-consuming way. Actually, we could turn off here, but the scenic route is more fun."

"Amazing!" Mordr exclaimed as the full tacky, neon-blinking extravaganza of the Strip began to emerge.

She nodded. "I've been living here since I graduated from college, and I'm still floored every time I see the Strip at night. There's round-the-clock action, of course, but its over-the-top glitz is best seen at night."

"Why would you choose to live in such a place?"

"I had a lot of college loans to pay off, and the offer here was better than any others. And, actually, I like this area. That's why I stay. It's not all casinos and gambling. There are neighborhoods. Everyday people who go to work and coach Little League or take their daughters to ballet. Teachers, secretaries, lawyers, accountants, chefs. True, much of the population is dependent in some way on the casinos or big hotels for employment." She noticed him glance her way with raised brows. "Sorry. I guess I sounded defensive."

"Is it the best place to raise children?"

"Now I *am* defensive. How dare you—"

"My words were ill-chosen. I did not mean to give offense. It is just that I picture this country's children being raised best in small towns where they do not lock doors. Where there is a smiling sheriff who knows everybody. And an aunt who bakes and cooks."

She stared at him, perplexed. Then she laughed. "Mayberry! I can't believe you." She laughed some more, dabbing at her eyes. "You watch a lot of TV, huh?"

She could swear he blushed, but she couldn't tell for sure in the fading light.

"Yes," he replied. "Between missions, vangels have a great amount of down time, as you say in this country. Since we are not allowed, or leastways not supposed, to fornicate, or drink to excess, or engage in other worldly activities that almost certainly involve sin, television makes the days and months and years go faster. We entertain ourselves in other ways, too, depending on our interests or talents, but mostly we must remain in seclusion to avoid detection."

Back to that vampire angel business! "No raping or plundering, either, I suppose," she teased, reminding him of his Viking heritage.

"That, m'lady, is a myth perpetuated by the biased monk historians of that time. Truth to tell, some Norsemen did such when they went a-Viking, but not all, and not all the time. Besides, men of other countries did the same, or worse. I know of some Saxon soldiers who skinned a man alive and pinned the skin to a church door."

She shivered with distaste. "Did you?"

"Skin my enemies?"

"No! Rape and pillage?"

At her nod, he replied, "No raping. There were willing women enough at home and abroad, but I do admit to the plundering. Especially churches and monasteries where the priests had no business hoarding gold chalices and silver crosses, not to mention fat sheep and very good cheeses."

"Cheese? You went a-Viking for cheese?"

She could swear a smile twitched at his lips. Could the man actually have a sense of humor?

After that, they were mostly silent as he drove slowly through the town, passing the big luxurious hotels. The Luxor, Tropicana, MGM Grand, Bellagio, Bally's,

Flamingo, Mirage, Harrah's, Casino Royale, Wynn, Fontainebleau. Also, the themed hotels, that replicated medieval castles, volcanoes and tropical gardens, or those reminiscent of cities around the world, like the Excalibur, Planet Hollywood, Caesar's Palace, the Venetian, Treasure Island, the Riviera, and Circus Circus. Then there were the dozens of wedding chapels, many of them Elvis-related.

"Hey, we could drive through the Hunka Hunka Burning Love Chapel and be married in less than an hour." She pointed to a sign for the neon pink chapel whose sign proclaimed. "In-Car Weddings Quick and Cheap. Elvis Minister Extra."

"Married!" Mordr exclaimed, and almost rammed into the car in front of them, which was in fact slowing to turn into the Hunka Hunka. "I will never wed again, even if I were permitted to do so, which I am not."

"Hey, it was a joke, all right? Don't get your Dracula cloak in a twist." Even though she wasn't serious, Miranda was somewhat miffed that he'd reacted so strongly to the idea of marriage with her.

"I do not joke about marriage," he said.

"No kidding! You don't joke about anything, as far as I can tell." Before he had a chance to respond, she added, "Of course, I understand why you would feel the way you do, considering your circumstance."

In a clear attempt to deflect her away from that forbidden subject, he asked, "Have you never wed?"

"Nope."

"Why?"

"No time, no right man."

"But there have been men?"

"Are you trying to find out if I'm a virgin? A thirty-four-year-old virgin?" She should have been insulted, but instead was just amused.

"No." He paused. "But I would not be averse to hearing your answer."

She said nothing.

"Well?" he prodded.

"It's none of your business."

"Neither is my 'circumstance,' but that does not stop you from barging in."

Okay, so he didn't want to talk about the tragedy in his life. She could respect that, even if she was curious. Maybe later he would open up to her. In the end, most of her clients admitted that talking about their problems really did help. "We're almost to the end of the Strip," she pointed out. "Turn right at the next light and go over one block, then right again. My office will be about a half mile after that." When he pulled up to the curb outside her building, she asked, "Do you want to go in? We're on the fifth floor."

"No. I've already seen it." He put the car in park but did not turn the ignition off.

Now, that was alarming! She was still suspicious of the man, somewhat. Had he been stalking her? "When?" she asked in a voice she couldn't stop from being icy.

"Earlier today, when the children were in school."

"I didn't see you."

"You were at the courthouse."

She pondered whether he could be telling the truth or not. "It's impossible for you to have done everything you did today and drive into the city, park your car, take the elevator to my office floor, then walk around and survey my work space."

"I did not drive."

This story was getting more and more bizarre. "Okay, I'll bite. How did you get here? Fly?"

He should have smiled, but then, he never smiled. "I probably would not mind a bite from you." Again, no smile. "No, I did not fly. I teletransported. By the by, I do not like your sarcasm."

"What? First you are a Viking. Then a vampire. Then an angel. Now you teletransport, like a bleepin' 'Beam me up, Scotty,' or whatever the hell teletransporting is. And don't forget, a nanny-slash-house manager. I'll tell you what I don't like. The way you—"

She had no chance to continue because he leaned over and placed both hands on either side of her face, turning her for a kiss. Just before his lips met hers, he murmured against her mouth, "You talk too much." They were both constrained by their seat belts, but that didn't stop the kiss from being a powerful expression of the sexual chemistry that sparked between them at first touch.

He groaned his pleasure, which acted like an aphrodisiac to her, proof that he found her desirable, that he wanted her. Because, God help her, she wanted him, too.

She felt the muscles of his arms bunching as he held a tight rein on his passion. He was attempting to resist her. She, overcome with passion herself, would not let him and licked the seam of his lips.

"You, my lady witch, are as tempting as Eve ever was in the Garden of Eden," he said.

Whether it was a complaint or a compliment, she wasn't sure. And didn't care. "That would make you Adam," she responded with another teasing lick.

"Or the snake." He reclaimed her lips then, molding her mouth to his this way and that in changing patterns 'til he got the exact position he wanted. Then he proved that he was the master in this game of sex play, kissing her so expertly and thoroughly that her toes literally curled in her high-heeled sandals. Ribbons of molten heat unfurled throughout her body causing her to feel his lips in places he wasn't even touching.

Like her breasts, the arches of her feet, the backs of her knees, the tips of her fingers, her inner elbow, and definitely at the juncture of her thighs, where the sweet burn of desire was a throbbing beat. She had never become so instantly aroused by a man in all her life. For that matter, she'd never been so aroused, period.

Who knew what would have happened next, how far they would have gone, if there hadn't been a sharp rapping on the window. Mordr jolted back to the driver's seat and she straightened from the puddle of hormones she'd melted to in her seat. With mortification, she realized it was a policeman who'd tapped on her passenger window and was motioning for her to open the window.

Mordr opened it electronically from his side.

The cop, whose name badge read Officer John Berry, leaned in. "Aren't you folks a little old for this?"

"Is a man ever too old for *this*?" Mordr replied, clearly unhappy at having been interrupted.

"What . . . what did he say?" Officer Berry asked her.

"Shh!" She motioned to Mordr, then told the cop, "Sorry, Officer. My . . . uh, boyfriend just got home from military leave and we haven't seen each other for . . . a long time."

"Oh." Addressing Mordr now, the policeman said, "Afghanistan, huh?"

Mordr, thankfully, caught her warning scowl, and nodded.

"My son is over there now." He cleared his throat and added, "Anyhow, kids. Time to get a room, okay?"

She and Mordr agreed quickly, she because she was glad to escape a ticket for public licentiousness or something, and Mordr probably because he feared all his weapons being discovered under that cloak. And, by the way, what kind of law enforcement person was he to not think it strange that a soldier would be wearing a cloak. On the other hand, it was Las Vegas. He no doubt saw stranger things.

Actually, that wasn't what Mordr was thinking, she soon realized, as he put the car in gear and began to drive away from the curb. He muttered to himself, "I cannot believe I allowed her to entice me so. I cannot believe that I am suddenly so weak I cannot control my urges. I cannot believe after all these centuries my sap rises instantly like an untried youthling. I cannot believe Mike is inflicting this new torture on me. I cannot believe—"

"Believe this," she said, and punched him in the arm. It was like hitting concrete, but she didn't want to rub her sore knuckles and give him any satisfaction. "You are the one who enticed me. You turn me on just by looking at me, and I am not easily turned on. Having five kids, a job, and not enough time in the day to take a breath kind of dampens the libido, you know. Furthermore, I haven't made out in a car since I was a teenager and I let Billy Jordan cop a feel after the junior prom."

He slanted her a quick sideways glance as he maneuvered through traffic. "I turn you on?" he asked, and she could swear that Mr. Grim almost grinned.

"Like a faucet." She folded her arms over her chest, then dropped them to her sides, when she realized that her breasts were still full and achy. If she didn't know better, she would wonder if he had dropped some kind of drug in her drink, except that she hadn't drunk anything. Truthfully, she had only herself to blame. "It's probably just sex deprivation that made me act so out-of-character."

"Right," he said, not believing it any more than she did.

"Where are we going?" she asked then as he turned

into an underground parking garage of a hotel on the Strip.

"I promised to show you some demon vampires, and that is what I will do," he said.

Oh crap! They were back to that nonsense. She glanced up at the hotel sign and laughed, "At Valhalla?" It was the new themed casino hotel. She'd never been there, but she'd heard it had a lot of hokey Viking decor.

He shrugged. "It's as good a place as any."

"Isn't Valhalla a kind of Viking heaven?"

"You could say that."

"Been there. Not interested in a repeat."

As he pulled into a parking slot and turned off the engine, he looked at her with a frown of confusion. When he finally realized that she was referring to their making out a short time ago as a bit of Viking heaven, he did something he hadn't done since she'd met him.

He smiled.

Twelve

Tears of a Viking . . .

Mordr laced his fingers with Miranda's as they walked toward the elevator in the parking garage.

When was the last time I held a woman's hand? Did I ever?

He continued to hold her hand, the pulse at their joined wrists seeming to offer a point/counterpoint of erotic rhythm, as they stood in silence in the intimate confines of the box as they rose to the lobby level.

Are my passions really being ignited by the mere touch of skin on skin?

Yes! Like sparks to long-dead tinder! Like lightning strikes to a desolate tree! Like fire to a death pyre! Like hearth heat to a bone-cold body! Like . . .

Aaarrgh! I am turning into a foppish, poor excuse for a Viking. Next I will be spouting poetry like a drukkinn *skald.*

He tightened his hold on her hand, alert to impending danger. As the elevator doors opened, they were assaulted by the cacophony of casino noise and color and flashing lights and conversation and smells.

Something had changed betwixt him and the red-haired witch at his side whose changeable green eyes darted this way and that, taking in all the sights. And that change was surrender, pure and simple. His.

At least for now, he was no longer fighting the compelling attraction he felt for this woman who'd come into his life with the suddenness of a North Sea storm. Even knowing that, sure as sin, such an attraction could be perilous to him. Mike would have a bird. Or an angel fit.

He was not sure when that change had come about. Was it when he had kissed her? Or had his long-dead passions begun to rumble back to life the moment he first saw her? Or could it be when her woman scent, that tantalizing mix of lilies and cloves, first swirled about him like a carnal mist?

But then, it did not matter when. It just was.

He was jolted out of his reverie when Miranda muttered, "Good Lord!"

If Mordr were permitted to swear, he would have said the same thing.

Actually, he had experienced similar shock the day he had wandered into this hotel casino. A full-size longship was rocking on the waves of a pool in the hotel lobby. Murals of Norsemen in battle adorned the walls. A wild boar bellowed from a cage on one side. In fact, the menu posted outside one restaurant offered wild boar barbecue. In other words, pig. A miniature Viking village, complete with longhouses and pretty, scantily clad Norsewomen bending over cook fires, ranged along the other side. Over the hotel loudspeakers, haunting music played, presumably played on instruments he'd never witnessed in his time, but some entrepreneur's idea of ancient Norse melody.

Male waiters in the casinos wandered about, wearing naught but knee-high boots, leggings so tight they must use a crowbar to get into them, and the most ridiculous headgear. Nothing on their oiled, hairless upper bodies. Like no Vikings of his acquaintance!

"Vikings did *not* wear horned helmets," he asserted vehemently.

"What?" Miranda, who had been gawking at said men, asked.

"Horned helmets. Where in the name of all the saints did modern folks get the idea that Norse soldiers wore such ridiculous attire? Not only would vain Viking men decline to cover their well-groomed hair with such monstrosities, but enemies in battle could latch on to those horns and bring a man to his knees. Although I suppose, if they lost a weapon in the midst of fighting, they could gore a man to death by head-butting him in the gut."

Miranda looked at him with amusement.

He supposed he was fixating over minutiae when there were so many other inconsistencies in this fake Viking world.

"I believe it might have started with some opera about Beowulf," she said.

Just then, a man stepped up to Mordr and asked, "Can you tell me where I can cash in my chips?"

To Mordr's chagrin, he realized that the man thought he worked here. In his cloak, with his Norse features, he must look like the Viking he was. He stepped around the man and walked away, taking Miranda with him.

"That was rude," she commented.

Like he cared! "Stop!" he ordered suddenly, dropping their linked hands and tugging her tightly to his side, an arm wrapped protectively around her shoulders. He raised his head and sniffed the air, this way and that, like a hunting dog on point. "Over there," he whispered in her ear. "Those two are Lucies."

"Where?"

"The couple standing together at the roulette table. They are interested in the man betting wildly beside them. Probably an addicted gambler, risking his family's last coin for the thrill of the sport. Afore the night is over, the poor fool will be in Lucie land."

"Are you saying that gorgeous hunk in green T-shirt and camouflage pants and his blond girlfriend in a tank top and designer jeans are demon vampires?"

"Shh," he warned. "Yes, they are."

"But they're beautiful."

"Only in their humanoid forms. You would not want to see them when they morph into scales and slime and red eyes and tails."

She rolled her eyes.

"Let us move on before they notice me. I do not want to fight them here in public."

"Fight?" she gurgled, glancing pointedly at his cloak, which she knew by now hid many different lethal weapons.

"Besides, now that I look around, I see Lucies all over the place. That pit boss yelling at one of his underlings. The Valkyries carrying drinks to the baccarat area. By the by, Odin would nigh explode with anger if any of his Valkyries walked about with breasts and buttocks nigh exposed to one and all. On the other hand, certain parts of his dead warriors might come to life in appreciation."

She rolled her eyes again, a habit he was beginning to find annoying, although he did like the way she turned in the cradle of his arm, still wrapped protectively around her shoulders, to look up at him, her mouth almost touching his. "I thought Odin and all those gods were a myth. Isn't it kind of sacrilegious for an angel, even an angel vampire, to believe in other gods?"

"I did not say I believe in Odin. 'Twas just a . . . never mind." He walked them out the doors and onto the crowded sidewalk of the Strip. They walked for blocks and blocks, she taking in the sights of Las Vegas, he taking in the sight of Lucies. "Stay close to me. That policeman over there . . . that prostitute on the corner . . . both Lucies."

"How can you tell?"

"Mainly their scent, but also, we vangels can sense a Lucipire in the vicinity. The presence of evil hangs in the air. And they look a little different than humans, to us vangels."

They walked into another hotel, this one lush with crystal chandeliers and velvety furniture. No bizarre themes, but the usual raucous noise of gambling—clanging slot machines, loud music, shouts and laughter, dealers calling out, "Place your bets, place your bets." Here and there, he noticed Lucies working. A desk clerk. A concierge. Waiters and waitresses. With his free hand, he pulled out his cell phone, tapped one button, and sent a voice mail in Old Norse, "Lucies everywhere. Massive infiltration. Air filled with scent of sulfur and lemons. Send vangels."

"Who are you talking to?" she asked.

"My brothers."

She tilted her head to the side in silent question.

He didn't have to answer, but he did. "There are demon vampires everywhere. Not in great numbers in any one place, but scattered about like a Satanic net. This city is in peril." At the look of disbelief and pity on her face, he added, "Can you not smell them? The demons reek of sulfur. The sinners—those already fanged and on their way to being drained at first opportunity, or those already wallowing in their bad deeds, or those contemplating some great sin—they smell of lemons."

"The only thing I smell is your cologne. Sandalwood and lime."

"I told you afore, I do not wear cologne." That damn life mate lure! "But that is neither here nor there. I must get you out of this town. All hell is going to break loose, and I mean that exactly as it sounds."

"You're starting to scare me, Mordr."

"You should be scared."

"Not that I believe there are such things as demon vampires, or vampire angels for that matter. The fact that you believe there are is what I find alarming."

Just then, they got caught in a mob of folks shoving to enter a nightclub where a popular country music band was playing. Luckily, there was no smell of Lucies, just human body odor covered with vast amounts of deodorant, soap, and bottled scents.

Miranda escaped the half circle of his arm and stood before him, looping her hands behind his neck. Then she began to sway from side to side, smiling up at him. "Forget all that nonsense about demons. Let's dance."

The band began to play a song called "I Melt."

For a certainty!

"What? Oh, no! I do not dance. I am too big and clumsy and . . . oomph!"

She yanked him flush with her body, her face resting on his shoulder. With each sway of her hips, she brushed his already burgeoning erection. An easy task with his parted cloak; the thin silk of her dress and the lightweight fabric of his braies provided no barrier at all to the size and power of his enthusiasm. He saw flashing lights behind his eyelids for a moment, but, no, it was the disco lights in the ceiling.

In another feat of surrender, he put his hands on her hips and yanked her even closer. All he did then was shift from foot to foot. If this was dancing, he was a sudden expert. A dancing fool!

In a futile effort to reinforce the crumbling wall of

his defense against her attraction, he blurted out, "I do not like red hair."

She lifted her head off his shoulder and glanced up at him. "Neither do I."

So much for that attempt! "And I do not like it skinned back off your face like a drowned cat."

"Meow!" Instead of being offended, she told him, "I only wore it this way because it was wet. It would have gone frizzy if I hadn't."

Huh?

While the band moved without break into "The Way You Look Tonight," she tugged out some pins and let them drop to the floor. Then she shook her hair into a mass of flaming waves.

He groaned.

"Is that a groan of disgust or a groan of pleasure?"

"Definitely pleasure . . . if you consider that I am probably adding dozens of years onto my penance."

"You might be punished for liking something about me?"

"No *might* about it. I *will* be punished but not for liking your hair down. Nay, 'twill be for all the bad things I am imagining that I could do to you. Many of them involving red hair." *And not just on your head.*

They continued to engage in the foresport called dancing for several long seconds before Miranda looked up at him again. "What kind of bad things?"

He laughed, something he could not recall doing in years, or leastways not very often. It felt good. In this moment, there was no soul-searing grief, no darkness of spirit, no rage at his fate, just a warm joy.

"You are so good-looking when you smile," she observed.

"And when I do not smile?"

"Trolling for compliments now?"

He shook his head, enjoying this light banter. "No, just being a troll."

In silence, they danced then, so close their two hearts seemed to beat as one. Meanwhile, the band moved from one slow song to another on the crowded dance floor.

"You Were Always on My Mind."

Yes, she was.

"Shameless."

Yes, he was.

"Must Be Doin' Somethin' Right."

It would seem so.

"Come a Little Closer."

Any closer and he would be inside her.

Then, in what could have been a message from you-know-who, "God Gave Me You."

No, He did not, a voice in his head disagreed.

"Then why offer her to me in such an enticing package?"

"Are you talking to me?" Miranda murmured.

"No. Just to myself."

"I know how you feel. I keep telling myself that this is a bad idea, that I should hotfoot it home and take a cold shower."

"Together?"

She never had a chance to answer because the band struck up a loud, raucous trill on electric guitars, and the leader announced, "Enough of these hokey slow songs. Time to liven up this party." With a bit of applause from the customers, they began to sing, "The Devil Went Down to Georgia."

Mordr figured that was his cue to leave. A reminder of why he was there tonight. Not to mention he did not do wild, dervish-style dancing like what he was now witnessing around him. Really, some men had no sense when it came to their attempts to seduce women to their bed furs. "Come. Let us leave this place." And, no, it was not cold showers he had in mind. If he had a mind at the moment!

They were not alone in the elevator down to the parking garage. They were not even touching. But a sharp awareness of each other resonated in the air, a promise of things to come. Things long forbidden to Mordr. Things still forbidden, but contemplated just the same. Like Adam, who was done salivating over the crisp, juicy, red apple and about to take that first bite.

The door binged open and everyone exited, leaving Mordr and Miranda to come out last. Instead of heading to the right where his car was parked, Mordr tugged Miranda into a dim alcove on the other side of the elevator. Backing her up against the wall, he succumbed to the taste of her rose-petal lips.

The apple was never so sweet. *Note to self: Apples are red. Miranda is red-haired. Both are sweet temptation.*

A fog swirled around them, carrying the scent of lilies and cloves. Or in her case, he would wager his sword arm that she was smelling sandalwood and lime. His lips did not need to persuade hers to open. She was already parted and welcoming him in. With fingers tunneling through her hair, his mouth came down hard on hers, and the fierce drugging kisses that followed almost caused his knees to buckle.

Never had a kiss been so powerful. As intimate as the sex act itself, but not nearly as satisfying. Like the dancing they had just engaged in, they sought each other's rhythm, then created a new, blended one of their own.

He tore his mouth from hers, and his head shot up with sudden alertness. He had heard something. Then he caught a faint whiff of something familiar. Sulfur. Lemon.

"Stay here, and do not move," he ordered. Pulling a compact metal object from an inside pocket of his cloak, he flicked a switch and it snapped into a full-length sword. Like magic it would appear, but actually an engineering marvel created decades ago by an especially talented vangel blacksmith. In the other hand, he already held a throwing star. Both had been specially treated with the symbolic blood of Christ, which would destroy any Lucie when wounded. Only then did Mordr shoot with uncommon speed to the far, dark area of the parking garage where two Lucipires were engaged in fanging and draining a man to not just death, but a fate far worse than the ending of human life. A fast track to Horror.

"Halt!" he shouted, causing both Lucies, a man and a woman, to raise their heads. Blood dripped from their huge fangs. Although he had identified them as male and female, it was sometimes difficult to tell the difference when demon vampires were not in humanoid forms. These were mungs. Huge in size, at least seven feet tall, they were covered with scales that oozed slime. Their eyes were red with bloodlust, and their hands were clawed. And tails. How could he forget the tails? If Mike had thought of it, he probably would have given vangels tails, too. As if fangs were not bad enough!

First things first. He must offer the victim—a terrible sinner, he sensed—a chance to repent.

The female mung lunged through the air toward him, and he finished her off quickly with a throwing star to the heart. "Good-bye, Lucie. Give Satan my regards." Immediately, she began to dissolve into a pool of sulfur-smelling slime.

The victim, half-drained of blood but not yet in stasis, let loose a terrible scream. "Help me," he pleaded.

The other mung was still trying to feed on him.

Mordr kicked the Lucie aside, and the beast hit the concrete wall with a loud cracking noise.

Mordr retrieved his throwing star and turned his attentions to the dying man, and there was no question he would be dead shortly. The question was whether he would die after repenting and await God's judgment on the Final Day. Or go to Horror today and eventually become a Lucie.

Through mind reading, something vangels were able to do when in the midst of saving souls, Mordr knew that this man, Lewis Robideaux, had profited for many years on child pornography. One of the worst kinds of sinners. Still, Mordr had to offer the man a chance to repent before his death. "Do you, Lewis, repent of your sins? Do you revile Satan and take Christ as your Lord and Savior?"

Robideaux's bleary eyes tried to focus on Mordr, whose fangs were out in preparation for a fanging to save his soul, if possible. Once he was able to bring Mordr into focus, not too happy with another fanged being, Robideaux laughed, blood gurgling from his mouth, and said, "Fuck you!"

"So be it!"

Mordr turned away from the man to find that the other mung had only cracked his head open, not a deadly blow for a powerful Lucie. They just stuffed their brains back in and resumed normal evil activities, like charging at Mordr with a battle-axe raised on high. Swinging the instrument in a wide arc, he almost decapitated Mordr, who jumped back just in time. The force of the heavy weapon pulled the mung with it, not having made purchase with Mordr's neck—thank you, God—and Mordr was able to thrust his sword into the miscreant's heart. The Lucie soon joined his partner in slimeville.

Through his side vision, Mordr noticed that yet another Lucie had come on the scene and was draining Robideaux to the point where his body was evaporating into thin air. Another convert for the other side. This Lucie was a haakai, older and stronger than the mungs. Mordr knew him well. Quintus, a former Roman soldier, had delighted in feeding Christians to the lions back in Colosseum days.

"Ah, Mordr, so we meet again," Quintus drawled, pulling a pattern-welded long sword from its jewel-encrusted scabbard at his side.

Mordr assumed a battle stance, legs spread, knees bent. He wished he had his old broadsword with him, Vengeance, but this thinner, more flexible rapier would do.

They both thrust and parried several times, getting their bearings, testing each other.

But then, Quintus made the mistake of taunting Mordr. "I met a fellow the other day down in Hell, Olaf Hordsson, he who raped your daughter and cleaved your son's skull through like a melon. Tasty treats, they both were, according to Olaf."

Mordr could not control the berserk rage that came over him then. With a roar of fury he cleft Quintus from skull to groin, watching with satisfaction as the Lucie's skin turned bright red and began to dissolve. Even then, Mordr continued to hack away at what was left of the man until there was naught but a puddle of slime. Bending over with palms on his thighs, he scanned the area to see if there were any more Lucies about. There were not. He panted for breath, trying to force his berserkness back inside. Otherwise, the bloodlust would be on him for any killing, not just demon vampires.

Only when his heartbeat slowed down to a hundred beats a minute, give or take, and the roar in his head calmed down to a mere rumble did he replace his soiled weapons to their special pockets inside his cloak. He turned then and began to walk back toward Miranda. And saw her standing not where he had left her in the protective enclosure of the alcove, but a short distance away. Watching him.

How long had she been standing there? What had she seen?

He reached out a hand to comfort her and she flinched, drawing back several steps. "Don't you dare touch me, you . . . you monster."

He could not argue with that. He *was* a monster of sorts. Why else would he have been made a vangel?

But then he saw something else in her eyes and horrified expression. She was afraid of him. Or repulsed. Or both.

She stared fixedly at his bloodied hands and the bits of demon vampire slime on his cloak and his fangs, which were still extended. He ran his tongue along the edge of his teeth, causing the fangs to retract. With a grunt of disgust, he went over to the SUV, where he popped the tailgate. Taking off his cloak, he placed it carefully in the back. Then he went around to the passenger side and opened the door. He took several holy water wipes from a special box in the glove compartment, using them to wipe his face and hands, then tossed them in a nearby trash bin.

Motioning toward the still-open car door, he said, "Come. I will take you home."

She shook her head. "Who are you? Are you one of them?" She motioned with her head toward the piles of slime.

"No, I am not a demon vampire. I am a vangel, as I told you afore. A Viking vampire angel."

"But . . . but you killed those . . . things."

"I did. The first two were the man and women you

saw in the Valhalla casino. I recall you saying they were a beautiful couple, that he was a gorgeous hunk."

"No!" she said with utter disbelief.

"Yes," he replied on a sigh.

"Do you enjoy doing this kind of thing?" She was still clearly in a state of shock.

"Get in the car, Miranda. I'll answer any of your questions when we are not out in open view. Where there is one Lucie, there may be others."

She scurried over and into the passenger seat so fast her dress rode up her thigh, giving a clear view of an almost transparent undergarment. Apparently, she was red all over, as he'd already surmised. Not just on her head.

Once in the driver's seat, he turned to her. "No, I do not particularly enjoy killing, even when it is ridding the world of demons whose evil is beyond human comprehension."

"Then why—"

"It is my job."

"You didn't just kill that last one. You were like a madman, hacking away when he . . . it . . . was already dead. Why?"

He swallowed several times. He should not reply. He really should not. But did he listen to good sense? No. "The demon mentioned something horrible, something particularly offensive to me."

"Words? You let words rile you to that extent? Clearly, you are in dire need of anger management, Mordr. I did my master's thesis on rage resolution. You need help. Believe me, I know about out-of-control anger issues."

He felt the anger rising in him again. He waited several seconds before turning to her. "You know nothing," he spat out. "That demon, Quintus by name, told me that he spoke with the man who murdered my children. How he repeatedly raped my little Kata, only six years old, and watched her bleed to death. How he cleaved my five-year-old son Jomar's little skull with a broadaxe like a melon. A melon!"

To his mortification, Mordr felt tears well in his eyes. "Even after all these years, I am shattered by the memory of their bodies as I found them on first coming home."

He could not face Miranda in his weakened state, but then he heard a soft sound and had to look. She was openly sobbing. For him? For his dead children?

This was just too much. More than he could bear. He was about to open the car door and call for Harek or Cnut to come get Miranda, but before he could get his cell phone out, she launched herself at him and somehow wedged her body between his chest and the steering wheel. Her ass sat on his lap.

"Oh, Mordr," she said, gazing at him through green pools of sympathy. "I am so, so sorry." Tucking her face into the crook of his neck, she wept voluminous tears. No one had ever cried for him before.

To his shame, his own tears streamed down his face and over his chin and blended with hers, a precious sharing of sorrow.

A proverb came to him of a sudden. Something he had heard one time in the Arab lands. "You may forget the one with whom you laugh, but you will never forget the one with whom you cry."

That was what he was afraid of.

Thirteen

Here a demon, there a demon,
everywhere a demon . . .

Miranda was shocked and stunned. In a walking daze. Alternately disbelieving and convinced she had entered some other universe. And scared to the bone.

How could she ever walk down the street again without wondering if this or that person was a demon in disguise? Did the cute bag boy at the grocery store have scales and a tail? Did her hairdresser drink blood after dark? What about the people she worked with? Especially that slimeball lawyer Jerome "Call Me Jerry" Daltry. But, no, if demons could take any human form, they wouldn't pick an overweight, bad-breath, balding persona. Would they?

"I'm losing my freakin' mind," she muttered as Mordr pulled into her garage and turned off the car lights. The interior garage lights went on automatically, so she could see him clearly.

"It happens to the best of us," Mordr replied, back to his old dour self.

She could tell that he regretted having taken her to town and revealing the dark underbelly of casino life. As if its underbelly wasn't dark enough already! And besides, these creatures were apparently everywhere, not just Las Vegas. It was enough to make a person live in a bomb shelter and never come out.

She'd always been a pragmatist, wanting to know what she was facing so she could prepare for the worst. Now she was thinking Pollyanna syndrome had a certain appeal.

A lapsed Catholic, she decided that going to church again might be a good idea. And holy water . . . she was going to get a gallon first chance she had. Where did one buy holy water, anyhow? And did holy water repel demons, or was that vampires? How about stakes? Oh Lord! She didn't think she could ever stake anyone, even Satan himself.

And there was another thing. Mordr definitely regretted having told her about his children. The poor man! How could any person witness such atrocities having been done to his children and not be warped for life? Not that Mordr was warped. Just a little bent out of shape. Or a lot, she conceded, given his grim, no-smile demeanor.

Except she had made him smile, she thought with inordinate pride, remembering their kisses. Both times. Before her world came crashing down.

She followed Mordr into the house, where they found the children were all safely asleep, and Mordr's brothers were watching some *Bourne Identity* flick on the TV in the den. Mordr exchanged a meaningful look with Harek and Cnut, and she knew that they knew she now knew their big, dark secrets. Well, some of them.

She went into the kitchen and sat down at the table, waiting while Mordr walked his brothers to the door. The sound of their soft conversation drifted her way, but she couldn't hear what they said. She couldn't think about that. So many other things riddled her brain. Questions, question, questions.

Mordr came into the kitchen, took one look at her face, and put two cups of water into the microwave.

"What are you making?"

"Tea. My sister-by-marriage, Alex, always drinks tea to calm her nerves when Vikar does something outrageous or dangerous or just annoys her."

She gave a short, humorless laugh. "Honey, a gallon of tea and a pigload of Prozac wouldn't calm me down now."

"Do not call me . . . endearments," he said.

Of all the things to home in on, that was the least important. "Why not?"

"Because it denotes a relationship, which we do not have."

"Really? *Honey*, you don't kiss a girl 'til her toes curl and her bones melt and then tell her there's nothing between them."

Before he could stop himself, Mordr's glance shot to her toes, which were exposed in her high-heeled sandals. A grin tried to tilt his rigid lips, but he held firm. Darn him!

The microwave pinged, and he put a tea bag in one mug and placed it on the table in front of her, along with a slice of lemon and some honey, a combination he must have seen his sister-in-law make. He then eyed the other mug, seemed to consider whether to put in a tea bag, or not, then dumped the water into the sink. Instead, he reached the cabinet high above the fridge and got a bottle of Scotch whisky which she'd received from a client one Christmas and never opened. "Ah, *uisge beatha*." He poured it into his mug, half full. "Did you know the Scots invented this particular brew? Water of life, it was called."

When he sat down at the table across from her, she switched mugs and said, "I need this more than you do, babe."

She saw him consider whether to chastise her for the "babe" endearment, then shrug as if it weren't worth the trouble.

Mordr sighed in resignation. "You have questions?"

"That's an understatement."

He took a sip of the tea and grimaced, taking back his cup of booze. She didn't care. Scotch tasted like medicine to her, even the good kind like this one apparently was.

"Assuming I believe all this demon/vampire/angel crap, how old are you?" she asked.

That question caught him off guard. He'd obviously been expecting something more important. "I was thirty-one when I crossed over in the year 850. So, that would make me roughly one thousand, one hundred, and ninety-five years old."

Her eyes widened. "And here I was worried about being an older woman, thirty-four to your thirty-one."

He appeared puzzled. "Why would that matter?"

"Things like that bother women. Like being taller than her lover. Or older. Or fatter. Or smarter."

"I am not your lover."

"Yet."

His jaw dropped.

"Oh, get a life! I was just kidding. You have a serious case of commitment issues, buddy. If you're interested, I have a group that meets about this problem every two weeks."

"You have a group about everything," he groused.

"Tell me how you came to be a . . . you know, angel with fangs."

"It is a long story."

"I have time."

"God was angry with the Vikings. Too proud. Too vain. Too vicious. Too many bad things. He was especially angry with my family because I and my six brothers each committed one of the Seven Deadly Sins in a most heinous manner. My sin was wrath."

"Surprise, surprise!"

"Your attempts at humor fail to impress me."

"Big, fat, hairy deal!"

He almost laughed.

She waited for him to explain more.

"In my fury over . . . you know . . . I killed many people. *Many!*"

She didn't think she needed to know more about that. Not at this point, anyhow. "So, God just decided one day that He would punish you all by making you vangels for eternity."

"Not exactly. Originally, he sentenced each of us to seven hundred years to make up for our sins, but being Vikings we have difficulty being pure. Every time we sin, more years are added to our original seven hundred."

She let out a burst of laugher. The idea of Viking men trying to be pure did pose funny possibilities.

She yawned. A combination of shock and information overload was finally catching up with her.

"Come. You need to sleep," Mordr said. "We can discuss everything in the morning."

She agreed and let him lead her up the stairs. "The only thing that matters, or the most important thing, is that my children are safe."

"Agreed," he said, opening her bedroom door and steering her inside. "I give you my solemn vow. The children will be safe. I failed to protect little ones under my shield once before. It will never happen again."

"Oh. Mordr, that wasn't your fault."

"It most definitely was my fault. If I had been there to protect them, they would not have suffered such violent deaths." He put up a halting hand. "No more! That subject is closed.

She sat on the edge of her bed and removed her shoes. He stayed in the open doorway, watching her. His posture, leaning one shoulder against the door frame, legs crossed at the ankles, was one of lazy indifference. But the light in his silvery blue eyes said something entirely different.

"Are you afraid I'll tackle you to the bed if you enter my bedroom?"

"I am afraid I will tackle *you* to the bed," he replied with uncommon humor, for him.

"And that would be a bad thing . . . because?" She couldn't believe she was being so aggressive.

"Oh, lady, tempt the lion and it will bite."

"Are you the lion?"

"Wouldst like to hear me roar?"

Miranda liked this light banter with the usual dour Viking. Just then, something more important occurred to her. "In the midst of all this stuff about a demon vampire threat, I forgot the biggest threat to my family."

He arched his brows at her.

"Roger."

"Of course."

"Is it possible . . . I mean, this will sound insane . . . but is it possible that Roger is a Lucipire?"

Lemonade, anyone? . . .

Roger had been in Las Vegas for a week and he was ready to kill someone. Miranda, of course, once he got his hands on her. But first of all, Clarence, who was the biggest, most disgusting pain-in-the-ass Roger had ever met, and there had been plenty in prison.

Among Roger's many complaints against his self-proclaimed, new best friend, none of which he had the nerve to voice, were these facts:

—Turned out Clarence's friend Lamar was actually his second cousin, maybe third. No one seemed sure, or cared.

—Turned out Lamar was a pimp and his apartment was a two-bedroom dump above a pizza shop where skanky women came and went as if there was a revolving door. Clarence offered to share the double bed in the guest room—a glorified closet—with Roger, but Roger had declined and spent his nights wrapped in a blanket on the dirty floor.

—Turned out Clarence had a violent temper that could ignite at the least little affront. A guy at the gas station who'd commented on Clarence's gold tooth ended up with a broken jaw and black eye. A bouncer at the cat house they visited on the way from Ohio got a bullet hole in the thigh, up close to his hairy balls, because he'd accused Clarence of unnecessary roughness with one of the "girls." Roger had no idea where or for how long Clarence had been carrying a weapon. Scary! And he'd made the cook in a diner shit his pants by lifting him off the floor and banging him against the wall, all because he'd burned Clarence's burger.

—Turned out Clarence's habit of openmouthed, loud eating was not confined to ice. Hard pretzels, potato chips, carrot sticks, apples, popcorn, and bread sticks also fit the bill. *Crunch, crunch, friggin' crunch.* The only time Clarence wasn't crunching was when he snored like a locomotive.

—Turned out Clarence was addicted to porn. Child porn. The younger the better. Now, Roger had nothing against porn. He'd jacked off to Anna Nicole Smith a time or two or twenty. But kids? Yuck!

Just then, Clarence walked in, a big smile on his

face. "Whatcha doin'?" He'd gone out with Lamar earlier for breakfast at a McDonald's down the street. In
fact, he carried a big-ass container of soda in one hand.
Roger knew what that meant. Ice.

Roger was sitting at the kitchen table. The apartment had been empty for once, but then it was only
eleven a.m. By late afternoon, it would be a zoo, once
again.

"Balancing my checkbook. I'm running out of cash,
fast." The minute he'd left the halfway house, Roger
had taken two thousand dollars out of the account he'd
once shared with his wife, which left a balance of five
thousand and some dollars. Not enough to even buy
a car. His own vehicle had been repo'ed while he was
in prison. Another thing he could blame on Miranda.

"Well, you know where we can make good money,"
Clarence said, slurping the last of his soda, and opening the lid.

Lamar was looking to expand his business and had
offered to set them up as pimps on the other side of
town. All they had to do was work the bus terminals
and homeless shelters for desperate women to start
their own stable of hookers. "Easy as fucking a blind
monkey," Lamar had assured them.

Nice picture! "No offense, but I'd rather get a job as
an electrician."

"Rog, Rog, Rog! How much can you earn as an electrician?"

Crunch, crunch, crunch.

Roger shrugged. "Twenty-five, thirty-five dollars an
hour."

Clarence laughed and crunched some more. "We
could earn a thousand dollars a night, each, on the
street. Fast money."

Where Clarence got this "we" business, Roger
wasn't sure, but he hesitated to point out that they

were not a team. Honestly, he wondered how long it would be before Clarence landed back in prison. He was a walking cop magnet.

"I can't think about that now. I've got to take care of other matters first. Don't forget, that's why I came to Vegas."

"The bitch," Clarence nodded. *Crunch, crunch, crunch.* He emptied the cup and tossed it toward the waste can. No Michael Jordan was he! He missed, and left the cup on the floor. "I ain't forgotten nothin', bro. Jist look out that back window and see what I got for us to do the job."

Bro? Roger gritted his teeth. How had he gotten himself mixed up with this guy? If he wasn't careful, he would land in the slammer again, just for associating with the creep.

Roger stood and walked over to the grimy window. All he saw in the alley was a heap of garbage overflowing the Dumpster and a battered van marked "Harrison Plumbing. No Job Too Dirty or Too Small." Comprehension came to him slowly. "You stole a van?"

"Borrowed it." Clarence beamed.

"Jeez, Clarence, you're gonna get us both arrested. Grand theft auto."

"No prob. By the time Harrison reports it missing and the cops get around to investigating, we'll have abandoned it outside the city."

He was probably right.

Clarence was scratching at a red mark on his neck. No doubt he'd been bitten by one of the mouse-size cockroaches that prowled the apartment at night. "What say we cruise the bitch's neighborhood and case out the situation?" Clarence suggested. "No one will notice us in the shit mobile."

"Great!" That was the first good idea Roger had heard all day. He closed his checkbook and put it in his back pocket as he stood. Walking toward the door with Clarence, he noticed something odd, and it wasn't the pistol Clarence was checking for ammunition. "You smell like lemons."

It wasn't a longboat, but . . .

𝔄 week after her "date" with Mordr, Miranda awakened on Saturday morning at seven a.m. to complete silence. No shouting kids. No banging doors. No running water. Not a peep.

It could mean the children were overtired and overslept past their usual break-of-dawn risings. Or it could mean they were in trouble or were causing trouble. Probably the latter. She recalled one time awakening to what sounded like a herd of mice—i.e., barefooted children running on tiptoes from one end of the house to the other, over and over. Turned out they were chasing Ben, who held a mixing bowl full of strawberry ice cream that he refused to share. Strawberry ice cream for breakfast? A mixing bowl full for one small person?

Roger had made no contact since that call more than a week ago. That didn't mean he didn't still represent a danger to her, especially since her neighbor Mrs. Edmonds from across the street and down a ways—she of the nude vacuuming—had reported two strange men in a plumber's van parked in her driveway a few days ago when she'd returned from the hairdresser. They'd had binoculars pointed toward Miranda's house. When Miranda had tried reporting it to the police, they told her she needed more than a suspicion that Roger was involved before investigating.

Equally alarming—yesterday's *Review-Journal* reported a large number of missing persons in Las

Vegas. The law enforcement party line was that gamblers often disappeared for a while if they didn't want family or friends to know they'd bet the family farm, so to speak, and lost.

To her surprise, when she went downstairs wearing a quickly tied robe over her nightgown, she found four little souls in the den. Maggie was working on a puzzle, and the boys sat like wooden soldiers at attention on the sofa watching cartoons.

At her arched brows, Maggie said, "Mordr promised to take us on an adventure today if we were quiet for one whole hour."

An adventure? Without consulting me first? I don't think so! "That's nice. What kind of adventure?"

"It's a surprise," Maggie informed her.

We'll see about that!

The boys looked at her and made zipping motions on their lips, as if they couldn't speak on pain of . . . something. So, bribery was Mordr's secret tactic for silence. It never worked for her. Maybe she'd offered the wrong rewards.

She stomped toward the kitchen, though it was hard to stomp in fuzzy sheep slippers, a gift from the children last Christmas, but she stopped just outside the kitchen doorway at what she saw. Mordr, wearing shorts and a "Vikings Rule" T-shirt, was sitting side by side at the table with Linda. They were coloring in Linda's new Barbie Princess coloring book. Coloring? A Viking coloring? Somehow the idea of those big fingers holding a tiny crayon just didn't fit.

Or maybe it did.

Her heart swelled almost to bursting. You had to love—well, admire—a man who didn't mind putting himself on level with children.

"You hafta color inside the lines," Linda advised Mordr in a gentle reprimand.

"Why?"

"Because it looks better that way."

"I like my way better."

"And Prince Ken doesn't have a mustache."

"My Prince Ken does. Without facial hair, he looks like an untried youthling."

Linda giggled.

"Hey, I didn't know we had a silver crayon for Barbie's crown. Did you hide it from me?"

"It's not a crown. It's a tiara."

"You would look good with a crown . . . uh, tiara. I wonder where we could buy one."

"Maybe at the mall. What's your favorite color?"

Mordr glanced up just then, sensing her presence, and said, without skipping a beat, "Red."

Miranda felt her face heat, with embarrassment as much as pleasure.

"Mine is blue. G'mornin', Aunt Mir. Mordr is gonna take us all to McDonald's for breakfast."

"How nice!" *Without asking me. Again.* At least, Linda wasn't calling him Daddy anymore. "Is that the big adventure I heard about?"

"No, there's another big adventure." He waggled his eyebrows at her.

Holy moly! He's gone from Mr. Grim Reaper to Flirty Fred. Did someone give him a happy pill?

"I'm havin' pancakes. Mordr is havin' the Big, Deluxe, Super-Duper Breakfast 'cause he's so hungry he could eat a bear, and he did one time. Eat a bear. It tasted gross. He has a big tummy an' it gets so empty sometimes they kin hear the rumbles for miles. Some folks think it's thunder. Isn't that silly?" She gazed up at Mordr for his approval.

He nodded and motioned with his head for Miranda to get a cup of coffee from the machine he'd already started. Just for her? Must be since he didn't particularly like the "bitter brew" himself. As she walked into the room he studied her appearance and made a mock gesture of dismay, forearm to forehead, "Oh no! Another bow!"

She glanced down to see the belt of her terry-cloth robe tied at her waist with a bow. It was the least sexy garment she could imagine, but he was looking at her like she was sex on a stick. "Puh-leeze!" she said, and took her first sip of the "bitter brew." And, boy, was it bitter! He must have used double the amount of coffee grounds needed. She tried her best not to grimace.

"And how many sheep had to die for your feet to be shod?

"An animal rights activist, are you now?" She knew perfectly well that he was a meat eater and had been a hunter, in his time. *His time?* Oh Lord, she didn't want to think about *that*. "Just for the record, these are made of fake sheepskin."

He grinned. He'd been teasing her. Would wonders never cease?

"Can we talk yet?" one of the boys yelled from the den.

Maggie walked in and sat down at the table, figuring she wasn't the one who talked too much and therefore didn't fall under the zipped lips threat. She had braided her long red hair into a single braid down her back and wore a clean tank top with Bermudas. Linda sported a braid, too. One blond braid on each side of her freckled face. She wore the new shorts set Miranda had bought on sale last month.

Did Mordr help them do all this? Even the hair braiding?

Her heart melted just a little bit more.

Just then all three boys came skidding into the kitchen, each trying to talk over the other.

"I'm the winner. I'm the winner," Sam proclaimed.

"I bet Ben that I could be quiet the longest. And I was. Thirty-three whole minutes."

"I was quiet just as long as you were," Ben contended.

"No, you weren't. You said, 'Holy shit' when Larry let loose a smeller feller."

"I did not," Larry protested. "It was just the sound of my bare legs on the leather couch. The smell came from your pickle breath."

"Loser!"

"Dickhead!"

"Swear jar!"

Someone, possibly Larry, dug into a pocket, and the clink of a quarter could be heard in the jar.

"I'm hungry."

"You ate a whole jar of pickles."

"Did not!"

"Did so!"

"Sam has cards in his back pocket. He's practicing so he can get up a game of poker with Johnny Severino. For money," Maggie said, raising her chin sky-high with superiority.

"Tattletale!" Sam spat out, giving Maggie the evil eye.

"It was only gonna be for pennies," Ben defended his twin.

"Unless Johnny wants to bet his new snake," Larry amended. "It's in an aquarium and everything. He feeds it mice."

"You guys are dumber than dog poop," Maggie proclaimed. "Aunt Mir would never let you bring a snake into the house."

Which reminded Miranda of something. "Where's Ruff?"

"He's having a quiet time on a leash out by the shed," Maggie said.

"He ate Mordr's underpants and then barfed them up on his shoes," Linda explained, "an' I almos' puked when I saw the pile. It had pickles in it."

"Mordr made us hose off his shoes," Larry added. "He said they were his second best boots for goin' a-Viking."

"Ahem!" Mordr cleared his throat, but no one heard him over their own chatter. She was used to being ignored when the kids were all excited like this. Mordr was stunned.

Miranda put her forehead on the table, trying to pan out the noise. It was too early in the morning and she didn't have enough caffeine in her to fortify her for the day to come.

Slowly, she heard silence come over the room. Without any shouting from Mordr, which was her usual way to make the little ones shut up. She raised her head and saw that Mordr just sat, arms folded over his chest, glaring.

The five children, even Maggie and Linda, stared expectantly at Mordr.

"Is this the way you behave when you want something?"

They all ducked their heads.

"Was I being good?" Linda asked tearfully.

"Yes, little mite," he said, patting her on the head.

"I was being good, too," Maggie said, indignant that Linda would be the only one complimented.

"You too, Maggie, though you have a habit of telling on others." Mordr reached over and squeezed Maggie's hand to soften his criticism.

For a man who abhorred being around children, he was doing a lot of touching today, Miranda noticed.

"Maggie's a snitch," Sam declared with disgust.

"Yeah, Maggie's a snitch," Ben and Larry echoed.

"What's a snitch?" Linda wanted to know.

"Mayhap your sister would not snitch if you did not give her reason to," Mordr said to the boys. "Be nice to her."

"Huh?" the three of them said as one.

"You can gain more with honey than vinegar. Sweet trumps sour any day," Mordr went on.

What? Who is this alien talking about sweet talk? Miranda was looking at Mordr, wondering what had come over him suddenly. Not that she didn't like it.

Time for Miranda to get her two cents in. "What's this I hear about a big adventure today, Mordr? I don't recall anyone asking me for permission to take the children on an adventure." Besides which, they were supposed to be sticking close to, preferably inside, the house until the danger of Roger and/or vampire demons subsided. She felt silly just thinking the words *vampire demon.* Anyhow, she couldn't conceive of any big adventure that would take place inside the house.

The kids went blessedly quiet, but she could see their excitement and the fear that they might have put the kibosh on it with all their squabbling.

"I had been thinking of taking you all on a voyage today," Mordr revealed to Miranda. "With your permission, of course."

"A-Viking?" three little boys asked hopefully.

"No, not a-Viking. More like a-boating on Lake Mead."

"Yippee! Speed boating!" Ben did a little Snoopy dance around the kitchen. "Varoom, varoom, varoom!"

"Waterskiing? Oh, man! I always wanted to go water-skiing." Sam was beaming from ear to ear. "That would be better than five-card stud for a snake any day."

"I could wear my water wings," Linda said in a weak voice. Even though she'd had swimming lessons, she probably feared being tossed into the lake, something her brothers might very well do.

"No, it would not be speed boating," Mordr said, shaking his head at how any comment exploded into a discussion with these kids. "I have rented a pontoon boat for the day." Realizing his mistake, he immediately turned to Miranda and added, "If you agree."

"A pontoon? That's booor-ing!" Sam declared.

"Well, you could always stay home with a babysitter." Mordr yawned as if he could not care less, either way. "I am sure one of my brothers would come watch over you. I, on the other hand, am looking forward to boating and swimming and fishing."

Sam and all the others agreed that sounded like a wonderful adventure and they turned expectantly to Miranda.

"Are you sure it would be safe?" she asked Mordr. The unspoken question was not just the safety of boating on a lake, but the danger from Roger or the demon creatures.

"Very safe," Mordr assured her.

"Well, okay, I guess."

The words were barely out of her mouth than the children shot off in all different directions to get beach gear—towels, flippers, goggles, swimming suits, etc.

"Do you know how to drive a boat?" she asked Mordr as he went out into the garage to get an ice chest for drinks and snacks.

"Miranda! I grew up on boats. I am a Viking."

"Yeah, but are you familiar with motorized boats, like a pontoon?"

"Of course," he said. At her look of doubt, he admitted, "Not so much. But how different could they be?"

She rolled her eyes. "You seem so different today. You'd never recognize you from the man who came here, reluctant to even be around children."

He shrugged. "I have decided not to fight fate anymore. What will be will be."

"Really?"

He came up behind her where she was dumping ice cubes from the ice maker bin into a large zipper bag. Wrapping his arms around her waist, he kissed her neck.

She turned in his arms and realized that he'd undone the bow of her robe. His hands were already inside, rubbing against her butt. With the thin barrier of her nightgown, she felt almost naked. And the evidence of his attraction to her pressed against her belly, his cargo shorts hiding nothing.

She put her arms around his neck and leaned back so that she could see his face. "Does this surrender to fate apply to us, as well?"

"Do you doubt it, wench?" He rubbed himself back and forth against her. While he seemed to turn her on with just a look, let alone such blatant action, she was more turned on by her effect on him. His eyes—always a clear, stunning blue—turned silvery blue. His lips parted. She could feel his strong heartbeat. And, God help her, but his incisors seemed to be slightly elongated with arousal.

"You said you would be in big trouble if you got involved with me," she squeaked out in a lame attempt to slow down this speeding train of sexual attraction.

"True," he said, and nipped at her ear.

Just his breath at her ear caused ripples of pleasure to skim over her skin and lodge in her girl places. His hands were another story altogether. They explored her body with lazy, long-fingered expertise. Her bottom, her breasts, the small of her back, her shoulders. Slow hands! Just like that old Pointer Sisters song.

"You are smiling," he noted, and kissed her softly. "Does that mean you agree?"

"To what?"

He chuckled. "To boating on Lake Mead."

She frowned with confusion. "I thought we were talking about something else."

With a teasing grin, he told her, "That is the best thing about us Vikings. We can do more than one thing at a time."

"Multitaskers?"

"Definitely. The more erotic the tasks, the better."

And, yes, he was stimulating her in more than one place at a time, in more than one way at a time. Oooh! She was the one who was in trouble here.

Just then Larry rushed into the kitchen, about to ask Miranda a question, "Aunt Mir, where is my—? Mordr! You're playin' kissy face with Aunt Mir. Yuck! Aunt Mir, he has his hand on your bum. Double yuck!" On those words, he rushed back out, no doubt to report their carnal activity to his siblings.

"We will finish this later," Mordr promised her as he stepped back and retied the belt to her robe.

"Finish what? The discussion?"

"The time for talk is long over."

She tilted her head to the side in question. "And the time is now for . . . ?"

"Surrender."

Fourteen

Sweet surrender . . .

It was a day out of time like no other. Being one thousand, one hundred and ninety-five years old, that was saying a lot.

After some initial fumbling and flooding of the pontoon boat's motor, Mordr had learned to handle the vessel. He'd spent hours cruising the manmade lake, stopping here and there to set the children up for fishing with the rented equipment. It amused him tremendously to find modern folks fishing for entertainment. In his time, Vikings fished for subsistence and found it to be woefully hard work.

The whole time they were riding on the boat, the song "Pontoon" by some band called by the lackwit name of Little Big Town kept blasting out on the sound system. Something about making waves out on the ocean with a catchy refrain, "Mmmmmmm . . . motorboatin'." Soon all the children, and Miranda, were singing along.

If Mordr heard the expression "Are we there yet?" in the car or the boat, he was thinking about wrapping that wonderful modern invention over each of their mouths. Duct tape.

Sam was, of course, betting that he would catch the biggest fish, and he did—a bass almost as big as he was, which broke his line. An argument ensued over whether a fish actually had to be brought on board to count. Mordr finally had to intervene and threaten to toss both Sam and Ben overboard if they didn't behave.

On the other hand, what a joy to watch Linda catch her first fish! Not so joyful was her crushed demeanor when she was made to throw the baby crappie back into the water. She'd wanted to bring it home in a bucket and keep it as a pet.

All of the children had been required to wear life vests, something Ben and Sam protested vehemently, claiming to be expert swimmers. Which they were, all of them, actually, but it was a regulation, and it allowed Mordr the freedom of not having to watch their antics every single minute. Like the time Ben fell overboard trying to loosen his fishing hook from some seaweed. Which, of course, prompted Sam to do the same. Before he knew it, five children were in the water, and Mordr had to stop the boat and go back for them.

Mordr couldn't recall children being so much trouble when he was growing up. But then, he was probably recalling the past through a different prism. Besides, under no circumstances, would he ever recall those as the proverbial "good old days."

By late afternoon, they'd boated, fished, ate the food Miranda had packed, swam, boated, and fished some more. Now the boat was anchored in a small cove. He was lying, elbows braced, on a blanket on a grassy knoll, watching Miranda scamper about in the shallow waters playing dodgeball with the children, boys against girls.

Laughing, she finally yielded victory to the boys and said she was getting too old for such energetic play. Walking up toward him, she dried her wet hair with a towel, causing a mass of long, damp waves to spring out, framing her sun-warmed face with its newly emerged scattering of freckles. Her jade-green eyes flashed with pleasure at his blatant perusal of her as she sank down beside him, the same green as the one-piece bathing suit she wore, with two thin straps over the shoulders. (By the by, to a Viking, thin straps were just as appealing as bows.) The garment was high on the hips and low on the breasts, hugging her thin frame, leaving little to the imagination. She probably thought to dampen his ardor by wearing such a modest swim outfit, compared to the bikinis many women wore, but he had news for her. She was more enticing for what she hid.

"This was a wonderful idea," she said, flopping onto her back, arms extended over her head and eyes closed, letting the still-warm sun bake her skin. Modern folks were strange in that way, always wanting to tan their skins, like leather.

He chuckled then.

"What?" She cracked one eye open.

"There is one practice of modern women that I like. Well, several, but in this case, the shaving of armpits." He glanced pointedly at hers.

Her eyes were both wide open now, and she arched her brows in question.

"My wife was dark-haired, and, whew! She had a virtual forest hanging from her armpits."

"Thank you for sharing that." She closed her eyes again, but a small smile curved her lips. She remained silent for several moments before saying, "Thank you."

"It was my pleasure."

"Aside from the fun of being out in the sun and water, it's such a relief just to be away from all the stress back in Vegas."

"The danger will still be there when we return."

"Don't rain on my parade."

At first he didn't understand. These modern phrases! "I promise not to rain, if you promise to be careful."

She nodded. "How much longer do you think this will go on?"

"The Lucipire threat should be over within a week. As for Roger, I am not sure. One thing at a time. Hopefully." He laughed when his attention was caught by the children playing leapfrog in the shallow water. Ben had stood suddenly when Larry was leaping and caused Larry to be riding his shoulders until the two of them fell over and under the water.

"You don't seem to have as much trouble anymore . . . you know, being around children."

"It is still difficult. The enjoyment of being with your children does not wipe out the pain of losing my own." He thought about what he had said, and it was true. "My grief is no less for Kata and Jomar, but it is tempered somewhat."

"Do you mind talking about them? What were they like?"

He lifted his elbows and eased back onto the blanket, folding his arms under his head. He did not discuss his dead children. Never. Not even with his brothers. Still, he found himself saying, "A joy, they were. Kata, the older at six years, was a bossy little miss. Fearless, a born leader. Always up to some mischief. Jomar, a year younger, adored his sister and followed her about like a playful puppy. More serious than Kata, Jomar did not act impulsively. He thought things out, remarkable for one so young." He paused, finding that instead of feeling pain at speaking of his children, there was a relief of sorts. Turning on his side to face Miranda, he said, "Kata was blonde like Linda. Jomar had black hair, but he resembled Larry in some ways, especially the way Larry is always tugging up his sagging braies—I mean, pants—having no buttocks to speak of, to hold them in place."

"Oh, Mordr!" Miranda had tears in her eyes as she listened to hm.

"I never had a chance to give them the gifts I had brought from my journey. A rainbow of different colored ribands for Kata and a small wooden sword for Jomar. I threw them into the flames of their funeral pyres."

"Being a close acquaintance of an archangel, did you ever ask about your children? I mean, if it were me, I would want to know if they are all right."

Mordr nodded. "Michael told me at our first meeting that Kata and Jomar are in a safe and happy place."

"That should be some comfort to you."

"It is, except I cannot rid my mind of the way I saw them last. And when I see their ravaged bodies, a rage like no other rises in me and . . ." He let his words trail off, and he shrugged. "I am what I am. I am what I became."

"I could help you."

"What? No! I do not want or need your sympathy."

"That's not what I'm offering. Oh, of course I sympathize, but what I had in mind was more professional help. Don't pooh-pooh psychology and the good it can do. You would be surprised at how much help we psychologists can be to grieving people."

"Pooh-pooh? Me?" He laughed, and in a deliberate ploy to change the subject, leaned over her and asked, "Do you psychoanalyze your lovers when you take them to your bed? Do you offer to 'cure' them?"

"Tsk, tsk, tsk!" she said. "The only thing I needed to cure them of is a bad case of sexual need."

"I have sexual needs."

"I'll bet you do. Actually, there haven't been very many lovers in my life and hardly any ever since I got the kids. Believe me, an Internet profile showing five children does not garner a lot of hits."

"You tried Internet dating?"

"No. I'm just using it as an example. Be honest, would you want to hook up with a woman responsible for five kids?"

"Depends on what you mean by hooking up. If you mean one night of hot sex, or two, or even five, that would be fine . . . in fact, perfect. A lifetime commitment, that would be another thing."

"See. Single mothers face daunting battles in the dating jungles. Single mothers with two or three kids, the jungle gets thicker and harder to traverse. Single mother with five kids, even a machete wouldn't get her past the first date."

He had to smile at her choice of words. "You missay me, Miranda. I did not mean that I personally would be daunted by a woman with children, not if I wanted that woman. Nay, I referred to the fact that vangels are forbidden love or sex relationships. In fact, we have been made sterile to ensure our compliance, except for Ivak, who is the exception to just about everything in the world. You would know what I mean if you ever met the handsome knave. Leastways, women consider him handsome. Never did he have trouble attracting anything with breasts, like bees to a honey pot. He is a prison chaplain, married, with a soon-to-be born baby, and Mike is as outraged with him as an angel with a thorn up its . . . wing. We are all suffering because of Ivak's missteps in the sexual arena."

She blinked several times at his rambling discourse. He was becoming a regular blathering machine. Then she asked, "Sterile? Do you mean impotent? I already told you—"

He put his fingertips over her lips. "Can you doubt my . . . uh, potency?" He glanced downward toward the tenting in his swimming shorts.

Her blush said it all. No more questions about could he or couldn't he. The question was: Would he? He hoped so. Provided Mike didn't catch on to his intentions beforehand.

"Wanting you has become a pounding need in my body. I was dead to feeling, but now, like a hibernating bear, you are provoking me to wake up. You are making me crazy. You know that, don't you?"

Normally, she would berate him for using the word *crazy*. Apparently it was not a proper word for folks in her mind-healing profession. Instead, she pondered his words and said, "I know what you mean. All you have to do is give me one of your smoldering looks, and you turn me on so much you make my knees sweat."

A slow, lazy grin emerged on his lips as comprehension sunk in. "I smolder? That settles it then. We must do something about your sweaty knees."

The children came up then, cutting off any further conversation. Or carnal activity. They were hungry. Again.

He came to his feet in one fluid movement, then held his hand out for Miranda, helping her stand. It took all his self-control to restrain his baser impulses when what he wanted to do was pull her into a tight embrace and have his carnal way with her. In the end, all he did was lean down and give her a soft kiss of promise.

"Kissing again! Yuck!" Larry said, opening the ice chest to see if there was anything left.

"He's probably going to boink her," the all-wise Ben told the others.

"What's boinking?" Linda wanted to know.

Maggie made a sound of disgust, and Sam was rolling on the ground, laughing. Larry was using a tongue-wetted finger to get the last of the crumbs from the potato chip bag.

"It's when a guy takes out his wiener and—" Ben started to explain, but Mordr put a hand over his mouth.

"Your brother was just teasing," Mordr told Linda.

"Johnny Severino says it starts with putting your tongue down a girl's throat 'til she can barely breathe. That makes her want to show you her pee place." This wisdom came from Larry, who hitched up his wet swim pants which were so low the crack in his buttocks was exposed.

"Someone needs to do something about Johnny Severino," Miranda said in a choked voice.

He and Miranda laid out the remaining food. Granola bars. Some tiny oranges called Cuties. Two peanut butter and jelly sandwiches, cut into quarters. An Oreo that Mordr ate quickly before anyone could grab it first. Several squeeze yogurts. Thin string cheese cylinders. All washed down with two shared bottles of water.

A day in the sun had turned them all sun-bronzed, except for Mordr, whose skin was getting lighter. He must feed soon by saving a sinner or by killing a Lucie, the best way vangels could get that suntanned look so prized in this modern world.

By the time they got home just before dusk, all the children were fast asleep, slumped over one another in the backseats of the van. He carried Linda out of the car, pressing buttons on the security panel to open the front door, then carried her upstairs to lay her on her bed. She never once opened her eyes. For a moment, he just stood, staring down at the little bundle of innocence. He was pretty sure he loved the little girl, and that could mean heartbreak for both of them when he left as he must, eventually.

He could not think about that now.

Miranda had awakened the rest of the children and brought them inside. They dragged themselves sleepily to their respective beds, needing no prompting tonight.

"You should take showers, but I think we'll skip those tonight. You're all so tired," Miranda said, to the children's relief.

"G'night," they said sleepily to Mordr as they passed by.

"Why don't you go take a shower," Mordr suggested to Miranda. "I'll bring the rest of the stuff inside and lock up for the night."

She nodded. "Thank you. All that sun and a long day. I'm beat, too."

He hoped not too beat. He had some smoldering to do. Among other things.

He should take a shower himself. A cold one.

He should call his brothers and get an update on the Lucie situation.

He should find out if Cnut had discovered anything more on Roger's whereabouts.

He should remember that he was a vangel and not permitted to do what he was considering.

He should remind himself that this was an assignment with an end date. At some point, probably soon, he would be leaving.

But it was too late. Like a heat-seeking missile the military used today, he was set on his course. No stopping now. His desire for Miranda overrode everything, especially his good sense.

God help me! Mordr thought.

The voice in his head that should be telling him to stop remained silent.

The history books didn't mention THAT about Vikings . . .

Miranda had been under the shower for so long the hot water turned tepid. It felt so good to wash the grime of the day off her body and to relax all the muscles she'd been unaccustomed to exercising on a regular basis, as in swimming, climbing on and off the boat, and playing games in the water with the children.

Squeaky clean and no longer drained of energy, she wrung the water out of her hair and was about to step out into the bathroom when she heard the sound of a door opening and closing. Without invitation, Mordr stepped into the shower stall with her. Naked.

His eyes devoured her.

Her eyes devoured him. For a second, panic assailed her and he was about to bolt. She couldn't help her anxiety. He was big. All over.

"Stay," he said, picking up a bar of soap. Wrinkling his nose at the floral scent, he shrugged and stepped under the showerhead, lathering up his hair and face and upper body.

She watched, fascinated. No longer in a panic. In fact, just the opposite. "As if I have any intention of going anywhere when I have a Christmas gift, birthday present, and a surprise party standing before me in all his naked glory."

"The things you say!" He shook his head, causing

droplets to hit her in the face. His eyes glowed with a savage blue fire, Viking to the bone, wounded man to the soul, and yet there was a deliberate calmness there, as well.

He took his time, leisurely soaping and rinsing his chest and abdomen, his underarms and belly. When he got to his genitals, he took special care, holding her eyes the entire time, as he cupped himself, then ran a fist over the soap-slick, blue-veined length of him.

Clean now, he gave his full attention to her as she stood pressed against the corner to the right of the showerhead. She didn't cower under his study, knowing instinctively that he found no problem with her thin body and small breasts. He kept his lips pressed together to hide his elongated incisors, which she'd had a peek at a moment ago when he'd raised his face to the shower.

Setting the soap aside and finger-combing his hair back off his face and over his shoulders, he flicked his fingers at her, motioning her to step toward him.

What an arrogant, presumptuous, male thing to do!

She did just that, stepping into his open arms. What a submissive female she was turning out to be!

At first, he just held her tightly against him, his face pressed down into the curve of her neck and shoulder. Then he turned his head slightly and whispered against her ear, "I have never wanted a woman as much as I want you."

Okay, she'd been half turned on all day and more turned on at first sight of his blue steeler, but this huskily spoken declaration was the bow on her birthday/Christmas present. She squeezed his shoulders and leaned back to look at him.

He put a hand over his mouth to hide his incisors . . . um, fangs.

"Don't," she said, pulling his hand away. "They are

who you are, whatever that is. Besides, we all have our flaws."

"And yours are?" he asked, clearly grateful for her acceptance.

"Come on. You have eyes. My small breasts."

"Odd you should mention them. Seems I've developed a preference for small over large." He cupped both breasts from underneath and they only half filled his big hands. When he flicked his thumbs over both nipples, they rose to attention, begging for more.

She sighed at the sensitivity of her breasts and his expert ministrations.

"Besides, your sweet nipples more than compensate for any lack."

Instead of leaning down, he lifted her by the waist so that her feet dangled a foot off the floor and his mouth could latch on to one breast and suckle her deep into his mouth.

"Oh. My. God." A keening sound of intense pleasure ripped from her arched throat. She threw her head back farther in ecstasy, which caused her breasts to press forward, begging for more.

"You like that, do you, sweetling?"

"No, I practically climaxed because I hate it so," she gasped out.

"You have a sarcastic mouth on you, wench," he said, grinning at her.

Grabbing his head, she planted him on her other breast. In the midst of chuckling, he licked and kissed and sucked on that nipple, too.

Backing her up against the wall, he turned off the shower and moved his attention to her mouth and spent considerable time showing her that there were dozens of ways of kissing, each of them worthy of praise, not that she was coherent enough to utter a word of praise. The whole time he was kissing her, his hands were busy searching for all the erotic spots on her body. And finding them!

At some point she must have raised her legs and wrapped them around his waist. Or maybe he had done it for her. In any case, his long fingers were stroking her from behind as she undulated against his balls and the underside of his penis that rose upward toward his navel.

A kaleidoscope of colors burst behind her eyelids, and her entire body went stiff. With the last bit of sanity she still held onto, Miranda asked, "Do you have a condom?"

"I do not need a condom. I carry no disease, and I told you before that I am sterile."

Mordr wasn't the first man to claim sterility or a vasectomy when in the throes of sex, but somehow she sensed that he was telling the truth. And so she nodded.

With her hands on his shoulders and her legs still wrapped around his waist, he walked them into her bedroom where a bedside lamp provided a dim, subdued light. He didn't bother to towel them dry. Their body heat would take care of that in no time, Miranda mused.

She thought he would lay her on the brass bed, but instead he sat her at the bottom edge and dropped to his knees before her, spreading her knees wide.

"No," she protested. Then more vehemently, "No! Not like that the first time."

"I just want to look at you. It has been a long, long time since I've gazed at a woman's secret place." He smiled and winked at her. "So pretty. Pink. Like the petals of a flower."

Then, before she could guess his intention, he stood, picked her up by the waist, and tossed her to the center of the mattress. He crawled up and over her, settling his body in alignment with their respective body parts.

"My need for you is fierce," he said, using his furred legs to rub against her calves.

She hadn't realized she was so sensitive there. But then he used his ankles to spread her wide, exposing that area she *had known* was sensitive. Sex Central, so to speak.

"I am afraid I might hurt you," he said against her ear where he licked the outer shell, then blew softly.

Her body lurched at the intense sexual pleasure that rippled out, igniting other parts of her body. Her lips. Her breasts. And lower.

When she was able to put two words together without blubbering, she put a hand to his face. "I need you, too. If there's something I don't like or if I'm hurting, I can use a safe word."

"Miranda," he said with exaggerated shock. "Have you been reading *Fifty Shades*?"

She felt herself blush but then countered with equal exaggerated shock, "Mordr! Have *you* been reading *Fifty Shades*?"

"Only the good parts," he admitted with absolutely no embarrassment, nibbling a path along her jaw, an especially diverting exercise because of his fangs. "An angel, even a vangel, must understand modern sins in order to avoid them."

"Is that theory accepted by Michael . . . the, uh, archangel?"

"No. What will your safe word be?"

"Oreo."

They both laughed, and then they were not laughing at all as Mordr braced himself on extended arms and used his erection to stroke the moist folds between her legs. It must take an incredible strength to do that, Miranda thought with what had to be feverish irrelevance.

Giving her no warning, he plunged into her, filling her, causing her inner muscles to expand to accommodate his size, and, yes, to her mortification, to have a mini-orgasm, just from that alone. But Mordr didn't notice, he was busy lifting her legs by the knees and pressing them up against her chest, giving him even more room to impale her fully, pubic bone to pubic bone.

"Holy Sex in the City!" she murmured.

Mordr's face was transformed in the sex act. His normally blue eyes turned almost silver. His nostrils flared. His lips parted, exposing the fangs. She assumed that fangs played some role in sex, as they did in fighting demons or saving sinners, but she wasn't about to ask that now. Maybe never. She wasn't sure she wanted to know.

He began long, slow strokes that about had her eyes rolling up into her head.

"You feel like a tight glove of warm honey down there," he informed her on about the fifth stroke. Or was it fifty. Her brain was no longer operating on a full tank.

"You feel . . ." She tried to reply with equal vividness, but all she could think of was ". . . so damn good."

His little half smile told her the compliment was well taken.

The force of Mordr's shorter strokes was so hard they moved her up the mattress, almost hitting her head on the spindles. Without breaking stride, he sat up on his knees, still inside her, with her butt resting on his thighs, and turned so that when he came down over her again, their feet were on the pillows. Which must have given him an idea—and, boy, did he have ideas—because he reached behind him for one of the pillows and placed it under her hips, canting her body at an angle off the bed. With this position, Mordr's public bone hit her clitoris every time he plunged in.

Instantly, without warning, her vagina began to spasm, clutching him in nature's vain attempt at keeping the man inside if he was so inclined to withdraw. Not that Mordr was. So inclined, that was.

When Miranda began to come down from the high of that orgasm, she noticed that Mordr was unmoving inside her, and still big as a horse—well, not a horse—but big. The man had not climaxed himself. Darn it! Instead, he was waiting out her mind-blowing peak before resuming his long strokes. At the same time, his fingers were busy playing with the nipples of her breasts. Rubbing, flicking, pinching, tugging.

As if she were a puppet, he played her body, directing her to move this way or that, sometimes in positions she would have balked at in the past. Before Mordr.

So much was going on in so many different places that Miranda didn't know where to concentrate. His hands at her breasts. His erection inside her. His lips kissing her. She wanted to swat at him and order him to do one thing at a time, and then she wanted to tell him, *Whatever you want, baby*.

Her vision went blurry. Her legs, which were looped over his shoulders—*How did that happen?*—went rigid. She was fast climbing to another climax, heightened by the slapping, wet sounds of his private male parts smacking against her female no-longer-private parts. And, yes, it did hurt. A little. But in a good way. For the love of *Fifty Shades*!

When she rose toward an orgasm this time, every nerve ending on her body felt titillated. Her heart was racing. Blood drained from her head. She would have fainted if she were on her feet. She bucked against him, seeking the ultimate reward, an explosion of the senses. For the first time in her life, she experienced what was called female ejaculation.

No sooner did she peak than Mordr pounded hard, hard, hard into her still convulsing channel. Thick cords stood out on his neck as he arched it back and he climaxed with a triumphant roar.

When she came back to her senses (she hadn't fainted, but was definitely dazed), she was splayed out flat on her back with Mordr's heavy weight pinning her to the mattress. His face was at her neck where she could feel his fangs pressing against her skin. Not biting, just letting their presence be known.

After what seemed a long time, Mordr lifted his head and smiled down at her. "That was good for a start."

She did faint then.

Fifteen

He was rusty but no longer broken . . .

$\mathfrak{M}$ordr waited for what seemed a really long time, but was probably only five minutes, for Miranda to wake up. He saw by the bedside clock that it was only midnight. He could have sworn they'd been at it all night.

He eased himself off her and moved them both to the head of the bed, resting on soft pillows. His arms were extended over his head, touching the spindles of the headboard, which, incidentally, gave him some ideas. Miranda was cuddled up against his side, her hand unconsciously lying over his flat belly, which also gave him some ideas.

As sated as he was, he wanted more.

In the meantime, his emotions were banging against the walls of his heart. This had been a life-altering sexual experience for him. The best sex he had ever had. The best sex he would ever have. But more than that. He liked Miranda. She made him smile when he had thought he could never smile again. *Oreo*, he thought, grinning like a lackwit. They could give *Fifty*

Shades a run for its money and then some. His heart swelled just thinking about Miranda.

It was a losing proposition for him, of course. Mike would never allow him to have more than this. In fact, he would cut him off as soon as he found out. The best he could hope for was to build up memories to last him a lifetime and then some.

He dozed off for a moment, his slumber interrupted by the feel of Miranda moving beside him. With one eye cracked open, he observed her trying to crawl away from him and off the bed. He caught her by the ankle just in time and yanked her back to the center of the mattress.

"Where do you think you are going, sweetling?"

"Um," she said, trying to pull the bed linen up and over her nakedness, which he would not allow, flipping it up and off the bed.

What was it about women that they could perform the most outrageous acts in the dead of night, then turn modest as a pure maiden the next morning?

"I was going to the bathroom. I should wash off this . . . wetness."

He put a big hand over the springy curls of her mons, which were indeed damp, and said, "I like your wetness." And that was the truth. He who had once disdained red-haired women now preferred fiery hair, especially down there where slick, crimson curls beckoned him like a lantern on the shore to a lost sailor.

By the runes, I am turning womanish with all these flowery thoughts.

"Mordr," she chided. That was another thing. Women did not like to talk about bodily fluids, like the ones they exuded before and during sex. Men, on the other hand, found it a sign of their sexual expertise. The more the better.

"You're smiling."

"I am happy." For some reason, he was surprised at that admission. In truth, he could not recall many such occasions in recent years when he could say that.

She glanced over to him and couldn't help but notice the size of his continuing enthusiasm. "Mordr," she repeated.

"What?"

"You can't be thinking . . ."

I most definitely can be thinking . . . "Why not? That was just a little bedplay to take the edge off."

"A little! In what world is that little?"

"Remember, I am not of this world exactly."

"I forgot."

He was pleased that she'd forgotten. It made him feel almost normal.

"Aren't you tired?"

"I do not require much sleep. Besides, sex energizes me."

She groaned.

"Go back to sleep," he said, as disappointed as one of the children when told they couldn't stay up late for their favorite TV show. He was pathetic, he decided.

"And what will you be doing while I sleep?"

"Watching you."

She stared at him. "Are you serious? Do you really think I want you watching me when I'm probably drooling in my sleep or some other unattractive thing?"

"I like looking at you. I like looking at your bed-mussed head, knowing that it was created by your thrashing in the heat of lovemaking. With me. I like seeing you snore softly through lips that are swollen from my kisses. I like that your nipples are still engorged and standing out, calling for more attention. I like the few freckles that bloom on your face after a day in the sun. I like the sex flush that still colors your face and neck."

With each reason he gave for watching her, Miranda's jaw dropped lower and lower. But what she said was "I do not snore."

He grinned. "Whatever you say, dearling."

"Said like a man who wants more sex."

He shrugged. "I do."

"Oh, all right."

Her lack of enthusiasm deflated his . . . enthusiasm. "I will not take an unwilling woman, or one not interested in bedplay."

"Are you kidding? I'm a modern woman. You had me with 'I like looking at you.'"

He needed no more encouragement than that and rolled to his back, taking her over with him. Then he lifted her up and over to straddle him, his staff enveloped up to the hilt in her convulsing folds. He saw stars at the intense bliss that suffused all parts of his body, but especially his thankful cock.

Meanwhile, Miranda looked like a bloody queen sitting on a throne. No longer sleepy, her green eyes twinkled with mischief as she wiggled her ass from side to side, presumably to get the right fit, but probably to tease his already heightened senses.

"Witch," he said, putting his hands on her hips to hold her in place until he got his bearings.

"Wretch," she said, and put her hands under her small breasts, lifting them saucily.

His cock twitched inside her.

Which caused her eyes to go wide.

You give, you get, dearling.

He took her hands, guiding her on how he wanted her to explore his body. She did more than that. She whispered praise to every part of his battle-scarred body that she touched and caressed and even kissed, the whole while with him still imbedded in her depths.

"Ride me," he directed.

And she did, bless her modern woman's heart.

This time he let her sleep and went into the bathroom to shower again. When he came out, he hoped selfishly that she was awake and they could have another bout of sex. Yes, he was a brute demanding so much of her, but he was a long-hungry man who could not be satisfied with just one meal. His window of opportunity might be slamming shut any minute now. Once Michael discovered what he was about.

She slept peacefully, though, with a small smile on her lips that he had put there, he hoped.

He dressed quietly in the short pants he'd worn that day, and nothing more. It was only two a.m. Checking on the children, he noted that they were all asleep. He could not dwell for very long in the room where Linda slept, her arms wrapped around a stuffed woolly lamb. She reminded him too much of Kata.

He made his way barefooted down the stairs. The kitchen light was on. He couldn't recall having left it on, but he might have. He wasn't unduly concerned about intruders, so secure had they made Miranda's house. Even so, he opened the hall closet and took out the sword he'd hidden there.

He wasn't totally surprised to find, sitting around the table, drinking what had to be the last of his beer, not just Cnut and Harek, but Ivak and Trond, as well. The fierce guard dog Ruff was on his back, legs in the air, fast asleep on his rug by the sliding patio doors, dreaming doggie dreams, interspersed with drips of drool and occasional grumbles. Wet dreams, Mordr presumed.

But that wasn't the important thing. Mordr went immediately alert. Why were his brothers here?

Ivak was the first to notice him. "Well, well, well. Someone has been getting some."

"Some what?" Harek asked, and turned to see him.

"Oh, that. He has been mooning over the lovely Miranda ever since he got here."

"And she has red hair!" Cnut told them. "You all know how Mordr mislikes red hair on his wenches."

"Apparently, not so much anymore if those scratch marks on his shoulders are any indication," Ivak commented.

Mordr propped his sword against the wall and barely restrained himself from touching those scratches, with pleasure that his woman had marked him so. *No, no, no*, he thought, *she is not my woman. Just my woman of the moment. Bloody hell, I am losing my mind*.

"Why are your eyes crossed?" This from Harek, who had found his spare package of Oreos and was gobbling them up. Beer and Oreos . . . what a combination!

"So, have you regained your virility?" Trond wanted to know.

"I never lost my virility," Mordr growled.

Four sets of eyebrows rose at that declaration.

"I just lost the inclination," he contended, knowing how dumb the words sounded even before they left his mouth.

"And now you have it back?" Cnut inquired.

Mordr let a smile emerge slowly on his lips. That was all he would say on the matter.

"Praise God!" Ivak exclaimed. "The gruesome one is smiling!"

"We finally have our brother back," Harek said, "and it only took one thousand, one hundred, and sixty-four years."

"To Mordr!" Trond raised his beer bottle in the air. The others did likewise.

But then Cnut asked the all-important question, "What will Michael say?"

That put a damper on their moods. None of them liked to be in the archangel's crosshairs.

"So, why are you all here?" Mordr asked.

A voice behind him said, "Jasper's Sin City mission ends on Wednesday night with the culmination of the Perverts Anonymous convention." It was Zebulan the Hebrew, their Lucie special agent.

Mordr was getting kind of tired of Miranda's house being an open turnstile for his comrades. Locked doors and security alarms meant nothing to creatures who could teletransport. But Zeb was a friend. Of sorts. In any case, he always brought valuable information. He was not in his Lucipire persona tonight, but instead wore jeans, a white T-shirt, and his familiar Blue Devils baseball cap. Typical two-thousand-year-old twenty-first-century jock.

"Whatever you are going to do will have to be done before that time," Zeb continued. "I have to say, this project for Jasper has been highly successful. He's preening about, crowing like cock of the roost. Between Las Vegas, Reno, Macau, and Monaco, he's had about six hundred kills. Dead humans now in Jasper's killing jars. He's expecting to hit a thousand over the next four days."

This was bad. Very bad. Every new Lucipire was a challenge to the vangels. Jasper's troops would far outnumber the vangels now. Michael would be livid. Hell and damnation! Mordr was livid himself.

They spent the next hour discussing a strategy for destroying the most Lucipires and saving as many redeemable sinners as possible. Mordr was especially talented at battle planning and they were all satisfied with the preparations when they were done.

"Well, I must be off. A devil's work is never done," Zeb remarked with dark humor as he stood and stretched. "By the by, you're looking rather pale tonight, Mordr. Mayhap you need to come back into the city with me. I can point out the not-so-bad sinners if you are losing the touch."

"Dost think so, Zeb?" Trond asked with tongue firmly planted in cheek. In other words, humor at Mordr's expense. "I'm thinking he looks flushed."

"And he smells like a flower in case anyone hasn't noticed," Ivak added.

"Shouldn't you be home with your pregnant wife?" Mordr asked Ivak.

"She is not due yet, and she will let me know when I am needed." Ivak grinned at Mordr. "Thank you for asking."

"That is not why I asked," Mordr grumbled.

"I know," Ivak said.

"Congratulations," Zeb said to Ivak with a decided glint of envy in his eyes. Rumor was that the former Hebrew Roman soldier—*and wasn't that a contradiction in terms?*—had lost several children in his human life. Like Mordr.

Leave it to Trond to not drop the subject. "Mordr has five children now, did you know that, Zeb?"

"No!" Zeb appeared shocked. He knew Mordr's history well.

"They are not my children. They are the children I was sent here to protect." Mordr's explanation sounded weak even to his own ears.

Just then a female voice could be heard calling out from the stairway, "Mordr? Are you down here?"

Mordr put his face in his hands, knowing what was to come.

Four beaming faces, no, five, including Zeb's, turned to the doorway where Miranda soon stood, wearing naught but his "Vikings Rule" T-shirt, which extended only to mid-thigh. Her red hair was wild and sex-mussed. Her lips appeared bruised and ripe from kissing. The sex flush remained on her face and neck. He hadn't fed on her, but she had the imprint of his fangs on her neck, nonetheless. She had a suck mark on the inside of one knee. She was Playboy Bunny of the Year, Bimbo Barbie, and Male Fantasy Number One, all in one neat come-to-bed-lover package.

"There is a God," Zeb said into the stunned silence.

"Amen!" the rest of them concurred. Except Mordr. He was speechless.

And that wasn't the worst thing.

The motion detectors caused all the outdoor lights to go on suddenly, followed by the ringing of the doorbell. At four a.m.!

"It wouldn't be a Lucie," Zeb told them quickly. "We don't announce ourselves with doorbells or knocking or other civilized greetings."

Miranda gasped. By use of the word *we*, Zeb had outed himself as Lucipire.

"Roger wouldn't come knocking at four a.m., either," Mordr concluded, "unless he's a total idiot."

"He *is* an idiot," Miranda said, and with no sense at all when it came to her safety, headed back down the hallway toward the front door. Mordr practically tripped over his feet racing after her, with his brothers and a demon vampire close on his heels. Ruff shuffled along after them, bringing up the rear reluctantly, giving only an occasional halfhearted bark. The dog obviously did not like having his sleep interrupted.

"You are going to give me a heart attack." Mordr hauled Miranda back with a hand on her upper arm just before she reached the door. Pushing her behind him, he gazed through the peephole, then cursed, "What a dragon fuck this is turning out to be!"

"Swear jar!" Harek said behind him.

"What's a swear jar?" Ivak wanted to know.

"Ruff!" Ruff said.

"Would you all shut up?" This from Miranda, who surprised them all.

"Ruff, ruff, ruff!"

"Somebody grab the dog by his collar before he bites one of you by mistake." Mordr was already undoing the dead bolts and high-tech locking systems on the door. Before he opened the door, he turned to the others and said, "I forewarn you all. Do not make rash judgments about what . . . who you are about to meet."

The door swung open and there stood a six foot two male in a red spandex miniskirt, hooker high heels, huge fake boobs, a blond wig, false eyelashes, and siren-red lipstick. "Hey, Mordr," Jack Trixson said in a deep male voice. "Just finished working and was passing by in the neighborhood, saw your lights on, and thought I'd drop by."

"I forgot you lived in the neighborhood," Mordr said dumbly.

Jack, his square jaw gaping with amazement, was enjoying his first view of Miranda the Sex Wench as she stepped around him. That, combined with five big Vikings and an equally big demon, must have appeared like an orgy. In fact, Jack said, "I didn't mean to interrupt your party."

His brothers and Zeb were enjoying this scene and his discomfort immensely. Ruff was just sniffing the newcomer.

"I cannot wait to tell Vikar," Harek hooted.

"Forget Vikar. I cannot wait to tell all of vangeldom about Mordr's unusual friend," Ivak said. Then he addressed Jack, "No offense, but you have to know our brother Mordr to understand how funny this is."

"Mike must be having a coronary," Cnut contributed.

Miranda made a gurgling noise, then turned on her heels and started back toward the stairs. "I'm going back to bed."

"Good idea," Mordr called after her as he waved Jack inside. "I'll be up shortly."

She turned and gave him a look that would melt concrete.

"Or mayhap not."

Once she was gone, and Ruff had gone back to his rug in the kitchen, Jack said, "Actually, there's a reason I stopped by. Do you know some guy named Roger Jessup?"

Bad and badder . . .

"The trouble with you, Rog, is that you haven't thought this thing through," Clarence said, and cracked his knuckles . . . his new favorite, irritating habit.

"That's all I've done. Think." *And no action.*

He'd gone to Miranda's neighborhood every day and hadn't found a way to gain entry to her house without setting off alarms. He was a master electrician and probably could have figured out a way to bypass the alarm system given enough time and access, neither of which he had.

He *had* managed to see his kids playing in the yard, but only from a distance. He'd discovered, also via binoculars, that some big blond dude was living there in his house, probably nailing the bitch in front of his kids. And, yes, he thought of it as his house since it had no doubt been purchased with his money from the sale of his house. Not to mention the big-ass, expensive Lexus SUV that came and went. Also probably purchased with his money.

It was enough to make his blood boil.

Clarence cracked his knuckles. Again. He was standing in front of the mirror on the wall between the kitchenette and living room, admiring the fake diamond earrings in the ears he'd had pierced yesterday. He thought he looked cool ever since he'd starting wearing Lamar's clothing, but Roger thought he looked like a bad Hollywood caricature of a black ghetto pimp. A long-sleeved, red nylon shirt, unbuttoned to the navel, tucked into hip-hugging black pants, and of course the requisite gold chains around his neck.

"You gotta think like a criminal, Rog." Clarence turned away from the mirror. "No pussyfootin' around, worryin' 'bout this or that possibility. Jump right in, guns blazin'."

Crack, crack, crack.

"Take me, fer instance," Clarence said. "I decided that Vegas was the place for me to settle down. Pimpin' was a job that suited me just fine. But my cuz Lamar was becomin' a royal pain-in-the-ass . . . get it, Vegas, royal flush, royal pain. Ha, ha, ha!" *Crack, crack, crack.* "So, I eliminated my cuz and now I'm king of the roost." He beamed at Roger, as if he'd accomplished some great feat.

Roger assumed that Clarence had killed Lamar, but he hadn't asked for details. All he knew was that Lamar was missing and Clarence—who smelled more and more like lemons these days, which was better than his prior B.O.—had taken over the pimping business. Roger was handling the accounting, such as it was. Scheduling which hooker went to what corner, and raking in the cash, which Clarence kept in a safe bolted to the floor in the hall closet.

The only good thing in this mess that had become his life was that Roger had ordered one of the whores, Carlotta, to clean up the apartment and keep it clean. Carlotta had even called in an exterminator to get rid of the cockroaches, which had infuriated the pizza operator on the ground level because apparently the roaches up here scurried on down there. To which Carlotta had said, "Go suck your own dick, Luigi."

Carlotta, overaged for a hooker at thirty, was grateful for work that didn't involve lying on her back with her legs spread. Actually, he kind of liked Carlotta, and not just because she gave a good blow job. She knew his history and sympathized over his anger toward Miranda. "The bitch needs to pay," Carlotta had said more than once in the midst of licking his balls. Yeah, you had to appreciate a good woman.

"What would you suggest?" Roger asked Clarence.

Clarence flashed him a sly glance and went to the freezer to get himself a glass of ice, over which he poured his usual Pepsi.

Roger barely stifled a groan. The next half hour would be filled with cracking and crunching,

"Let me see that picture again," Clarence said. *Crunch, crunch, crack, crack.*

Roger knew which picture he meant. It was a photo of Miranda in their backyard playing croquet or some shit game with his kids, all five of them. It had been taken with a zoom lens from the upper floor of a vacant house for sale a half block away.

"Here's the first thing you need to decide," proffered the all-wise Clarence, or so he thought he was. *Crunch, crunch, crack, crack.* "What are you gonna do with five kids once you off Miranda?"

"Huh?"

"Do you want custody of your kids?"

"Well, yeah. I mean, sure."

"Where would you live?"

"In that house . . . my house," he said tentatively. "Or I could sell it and move somewhere else."

"You're assuming the court would give you custody."

"Sure. Why not? I'm the father. With Miranda no longer around, why wouldn't they?"

Clarence shrugged, not so certain, but then Clarence was skeptical about the fairness of the court system. Roger was, too.

"What are you getting at, Clarence?"

"Be honest, bro. What you'd really like is Miranda out of the way, the kids in foster care, and you with the cash to do whatever you want, probably far from Vegas. Seriously, some men are made to be fathers. I don't see you caring that much about your kids."

Clarence was probably right, but Roger didn't like his pointing out his shortcomings.

"It's no crime not to be wanting snot-nosed kids hanging on you for the rest of yer life. And they cost a shitload of money to raise. Clothes, food, all that crap."

"It's just that my wife turned the kids against me. All I had to do was holler and they jumped to her defense. Hard to love children who don't love you back."

Clarence nodded. "Here's the deal. I can take care of Miranda for you. They'd never find her body or be able to trace her disappearance to you. Child protective services would be on your family like flies on a manure pile, taking your kids away, unless you decide to fight for them. You'd get the house and car and money to go off for a new start somewheres else. Maybe the Bahamas. Yeah, that would be cool. Sun, beach, hot women, no kids."

That sounded incredibly good to Roger, who wanted desperately to escape from this shithole of an apartment and shithole of a life. A new beginning, that's what he wanted. But he also knew that Clarence wouldn't do this for nothing.

He looked up at Clarence, who'd stopped crunching and cracking. The icy expression on his face chilled Roger, who should have been accustomed to Clarence's mood swings by now. He was a schizo just waiting to happen.

"What would it cost for you to do this 'favor' for me?"

"A 'date.' I want you to set me up on a 'date.'"

"With Miranda?" Roger asked incredulously.

"Hell no. With yer daughter."

"What?" Roger was shocked. "*What?*"

"You heard me."

"Maggie's only ten years old."

"Not that one," Clarence said with absolutely no shame. "The other one." He walked over and tapped a fingertip on the photograph, dead center on his five-year-old daughter, Linda.

"You are one sick bastard," Roger said before he had a chance to curb his tongue.

"Yeah, but I'm the sick bastard who can save yer lily-white ass a whole lot of trouble. Besides, you're a wife beater who wants to murder someone. Who's the sick bastard here?" He flicked a fingertip against Roger's ear as he passed by on his way to the doorway, where he picked up one of Lamar's old Panama hats from the coatrack. "And, by the way, you have until tomorrow to decide, or get the fuck out of here. Find another place to freeload. George and Ginette are looking fer a place."

George and Ginette were a weird couple that Clarence had become chummy with. Sometimes they were practically movie-star gorgeous with great clothes and pleasing personalities. Other times they appeared to have fangs and a rotten egg smell about them. The creepy thing was, they wanted Clarence to let them suck his blood, just a little. In fact, Roger had awakened one night to find Ginette in bed with him, naked, trying to fang his neck. She'd even gotten a little bite in before he'd managed to shove her out of the bed.

The door slammed behind Clarence.

Roger just stared at the closed door. He needed to get out of this place.

But how could he "sell" his own child?

Roger thought it over and realized he had no particular fondness or bond with the little girl, even if she was his own blood. It was the idea of a grown man having sexual activity with a child that grossed him out, and there was no doubt that was what Clarence had in mind when he mentioned a "date."

But what could it hurt if it was only for one night? Would that be so bad? Over and done with in a matter of hours. Maybe they could slip the kid a roofie or something, and she wouldn't suffer too much.

No, he couldn't do it. There had to be another way.

Rubbing the mosquito bite on his neck that was still itchy, Roger pondered the situation. Maybe he could pretend to Clarence that he was willing. Wait for him to kill that damn Miranda, then renege on the deal. Of course, the only way that would work would be if Roger then killed Clarence, too. Now, there was an idea that held some appeal.

Roger had a lot to think about.

But, first, he had a sudden yearning for a glass of lemonade.

Sixteen

The Energizer Bunny had nothing on them ...

The following day was a Sunday, so Miranda was home all day.

Despite her mortification over Mordr's brothers and the cross-dressing neighbor seeing her post-sex, Miranda couldn't stay mad at Mordr.

She was insatiable. Mordr was insatiable. Together they were like a pair of sex-starved rabbits. She swore she would be walking bowlegged to work the next day. Mordr swore his cock would be worn down to a nubbin.

Even with five sets of curious eyes, they managed to have sex every other hour. The key was finding a place to be alone, which they managed. Boy, did they manage! In the laundry room on top of the washing machine during the spin cycle. In her office with him on the desk chair and her kneeling on the floor. In her office with Mordr taking her on top of the desk, from behind. Near-sex in the shed when she'd gone out to search for some clay pots; Ruff had interrupted what he must have considered a game; he'd wanted to play, too. They were saving the den recliner for later.

Mordr had tried to talk the kids—okay, bribe the

kids—into taking a nap to recover from their long time in the sun the previous day . . . to recharge their batteries, so to speak. They'd looked at him like he'd lost his mind. They were children. They didn't need to recharge anything, their energy supply being endless.

Fortunately, or not so fortunately, Darla showed up late in the afternoon. To return a blouse she'd borrowed last week, she said, but really in hopes of catching a glimpse of one of the Viking studs Miranda kept telling her about. No such luck! The men were gone for now, except for Mordr.

After pouring two iced glasses of sweet tea, Miranda went out on the patio to chat with Darla.

The children were down in the basement, which Miranda used for a storage area, never having gotten around to renovating the space. Mordr had cleared one part of the large room between their bouts of sex today and somehow managed to have a Ping-Pong table delivered on a Sunday. The kids and Mordr were engaged in a tournament at the moment. He'd suggested that he and Miranda play strip Ping-Pong later. Like strip poker, but more energetic.

That energy thing again!

"So, I take it that your undercover bodyguard is doing a good job," Darla said, her eyes twinkling with mischief. "Emphasis on undercover."

No use trying to hide anything from her good friend. Darla knew her too well. "An excellent job. Above and beyond."

"Don't you mean above and below?"

"You are bad, Darla."

"And he knows his way around the bedsheets?"

Miranda rolled her eyes.

"That good?"

"Oh. My. God!" That's all she would say on the subject, but Darla got her drift.

"And he has brothers?"

"Six, but only three of them eligible."

"Three is enough." Darla sipped at her tea, then spoke again. "No more threats from Roger?"

"Nothing direct." She told Darla about the neighbor who found a van parked in her driveway with the occupants watching Miranda's house. And then, last night, Jack Trixson mentioned rumors were circulating on the Strip about some really vile character named Clarence, a new pimp on the street, who was talking about a hit he was going to perform for his good friend Roger. Miranda's name had come up.

What kind of criminal announced his crime ahead of time? An inept one, she concluded, but even inept criminals could be dangerous.

Mordr had advised Jack to take a vacation this week, that it wasn't safe to be in the city over the next few days. When Jack had asked him to elaborate, Mordr refused but emphasized, "Trust me."

"If this is true, shouldn't I be warning other people? My boss? Other members of our dance revue?"

Mordr had shaken his head. "I'm already out of line telling you of the threat."

"Must be terrorists," Jack had muttered, and Mordr had not bothered to correct him. In a way, they were the same thing.

Miranda felt the need to do the same favor for Darla. "I want you to take a leave from work this week, Darla. Come and stay here with me."

"Three's a crowd, honey."

"Crowds R Us. There are already seven of us here, and people coming and going like a revolving door at Macy's."

"I don't understand why you would warn me away from the city. Roger has no bone to pick with me. I doubt he even knows we're friends."

"It's not just Roger. Something bad is going down in Vegas any day now, and take my word on it . . . you don't want to be around."

"And you're not going to tell me what this something bad is?"

Miranda shook her head. She wished she could tell Darla about the vangels and the Lucipires and the whole St. Michael the Archangel business, but she'd promised Mordr that she would say nothing. Besides, Darla would never believe her. Miranda wasn't sure she believed it herself.

Mordr opened the sliding glass door to the kitchen and, without greeting, addressed Darla, "Did you bring a weapon with you? Can you stay for a few hours until I get back?" He had a high-tech cell phone in hand and appeared to have just finished a call. "I need to go out, but I can't leave Miranda and the children without protection."

"Uh, I'm standing right here," Miranda said.

"I know you are, sweetling." He leaned down and kissed her smack on the lips before turning back to Darla, whose mouth had dropped open at such open affection. His kiss must seem like a declaration of some sort, but Miranda knew better. It was just Mordr getting horny again.

Darla clicked her jaw shut. "Yes, I have a pistol in the glove compartment of my car, and I can stay as long as you need me. Is it Roger? Jeez, I'd love to nab the creep myself. A bullet to his family jewels, for a start." She made a gun with her forefinger and thumb. "Bam, bam!"

Mordr fought a grin at Darla's bloodthirstiness. "No, it's not Roger this time. Leastways, I do not think it is. This is another danger."

Darla exchanged a quick glance with Miranda.

"I do not think there is any threat out here in the

suburbs, but do not take any chances. Keep all the doors and windows locked. Open to no one."

"Except for you and your brothers, right?" Miranda asked.

"Not even for us."

The implication was they could teletransport inside, if need be. *Oh boy!*

"Keep your weapon at hand at all times, preferably on your person. Miranda can give you a shirt or something to hide it from the children."

"Wow! You're really serious about this danger, aren't you?"

"Serious as sin."

"And you're not going to tell me jackshit about what's going on. I don't like being kept out of the loop when my person and that of my friends and associates are in peril."

"It has to be that way."

"Sort of like, if you told me, you'd have to kill me."

"Exactly like." He waggled his eyebrows at Darla to confuse her about whether he was serious or not.

After giving Darla more instructions, Mordr flicked his fingers for Miranda to follow him upstairs. Under normal circumstances, she would tell him what he could flick, but he added, "Come, talk to me while I change my clothes, sweetling."

Sweetling? Darla mouthed at her, but Miranda suspected that, despite the endearment, Mordr had something else in mind.

Man in Black. Cloak and weapons. "I thought this was supposed to happen tomorrow night."

"Schedule change. Jasper and his demon vampires will be gone by midnight."

Once they were upstairs, he shut the door behind them and tossed her onto the bed before she could blink. He spread her legs and knelt between her knees.

"I thought you were in a hurry." Men! she mused. Even in the midst of impending danger, or perhaps because of impending danger, they had to have one last roll in the hay.

He pulled his T-shirt up and over his head, tossing it over his shoulder. "I have a half hour. I can be re-clothed in three minutes. That leaves me twenty-seven minutes with nothing to do. Any suggestions?"

"Not as many as you have, I'll bet."

"You have no idea." He pulled the claw comb from her hair and spread the tresses out over the pillow. Mordr had developed a liking for wavy red hair.

What could she say? She'd developed a liking for grim Vikings.

"So many things I want to do to you," he murmured. "So many things I want to show you."

"How about the things I want to do to you?"

He smiled. "I haven't even shown you the Viking S-spot yet."

"I can't wait."

"Or doggie sex."

"Uh."

She loved this playful side to Mordr. But he was scaring her a little bit, too. Like time was running out and he was trying to cram in all the memories he could. She'd known theirs was not going to be a long-term relationship. Still . . .

He unbuttoned her blouse and undid the front closure on her black silk bra, staring down at her. Rubbing his palms in a circular fashion over her bare breasts, he said, "Mine."

She cupped the bulge in his shorts. "Does that mean this is mine, as well?"

"Always."

That sounded promising. Maybe she was misreading his rush to fill every moment.

Unzipping but not removing his shorts, he released himself. No underwear, but then why would there be with all the sex they'd been having? More convenient.

He did help her shimmy out of her shorts, though, leaving just the opened bra and matching black silk bikini panties. Wasting no time, he moved the crotch of her panties aside, took his erection in hand, and slid right in.

Whoa! Miranda hadn't realized she was so ready. She hadn't realized she wanted this as much as he did.

He rocked her then. Back and forth. Back and forth. With deliberate, torturous slowness.

She wanted to caress his body, to lean up for a kiss, but he would not allow that. In fact, he laced her fingers with his and extended them above her head. The whole time he held her gaze. "Your eyes tell all your secrets. Do not hide from me."

She writhed and tried to get him to move faster, to touch her in those special places, but he remained firm. Just slow rocking, back and forth.

But then she realized that the rocking was going a little bit more forward and touching her most sensitive place. Her eyes went wide, and she gasped at the pleasure that was so much more intense because it came and went. Touch, release. Touch, release.

She moaned.

"Tell me," he said. "Tell me what you want."

She did, but he was not satisfied with a mere "harder" or "faster." He forced her to tell him in graphic detail what she wanted him to do and how it felt when he did. She used words she'd never said aloud before.

Still, he rocked them slowly, and she felt the mounting tension in her become a delicious agony. She arched her back so that her nipples could abrade the blond fur of his chest. So aroused was she in the end that she became disoriented.

"Please, please, please," she begged.

When he paused in rocking, she could swear he grew even larger inside her. Then, leaning down, he took one nipple in his mouth and drew on her, hard. At the same time he withdrew his penis, then slammed into her.

Her orgasm was immediate and shattering, ripping across her entire body. She would have screamed, except he put a gentle hand over her mouth, "Shh, shh, that is the way. Relax. Do not try to control the peaking. Surrender. Sur-ren-der!"

He stopped speaking abruptly because his own climax was approaching. She would have liked to turn the tables on him, to tell him to relax, to surrender to the orgasm, but she was speechless as the folds of her vagina continued to clutch and unclutch him until he roared out his own release.

It took several moments for their heavy breathing to slow. Easing out of her, he rolled over. With his arm around her shoulders, he tucked her into his side.

She laid her face against his chest, feeling the steady beat of his heart. A comfort of sorts. He was alive, no matter what he said, no matter what he was.

He kissed the top of her head. "Thank you, Miranda."

"For what? Sex?"

He pinched her bottom. "That, too. But, no, I thank you for bringing me out of the dark. I will be forever grateful for that."

"That sounds an awful lot like good-bye."

"I must go soon," he said, deliberately misinterpreting what she meant and rising from the bed.

"You will come back, won't you?"

"Of course. My main mission here is incomplete. Roger is out there, a threat."

Pride kept her from asking if that was the only reason. Pride kept her from telling him that she was falling in love with him, fearing it was one-sided. Pride had her reclipping her bra, adjusting her panties, and watching as he dressed quickly and efficiently. He unlocked a long, flat chest he'd fitted in the back of her closet and took out various weapons, which he placed in strategic pockets of his pants. A knife went into his boot. A gun in a shoulder holster. And that was just the arsenal on his person. When he put on his long cloak with the silver angel-wing epaulets, she couldn't help but notice the firearms. A folding sword, throwing stars, a wicked-looking stick covered with sharp points. His fangs kept trying to emerge and she could see the constant effort he made to retract them until he was away from here.

If she hadn't realized it before, she did now. He was facing danger tonight. Mortal danger. "Mordr, could you die while fighting the demon vampires?"

"Death holds no fear for me. If I 'die,' I will either recover or go to that holding place in the heavens for vangels, Tranquility, until the final reckoning. No, the biggest fear for a vangel is that we be taken by Jasper and that he attempt to torture us into turning to his side." He shivered as he imagined some horror Miranda couldn't possibly comprehend, but it must be bad.

"You look very pale, Mordr. And I notice you swaying on your feet occasionally. What's wrong?"

He shrugged. "I need to feed, by saving some sinner or killing some Lucies. Never fear, I will have my strength back shortly."

"But you shouldn't be going into battle, or whatever this will be tonight, in a weakened state. It would make you vulnerable," she guessed. Something occurred to her then. "Would it help if you took some of my blood?"

Mordr had been bent over, tying some kind of cross-gartered scabbard onto one thigh. His head shot up and he looked at her, his blue eyes more silvery gray than normal. She had noticed that they changed when he was aroused, but this was even more extreme. Must be some kind of bloodlust thing. "It would help, but I would not ask that of you."

"I am offering," she said with more outward bravery than she actually felt inside. Let's face it. She had no idea what exactly she was offering.

He was about to refuse, she could tell, but she got up off the bed and walked over to him resolutely. Taking his face in her hands, she said, "Do what you need to do."

He hesitated but then lifted her in his arms and carried her across the room. Sitting down in a chair with her on his lap, his cloak puddled out and around them onto the floor. "I will only take a little," he said huskily.

"Will it hurt?"

A smile tried to emerge on his lips. His fangs were fully extended. "Just a pinch. Usually, when there is a blood giving between a man and a woman, it is done during the sex act."

"What? No way are we having sex again! I couldn't possibly . . ."

He did smile then, and that wonderful aura of scented fog surrounded them, sandalwood and limes. He sniffed the air, noticing the same thing, except what he would be smelling was lilies and cloves. The perfumes that life mates supposedly put forth, like pheromones. *Good heavens! When did I become a believer?*

He turned her head so that it was arched to one side, exposing the long sweep of neck from ear to shoulder.

He licked her then, and it felt like warm oil heating the skin, tingling. When he put his mouth to her and bit into the skin, there was a pinch. But then, as he sucked softly, she felt a hot, gushing sensation through her veins, from that spot to all her extremities, lodging especially in her lips, and breasts, and hands and toes, and inside her most intimate place. The sensations were so intense she lost consciousness, but only for the few moments that Mordr sucked on her.

As he laid her back on the bed, she could see that Mordr's skin tone had already changed to a healthy tan. His fangs had retracted and there was no blood that she could see in his mouth.

"I must go," he said. Then he did the oddest, most touching thing. He placed a palm over his heart, then opened the hand, extending it toward her in an ancient gesture.

She must have fallen asleep then, for when she opened her eyes again, he was gone. She dressed in biking shorts and a long T-shirt, tying her hair back into a ponytail. The house was quiet when she went downstairs. In the kitchen, she was making herself a cup of herb tea when Darla came up from the basement. "Those kids are ruthless," she said. "I lost five dollars to Sam over a stupid Ping-Pong game. I know, I know, I shouldn't be encouraging his betting."

Darla, bless her heart, was making an effort to divert her attention from Mordr's departure and what it might mean, although Darla didn't have a clue as to the extent of the danger he faced.

"What do you say that we have quick spaghetti for dinner?" Miranda asked. "There's garlic toast in the freezer."

"Sounds good to me. I'll make the salad."

Just then there was a buzzing noise, indicating the motion detector had gone off outside, followed by the ringing of the doorbell. She and Darla exchanged worried glances. They both approached the front door with caution, Darla having grabbed her pistol from a purse above the fridge.

Looking through the peephole, Darla said with surprise, "It's a policeman. Were you expecting one?"

Miranda shook her head. "But Mordr said not to open the door to anyone."

More ringing of the doorbell, followed by knocking, and a male voice saying, "Las Vegas Police Department. Open up, please."

Darla opened the door slightly, leaving the chain in place. "Pass me your credentials."

"Yes, ma'am." The big black man in uniform handed through a leather folding case holding a LVPD badge on one side and a card identifying him as Sergeant Amos Doram on the other side. Through the partially open door she could see a police car parked at the curb with another cop inside.

Darla handed the credentials back and asked, "What's the problem, Officer?"

"We had a report of a suspicious character lurking about this address. We have him down at the station right now for carrying a weapon without a license. He claims to know a Ms. Miranda Hart. Are you Ms. Hart? You need to come down to the station and see if you recognize him. I have a photograph here."

Miranda and Darla exchanged glances and both said, "Roger" at the same time. Sure enough, the wallet-size picture the cop handed through was Roger in all his slimy glory, smiling at the camera in a police mug shot. The date stamp said it had been taken today.

Darla undid the chain and opened the door for the cop to come in.

Officer Doram smiled then. Their first clue that they might have made a mistake came when they noticed that he sported a gold-filled front tooth and diamond ear studs the size of peas. What kind of cop had gold teeth and earrings?

The second clue was when they saw that his smile wasn't directed at them, but at Linda, who had come up from the basement and was watching them from the kitchen. "Come here, baby girl," the pseudo cop crooned. The expression on his face was pure evil.

Darla began to raise her pistol, but Doram was quicker. He raised his own weapon and whacked Darla over the head, causing her to crumple to the floor.

"Aunt Mir!" Linda screamed, running into Miranda's arms and hiding her face in her neck.

Doram grabbed Miranda by the upper arm and dragged her out of the house toward the waiting car, where the other "officer" was holding the door open.

"Daad-dy!" Linda shouted joyfully on seeing that the guy in police uniform was Roger.

Just then a bunch of things happened at once. Miranda and Linda were shoved into the backseat, where the doors automatically locked.

Another police cruiser pulled up behind them, and two other officers, a man and a woman, stepped out.

"George, Ginette, what the hell are you doin' here? Are you followin' me?" Doram bellowed.

"Your time is up, Clarence," the woman said.

Clarence? Who's Clarence? Miranda wondered. *Oh. The cop's real name must be Clarence.*

"It's come-to-Jesus time, Clarence. Or rather, come-to-Satan time. Ha, ha, ha!" the man said.

With those words, the most amazing, frightening thing happened. Before their very eyes, the couple transformed into these huge fanged beasts, with oozing scales, red eyes, and tails. Clarence shot several rounds at them, to no avail. The bullets just bounced off their leathery hides. The beasts . . . demon vampires

like the ones Miranda had seen in the city with Mordr
. . . immediately began to fang and gnaw at Clarence.

"Holy crap! Holy crap!" Roger exclaimed, as shaken
as Miranda at what they were witnessing. He ran
around to the driver's side, putting the car in gear and
zooming off. But he had to turn around at the cul-de-
sac.

Miranda tucked a crying Linda into her chest, hiding
her face, but Miranda glanced over on the return past
her house to see the big black man being devoured and
slowly dissolving. That was the only way she could describe it. When the beasts were done, they transformed
back into their human forms, got back in the police car,
and drove away, leaving behind Doram's . . . or Clarence's . . . cop clothes, a gun, and a pile of slime.

What would her neighbors think? Had any of them
even seen what was happening?

Turning back to the wire screen between the backseat and the front seat, she asked, "What in God's name
have you gotten yourself involved in, Roger?"

"I don't know, I don't know." Roger seemed stunned.
Well, who wouldn't be, seeing two beasts devouring a
man, even a bad man? Roger was driving erratically. If
he wasn't careful, they were going to be stopped by—
oh, this was too bizarre—the cops.

"Where are we going, Roger?"

"I don't know, I don't know."

"Why don't you just take us back and we'll forget
this ever happened?"

"Can't do that."

"So, what's the plan?"

"The plan was . . . is . . . to kill you and get back
all the things I'm entitled to. Money, house, car . . . a
Lexus, ferchrissake."

"The Lexus doesn't belong to me."

"Huh?"

"It belongs to my . . . um, friend, Mordr."

"Whatever! The house does. You stole my house and bought this house so, technically, it belongs to me."

How could you reason with such illogic?

"So, after you get rid of me, what about Linda?"

Linda turned in her arms and smiled. "Hi, Daddy."

Roger groaned. "The kid was never supposed to be involved. Clarence was going to gain me entry to your house. I was gonna kill you and Clarence, then go into hiding for a couple weeks, then come claim my 'inheritance.' But I never counted on those . . . those . . . things arriving. I knew there was something strange about George and Ginette, but . . ." He shivered with revulsion.

"You can't kill me now," she said.

"Why not?"

"Because Linda recognizes you—" She cut herself off when she realized that she was pointing out to this madman that if he offed her, he would have to do the same to his own daughter. And he was just deranged enough to do it.

Soon Roger pulled onto a side street in Vegas in front of Luigi's Pizza Parlor, then he went around to an alley behind the shop.

"We're stopping for pizza?" she asked incredulously. "I'll have sausage and mushroom." Her attempt at humor fell flat.

"No food, bitch. We're going to the apartment upstairs. And here's the deal. You come voluntarily and quietly or I take Linda, and you don't want to know what I will do with her, daughter or not."

Holding Linda's hand, Miranda followed Roger up the back stairs to the apartment above the shop, which was permeated with the scent of tomato sauce and cheese and baked crusts. To her surprise, there was another coconspirator in this crime spree.

A bleached blond woman wearing a short skirt, and no underwear, had her feet propped on the coffee table, knees widespread, and was painting her toenails a flaming red.

"We have company, Carlotta," Roger said. "Where are those velvet handcuffs I bought you yesterday?"

Carlotta summed the situation up perfectly. "Oh shit!"

Seventeen

Even the mighty do fall . . .

By ten p.m. nets of vangels were covering the cities of Las Vegas, Reno, Monaco, and Macau, trying to catch any Lucipires attempting to escape. And at the same time, walking the streets and strolling the casinos, looking for sinners about to be taken who might be up for redemption. All of this needed to be done with as much secrecy as possible.

It wasn't a perfect plan, and many of the Lucipires would escape to wreak more havoc in other places, or even back to casino cities in the future. But still, Mordr estimated that many hundreds of them would meet their doom.

He and Vikar were heading the Las Vegas operation with two hundred vangel soldiers. Ivak and Harek were in Reno, Sigurd and Cnut in Macau, and Trond in Monaco, with similar contingents of vangels working under them.

With the special secure cell phone to his ear, the one only vangels could transmit on, Mordr waited for Vikar's signal to begin. With a slash of his arm downward, Vikar teletransported to the far side of the city, while Mordr relayed directions to his brothers and then began his own battles. Bloody pandemonium ensued, or you could say slimy pandemonium.

Even after all these years, it was intimidating sometimes for Mordr when he first came upon a Lucie in full demonoid form. Often heads taller than his six foot four, strong as *drukkinn* dragons, stinking like rotten eggs, whipping their massive tails, and waving their claw-like fists.

Vikings were not happy at all with their fangs, but imagine how horrible it would have been if Michael had given them these other beastly attributes as well. And Michael could have done it, too, not having a particular liking for Vikings as a whole.

Mordr, along with six of his best fighters, swooped down to the Strip and the hotel where Jasper and his mung assistant Beltane were supposed to be staying. He caught them leaving the penthouse suite with an entourage of twenty or so hordlings and imps who kept bumping into one another, creating chaos. Jasper must be overconfident to have no powerful haakai with him or more mungs.

He did have in hand an unsuspecting call girl. Well, unsuspecting but not innocent. The woman headed a notorious agency that catered to perverted tastes. She no doubt thought the designer suits Jasper and Beltane wore translated to a ticket for her to international wealth and travel, where in fact her ticket would be to Horror and a life far worse than that she inflicted on the women who worked for her.

"Jasper," Mordr called out, a sword in one hand and a rifle in the other.

Suddenly alert, Jasper's eyes, quickly morphing into a bright red, latched on to Mordr with evil malice. "A Sigurdsson!" He licked his bloodred lips. "Just what I wanted for dessert." He motioned for Beltane to take the girl aside, and Jasper's troop, such as it was, lined up against Mordr's vangels. It was Jasper against Mordr, though.

The woman let out a scream when she saw what beasts the Lucies were turning into. Not the high-class boss man and mob, as she'd assumed. Beltane merely slapped her aside the head with one of his big paws and she slunk down to the floor.

Mordr and Jasper faced off against each other. The king of the Lucipires wielded a heavy broadsword against Mordr's thinner-bladed dueling sword. While not so heavy, Mordr's weapon was equally lethal in its own way. Through his side vision, he saw one of his vangels approach the woman, offering her a chance to repent. She spat her refusal at him. The vangel shrugged and turned away, thus leaving her to a bunch of hordlings who gnawed on her flesh, quickly reducing her to a pile of empty clothing on the floor. Win some, lose some, Mordr thought.

Mordr delivered a number of wounds to Jasper that would be fatal to a human, but not to a demon vampire. The master Lucie was merely weakened, but still in fighting form. The only way to really get rid of Jasper would be a specially treated blade or bullet to the heart, neither of which Mordr had managed thus far.

And then Jasper struck hard on a backward swing, catching Mordr off guard. Mordr fell backward, tripping over an imp who was rolling about the floor licking up blood. That's when Jasper delivered what could be a final blow to Mordr, the broadsword almost severing his arm at the shoulder. Jasper knelt, about to fang the blood from Mordr, which would bring him to a numb-like stasis, a fate worse than death because it would mean Jasper could take him to Horror and conceivably turn him into a Lucipire after days or months of torture.

Mordr began to fall into unconsciousness, which he knew, even with his dazed senses, would give Jasper the opportunity to feed on him, sealing his fate in the worst possible way. With one last agonized cry, as Jasper's fangs lowered toward his neck, Mordr pleaded in a loud cry to the heavens, "Help me!" Whether he was praying to God or Michael was unclear. All he knew was he'd rather be dead than a demon.

So grievous were his injuries he was unaware that his brother Vikar heard his plea and came to his rescue. Swords flying right and left, Vikar and his troop slew one Lucie after another until they reached Mordr, who was already near "death."

A limping Jasper and the severely wounded Beltane escaped as Vikar lifted Mordr and immediately teletransported him back to Transylvania with an urgent call to Sigurd, their physician brother, to come help save Mordr.

Mordr's last thought, in his dream-like—rather nightmare-like state—was *I never got to tell Miranda that I love her.*

The half-severed arm would heal, but there were other worries. Although Jasper hadn't yet fed on Mordr, his sharp fangs had scraped the skin, oozing poison into his flesh. Without expert vangel help, Mordr would perish. Even the saliva of a demon vampire was deadly potent.

It was one day later before Mordr discovered that Miranda and Linda had been taken by Roger. His brothers, anticipating his reaction, had tied him to the bed in order for him to recover.

It was two days before Mordr broke his bonds and teletransported back to Las Vegas, where he discov-

ered an empty house. Not only were Miranda and
Linda nowhere to be found, as he'd been informed by
his brothers back in Transylvania, but the rest of the
children were gone, as well. Even the dog was absent.

"I could have told you, if you had asked, that the
children are with Ivak in Louisiana. And the woman,
Darla, is in the hospital recovering from a head wound,"
Vikar grumbled, having followed after Mordr. "Your
friend Jack is caring for the dog. Apparently, he has
become quite the Olympic swimmer, spending half
the day in the pool."

"What? Jack is an Olympic swimmer? What has
that do with Miranda and Linda?"

"No, lackwit! Ruff has become an avid swimmer.
And it has naught to do with Miranda or Linda. I was
just trying to lighten your mood."

Mordr told Vikar what he could lighten. Then he
choked out, "What of Miranda and Linda? Has there
been no ransom demand?"

Vikar shook his head, sadly.

Once again, Mordr felt like such a failure. Once
again, he'd failed to protect those under his shield. Especially Linda, who was so much like his own Kata.
How would he ever bear the guilt if he lost these two?
Clearing his throat, Mordr asked, "Do we know for
certain that it is Roger who has them? Or, please God,
do not let them be with Jasper."

"We're fairly certain there is no tie to the Lucies."

Fairly certain? Oh, that is reassuring! "Just Roger, who
wants Miranda dead."

Vikar acknowledged with a nod that this was true.

"But why would he take Linda, and not the other
children?"

Vikar hesitated to tell him.

Mordr made a growling noise indicating he was in
no mood for soft soaping.

"We do not think Roger wanted the child. We think his friend, a fellow inmate from prison, wanted the little girl."

"Why?" Mordr tilted his head in question. "Why would an ex-convict want a five-year-old child?" When understanding seeped in, Mordr let out a roar of outrage, the blood drained from his brain, and he felt himself begin to faint. *Me—one of the fiercest Vikings in all the Norselands—fainting like a milksop youthling on first sight of his own sword dew? What is happening to me?*

He was just barely caught by his brother before he fell to the floor and sustained even more bodily damage, especially to his left arm, which was still in a sling. "Holy clouds, Mordr! You weigh as much as a warhorse. I think I sprained my back, and I was planning some energetic bedplay with Alex tonight," Vikar complained.

Apparently Mordr wasn't as healed as he'd thought he was. He really did faint then.

Even unconscious, his mind kept crying out, *Miranda! Linda! Hold on. I am coming for you.*

Some days you're the hook, some days the hooker . . .

𝕿wo days with Roger and Company, and Miranda felt as if she'd fallen in with a bunch of nutcase criminals.

Roger, an antacid-popping Nervous Nellie, kept looking over his shoulder, expecting the demon beasties to come after him. For all Miranda knew, they might.

In the meantime, Roger had her velvet handcuffed to the headboard in one bedroom. Linda came and went throughout the apartment, the darling of all the visitors (aka prostitutes). Roger, on the other hand, had the paternal genes of a gnat.

Roger still claimed he was going to kill Miranda, but she was beginning to think he didn't have the gonads for the job. To avoid any detection of his friend Clarence's disappearance, Roger had taken over Clarence's pimp business. Imagine Don Knotts as a pimp and you got the picture.

Carlotta, on the other hand, was a vicious, greedy witch who kept harping on Roger to do "the job" so they could zip off to the Bahamas with all of Miranda's cash. Miranda had news for Roger and Carlotta. There was no cash, or little of it, and the house was tied up in a thirty-year mortgage that would take months to sell in this depressed housing market. In truth, she was probably upside-down on her mortgage.

If only she could get hold of a phone, Miranda would call for help. To Darla, whom she could only pray was all right. Last time Miranda had seen her, her friend had been lying on Miranda's hall floor, blood flowing from a head wound. Or she could call the police, who must surely be searching for her and Linda. No. The one she would call first would probably be Mordr.

And, by the way, where was her favorite Viking anyhow? She'd thought Mordr was supposed to be her protector. You'd think he would have traced her by now. Surely, the showdown with the demon vampires was over. In fact, Roger had devoured the local newspapers the first few days, looking for news about the missing Clarence, and what he'd found was lots of missing folks in and around Las Vegas, leaving behind clothes, jewelry, watches, wallets, and nothing else. In still other places, piles of strange, smelly slime puzzled the authorities. FBI and other authorities were flooding the city, seeking answers, none of which they'd shared thus far with the public. Alien aficionados were having a heyday, claiming an invasion from another planet.

Roger came in with a lunch tray for her then and said, "I know that you know more than you're telling me. Who or what are George and Ginette? I mean, did you see them turn into those fucking animals? And Clarénce just dissolved into a pile of nothing."

Miranda chewed on her pizza—the usual fare here above Luigi's. "Demon vampires," she told him, not for the first time. "That's what George and Ginette are. They live in a place called Horror with a king named Jasper and they come hunting for bad guys like you."

"Yeah, and I'm a fucking acrobat," he replied with his usual disbelief, stomping off to work on his pimp duties.

A subdued Linda came into the bedroom then. She was getting a stomachache from all the junk food she was eating, thanks to her ladies-of-the-night friends. Candy, sweet soft drinks, cupcakes, and the like. "My tummy hurts," Linda whined until she finally fell asleep on Miranda's bed. With her hair teased and sprayed into some hooker's idea of what a little girl should look like, and her fingernails and toenails painted a scarlet color, and her lips tinted with pink gloss, and her eyelashes mascaraed into black smudged fans, Linda looked like a caricature of a mini-adult, like one of those entrants in a child's beauty pageant you saw on TV.

Miranda leaned down and kissed the little girl on her forehead, brushing some of the waves off her face and behind her ears. *Soon*, she promised. *Soon we'll be out of here, honey, and back home where we belong.*

With or without Mordr? she wondered.

Well, that was irrelevant for now, Miranda decided. She had more important issues to deal with. Like, she desperately wanted a shower since she was beginning to smell her own body odor, especially when she perspired day and night with the heat from the pizza ovens down below. AC ran nonstop but didn't accomplish much of anything.

Carlotta came in next and put the capper on Miranda's crappy day. "I think Roger should put you to work."

"As a psychologist. Yeah, I can see how some of you people need my help. Hookers Anonymous meets in my office once a month, if you're interested."

"Not as a psychologist, bitch. As a working hooker."

Miranda burst out laughing and couldn't stop for so long that Carlotta stormed out of the room, slamming the door behind her.

Later that day Linda walked into the bedroom playing with a handheld game. "What's that, sweetie?" Miranda asked.

"Nothin'," Linda answered sheepishly.

"Linda?" she inquired, recognizing child guilt when she saw it.

"I dint take it," Linda said. "It was just sittin' on the counter."

Miranda took the electronic device from her to see exactly what it was and realized she was holding a cell phone. Quickly, before anyone could catch her, Miranda punched in some numbers.

"Hello, who is this?" a male said in a questioning voice, not recognizing the caller ID.

"Some protector you are, Mordr! Where the hell are you?"

"Sweetling?"

"Don't you sweetling me. Get your butt over here before I die."

"Die? Oh no! Did that bastard shoot you?"

"Idiot! Die of heat stroke."

The wrath of God . . . um, an archangel . . .

𝕿o Mordr's chagrin, it was not he who went to rescue Miranda and Linda.

Just as he was arming himself and preparing to go out to the Lexus parked in Miranda's garage, Mordr heard a familiar voice yell, "Mordr Sigurdsson!"

Mordr stopped in his tracks and waited. He didn't have long to wait.

Michael appeared in a puff of feathers. He hadn't even bothered to change from his heavenly robes. His fury was obvious, from his glaring face to his quivering wings.

Stepping back into the kitchen to make room for the archangel, Mordr said, before he lost his nerve, "I must go to rescue Miranda and the child."

"You must, you must," Michael mocked. "Thou must obey my orders, in case you have forgotten, Viking. Ivak has already been sent to take care of them. You and I have our own business to attend to."

Uh-oh!

"What have you to report on the casino mission? Have you wiped out all the Lucipires?"

"Me? Personally?"

"Do not be flip with me, Viking. Is Jasper gone and condemned to shoveling coal for Satan's fires?"

"No. As far as I know, he is back at Horror, planning new evil deeds."

"As far as you know?" Michael mocked, walking about the kitchen, idly picking up and examining various objects. A bottled water. The can opener. A wooden block of steak knives. The coffeemaker, which he sniffed with distaste. "As far as you know," he repeated.

"I have been rather . . . indisposed." Mordr felt his face heat at his choice of such as weakling word.

Michael arched his brows. "Really?" He pointed a forefinger at Mordr's shoulder.

The sling fell off and the persistent ache was gone. Rolling his shoulder, Mordr realized that the wound was healed. "Thank you."

"I do not need or want thy thanks. How many Lucipires were destroyed in the casino mission?"

"Five hundred and fifty, I have been told," Mordr answered.

"And how many human sinners were added to Jasper's ranks?"

Mordr saw where this was going now. "As many as a thousand," he admitted.

Michael pretended to be counting on his fingers and came up with a net gain for the bad guys of "Four hundred and fifty!" The archangel shook his head from side to side with apparent disgust. "And do you consider that a successful mission?"

Mordr was about to utter that modern phrase, "Win some, lose some," or to remind Michael that his mission had been to protect Miranda and the children, not the casino project. But look how that turned out! Linda and Miranda were both missing! In the end, he decided discretion might be called for. He opted for silence.

"Is it possible you were distracted during this mission?"

"What?" One of the worst things about talking with Michael was how his conversations changed direction so rapidly. A tactic designed to put the other person at unease. Mordr was definitely uneasy now.

"What have you done, Mordr?" Mordr knew that Michael was no longer talking about the mission, evidenced by his next question, "Have you been sinning?"

Mordr didn't even bother to deny the charge, although his lovemaking with Miranda had not felt like sinning.

"Excuses!" Michael said, reading his mind.

Mordr would have to be careful about that.

"Did I not tell you and your brothers that there would be no more fornication? Did I not forbid any more relationships with humans? Did I not warn you of the consequences? Did you think you were the exception?"

Mordr bowed his head, then raised his chin. "I was dark and empty for so long. I tried to avoid the temptation, but I was weak. In truth, I cannot regret having loved Miranda. Still love Miranda," he amended.

Michael threw his hands up. "What am I to do with you?"

"Punish me?"

"That goes without saying. Go immediately to the tower in the Transylvania castle and stay there until I have made a decision. Until then, contemplate your sins."

"Can I at least go and say my good-byes to Miranda and the children."

"Do not push me, Mordr."

Mordr did not need to teletransport himself. Michael did it for him with a lung-piercing whoosh that landed him on his arse on the cold concrete floor of the tower.

The oddest thing happened then. The scent of lilies and cloves filled the chamber.

Mordr chose to view that as a good omen.

Eighteen

Sometimes prayers do get answered . . .

Miranda and Linda were rescued, but not by Mordr. His brother Ivak and a contingent of what she assumed were vangels came to take them away, at the same time the police arrived to arrest Roger and Carlotta.

While Carlotta screeched like a banshee that she was innocent, Roger went willingly. In fact, he almost seemed to welcome a return to prison. His rambling went pretty much like this: "Hey, I don't mind being locked up, but are you sure you cops didn't arrest any couple recently named George and Ginette? I am *not* sharing a cell with those two monsters. In fact, solitary confinement would be good.

"I already told you, George and Ginette look like movie stars sometimes, but then they suddenly become about seven feet tall, with red eyes and fangs. And tails. Big tails. They killed Clarence by eating him. No, I'm not shitting you. They gobbled him right up, all except for his cop clothes.

"How do I know why they didn't eat the clothes! Of course I know Clarence wasn't a cop. Do you think I'm a moron? Why are you guys laughing?

"Clarence was a pimp. I've been filling in for the bastard. You ever tried to organize a herd of hookers? It's worse than trying to herd cats, I tell you. Which bastard? Clarence! Holy shit! How many times do I have to tell you? Clarence killed his cousin Lamar, the pimp, and then the Weird Couple killed Clarence, and Clarence was about to kill Miranda. Weird Couple, Odd Couple, get it? Ha, ha, ha!

"No, I didn't kill Clarence, though I would have liked to. It was George and Ginette, the demon dragons, who made a Happy Meal out of Clarence.

"Is anyone listening to me? I think Clarence's ice chewing and knuckle cracking must have finally pushed me over the edge.

"Hey, why are you putting that straitjacket on me?"

Apparently, Roger would be staying at the funny farm, not the prison farm, at least for the time being.

Ivak, the too-good-looking-for-his-own-good Sigurdsson brother, shielded Linda's eyes and ears from the sight of her babbling father being arrested. And, yes, Ivak was wearing the long black cloak with angel epaulets. He quickly escorted her and Miranda down to the Lexus SUV and immediately took off, wheels squealing. Other vangels rode in the backseat, weapons ready. Several others followed in vehicles behind them.

Recognizing the SUV as the one Mordr had been using while in Las Vegas, she asked, "Where's Mordr? Why didn't he come for us?"

"He's . . . uh, indisposed."

Now that she was free, she had time for other emotions. Like anger. "Indisposed? Like he has better things to do?"

"Like he has nothing to do," Ivak answered enigmatically.

"I want Mordr," Linda said. She was sitting on the

front seat, on Miranda's lap. Not the safest place to be, according to the law, but the little girl was holding on to Miranda like a life buoy in the middle of the ocean. She'd been through an ordeal most children never faced and never should.

"He had to go away for a while, sweetheart," Ivak said, patting Linda's hand.

"Is he coming back?" Linda wanted to know.

Miranda would like to know, too.

"I cannot say for certain," Ivak answered honestly, slanting a look of apology Miranda's way.

That look said it all.

Mordr had told her over and over that Michael would never let him stay with her. Until now, she'd thought it was still a possibility. "Michael?" she whispered.

Ivak nodded.

Anger was now replaced by worry. What would the archangel do to Mordr? There was sure to be some punishment for his involvement with Miranda. Mordr had told her so.

Suddenly, she realized that Ivak wasn't headed toward the suburb where she lived. "Where are we going?" she asked in a panic.

"The airport. When all hell broke loose last week, we took the other children to my home in Louisiana. For protection. That's where we're going now."

She couldn't believe that she hadn't asked about the other children, first thing. Maybe she was in more shock than she'd realized from this whole experience. Even though she was now out of danger, even though Roger would be gone for years to come, a delayed reaction was setting in, and she began to weep . . . silently, so as not to alarm Linda, who'd fallen asleep.

"Everything has a way of working out, Miranda. Just relax. Enjoy a few days at Heaven's End. Maybe you'll even get to meet our good friend Tante Lulu and her friend St. Jude."

Why that last statement brought a mischievous gleam to his eyes, she had no idea. "St. Jude? I thought St. Michael was the saint du jour."

Ivak laughed. "Mike is our saint du jour. Jude is Tante Lulu's."

That made no sense at all. "Heaven's End? Is that like some celestial planet or something?" she asked, just to make conversation. Oh God, she hoped they weren't going planet hopping now, on top of everything else. If they could teletransport, she assumed they could do that, too.

"Don't ask," Ivak warned. "You'll find out soon enough."

Turned out Heaven's End was the name of Ivak's run-down—really run-down—plantation in southern Louisiana. Mordr had told her about it one time, she recalled now. For several days, she and the children stayed with Ivak and his wife, Gabrielle, on the property they were going to restore as soon as she had her baby, which would be any day now.

Miranda learned a lot about vangels from Gabrielle, another human brought into this web of angel vampire beings, or whatever they were.

"No offense, but you're a lawyer, presumably an intelligent woman. And yet you married a vampire angel! Didn't you have reservations about that?"

"Plenty. Especially since vangels are sterile. But Ivak's swimmers never got the memo." Her eyes twinkled merrily as she relayed that information. There was a story there, Miranda was sure.

They were sitting out on the verandah, Miranda with a mint julep and Gabrielle with a cold sweet tea. The children were off with Ivak trying to trap more of the snakes that plagued the property.

"There are a thousand different snakes in the world, and nine hundred and ninety species are in residence here at Heaven's End," Ivak had told her on her arrival. Heaven's End, clearly an oxymoron, was the name of the former slave plantation.

"How does it work . . . this vangel/human thing? Don't they live forever, or for centuries anyhow?" Miranda asked Gabrielle.

Gabrielle nodded. "Michael allowed me . . . and my two sisters-in-law . . . to marry vangels. We will live as long as they do, and no longer. We will not age, same as them. If they die tomorrow, though, we would die, too. As for the baby . . ." Gabrielle's voice quivered. "Ivak and I will not age, but our child will. In other words, we will one day bury our boy. That is what we are having. A boy."

"That seems rather cruel."

Gabrielle shrugged. "It's a choice I made."

"Why aren't I being given a choice?"

"What do you mean?"

"Well, Ivak tells me that Mordr is being held prisoner or something back at the castle in Pennsylvania, that he's not permitted to contact me."

"It's not you personally. It's the whole idea that Michael objects to. Vangels and humans are not meant to mix, or at least that was the way it was originally intended. I think it has something to do with fallen angels having sex with human women in biblical times, or maybe that's just a story that has no merit. In any case, after Ivak and I married, Michael swore it would be the last time."

Miranda nodded. She'd been told this before, but somehow it didn't seem fair. "The children miss him so much. I don't know how he bonded with them so well in such a short time, but he did. To give him credit, he fought their touch a lot."

"And how about you?"

"Did I bond with him?"

"Do you love him?"

"I think so."

"How about Mordr? Does he love you?"

"I don't know. He never told me so." But then, she hadn't told him, either. She was so confused. "There is one thing." Miranda told Gabrielle about the heart sign Mordr made just before he'd left for the last time.

Gabrielle had tears in her eyes when Miranda finished. "Ivak never made that sign to me." He probably would before nightfall.

"What should I do?" Miranda asked.

"Pray!"

At first, Miranda thought it was Gabrielle who'd given that oversimple suggestion, but then she realized that someone else had stepped up behind them. It was a little old lady dressed in neon orange biking shorts with a purple tank top, sporting the logo "I'm Not Old, I'm Ripe," and white orthopedic shoes and pink ruffled anklets. An explosion of liver spots covered every inch of exposed, sagging skin. Her gray curls were held back off her face by a rhinestone-studded headband. Makeup filled all the crevices on her wrinkled face, accentuated by false eyelashes and bright red lipstick. Grandma Moses with a Mary Kay addiction.

"Tante Lulu!" Gabrielle said, pushing herself clumsily out of her chair and offering the seat to the old lady. She went to the verandah rail and pulled another chair over. Before she sat back down, Gabrielle poured a glass of sweet tea and handed it to her guest. "I didn't know you were coming today." Eyeing her outfit, Gabrielle raised a brow. "You been out jogging?"

"In this heat? I swear, it's so dry t'day, the bushes are followin' the dogs around. No, I ain't climbed on the crazy train yet." Smiling at Miranda, whose jaw had been hanging open, she extended a hand and said, "Hi! I'm Louise Rivard, but you kin call me Tante Lulu, like everyone does. You mus' be Miranda. Ivak tol' me 'bout you."

"Did you bring that snakebite medicine for Ivak?" Gabrielle asked, then explained to Miranda, "Tante Lulu is a famous *traiteur*, that's what they call a folk healer here on the bayou. Ivak and his workers have been getting some bites from the nonpoïsonous snakes that're causing rashes and nausea and stuff."

"I brought my Piss 'n' Boots remedy. Tee, hee, hee! It's made up of goat urine and boiled cowhide with a little gator fat ta bind it all t'gether."

"You're kidding!" Miranda said before she had a chance to bite her tongue.

"Pfff! I ain't got time ta be kiddin'. If I hesitate too long, I might find myself on the Other Side." She grinned to show Miranda that she wasn't offended. "Anyways," she addressed Gabrielle now, "I brought Jem Hawkins with me t'day. He's a professional snake catcher. I swear, that guy is so skinny if he closed one eye he could pass fer a needle. And stink? Pee-you. Smells lak swamp water all the time. Thass why we call him Stinky Hawkins. I'll hafta spray mah car with a gallon of air freshener."

After that ramble, the old lady took a long drink of her tea, then leaned back in her chair and studied Miranda. "So. You gonna take my advice, girl?"

"Huh?"

"Pray. Dint you hear me tell you ta pray?"

"Oh. That."

Really, the old lady's brain skittered around from one subject to another without warning, like a human Ping-Pong ball.

"Yes, that. I woke up this mornin'—most days I'm

jist glad ta wake up, truth to tell—and I felt St. Jude nudgin' me ta come over here. When I heard you soundin' kind of hopeless when I walked up, I knew you were ta be my mission."

Oh boy!

"Tante Lulu is a great fan of St. Jude. He's the patron saint of hopeless cases," Gabrielle explained to Miranda.

"Well, I'm certainly feeling hopeless."

"You came ta the right place, then. Tell me what the problem is." Tante Lulu leaned forward, waiting avidly for her to spill her secrets.

To Miranda's surprise, she did just that. For some reason, the old lady engendered trust . . . and, yes, hope.

Tante Lulu listened intently, especially interested in knowing that the man Miranda loved was Ivak's brother. She nodded here and there, and shook her head at other times. Of course, Miranda didn't mention all the vangel/Lucipire stuff.

When she was done, Tante Lulu squeezed her hand and said, "Sweetie, this is yer lucky day. I'm gonna be yer new best friend, and friends are God's way of takin' care of us, y'know."

Okaaay! "So, what do I do about this situation with Mordr?"

"Pray. Dint you hear what I said ta begin with. You mus' have cotton balls betwixt yer ears, bless yer heart."

"I haven't been to church in years, and I can't remember the last time I prayed," Miranda disclosed.

"Mebbe it's time ta start," Tante Lulu told her, wagging a forefinger. "Dontcha be worryin', though. You aim fer the Big Guy, and I'll be prayin' ta St. Jude fer ya, too. A double whammy, thass what it'll be."

"Speaking of double whammies," Gabrielle interrupted, "is it possible I'm carrying twins? I swear, I must have gained fifty pounds."

Tante Lulu put her hand on Gabrielle's tummy. "Nope. Jist one, but he's burstin' ta come out. Mebbe t'day."

"Really?" Gabrielle squeaked out.

"Did I say t'day? Could be t'morrow." Tante Lulu winked at Miranda, causing one of her eyelashes to go lopsided. It was hard to tell whether the old lady's wink meant she really did know when the baby would arrive, or she was just teasing.

Archangel's nose, out of joint . . .

Miranda hadn't really taken the old lady seriously when she'd mentioned prayer as the solution to all her problems, but when she was back in the house in Las Vegas the next night, and the children were crying for Mordr, she told them, "Why don't we pray? Ask God to bring him back?"

And that's what they did. Every night. For seven nights. On the eighth day, after dropping off the kids at Jack Trixson's house to swim in his pool with his children, Miranda came home to a too quiet house.

But then, she was surprised by what sounded like a flock of birds overheard. Pigeons? One of them dropped down onto to the patio with a grunt.

Going out carefully, she looked and saw the most amazing thing. A man—a beautiful man with long black hair, perfect skin, a fine build, wearing jeans and a pure white T-shirt—sitting at her patio table. There were feathers fluttering all around him.

"I do not like people going over my head. Let me tell you that right off. Usurping my authority is no way to get on my good side."

"Huh?" she said, and sank down into the chair opposite him.

"Did you not encourage your children to pray to God to bring Mordr back to them?"

"Well, yes."

"Did you not know that God cherishes little children? Did you not know that God would be touched by the pleas of his smallest creations?"

"Um. I never thought about it. Who are you anyway?"

"Michael."

"Jeesh! Am I really sitting here talking to an angel? Not just any angel. The primo angel of all time."

"Dost think flattery will gain thy ends?" he asked, but he was smiling.

There was nothing more glorious than an archangel smiling. The very air seemed to glow around him. Like a halo. Well, duh!

"Here's the deal," she said, figuring this was her one shot at getting Mordr back. "I love Mordr. I think he might love me. My children love him and need him. What's so wrong with that?"

"What is wrong is that? Mordr is a vangel! He will probably go on being a vangel for centuries to come. You will never have children, that I guarantee. There will be no more mistakes like Ivak, not that babies are a mistake, but . . ." He scowled at her.

"I have five children. I don't need any more."

"And when they age and you do not?"

She gulped. She hadn't thought of that. "I think I could live with that."

Michael threw his arms out helplessly. "Well, 'tis out of my hands anyhow. God has spoken."

"Huh?"

Talking with this archangel was like talking with Tante Lulu. A person wasn't really sure what was being said but suspected it was important.

The archangel disappeared in a cloud of the most wonderful fragrance, unlike anything she had ever smelled. Not perfume precisely. Just heavenly air. She smiled at the fancifulness of her thought, then frowned. Now, she smelled sandalwood and lime.

Was that a sign of some sort?

Gamblers come in all sizes . . .

Harek was sitting at the high-stakes blackjack table in the Silver Nugget Casino.

He had a pile of winning thousand-dollar chips sitting in front of him on the green baize, along with a Jack Daniel's in a tumbler, beaded with condensation. On his one side was a hot widow from Iceland who kept putting her free hand on his thigh, high up. On his other side was this entertaining fellow, P. Jack something-or-other, who had recently married for the fourteenth time. Harek and everyone else at the table, including the young dealer, were having a grand old time.

In fact, Harek hadn't had so much fun in ages. Literally. His sin had been greed, very bad greed, and he'd been forbidden by Michael to gamble anymore. Who was he hurting? No one, except the casino owner, who was probably a mob boss or something, Harek justified. Besides, what Michael didn't know wouldn't hurt Harek. Another justification to himself.

Just then, as the dealer cut a new deck of cards, and was placing it in the shuffling machine, Harek glanced over to the walkway that surrounded the casino proper, cut off by a velvet rope. Then he did a double take.

Five midgets stood there waving at him. Midgets? Well, little people. And the most bizarre little people he had ever seen in all his thousand-plus years.

The two girls or women, it was hard to tell from this distance, wore wigs and wobbly high heels, and enough makeup to plaster the ceiling of the Sistine Chapel. Their spandex dresses highlighted breasts that were either bad boob jobs or nature's mutants. The boy-men wore little suits and hats . . . a beret, an over-size Stetson that kept falling down over the person's eyes, and a baseball cap. Two of them had mustaches and one of them had freckles . . . a lot of freckles.

But why were they waving at him? And one of the females was squealing in a decidedly girlish, not womanish, manner, "Har-ek!"

"Oh. My. God!" he muttered when understanding seeped into his thick skull. It was Miranda's kids.

And among the security guards who were rushing to the site was one who could be a twin of Mike. Or Mike himself. He knew the answer to that question even before he noticed the guard's fierce scowl directed his way.

Oh, he was in big trouble!

"Cash in," he told the dealer.

Everyone at the table protested his leaving in the middle of a winning streak, but he knew that he had no choice. Another minute and Mike would be over here dragging him off by the ear.

"What are you kids doing here?" he asked the minute he came up to them and steered them into a lounge area.

"What are *you* doing here?" Mike asked him.

"We were looking for you," Maggie, the older girl, said, as she adjusted her drooping décolletage.

"Me? Why me?"

Mike was looking at him like he was scum.

"Because we're trying to find Mordr, and we heard that you were here. We figured you would help us find Mordr." This was Sam, who was eyeing the slot machines even as he spoke. Given a chance, the kid—the one who had an inappropriate-for-his-age interest in gambling—was going to make a dash for the nearest Wheel of Fortune.

In fact, a heavyset woman sat down at that particular machine, put in a dollar, and the thing went wild. "Wheel of Fortune, Wheel of Fortune, Wheel of Fortune," its speaker kept saying, along with a lot of raucous bells and whistles. Apparently, she had just won a jackpot, as evidenced by casino personnel running to her side.

Sam looked as if he could puke. "That was my machine. I was gonna put in four quarters. See." He held out an open palm that held four quarters. "She stole my winnings." He was about to shoot across the rope fence and confront her.

"Oh no, you do not!" Harek said, grabbing him by the back of his suit jacket and tugging him back. "Where did you kids get these clothes anyhow? And how did you know I would be here?"

"Yes, Harek, curious celestial minds would like to know how they knew you would be here." Mike had his arms folded across his chest, glaring his way. "Could it be you are always here?"

"I am not!" he said vehemently. "This was my first time."

Mike rolled his eyes.

"Well, my second time. In a hundred years."

"We knew you were here because Mr. Trixson mentioned it to Miranda when she dropped us off at his pool this afternoon," Ben informed Harek.

"Mr. Trixson works in a dance club next door and he came here for breakfast this morning," Maggie added.

Mike glanced pointedly at his wristwatch. The message was clear. The archangel was now aware that Harek had been in the casino all day.

"Mr. Trixson has a whole closetful of costumes," Linda, the little one, with two missing front teeth, added further information to the kids' story of how and why they got here.

"Did Mr. Trixson bring you here?"

"No!" all five of them said with horror.

"He thinks we're down in the basement playing videos," Ben told him with way too much pride in their deviousness.

"We took the bus," Larry of the freckled face said. "Whoo-boy! It took us two hours to get here."

Harek sighed deeply, sensing that he was going to be blamed for the kids' misbehavior, as well as his gambling. "Where is Miranda?"

"At work."

Harek turned to Mike to ask if he should take them there, or would he? But Mike was already gone. Not that his heavenly mentor wouldn't deal with Harek later. No doubt about that!

A short time later, Harek arrived at Miranda's psychiatric clinic with five oddly dressed little people in tow.

The secretary, whose jaw dropped when he asked if he could see Miss Hart, just waved them on.

Miranda had been reading some document when they walked in.

"Um, Miranda, I have a little present for you. Five presents, actually," Harek said.

She glanced up, then stood abruptly, almost knocking over her desk chair. "What have you done?"

He wasn't sure if she was addressing the children or him.

It didn't matter. They were all in big trouble.

Nineteen

Beware thou ruffling the feathers of an archangel . . .

Mordr was cleaning his nails with the tip of his sword in the tower room of the Transylvania castle, bored to the point of berserkness. Really, this was a new situation for Mordr. Never before had he felt like breaking out into a rage of violence from the tedium of his own dull company.

He was worried about Miranda and the children. Oh, not their safety precisely. His brothers would have saved her from Roger's evil clutches, and he was fairly certain there was no Lucie presence in Las Vegas anymore. What he was worried about was how Miranda and the children were taking his absence. Oh, he'd warned Miranda that their relationship could end at any moment. That didn't make it any easier to bear. He'd thought he would have time to at least say good-bye. And the children . . . ah, the children! They would not understand how he could suddenly go away. Their hurt must be immense.

Mordr hadn't bathed or shaved in more than a week. Food was passed to him in silence through a slot in the door several times a day. Apparently the residents of the castle, his fellow vangels, had been forbidden to speak to the "prisoner."

He recognized the cackle of Lizzie Borden, the cook, on a few occasions when food was delivered. Lizzie never did like him very much, and must be taking extreme pleasure in his discomfort, as evidenced by her serving him peas with almost every meal. He hated peas, and Lizzie knew it. Not to worry. He had amassed quite a collection of the now dry peas which he was using to aim like bullets at a large spiderweb in the corner.

He had just flicked his last pea when he sensed a presence behind him.

Michael.

And he was in full-blown angel gear, too. Pure white robe, gold braided belt, sandals, halo, and, of course, the massive wings. Mordr was in for it!

Shaking his head at the peas scattered about the floor, Michael said, "What am I going to do with you?"

"'Twould seem to me that you have already done it," Mordr replied, glancing pointedly around the dismal tower room. "Besides, it's just a few peas. It's not like I'm depriving the poor children of China of their food."

"I swear, you Vikings have brains the size of a pigeon's. And that is an insult to pigeons, who are God's feathered creatures, just as we angels are."

Mordr nigh bit his tongue through preventing himself from remarking on the foul things pigeons did to holy statues. On a sigh, he asked, "What did I do now?"

"Your insolence knows no bounds. How could you, Mordr? How could you use little children to further your ends?"

"Huh? I was jesting about the poor children of China."

"Aaarrgh! I am not referring to those children. I am referring to your children, the ones back in Las Vegas who are praying for your return."

"They are *my* children now?" he asked, thoroughly confused. Michael was accusing him of doing something related to *his* children. But then, the rest of Michael's statement sank in. "They are praying? For me? To come back?" He couldn't help but smile.

Michael had not witnessed his smiles for more than a thousand years, but he was not touched. Oh no. Not him. And Mordr was accused of being grim!

"Forget pigeons. More like ants," Michael remarked. "Teeny tiny brains to fit in big fat heads!"

Mordr would have been insulted, except he was still back there with Michael's assertion that the children had prayed for him. "And you think I used the children for my own ends?"

"Why else would they be praying to God—to God! not me, by the by!—for your return?"

"Uh. Mayhap they are fond of me, small-brained as I am. Mayhap they see me as some kind of father figure to replace that nithing whose blood they unfortunately carry. Mayhap they suddenly got religion. Mayhap—"

Michael spoke right over him. "You usurped my authority, Viking, by going over my head, directly to my superior."

"I did nothing except sit here in this tower. Wait a minute. Are you saying that your ultimatum about no more human/vangel relationships has been overruled by a higher authority?" He pressed his lips together in an attempt to hide his glee.

"The Lucipires are growing in strength, no thanks to you vangels, who need to work harder. You will no doubt be a vampire angel for many centuries to come, and that does not even count your penance for your most recent sins."

"No less than I expected." Mordr shrugged.

"She might not have you," Michael said.

Mordr grinned. "I am a Viking. She will have me."

A declaration of war ...

𝕸iranda wanted nothing to do with Mordr.

He'd been gone for more than three weeks now. Not a word from him. Not even a secondhand message via one of his brothers, who'd taken to dropping in on her on occasion, except for Harek, who had been sent to Siberia on a mission of indefinite duration. And she knew that Mordr had been released from his "prison" exactly six days ago.

Then, all of a sudden, Mordr had shown up, sporting a new, neatly trimmed mustache above his lip and a soul patch on his chin. And a haircut! He'd trimmed off all that beautiful hair into a modern do, low on the neck, but lots shorter than his previous tresses. His clothing had to have come from some upscale men's shop. He was wearing a bleepin' suit, for heaven's sake. Black Hugo Boss over a crisp white dress shirt and a Ralph Lauren tie and Italian loafers. It was as if he was trying to expunge the Viking out of himself. Good luck with that!

"Miranda, dearling," he had drawled out, his voice oozing sex.

She'd give him "dearling"!

When his endearment didn't cause her to do handsprings toward him, he crooked a finger, beckoning her toward him. And then he winked.

She almost laughed.

Or cried.

The clueless Viking actually thought he could just pick up where they'd left off weeks ago. In bed.

She had news for him. That door had closed. It had taken her a week to stop crying. It had taken even longer to convince the children that Mordr wasn't coming back. No way was she putting herself or the kids through that pain again.

But Mordr wouldn't give up.

That first day, before he'd left, she told him, meanly, "By the way, I don't like facial hair. You look like you have a caterpillar on your lip."

Next day, he was clean shaven.

Every day, like clockwork, he showed up at her house, at her workplace, at the coffee shop at the lower level of the clinic building, even on the jogging path where she ran every morning. You did not want to see a six foot four, two-hundred-and-twenty-pound hulk come running up beside you at half past dawn, even if he did look like pure sex in his running shorts and shoes, and that's all.

And now, speaking to her through the narrow opening of the chain lock on her front door—not that he couldn't teletransport, if he'd wanted to—he tried to defend his absence, "But I was locked in a castle tower like some bloody medieval princess. I could hardly come to you, on a whim."

Excuses! He could have found a way if he'd really wanted to. "You ever heard of Rapunzel? You could have climbed down your hair or something."

He didn't even crack a smile. Great! They were back to the Grim Reaper again. Big deal!

"How about the six days after you were released?"

"I was making plans."

"Oh? Were there no phones where you were making those plans?"

"Yes, there were phones, but I wanted to have our future mapped out before I spoke with you."

"Are all Vikings so dumb, or is it just you?"

"Probably just me. What did I do wrong?"

"You were mapping out our life, as if I had no say in it."

"Of course you would have a say in it. After I decided what it would involve. Must you always be at cross-wills with me? A man takes care of those—"

"If you say, 'those under your shield,' I am going to scream," she interrupted. "I never asked to be under your frickin' shield, nor do I want to be."

"Where do you want to be?" he asked with a grin, probably thinking he was making inroads with her.

"Far away from you," she replied, and tried to shut the door.

He stuck his flip-flopped foot in the space to prevent the door from shutting. After the first day, he'd given up on the dressy duds and was back to shorts and a T-shirt, this one proclaiming, "Got Viking?"

"How are the children?" he asked to keep her talking.

"Fine. And Roger's going to be in jail for a long time. So, no problems there, either. Good-bye."

"You prayed for me," he pointed out, as if that meant she should welcome him with open arms . . . and legs.

"The children did." That was only a half lie.

"Miranda, I love you."

Her heart about melted, but she had to be strong. "Too late. Mordr, go away. I appreciate all you've done for me . . . for us, but we're better off without you."

He flinched at her harsh words. But then, he asked, "Can you say that you do not love me in return?"

When she didn't reply, he smiled. "I give you fair warning, m'lady." He took out his sword and planted it in the wooden threshold of the door frame. "I do now declare war against you, heartling. Raise the drawbridge, build a moat, bar the doors, I will be assaulting your defenses forthwith. You will surrender, or I am not Mordr the Brave."

She smiled inwardly. That had been his name before he'd gone berserk, according to his brothers. "And I am Miranda the Stubborn."

He put a fist to his heart and extended the open palm toward her before turning and walking away.

If he'd only known, that heart sign would have won him entry in a nanosecond.

And thus the mighty do fall . . .

A week went by with no sign of Mordr.

Did he really give up so easily?

She suspected something was up when Jack Trixson convinced her to let the children go on a weekend camping trip with his family. Even Maggie had developed a sudden interest in outdoor living.

And Darla had talked her into a day at the Mecca Hotel health spa for the two of them. Massages, facials, manicures and pedicures. Followed by dinner and entertainment at a male revue called Thunder From Down Under. While definitely hot, those Aussie hunks had nothing on Mordr.

She almost expected to see him parked on her doorstep when she got home. But no. No vehicle in her driveway or garage. No extra lights on in the house. Not even a love note in her mailbox.

The next morning, a Saturday, she dragged herself to work, where she had three group therapy sessions scheduled. Staff psychologists alternated who would supervise these weekend clinics.

It was contrary of her, Miranda knew, but she was

disappointed that Mordr had followed her orders to go away and stay away. And she hadn't even built a moat. So much for his declaring war against her!

After two cups of coffee, she managed to lead the first session on addictions, primarily gambling. It was a successful meeting with a dozen clients, even though half of them would probably head for a casino afterward. She considered it progress that they continued to show up.

After a fifteen-minute break, she led the next session on teenage self-esteem. It was sad to hear all the young girls bemoan their self-identities tied in with magazine and TV images of gaunt, too-thin body frames and outer beauty as an indicator of worth. Even more alarming was the bullying that went along with physical appearance.

Finally, the sexual dysfunction group filed in. Only six people came today and they sat on half the folding chairs arranged in a circle. Martin "Marty" Gallagher, a Marine vet who suffered impotency due to PTSD. Jenny Laird, a self-proclaimed nymphomaniac, although Miranda believed she got off just talking about sex in therapy. Bob and Helen Morgan, a couple who argued constantly about sex. He wanted less; she wanted more. And then there was Mordr, sitting there as if he belonged. Today he wore Harley-Davidson attire. All leather, right down to his big boots and a jacket that said, not "Hell's Angels," but "The Other Angels."

Despite being discomforted by Mordr's presence, Miranda started the meeting. "Jenny, did you try that exercise class I suggested as a way of working off some of your sexual energy?"

"Pfff!" Jenny said, tossing her long blond hair over one shoulder and eyeing the newcomer to the group, who had yet to be introduced. Mordr. "The instructor in the class was a male, and he had us doing these pelvic thrusts to the rhythm of some weird rap music. By the time the class was over, I was so hot I dry-humped him in the locker room. The little weasel reported me to the manager, but not before nailing me in the shower, from behind, and after I gave him a blow job under his desk."

Marty yawned. He'd heard Jenny's stories before, most of which were fabricated. Helen gazed at Jenny with envy, and Bob cringed, fearing that his wife was going to be demanding even more of him when they returned home today. Mordr, on the other hand, was gaping at Jenny.

"Thank you for sharing that, Jenny," Miranda said quickly before Mordr could speak, as he obviously was about to. "Do you think it was wise to engage in such activity in a public place?"

"Well—" Jenny started to say.

"All the sex books say that if it feels good, go for it," Helen interrupted. "And Jenny wasn't even doing it in front of anyone else, which would have been all right, too. Exhibitionism is a natural female fantasy. Bob wouldn't even do it with me in the bathroom of the country club."

"It was the men's room, and there were men in the other stalls," Bob said with disgust.

"Hell! If I could get it up, I'd do it in Times Square," Marty said. To Mordr, Marty explained, "Ever since I got back from Iraq, I've been unable to make the old soldier stand to attention. I keep seeing this kid who had a bomb strapped to his cock. Went off in a pink mist right in front of my whole company."

Mordr put a sympathetic hand on the man's arm. "I had men serving under me who suffered such after battles. Usually, it went away over time. Betimes, a bout of alehead madness helped, but mostly it was time and a patient woman who brought the staff back to life."

Miranda was amazed at Mordr's empathy. Most men would make a joke about such an affliction.

"Dr. Hart thinks I need a sex surrogate," Martin added.

"Dr. Hart?" Mordr frowned in confusion. It was probably the first time he'd heard anyone refer to her as a doctor.

"He's talking about me. I have a doctorate in psychology," she told Mordr.

"And a sex sir . . . whatever he said?" Mordr inquired.

Miranda explained what a sex surrogate did.

"Over my dead body!" Mordr declared.

Everyone sat up with interest now, sensing a spark between her and Mordr.

Spark? It was more like a bonfire.

"If you will be having sex, it will be with me, not another man," her Viking blabbermouth went on.

Miranda felt herself blush. "I'm not a sex surrogate. There are women who provide that professional service."

"Harlots?"

"No, there are trained women, and men, who have the clinical experience to help those suffering from sexual issues," she said.

"How do I get to be one of those surrogate things?" Jenny wanted to know.

"Yeah. Can we sign up here?" Helen asked.

Marty winked at Mordr, as if they shared some manly joke.

Enough of this nonsense!

"Mordr, group therapy is serious. What is your sexual problem? What brings you here today?"

Big mistake!

"Ah! You should finally ask!" He rolled his eyes meaningfully at the rest of the group. "I have had sex only ten times in the past thousand or so years. Four of those times in one night and six the following day. With Miranda, of course. I was especially fond of the mouth tupping under the desk. And now she has refused to see me again."

"Four times in one night!" Helen sighed with envy.

"I am not having sex under a desk," Bob asserted.

"Exactly what kind of sex is mouth tupping? Details, honey? Details?" Jenny was licking her red lips with anticipation.

"Bullshit!" Marty said with a sneer. "No guy can do it that many times in a day and a half."

"I am a Viking," Mordr told Marty. "We are better endowed than the average man."

"Bullshit!" Marty repeated.

"I did not even have a chance to show her the Viking S-spot." Mordr put on a woeful puppy-dog face. Where was Mr. Grim now?

"The whaaat?" Jenny was practically hyperventilating.

"Uh, I think we need to end this session early today," Miranda intervened, fearing what might come next. "Mordr and I have some things to discuss. Next time we'll stay an extra half hour, if that's okay with you all."

The others slowly exited with knowing grins and snickers.

When they were gone, Miranda put her hands on her hips and glared at Mordr. "This was outrageous, even for you. How could you, Mordr? I work here. You can't barge in and interrupt my professional work."

He shrugged. "You would not grant me entrance to your home. Come. I have something to show you."

"I'm not interested. Do you understand how improper it was for you to interrupt my work sessions?"

"Being proper has never been of much importance to me. Come." He held out a hand for her.

She swatted the hand away. "And what's with the motorcycle gear anyhow?"

"I bought a motorcycle. Is this not what one wears on a motorcycle?"

"You bought a motorcycle? What next? A longship?"

"How did you know?" At the expression of shock on her face, he flicked her gaping mouth shut with a forefinger, then disclosed, "No, I did not buy a ship . . . precisely. I did buy a motorboat. And I bought a car. Not a car . . . precisely."

"Enough with the 'precisely' crap. What did you buy?"

"A van which will easily hold a man, a woman, five children, and a dog. And a boat. A motorboat, not a longship. Actually, I went to the car market to buy the car, and saw the boat and motorcycle there. I made a good bargain. The family package."

She stamped her foot. "We are not your family."

"You should be," he said. "You *will* be."

She stamped her foot again. "No, no, no!"

He stamped his boot. "Yes, yes, yes!"

She frowned at him.

He smiled at her.

"Trond told me that motorcycles are a surefire way to melt a woman's heart, or leastways her female parts. Spread legs. Vibrations. Holding on to her man. Wind on the nether regions." He waggled his eyebrows at her.

"I cannot believe you said that."

"Believe it," he said. "Enough squabbling, wench!" On those ominous words, he picked her up by the waist, tossed her over his shoulder, then walked out of the office and over to the elevator, down to the parking garage where there was, indeed, a motorcycle with two helmets. Along the way when they passed stunned folks, Mordr told them, "Do not worry. The wench and I are playing a sex game."

"Are you going to kidnap me now?"

"If that is what it takes?"

In the elevator, a weary-looking cleaning lady asked Miranda, "Do you want me to call 911?"

Miranda craned her head up from where it was hanging down his back to better see the woman. "No. I'll call myself. After I kill him."

A half hour later—and, yes, certain body parts were feeling the effect of the vibrating machine—they arrived at a house sitting on about five acres of land. There was a stone fence with an iron gate surrounding the property. Using a remote, Mordr opened the gate and they rode through onto a curved driveway.

"You're trespassing," she sputtered as he cut the motor before the front entrance and lifted her off the bike. At first, he had to hold her up because her legs were so shaky.

"No, I am not. It is my home. *Our* home."

"I beg your pardon!"

"You should. It was not easy finding the perfect dwelling and buying it all within one week."

"Perfect for whom?" She tried not to stare at the house that was beyond beautiful. A two-story cedar home with long porches and a French door leading to colorful garden patios, and, if she was not mistaken, an in-ground pool in back.

"For all of us. I know that you are annoyed with me for not coming to you immediately after being released by Michael, but I am not a man prone to acting with haste."

"Haste? Pfff! More like turtle slow."

He pinched her butt for the interruption. "The sex betwixt us was good, you must admit—"

"I wouldn't know. It's been so long that I forget."

He pinched her other butt cheek. ". . . but I knew you needed more than that. A permanent man in your and the children's life was essential."

"Who says every woman needs a man? Sometimes a good vibrator will do."

"You have a vibrator? Never mind. We will come back to that later. So, I pondered the best way that I could show that I intend to stay around. A home, that is what I decided. Well, Vikar advised me on that course. Being wed with two children, he is much in favor of home and hearth these days."

"You're seeking love advice from your brothers?" she asked with a laugh.

"Hah! I will take any help I can get, even from my mocking, halfbrained brothers," he said. "And, of course, I had to provide a place of safety, Cnut reminded me. Sorry I am to say this, sweetling, but your home is not safe. I will always be fighting Lucipires, and I cannot have my family exposed to potential danger in a development such as yours. Besides, your children need a father."

"Who told you that?"

"No one. I thought of it myself." When she still stood before him, unmoved, he said, "Above all else, I am the one in need." He gulped, and his voice was raspy as he concluded, "I need you. All of you."

"Oh, Mordr!"

He could tell that she was melting, but to give him credit, he didn't immediately do a fist pump in the air for victory, or jump her bones. Instead, he took her hand and led her on a tour. The house was unfurnished but he had a vision for all the rooms, including a bedroom for each of the children, separate rooms over the garage for a housekeeper and a gardener, and a master suite with privacy for themselves.

His eyes gleamed with mischief for a moment. "That last was Ivak's idea. Much sex needs much privacy. Those were his exact words."

She was standing at the windows of the master bedroom looking out over the back lawn. It *was* a perfect house. Large, but not pretentious. Cozy, despite its dimensions. She should be offended that he'd made such a big decision without her input, but she couldn't find anything missing.

"I thought Mayberry was your idea of an ideal home," she said, swiping at a tear.

His face fell. "You would rather have a house in a small town? I thought you preferred being near your work."

"I was teasing."

"Oh." He stared at her. "Will you marry me?" he asked without preamble. Before she had a chance to answer, he said, "No. Do not say anything. Let me convince you." He was already peeling off his jacket and toeing off his boots.

"Which brother gave you that advice?"

"None. I am not entirely without imagination."

She backed up. "Wait. Sex isn't the answer to everything." *Did I really say such a dumb thing? Must be all that vibration loosened something in my brain.*

"Hah! It's damn near enough." His blue eyes were turning silver with arousal. Already.

To be honest, she'd been ready since she hopped onto that wretched motorcycle.

She should have been continuing to protest, but she was too fascinated by Mordr's striptease. At least, it felt like teasing to her. Actually, he was naked within moments. And hung like a horse . . . or was that "hung like a Norse"? *My brain really is falling apart to make such a crude joke with myself. Good thing I didn't say it out loud.*

"All of us Vikings are," he remarked.

Oh damn! I did say it out loud.

Instead of coming up to her then, he leaned against the opposite wall and said, "Your turn. Disrobe for me, sweetling. Slowly."

She laughed. "You're the one supposed to be seducing me."

"Betimes a man can seduce a woman just by watching her unveil her hidden body secrets. And, no, I did not learn that from one of my brothers. There are some talents I perfected on my own."

"Sex talents?"

He nodded and waved a hand peremptorily for her to begin her stripping.

Her pride and her hurt over his absence still had not been assuaged. And she had legitimate reasons for thinking their future together would be a shaky one. "No," she said, reminding herself that she had to make decisions for six, not just herself.

Instead of frowning, he smiled with satisfaction. "I thought you would say that." He walked over to a door, which he opened wide, causing an inner light to go on automatically. It was a narrow walk-in closet with a mirror at one end and hanging pegs along both side walls. From two of those pegs hung long silk scarves.

She made the mistake of walking in to examine the closet closer, realizing too late that the door was closing behind them, dimming the lights. Mordr was in the closet with her and he immediately turned on a manual light switch.

"*Now* the seduction begins," he purred.

And it did.

Boy, did it ever!

Despite her protests and squirming body, he stripped

her down, faster than a starving boy could peel a banana. Too soon, or too late, he had her hands tied to either wall and she was facing the mirror. Buck naked. With a buck naked Mordr standing behind her.

She cringed. "I don't like this, Mordr. Most women don't like looking at their nude bodies in a mirror. We see all our imperfections."

"Ah. Then it will be my job to extol all your perfections," he said, staring at her reflection over one shoulder while his arms encircled her from behind and his big hands cupped her breasts from underneath. "Like these sweet fruits." He flicked the nipples with his thumbs while still raising her breasts higher. "See how they bloom, like big pink berries. I cannot wait to taste them."

She made a gurgling sound, of pleasure or protest, she wasn't sure. It didn't matter. Her Viking was moving on to new sites.

"Do you still not like this?" he murmured as he kissed her shoulder and rubbed his erection against the crease of her buttocks. He had to bend his knees slightly to put them on the same level and spread to bring himself closer. Meanwhile, his hands were busy caressing her abdomen and belly and hips and—thank you, God—lower. "Sweet cream, your skin is. I cannot wait to lick you all over, like a cat. Your smooth skin, my rough tongue."

That image had just about sunk in when she felt a light sweep of calloused palms over her red curls. "Threads of fire, coated with honey. Mmmmm."

It was fascinating to see the contrast of his big hands against her smaller-boned body. It was tantalizing to hear his sex-husky voice murmur against her ear. It was heaven to see how much a man like him could want a woman like her.

"You did not answer me, Miranda."

"What?"

"I asked if you still don't like this mirror foresport? Never mind. I got my answer."

She turned her head and found his lips. Kissing him like this when she couldn't engage other parts of her body, just her mouth, was a novel experience. She moved right and left and back again, seeking the best fit. She parted his lips with her tongue and explored, even passing her tongue over his fangs, which seemed especially sensitive.

He growled, seductively, and took over the kiss. Masterfully.

She could barely stand when he was done with her mouth and moved his kisses to her neck, where he was licking and nipping, restraining himself from fanging her.

Staring forward, she could barely recognize herself. Her hair, which had been in a neat ponytail, was now loose and wild and curly. Her eyes were half lidded. Her lips were bruised and rosy hued from kissing. From this prism, she didn't look half bad, she decided. A male fantasy, for sure. Who was she kidding? It was a female fantasy, too.

"Don't you want to know if I'm seduced yet?" she murmured as she arched her breasts out to ease the ache that throbbed in them.

"Not yet."

"Touch me some more," she told him, rubbing her bottom against his erection, which felt hot and even bigger. Harder.

"I have a better idea, sweetling." He undid the scarves, but when she tried to turn in his arms, he stopped her. "Touch yourself."

"What? No."

"Do not go shy on me now, love. I want to watch when you bring yourself to peak."

Miranda had never done this before. Well, not in front of a mirror. And definitely not in front of a man. But Mordr wasn't any man. And he had called her "love."

So she caressed her own body and took the most pleasure in his glittering silver eyes, his flared nostrils, his parted lips, his hands which were fisted and pressed against either wall. When she could feel her climax coming, she turned and reached for him. "Not alone."

Braced against the wall now, he lifted her up and onto his penis. Slow, slow, slow until he filled her. His hands held her up from under the buttocks and guided the rhythm. Meanwhile he kissed her and whispered, "I love you, I love you, I love you." When her orgasm came with a pounding crash, she found herself lying on the carpeted floor with Mordr above her, neck stretched back, straining to his own climax. Before the end, he put his fangs to her neck and bit her. "Just a little, just a little." Which caused her arousal to rise all over again in shooting waves of the most intense pleasure as her inner folds locked around him, trying to keep him inside. She came again, and then again.

When Mordr's breathing slowed and she felt as if she might actually live, he raised his head and extended his arms, relieving his weight off her. "Will you marry me, Miranda?"

She put a loving hand up to his face. "You have a lot of baggage, Mordr. Marrying you is not as simple as marrying most men."

"I know. It would be asking a lot of you to share my kind of life. Selfish, in fact. But I cannot help but ask. The thought of living another year, let alone dozens . . . hundreds . . . of years alone is just too painful to contemplate."

Her heart ached for him, for the man he had been

when she first met him. Grim, sad, desperately alone with his guilt and rage. Could she condemn him to that fate again?

"I promise to love you and take care of you and your children. I cannot give you children of your own womb, but I will help you with those children of your heart. I will try my best to be a good husband and father."

Tears welled in her eyes at his heartfelt promises. "Will Michael allow us to be together?"

"I think so. He is not happy with me, but, yes, he will agree."

"What if he changes his mind, for whatever reason, next month or next year? I don't think I could bear to go through this kind of separation again. And the children, too. They are just now getting used to your not being around."

"I asked them for your hand in marriage, and they agreed."

She gazed up at him with mock indignation, "Don't you think you should have asked me first?"

"I did, but you said no."

She shook her head at his hopelessness. "Ask again."

"Will you marry me?"

She nodded and when he smiled—*Mordr had a wonderful smile*—she told him, "You had me with the heart bump."

"The what?"

"Heart bump." She showed him by pounding a fist over her heart once and extending the open palm toward him. A graceful gesture done best in slow motion.

"I do that?"

"You do."

They both glanced upward then. Michael.

Epilogue

A garden party, Viking style . . .

Mordr Sigurdsson and Miranda Hart were married three weeks later in the backyard of their new home.

A rental company provided a large tent to accommodate the fifty family members and guests who attended. Caterers provided a fancy buffet for the reception that followed. Some folks were surprised to see Oreos on the table. The bartender was told to make sure there was plenty of beer. Vikings did like their beer! There was also a case of Fake-O in the basement refrigerator for any vangels in need.

To show that he was a modern man and willing to live a modern life for his new wife, Mordr wore a black tuxedo, not the usual Norse wedding attire. Because he'd been out on a mission last week, saving sinners threatened by Lucipires in Atlantic City, his skin was a deep tan, a handsome complement to his blond hair, which was growing out, something his new wife encouraged. She had loved his war braids, which she preferred to call "love braids" when they were in the privacy of their own room.

His brother Vikar, his best man, and his five groomsmen, Trond, Ivak, Cnut, Harek, and Sigurd, wore tuxedos, as well. Darla, who was Miranda's maid of honor, said it was the best eye candy she'd ever seen and soon had everyone calling Sigurd Dr. McDreamy, to which he just smiled, not at all embarrassed. He probably got that a lot at Johns Hopkins. Also, Vikings liked to embarrass one another. It was in their genes.

Miranda wore a calf-length, long-sleeved, scoop-necked cocktail dress of cream-colored lace. Her red hair was piled atop her head, interweaved with a circlet of miniature cream roses and white baby's breath. Mordr whispered to her that the best thing about lace was the skin that peeked through. Pure temptation. She wore an amber heart in an ancient gold pendant about her neck, a bride gift from Mordr the night before. She'd thanked him appropriately.

Sam and Ben gave Miranda away. Larry served as a junior groomsman. All looked adorable in their child-size tuxedos.

Maggie and Linda were bridesmaids in frothy green dresses. Linda wore a tiara, as well, one Mordr had bought for her in a costume store. And Vikar's twin children, Gunnar and Gunnora, served as ring bearer and flower girl, when they weren't scurrying around, chasing a big white bear of a dog wearing a huge green ribbon. Green was the color theme of the wedding, to match the bride's eyes, Mordr told everyone.

The minister, who arrived to perform the ceremony and left immediately after, wore austere clerical garb, which only enhanced his almost celestial appearance. Some said the sun shone down directly on the priest as he stood at the improvised altar, creating the illusion of a halo, which was impossible, of course. When he was performing the rites, he used an aspergillum to sprinkle holy water over the rings the bride and groom would exchange. He managed to wave a goodly amount in Mordr's direction, too, dousing his entire face with holy water. "A Viking can never be too holy," the archangel explained, clearly unapologetic.

Mordr wiped off his face using a St. Jude handkerchief, passed up to him by an old lady from Louisiana sitting in the front pew. Tante Lulu, she was called. Miranda had met her during her short visit to Ivak's home after the kidnapping by Roger. Because the wedding was in Las Vegas, Tante Lulu was dressed like a ninety-year-old showgirl. (Don't ask!)

Before he left, Michael took Harek, Cnut, and Sigurd off to the side and he was seen, stern-faced, wagging a forefinger at them. Everyone surmised it was a warning not to follow their brothers' suit in pursuing mortal women.

The star of the day, aside from the bride, was two-week old Michael Sigurdsson, nicknamed Max, to distinguish him from that other Michael. The archangel who had been there soon after the birth—*possibly during, no one knew for sure*—had told Ivak, "Do not think to get on my better side by naming your child after me." To which Ivak had replied with wide-eyed innocence, "There is a better side?" Everyone could see how Michael doted on his namesake, appointing himself as the little one's personal guardian angel.

But the one who almost brought the house down—rather the tent—was a young vangel named Armod, who was an avid fan of Michael Jackson. He did a rendition of "Billie Jean" that had the crowd clapping and shouting for more. With that encouragement, he performed "Beat It," and "Don't Stop 'Til You Get Enough." After which he was seen teaching all the children how to do his killer break-dance routine. Jack Trixson, who'd provided a deejay for the event, said Armod could join his dance revue any day. Mordr said it was the dumbest thing he'd ever heard of, a Viking who break-dances, but he was seen to tap his feet during the songs, too.

Miranda told Armod how impressed she was with his dancing.

"If you think I am good, you ought to see the VIK dance!" Armod rolled his eyes at her. "They do a cool version of the 'Chains, Chains, Chains' dance from that John Travolta movie *Michael*."

"Who or what is the VIK?" Miranda asked, wondering how anyone could describe Mordr as "cool."

"The seven Sigurdsson brothers. Our commanders."

"Really?" Miranda turned to address Mordr who was talking to Tante Lulu. "Mordr, you told me that you couldn't dance. Now I find out that you do a wonderful Michael dance. And you're cool!"

Mordr shot Armod a scowl, and the boy hurried away, laughing.

"I saw Ivak do the chains dance one time in Loozee-anna when my family was doin' a musical revue at Angola Prison. Talk about!" Tante Lulu piped in.

There had to be a story there, Miranda decided.

"They were really, really good. Even better than Richard Simmons, my all-time favorite fella."

Still another story, Miranda thought.

Mordr steered Miranda away, toward the side of the house. "I am not dancing today. Do not even think of asking the deejay to play that song."

"Whatever you say, sweetling." She rather liked the Viking endearment, and by his grin, Miranda assumed that Mordr liked it, too, when she reciprocated. "Will you do the dance for me later when we're alone?"

"I intend to be naked when we are alone."

"That works for me."

"Miranda!" He grinned. "How daring you are when we are in the midst of a party! I will dance for you if you will do something for me."

She laughed. "I think I've already done *that*."

"This is something different. Will you ride the motorcycle with me around our property when everyone is gone?"

That sounded too tame for Mordr. She figured there had to be a catch.

There was.

"Naked."

"No way!" she said, ducking out from under his arms and returning to their guests.

"Have you never heard, wife, that it is unwise to challenge a Viking," he called after her.

In the end, a whole lot of shaking did go on, but it might have just been dancing. Or not.

When they were almost asleep in each other's arms way later that night, Mordr said. "I will love you forever, heartling."

The trouble was, he meant that literally.

Matchmakers ... and angels ... come in all sizes ...

Somewhere, high in the skies, Michael was sitting on a cloud with two small children. A black-haired boy of five, and a golden-haired girl of six.

"Is Father happy now?" the girl asked.

The archangel nodded.

"Good," the girl and boy said at the same time.

Michael, who was ofttimes referred to as the Warrior Angel, stood, "Come, Jomar, we will practice on your swing some more." He handed the boy his small wooden sword.

Kata preferred to stay behind and sort through the skeins of colored ribands a kind father had bought for her many, many years ago.

Reader Letter

Dear Readers:

Kiss of Wrath was a hard book to write. So many characters! Not just the hero and heroine, the six brothers, the heroine's friend, the Demon Zeb, the cross-dressing neighbor, the Lucipire king, and of course the five children, all of whom needed unique characteristics. But it was an especially satisfying story to write because of Mordr's poignant history. I hope you liked it.

So far, I've taken my Viking vampire angels to Transylvania, Pennsylvania (*Kiss of Pride*), Navy SEAL land in Coronado, California (*Kiss of Surrender*), the bayou with that rowdy Cajun LeDeux family (*Kiss of Temptation*), and now Las Vegas. Too late my editor suggested that a better title for this might have been *A Vangel in Vegas*. Wouldn't that have been great?

Next up will be Sigurd's story. He's the Viking brother, a noted healer and currently a physician at Johns Hopkins, who is guilty of the sin of envy. This is proving to be another hard book to write. How to make a man eaten up by envy into a heroic character? Methinks (Good heavens, I'm starting to talk like a Viking {grin}) Sigurd needs a good woman to turn him around, don't you?

There will be even more vangel books coming, of course. After all, there are two more Sigurdsson brothers left with stories to tell. Plus, Zebulan, the good demon, intrigues me with his tragic past. Don't you think he would make a good hero?

In addition, there are still a few Vikings dying (forgive the pun) to tell their stories in a historical setting. Alrek the clumsy Viking, Wulfgar the Welsh knight, Jostein the somber Viking with an estranged wife, Jamie the Scots Viking, Finn the Vain, or Tykir's brothers—Guthrom, Starri, or Selik. So many choices! Do you have a preference?

Please check my website, www.sandrahill.net, or my Facebook page, SandrHillauthor, for more details on all my books and continually changing news. There are often special promotions with bargain prices on books. I periodically have great Viking or angel jewelry giveaways on my Facebook page. Also, signed bookplates are available for any or all books by sending a SASE to Sandra Hill. PO Box 604, State College, PA 16804.

As always, I wish you smiles in your reading.

Sandra Hill

Glossary

Asgard—home of the gods, comparable to Christian Heaven

Aspergillum—liturgical instrument used to sprinkle holy water

A-Viking—a Norse practice of sailing away to other countries for the purpose of looting, settlement, or mere adventure; could be for a period of several years

Berserker—an ancient Norse warrior who fought in a frenzied rage during battle

Birka—Viking-age market town where Sweden is now located

Braies—slim pants worn by men

Brynja—flexible chain-mail shirt

Ceorl (or churl)—free peasant, person of the lowest classes

Cotters—farmers or peasants

Cubit—type of Biblical measurement, usually equal to roughly 17.5 inches

Drukkinn (various spellings)—drunk

Fjord—a narrow arm of the sea, often between high cliffs

Frankish—having to do with Frankland (as France was known at that time)

Gammelost—pungent Norse cheese with a greenish-brown crust

Garth—yard or courtyard

Haakai—high-level demon

Halogland—Northern Norway

Hauberk—long defensive shirt or coat, usually made of chain links or leather

Hedeby—Viking-age market town where Germany is now located

Hersir—military commander

Hird/hirdsmen—permanent troop that a chieftain or noble might have

Hnefatafl—a Viking board game

Hordaland—Norway

Hordling—lower-level demon

Housecarls—troops assigned to a king's or lord's household on a longterm, sometimes permanent, basis

Imps—lower-level demons, foot soldiers so to speak

Jarl—high-ranking Norseman similar to an English earl or wealthy landowner, could also be a chieftain or minor king

Jomsvikings—legendary troop of elite Norse mercenaries

Jutland—Denmark

Kaupang—Norse market town

Keep—house, usually the manor house or main building for housing the owners of the estate

Longship—narrow, open water-going vessels with oars and square sails, perfected by Viking shipbuilders, noted for their speed and ability to ride in both shallow waters and deep oceans

Lucifer/Satan—the fallen angel Lucifer became known as the demon Satan

Lucipires/Lucies—demon vampires

Mead—fermented honey and water

Mjollnir—Thor's hammer

Motte—a high, flat-topped earthworks mound

Mungs—type of demon, below the haakai in status, often very large and oozing slime or mung

Muspell—part of Nifhelm, one of the nine worlds in the Norse afterlife, Muspell is known by its fires guarded by Sert and his flaming sword

Nithing—a Norse insult meaning a person who is less than nothing

Odin—king of all the Viking gods

Purdah—practice in certain countries of screening women from men or strangers by wearing all-enveloping clothing

Sennight—one week

Seraphim—high ranking angel

Skald—poet

Stasis—state of inactivity, rather like being frozen in place

Svealand—Sweden

Sword dew—blood

Teletransport—transfer of matter from one point to another without traversing physical space

Thralls—slaves

Traiteur—Cajun folk healer

Trepanning—drilling a hole in the head for medicinal reasons

Uisge beatha—Scotch whiskey

Valhalla—hall of the slain; Odin's magnificent hall in Asgard

Valkyries—female warriors in the afterlife who do Odin's will

Vangels—Viking vampire angels

Vestfold—Southern Norway

VIK—the seven brothers who head the vangels

Wergild—a man's worth offered in payment

Read on for a sneak peek at

Vampire in Paradise

the next book in the

DEADLY ANGELS SERIES

from *New York Times* bestselling author

SANDRA HILL

Available in print and ebook
from Avon Books
December 2014

Prologue

The Norselands, A.D. 850 . . .
Only the strongest survived in that harsh land . . .

Sigurd Sigurdsson sat near the high table of King Haakon's yule feast sipping at the fine ale from his own jewel-encrusted, silver horn. Tuns of mead and ale and rare Frisian wine flowed.

Favored guests at the royal feast had their choice amongst spit-roasted wild boar, venison and mushroom stew, game birds stuffed with chestnuts, a swordfish the size of a small longboat, eels swimming in spiced cream sauce, and all the vegetable side dishes one could imagine. Honey oak cakes and dried fruit trifles finished off the meal for those not filled to overflowing. Entertainment was provided by a quartet of lute players who could scarce be heard over the animated conversation and laughter. Good cheer abounded.

In the midst of the loud, joyous celebration, Sigurd's demeanor was quiet and sad.

But that was nothing new. Sigurd had been known as a dark, brooding Viking for many of his twenty and seven years. Darker and more brooding as the years marched on. And he wasn't even *drukkinn*.

Some said the reason for Sigurd's discontent was the conflict betwixt two warring sides of his nature. A fierce warrior in battle and, at the same time, a noted physician with innate healing skills inherited from and homed by his grandmother afore her passing to the Other World when he'd been a boyling.

Sigurd knew better. He had a secret sickness of the soul, and its name was Envy. Never truly happy, never satisfied, he always wanted what he didn't have, whether it be a chest of gold, the latest, fastest longship, a prosperous estate, the finest sword. A woman. And he did whatever necessary to attain that new best thing. *Whatever.*

'Twas like a gigantic worm he'd found years past in the bowels of a dying man. Egolf the Farrier had been a giant of a burly man in his prime, but at his death when he was only thirty he'd been little more than a skeleton with no fat and scant flesh to cover his bones. The malady had no doubt started years before innocently enough with a tiny worm in an apple or some spoiled meat, but over the years, attached to his innards like a ravenous babe, the slimy creature devoured the food Egolf ate, and Egolf had a huge appetite, in essence starving the man to death.

"Sig, my friend!" A giant hand clapped him on the shoulder and his close friend and *hersir* Bertim sat down on the bench beside him. Beneath his massive red beard, the Irish Viking's face was florid with drink. "You are sitting upright," Bertim accused him. "Is that still your first horn of ale that you nurse like a babe at teat?"

"What an image!" Sigurd shook his head with amusement. "I must needs stay sober. The queen may yet produce a new son for Haakon this night."

"Her timing is inconvenient, but then a yule child brings good luck." Bertim raised his bushy eyebrows as a sudden thought struck him. "Dost act as midwife now?"

"When it is the king's whelp, I do."

Bertim laughed heartily.

"In truth, Elfrida has been laboring for a day and night so far with no result. The delivery promises to be difficult."

Bertim nodded. 'Twas the way of nature. "What has the king promised you for your assistance?"

"Naught much," Sigurd replied with a shrug. "Friendship. Lot of good that friendship does me, though. Dost notice I am not sitting at the high table?"

"And yet that arse licker Svein One-Ear sits near the king," Bertim commiserated.

I should be up there. Ah, well. Mayhap if I do the king this one new favor . . . he shrugged. The seating was a small slight, actually.

A serving maid interrupted them, leaning over the table to replenish their beverages. The way her breasts brushed against each of their shoulders gave clear signal that she would be a willing bed partner to either or both of them. Bertim was too far gone in the drink and too fearful of the wrath of his new Norse wife, and Sigurd lacked interest in services offered so easily. The maid shrugged and made her way to the next hopefully willing male.

Picking up on their conversation, Bertim said, "The friendship of a king is naught to minimize. It can be priceless."

Sigurd had reason to recall Bertim's ale-wise words later that night, rather in the wee hours of the morning, when Queen Elfrida, despite Sigurd's best efforts, delivered a deformed, puny babe, a girl, and Sigurd was asked by the king, in the name of friendship, to take the infant away and cut off its whispery breath.

It was not an unusual request. In this harsh land, only the strongest survived, and the practice of infanticide was ofttimes an act of kindness. Or so the beleaguered parents believed.

But Sigurd did not fulfill the king's wishes. Leastways, not right away. Visions of another night and another life and death decision plagued Sigurd as he carried the swaddled babe in his arms, its cries little more than the mewls of a weakling kitten.

Despite his full-length, hooded fur cloak, the wind and cold air combined to chill him to the bone. He tucked the babe closer to his chest and imagined he felt her heart beat steady and true. Approaching the cliff that hung over the angry sea, where he would drop the child after pinching its tiny nose, Sigurd kept murmuring, "'Tis for the best, 'tis for the best." His eyes misted over, but that was probably due to the snow flakes that began to flutter heavily in front of him.

He would do as the king asked. Of course he would. But betimes it was not such a gift having royal friends.

Just then, he heard a loud voice bellow, "SIGURD! Halt! At once!"

He turned to see the strangest thing. Despite the blistering cold, a dark-haired man wearing naught but a long, white, rope-belted gown in the Arab style approached with hands extended.

Without words, Sigurd knew that the man wanted the child. To his surprise, Sigurd handed over the bundle that carried his body heat to the stranger.

"Take her, Caleb," the man said to yet another man in a white robe who appeared at his side.

"Yes, Michael." Caleb bowed as if the first man were a king or some important personage.

More kings! That is all I need!

The Michael person passed the no-longer crying

infant to Caleb, who enfolded the babe in what appeared to be wings, but was probably a white fur cloak, and walked off, disappearing into the now heavy snowfall.

"Will you kill the child?" Sigurd asked, realizing for the first time that he might not have been able to do it himself. Not this time.

"Viking, will you never learn?" Michael asked.

He said "Viking" as if it were a bad word. Sigurd was too stunned by this tableau to be affronted.

"Who are you? *What* are you?" Sigurd asked as he noticed the massive white wings spreading out behind the man.

"Michael. An archangel."

Sigurd had heard of angels before and seen images on wall paintings in a Byzantium church. "Did you say arse angel?"

"You know I did not. Thou art a fool."

No sense of humor at all. Sigurd assumed that an *arch*angel was a special angel. "Am I dead?"

"Not yet."

That did not sound promising. "But soon?"

"Sooner than thou could imagine," he said without the least bit of sympathy.

Can I fight him? Somehow, Sigurd did not think that was possible.

"You are a grave sinner, Sigurd."

He knows my name. "That I freely admit."

"And yet you do not repent. And yet you would have taken another life tonight."

"Another?" Sigurd inquired, although he knew for a certainty what Michael referred to, and it was not some enemy he had covered with sword dew in righteous battle. But how could the man . . . rather angel . . . possibly know what had been Sigurd's closely held secret all these years? No one else knew.

"There are no secrets, Viking," Michael informed him.

Holy Thor! Now he is reading my mind!

Before Sigurd could reply, the snow betwixt them swirled, then cleared to reveal a picture of himself as a boyling of ten years or so bent over his little ailing brother Aslak, a five-year-old of immense beauty, even for a male child. Pale white hair, perfect features, a bubbling, happy personality. Everyone loved Aslak, and Aslak loved everyone in return.

Sigurd had hated his little brother, despite the fact that Aslak followed him about like an adoring puppy. Aslak was everything that Sigurd was not. Sigurd's dull brown hair only turned blond when he got older and the tresses had been sun-bleached on sea voyages. His facial features had been marred by the pimples of a youthling. He had an unpleasant, betimes surly, disposition. In other words, unlikable, or so Sigurd had thought.

Being the youngest of the Sigurdsson boys, before Aslak, and the only one still home, Sigurd had been more aware of his little brother's overwhelming popularity. In truth, in later years, when others referred to the seven Sigurdsson brothers, they failed to recall that at one time there had been eight.

Sigurd blinked and peered again into the swirling snow picture of that fateful night. His little brother's wheezing lungs laboring for life through the long predawn hours. His mother Lady Elsa had begged Sigurd to help because, even at ten years of age, he had healing hands. Sigurd had pretended to help, but in truth he had not employed the steam tenting or special herb teas that might have cured his dying brother. Aslak had died, of course, and Sigurd knew it was his fault.

Looking up to see Michael staring at him, Sigurd said, "I was jealous."

Michael shook his head. "Nay, jealousy is a less than admirable trait. Your sin was envy."

"Envy. Jealousy. Same thing."

"Lackwit!" Michael declared, his wings bristling wide like a riled goose. "Jealousy is a foolish emotion, but envy destroys the peace of the soul. When was the last time you were at peace, Viking?"

Sigurd thought for a long moment. "Never, that I recall."

"Envy stirs hatred in a person, causing one to wish evil on another. That was certainly the case with your brother Aslak. And with so many others you have maligned or injured over the years."

Sigurd hung his head. 'Twas true.

"Envy causes a person to engage in immoderate quests for wealth or power or relationships that betimes defy loyalty and justice."

Sigurd nodded. The archangel was painting a clear picture of him and his sorry life.

"The worst thing is that you were given a treasured talent. The gift of healing. Much like the Apostle Luke. But you have disdained it. Abused it. And failed to nourish it for a greater good."

"An apostle?" Sigurd was not a Christian, but he was familiar with tales from their Bible. "You would have me be as pure as an apostle? I am a Viking."

"Idiots! I am forced to work with idiots." Michael rolled his eyes. "Nay, no one expects purity from such as you. Enough! For your grave sins, and those of your six brothers . . . in fact, all the Vikings as a whole . . . the Lord is sorely disappointed. You must be punished. In the future, centuries from now, there will be no Viking nation, as such. Thus sayeth the Lord," Michael pronounced. "And as for you Sigurdsson miscreants . . . your time on earth is measured."

"By death?"

Michael nodded. "Thou art already dead inside, Sigurd. Now your body will be, as well."

So be it. It was a fate all men must face, though he had not expected it to come so soon. "You mention my brothers. They will die, too?"

"They will. If they have not already passed."

Seven brothers dying in the same year? This was the fodder of sagas. Skalds would be speaking of them forever more. "Will I be going to Valhalla, or the Christian heaven, or that other place?" He shivered inwardly at the thought of that latter, fiery fate.

"None of those. You are being given a second chance."

"To live?" This was good news.

Michael shook his head. "To die and come back to serve your Heavenly Father in a new role."

"As an angel?" Sigurd asked with incredulity.

"Hardly," Michael scoffed. "Well, actually, you would be a vangel. A Viking vampire angel put back on earth to fight Satan's demon vampires, Lucipires. For seven hundred years, your penance would be to redeem your sins by serving in God's army under my mentorship."

Sigurd could tell that Michael wasn't very happy with that mentorship role, but he could not dwell on that. It was the amazing ideas the archangel was putting forth.

"Do you agree?" Michael asked.

Huh? What choice did he have? The fires of hell, or centuries of living as some kind of soldier. "I agree, but what exactly is a vampire?"

He soon found out. With a raised hand, Michael pointed a finger at Sigurd and unimaginable pain wracked his body, including his mouth where the jaw bones seemed to crack and realign themselves, emerging with fangs, like a wolf. He fell to his knees as his shoulder blades also seem to explode as if struck with a broadsword.

"Fangs? Was that necessary?" he gasped, glancing upward at the celestial being whose arms were folded across his chest, staring down at him.

"You'll need them for sucking blood."

"From what?"

"What do you think? From a peach? Idiot! Fom people . . . or demons."

What? Eew! He expects me to drink blood? From living persons? Or demons? I do not know about this bargain.

"Thou can still change thy mind, Viking," Michael said.

Reading my mind again! Damn! "And go to hell?"

"Thou sayest it."

Sigurd thought about negotiating with the angel, but knew instinctively that it would do no good. He nodded. "It will be as you say."

Moments later, when the pain subsided somewhat, the angel raised him up and studied him with icy contempt, or was it pity? "Go! And do better this time, vangel."

On those words, Sigurd fell backwards and over the cliff. Falling, falling, falling toward the black, roiling sea. He discovered in that instant that there was one thing a vangel didn't have. Wings.

One

Florida, 2014
Sometimes life throws you a life
line, sometimes a sinker . . .

No one watching Marisa Lopez emerge from the
medical center in downtown Miami would have
guessed that she'd just been delivered a death blow.
Not for herself, but for her five-year-old daughter
Isobel.

Marisa had become a master at hiding her emotions. When she'd found out she was pregnant midway
through her junior year at Florida State and her scum-
bag boyfriend skipped campus faster than his two
hundred dollar running shoes could carry him. When
her hopes for a career in physical therapy went down
the tubes. When she'd found out two years ago that
her little girl had an inoperable brain tumor. When the
blasted tumor kept growing, and Izzie got sicker and
sicker. When Marisa had lost her third job in a row
because of missing so many days for Izzie's appointments. And now . . . well, she refused to break down
now either, not where others could see.

And there *were* people watching. Looking like a young Sophia Loren, not to mention being five-ten in her three-inch heels, she often got double takes, and the occasional wolf whistle. And she knew how to work it, especially when tips were involved at The Palms Health Spa where she was now employed as a certified massage therapist, as well as the Salsa bar where she worked nights at a second job. Was she burning the candle at both ends? Hell, yes. She wished she could do more.

Slinging her knock-off Coach bag over one shoulder, she donned a pair of oversized, fake Dior sunglasses. Her scoop-necked, white silk blouse was tucked into a black pencil skirt, belted at her small waist with a counterfeit, red Gucci belt. Walking briskly on pleather Jimmy Choos, she made her way down the street to her car parked on a side street . . . a ten-year-old Ford Focus. Not quite the vehicle to go with her seemingly expensive attire. Little did folks know that hidden in her parents' garage was a fortune in counterfeit and knock-off items, from Rolex watches to Victoria's Secret lingerie, thanks to her jailbird brother Steve. A fortune that could not be tapped because someone besides her brother would end up in jail. *Probably me, considering the bad luck cloud that seems to be hanging over my head.*

It wasn't against the law to wear the stuff, just so long as she didn't sell it. To her shame, she'd been tempted on more than one occasion this past year to do just that. Desperation trumps morality on occasion. So far, she hadn't succumbed, though all her friends knew where to come when they needed something "special."

Her parents had no idea what was in the green-lidded bins that had been taped shut with duct tape. They probably thought it was Steve's clothes and other worldly goods. Hah!

Once inside her car, with the air conditioner on blast, Marisa put her forehead on the steering wheel and wept. Soul searing sobs and gasps for breath as she cried out her misery. Marisa knew that she had to get it all out before she went home where she would have to pretend optimism before Izzie, who was way too perceptive for her age. Her parents, on the other hand, would need to know the prognosis. They would be crushed, as she was.

A short time later, by mid afternoon, with her emotions under control and her makeup retouched, Marisa walked up the sidewalk to her parents' house. She noticed that the Lopez Plumbing van wasn't in the driveway; so, her father must still be at work. Good. Marisa didn't need the double whammy of their reaction to the latest news. One at a time would be best.

Marisa had moved into her parents' house, actually the apartment over the infamous garage, after Izzie's initial diagnosis two years ago . . . to save money and take advantage of her parents' generous offer to baby sit while Marisa worked. Steve, who had been the apartment's prior occupant, was already in jail by that time, serving a two to six for armed robbery. The idiot had carried an old boy scout knife in his pocket when he'd stolen the cash register receipts at the Seven Eleven. Ironically, he'd never been nabbed for selling counterfeit goods . . . his side job, so to speak.

Unfortunately, this wasn't Steve's first stint in the slammer, although it was his first felony. She hoped he learned something this time.

Marisa used her key to enter the thankfully air-conditioned house. Immediately, her mood lightened somewhat in the home's cozy atmosphere. Overstuffed sofa and chair. Her dad's worn leather recliner that bore the imprint of his behind from long years of use. And the smell . . . ah! The air was permeated with the scent of spicy browned beef and tomatoes and fresh baked bread. It was Monday; so, it must be Vaca Vieja, or shredded beef, her father's favorite, which would be served over rice with a fresh salad. No bagged salads here. No store bought bread.

Izzie was asleep on the couch where she'd been watching cartoons on the television that had been turned to a low volume. The pretty, soft, pink and lavender afghan her grandmother had knitted for her covered her from shoulders to bare feet, but even so, her thin frame was apparent. There were dark smudges beneath her eyes.

Marisa put her bag on the coffee table and leaned down to kiss the black curls that capped her little girl's head. At one time, Izzie had sported a wild mass of corkscrew curls, all of which had been lost in her first bout of radiation. A wasted effort, the radiation had turned out. To everyone's surprise, especially Izzie, the shorter do suited her better.

With a deep sigh, Marisa entered the kitchen.

Her mother was standing at the counter washing lettuce, tomatoes, cucumbers and radishes that she must have just picked from the small garden in the back yard. She wore her standard daytime "uniform." A blouse tucked into stretchy waist slacks, and curlers on her head. Soon she would shower and change to a dress and medium pumps, her black hair all fluffed out, lipstick and a little makeup applied, to greet Daddy when he got home. It was a ritual she had followed every single day since her marriage thirty-two years ago. Just as she maintained her trim, attractive figure at fifty-nine. To please Daddy, as much as herself.

Her mother must have sensed her presence because she turned abruptly. At first glance, she gasped and put a hand to her heart. No hiding anything from a mother.

"Oh, Marisa, honey!" her mother said. Making the sign of the cross, she sat down at the kitchen table and motioned for Marisa to sit, too.

First-generation Cuban-Americans, they'd named their first-born child Marisa Angelica, after Grandma Lopez "back home," and Aunt Angelica who was a nun serving some special order in the Philippines. Steve was Diego Estefan Lopez. The louse!

"Tell me," her mother insisted.

"Doctor Stern says the tumor has grown, only slightly, in the past two months, but her brain and other tissue are increasing like any normal growing child and pressing against . . ." Tears welled in her eyes, despite her best efforts, and she took several of the tissues her mother handed her. "Oh, Mom! He says, without that experimental surgery, she only has a year to live. And even with the surgery, it might not work."

Izzie's only hope, and it was a slim one at best, was some new procedure being tried in Switzerland. Because it was experimental, insurance would not cover the expense. The two hundred thousand dollar expense might just as well be a hundred million, considering Marisa's empty bank account, as well as her parents, who'd second mortgaged their house when Steve got into so much trouble.

She and her mother both bawled then. What else could they do? Well, her mother had ideas, of course.

Her mother stood and poured them both cups of her special brewed coffee from an old metal coffee pot on the stove. No fancy pancy (her mother's words) Keurig or other modern devices for the old-fashioned lady. They both put one packet of diet sugar and a dollop of milk in their cups before taking the first sip.

"First off, we will pray," her mother declared. "And we will ask Angelica to pray for Izzie, too."

"Mom! With the hurricane that hit the Philippines last year, Aunt Angelica has way too much on her prayer schedule."

"Tsk-tsk!" her mother said. "A nun always has time for more prayers. And I will ask my Rosary Altar Society ladies to start a novena. A miracle, that is what we need."

Marisa rolled her eyes before she could catch herself.

Her mother wagged a forefinger at her. "Nothing is impossible with prayer."

It couldn't hurt, Marisa supposed, although she was beginning to lose faith, despite being raised in a strict Catholic household. Hah! Look how much good that moral upbringing had done Steve.

That wasn't fair, she immediately chastised herself. Steve brought on his problems, and was not the issue today. Izzie was. Besides, who was she to talk. Having a baby without marriage. "We'll pray then, Mom," she conceded. *If I still can.*

She let the peaceful ambiance of the kitchen fill her then. To Cubans, the kitchen was the heart of the home, and this little portion of the fifty-year-old ranch style house was indeed that. The oak kitchen cabinets were original to the house, but the way her mother cleaned, they gleamed with a golden patina, like new. Curtains with embroidered roses framed the double-window over the sink. In the middle of the room was an old table that could seat six, in the center of which was a single red rose in a slim crystal vase, the sentimental weekly gift from her father to her mother. The red leather on the chair seats had been reupholstered twice now by her father's hands in his tool room in the basement. A Tiffany-style fruited lamp hung over the table.

A shuffling sound alerted them to Izzie coming

toward the kitchen. Trailing the afghan in one hand and her favorite stuffed animal, a ratty, floppy eared rabbit named Lucky in the other, she didn't notice at first that her mother was home.

Marisa stood. "Well, if it isn't Sleeping Beauty?"

"Mommy!" Dropping the afghan and Lucky, she raced into Marisa's open arms. Marisa twirled Izzie around in her arms until they were both dizzy. She dropped down to the chair again, with Izzie on her lap, both of them laughing. "Dizzy Izzie!" her daughter squealed, like she always did.

"For you, Isobella." Her mother placed before Izzie a plastic Barbie plate of chocolate-sprinkled sugar cookies and a matching teacup of chocolate milk. Her mother would have already crushed some of the hated pills into the milk.

"I'm not hungry, Nana," Izzie whined, burying her face against Marisa's chest.

"You have to eat something, honey. At least drink the milk," Marisa coaxed.

After a good half hour of bribing, teasing, singing, and game playing, she and her mother got Izzie to eat two of the cookies and drink all of the milk.

"What did the doctor say?" Izzie asked suddenly.

Uh-oh! Izzie knew that Marisa had gone to the medical center to discuss her latest test results. "Doctor Stern said you are growing like a weed. No, he said you are growing faster than Jack and the Beanstalk's magic beans." At least that was true. She was growing, despite her loss of weight.

Izzie giggled. "I'm a big girl now."

"Yes, you are, sweetie," Marisa said, hugging her little girl warmly.

Somehow, someway, I am going to get the money for Izzie, Marisa vowed silently. *It might take one of my mother's miracles, but I am not going to let my precious little girl die. But how? That is the question.*

The answer came to her that evening when she was at La Cucaracha, the Salsa bar where she worked a second job as a waitress and occasional bartender. Well, a possible answer.

"A porno convention?" she exclaimed, at first disbelieving that her best friend Inga Johanssen would make such a suggestion.

"More than that. The first ever International Conference on Pornography: Freedom of Expression," Inga told her.

"Bull!" Marisa opined.

They were in a back room of the restaurant, taking a break. They wore the one-shouldered, knee-length, black Salsa dresses with ragged hems, La Cucharacha's uniform for women (the men wore slim black pants and white shirts). They were both roughly five foot eight, but otherwise completely different. Where Marisa was dark and olive skinned, Inga was blond and Nordic. Where Marisa's figure was what might be called voluptuous, Inga's was slim and boylike, except for the boobs she bought last year. The garments they wore were not meant to be revealing but to accommodate the restaurant's grueling heat due to the energetic dancing. They needed a break occasionally just to cool off.

Inga waved a newspaper article at her and read aloud, "All the movers and shakers in the pornography industry will be there. Multi-billion dollar investors, movie producers, Internet gurus, actors and actresses, store owners, franchisees—"

"Franchisees of what?" Marisa interrupted. "Smut?"

Inga made a tsking sound and continued, "—sex toy makers, instructors on DIY home videos—"

"What's DIY?" Marisa interrupted again.

"Do it yourself."

"Oh, good Lord!"

"Martin Vanderfelt—"

"A made-up name if I ever heard one."

"Please, Marisa, give me a chance."

Marisa made a motion of zipping her lips.

"Martin Vanderfelt, the conference organizer, told the Daily Buzz reporter, 'Our aim is to remove the sleaze factor from pornography and gain recognition as a legitimate professional enterprise serving the public.'"

Marisa rolled her eyes but said nothing.

"This is the best part. It's being held for one week on a tropical island off the Florida Keys. Grand Keys, a plush special events convention center, comes complete with all the amenities of a four-star hotel, including indoor and outdoor pools, snorkeling and boating services, beauty salons and health spas, numerous restaurants with world class cuisines, nightclubs, tennis courts—"

"I'd like to see some of those over-endowed porno queens bouncing around on a tennis court," Marisa had to interject.

Inga smiled. "So cynical! Becky Bliss will be there. You know who she is, don't you?"

Even Marisa knew Becky Bliss. She was the porno princess famous for being able to twerk while on top, having sex. "Are you suggesting we might learn how to do *that*?"

"It wouldn't hurt. Maybe it would enhance your non-existent sex life."

"Not like *that*!"

"Okay. Besides, John Rocket will be there, too."

Marisa had no idea who John Rocket was, but she could guess.

"Anyhow, this conference isn't for your everyday Joe, the porn aficionado. It costs five thousand dollars to attend. The only access to the island is by water. You can't drive there, of course. They expect to see lots of yachts and seaplanes."

"Okay, I give up. Why would you or I even consider something like this? Oh, my God! You're not suggesting I make porno films to raise money for Izzie, are you?"

"Of course not. Look. This article says they are looking to hire employees for up to two weeks at above scale wages, all expenses paid, including transportation. Everything from waiters and waitresses to beauticians to diving instructors ... even a doctor and nurse. Waiters and waitresses can expect to earn at least two thousand dollars, and that doesn't include tips. Upper scale professions, much more."

"I still can't see us doing something like this."

"Why not? We don't have to like all the people that come to the Salsa bar, but we still serve them food or drinks."

"I don't know," Marisa said.

"There's something else to consider."

"If you're going to suggest that I might find a sugar daddy to pay for Izzie's operation, forget about it." *But don't think it hasn't occurred to me.*

"No, but there will be lots of Internet types there. Maybe you could find someone with the technical ability to set up a website for Izzie to raise funds."

"I already tried that, but every company I contacted said it has been overdone. There's no profit for them."

"Maybe you've made the wrong contacts. Maybe if you met someone, one on one ... I don't know, Marisa, isn't it worth a try?"

"I'll think about it," Marisa said, to her ⁄ prise.

"Applications and interviews for employment are being held at the Marriott in Key West next Friday," Inga pointed out. "Don't think too long."

"Don't push," Marisa said.

They heard the Salsa band break out in a lively instrumental with a rich Latin American beat. A prelude to the beginning of another set of dance music.

As they headed back to work, Inga said, "I'll drive."

Two

Transylvania, Pennsylvania, 2014 A.D.
It was a male fantasy assignment ... or was it?...

*S*igurd was late arriving at the castle for the conclave called by St. Michael the Archangel.

He'd run into a traffic pile-up on the Beltway when he left his job as a cancer research physician at Johns Hopkins. Then he'd gotten behind a vampire parade in this whack-job touristy town that celebrated ... guess what? Yep. Dracula wannabes.

Hah! If they knew how inconvenient fangs actually are, Sigurd thought, running his tongue under his own pointy set, *they would keep their fool mouths shut and take up a saner hobby, like sword fighting. Try kissing a maid when the incisors are out. Or drinking a cold beer, modern man's wonderful invention that surely rivals our ancient Viking favorite beverage ... mead. I scare even myself when I happen upon a mirror and see how I look.*

He could have teletransported, but vangels were warned to use that talent only on special occasions. Like when they were needed quickly to back-up one of their fellow Viking vampire angels. (He still shuddered after all these years to consider himself one of those.) Or when a Lucipire was about to gobble them up.

He pressed the code numbers into the remote on his SUV dashboard and watched as the gates opened onto the massive property where his oldest brother Vikar was converting an old, rundown castle into one of the headquarters for all the vangels. Vikar was three years into the project, and the progress was slow, as evidenced by scaffolding around one of the towers. Sigurd parked his vehicle in the back courtyard, rather than going down into the underground parking garage. He didn't expect to be staying long.

He entered the kitchen, about the size of most longhouses "back in the day," a modern expression he was embarrassed to find himself using way too much lately. He wasn't that old. Well, actually he was. Twenty-seven human years, but a mind-boggling one thousand, one hundred and ninety-one years. His original sentence . . . uh, assignment as a vangel had somehow been extended, and extended, by a few sins he was unable to avoid over the years. Or a lot. But, really, did Mike (the rude name the VIK—acronym for Sigurd and his six brothers—had given their heavenly mentor) expect virile Viking men to remain celibate for decades, let alone centuries?

Sigurd shook his head to clear it. His mind seemed to be wandering so much today. Probably overwork on his latest medical project, not to mention having gone on a vangel mission in Baltimore over the weekend where a Lucie horde had been nesting in one of the slums, preying on drug addicts. Lucies was a nickname they had given to the demon vampires.

The scent of cooking food hit Sigurd first, and he noticed one of the vangels, their cook, Lizzie Borden (yes, *that* Lizzie Borden) hacking away at what appeared to be the hind quarter of a cow, then tossing the pieces to brown in a huge, sizzling iron skillet.

"Good morn, Mrs. Borden," he said.

"Pfff! What is good about feeding fifty ravenous Vikings?" Lizzie always complained about her cooking chores, but she guarded her domain like a Norseman protecting his longship.

He opened the commercial size fridge to get a bottle of Fake-O, the blood substitute he had invented several years ago to supplement the vangels' supply when it had been too long since they saved sinners or annihilated Lucies. Blood caused a vangel's skin to have a nice suntanned hue. Without it, their skin turned lighter and lighter until it was almost transparent.

"Where is everyone?" he asked Lizzie after quaffing down the thick beverage in one long swallow, then wiping his mouth with the back of a hand, fighting a shiver of disgust. One of these days, when he had more time, he would have to do something about the taste.

"In the front parlor. They started an hour ago," Lizzie pointed out with relish. She didn't care much for Vikings.

"Thanks, Liz," he said, just to annoy here.

She said something very unangelic as he walked away. Not that any of them were angels. More like fallen angels.

On the way down the long corridor he ran into Regina, who had been a witch back in the thirteenth century Norselands. A real witch, the kind who brewed potions in a boiling cauldron and issued curses hither and yon. She was always threatening to do unsavory things to the manparts of the various VIK when they displeased her.

"Why aren't you in the meeting?" he asked, in a very polite manner, if he did say so himself.

Despite his good manners, she sneered at him.

"Mike was done with us peons hours ago. He is dealing with the sins of you VIK now." She cackled. She actually cackled, and added, "Someone is about to have his arse chewed up good and well."

"Me?" he inquired with mock innocence and made a rude gesture at the hissing black cat that followed on Regina's heels.

The cat tried to piss on his boot but he managed to get away, unscathed. Regina was muttering something behind him, probably a curse. He would have to get a codpiece to protect himself when he left here today. Where did one buy a codpiece anyhow?

He tried to enter the parlor unobtrusively, to no avail.

His six brothers turned as one, eyebrows arched, lips twitching with humor at his expense. They sat in a semicircle before Mike, who was sprawled lazily in a throne-like, wingback chair, jeans-clad legs crossed at the ankles over a pair of athletic shoes. The latest, very expensive Adidas. Mike had a fascination with modern footwear. A large, gold cross hung on a thick chain around his neck, nestling on his pure white t-shirt. The only other indication of his saintliness was a rather halo-like glow about his long, black hair. No wings today.

"Ah! The prodigal vangel deigns to honor us with his presence," Mike said. Sarcasm was a favorite tool of Mike's, and it was usually directed at the VIK. None of them were immune.

"Sorry. There was a—"

Mike waved a hand, uninterested in his explanation. "Vikar, recap for the tardy one what we have been discussing."

Vikar winked at Sigurd, who sat down in the empty chair beside him. "It appears that Jasper and his demon vampires are growing in number. Well over two thousand, at last count. Whereas the number of vangels is closer to five hundred." Jasper was the king of the demon vampire, one of the fallen angels who had been kicked out of heaven along with Lucifer. "We are going to add more new vangels to our ranks . . . one hundred at a time, under the training of Cnut and Mordr. And there is a big event being planned by Jasper for next month."

Sigurd tilted his head in question.

"Let Harek show him," Mike directed.

Harek sat in the chair on Sigurd's other side. He was the computer guru in their ranks. He slid the laptop from his knees to Sigurd's and pointed to the screen. "St. Lucy Island."

"And is that not an appropriate name?" Mike interrupted.

Sigurd saw a picture of a lush, tropical island with what appeared to be a massive hotel complex from which bungalows stemmed out like the spokes of a wheel. Luxury yachts and sailing vessels were anchored in the clear blue waters.

"It is an island off the Florida Keys. That large structure there is a special events hotel. And, whoo boy, is there a special event being planned there." This from a grinning Harek.

"One which Jasper hopes to infiltrate where he will harvest more souls for his evil legions," Michael told Sigurd.

"The first ever International Conference on Pornography." Harek grinned at him.

Sigurd frowned, suspicious of that grin, and turned to Mike. "What has this to do with me? I am a physician at Johns Hopkins."

"Not any more," Mike said. "Thou art about to render thy resignation."

"Why? I do good work there," Sigurd protested.

"You do, but you have been in one place for twenty years, and you do not age. 'Tis time for a change."

Sigurd understood. "Then another hospital?"

Mike shook his head. "Thou art about to start a new . . . job. Thou will be the resident physician on St. Lucy Island for the duration of this vile affair."

Sigurd almost choked on his tongue, so stunned was he. His brothers barely stifled their snickers.

"Me? I am going to a porno convention."

"Thus sayeth the Lord," Mike pronounced.

Bullshit! Sigurd thought. *Thus sayeth Michael the Irksome Archangel.*

That was how Sigurd found himself the following week in Key West, Florida, applying for a new, unenviable position.

For the love of a troll! He was a fierce fighting warrior, a practicing healer and physician, a Viking vampire angel. He'd thought he could not be shocked anymore.

He was wrong.